WILDE LAKE

WILDE LAKE

A NOVEL

LAURA LIPPMAN

WM

WILLIAM MORROW
An Imprint of HarperCollinsPublishers

P.S.™ is a trademark of HarperCollins Publishers.

HarperCollins books may be purchased for educational, business, or sales promotional use. For information, please e-mail the Special Markets Department at SPsales@harpercollins.com.

A hardcover edition of this book was published in 2016 by William Morrow, an imprint of HarperCollins Publishers.

FIRST WILLIAM MORROW PAPERBACK EDITION PUBLISHED 2017.

Designed by Jaime Putorti

Library of Congress Cataloging-in-Publication Data has been applied for.

ISBN 978-0-06-208346-3

17 18 19 20 21   OV/RRD   10 9 8 7 6 5 4 3 2

PART ONE

When my brother was eighteen, he broke his arm in an accident that ended in another young man's death. I wish I could tell you that we mourned the boy who died, but we did not. He was the one with murder in his heart and, sure enough, death found him that night. Funny how that works.

It happened at the lake. Wilde Lake. Named not for Oscar, but Frazar B. *Who?*, you may well ask. I had to look it up myself and I'm a native to these parts. Frazar Bullard Wilde was president of Connecticut General, an insurance company. When longtime customer Jim Rouse decided in the 1960s that he wanted to build a "new town" utopia in Maryland farmland midway between Baltimore and Washington, D.C. Connecticut General provided funding and agreed that Rouse should acquire the land stealthily, parcel by parcel, keeping prices low. Rouse was a good man—churchgoing, modest, indifferent to his personal fortune, careful with his company's coffers. Yet Columbia, Maryland, the egalitarian experiment that he probably considered his greatest legacy, began in deceit.

Again: Funny how that works.

Frazar's reward was the lake. The lake and, a year later, the "village" that surrounded it. Man-made, dammed, Wilde Lake was the opposite of wild, even with several hundred high school seniors massed at its southeastern edge, celebrating their graduation from Wilde Lake High School. It was June 18, 1980. They were eighteen years old, the lake was fourteen years old, Columbia was thirteen years old. The gathering went about as well as any unsupervised party of adolescents ever goes, and at least multiple family rec rooms would be spared the trash, the vomit, the blood. This outdoor party was a tradition, to the extent that this young, raw suburb could claim to have traditions. On graduation night, seniors stayed out until dawn. Where they ended up varied, but they always started at the lake.

When AJ informed our father that he intended to participate in this annual ritual, our father was torn. He never wanted AJ to be the odd kid out. Yet he truly hated the teenage tendency to *ramble,* as he called it, with no particular destination or plan. And there could be no escaping the fact that AJ was the son of Andrew Jackson Brant, state's attorney for Howard County. It would be big news if AJ Jr. were busted for smoking pot or underage drinking. It would not have ruined AJ's life, the way such missteps can today, what with mandatory expulsions from school and sentencing guidelines. County cops probably would have trained their flashlights on AJ and his friends, confiscated their contraband, ascertained that no one was getting behind the wheel drunk, then sent everyone home. A nuisance, an embarrassment, nothing more. Those were the limits of my father's imagination in June 1980, when it came to his only son.

But he was a fair man, always open to reasonable debate, encouraging us to make a case for the things we wanted—later bedtimes, the family car, a private phone extension. So AJ sat down with him a few days before graduation and told him—*told* him—that his crowd planned to stay out all night, then crash at the home of his friend Bash, whose family had a renovated farmhouse in what was then considered "the country." Furthermore, AJ said, their friend Ariel, one of two girls in his group and by far the most sensible, had agreed to be the designated driver, although I don't think that was the term used. I'm not sure the term even existed back in 1980.

"I'm eighteen," AJ began in a stately manner, as if addressing a jury. "Born in 1962."

"I remember," our father said dryly. "I was there."

And I was there for this discussion, in our living room, pretending to read the evening newspaper, the *Light,* while listening to my father and brother talk. Eight years younger than AJ, I had a lot to learn about winning privileges. My high school graduation might be two entire presidential cycles away—elections were always a frame of reference in our political household—but I wanted to be prepared to argue for whatever would be the cool thing when my night finally came around.

"The law says I can drink beer and wine, but I'm going to be honest with you—my friends and I might drink other things if they're served. It seems only fair to me. If we lived in, say Wisconsin, I could drink whatever I liked at age eighteen."

"My job," our father said, "is to uphold the laws of *this* state."

"Are you going to forbid me to go?"

"No. You can go. And you can stay out. But I urge you to obey the laws, AJ. Whatever you do, I'm going to trust you to use common sense. You must understand that there will be no special treatment if you get in trouble."

"There never has been," AJ said.

Through no fault of his own, AJ ended up obeying the letter of the law. He spent most of the night in the ER at Howard County Hospital, where they did take his blood to test for alcohol and drugs, come to think of it. PCP was a big concern at the time. They probably thought my brother had superhuman strength, given what he had done. But he had managed only a sip of beer before the trouble started.

The night had begun in the auditorium of Wilde Lake High School. With more than three hundred kids graduating, the seniors had been given only two tickets, a hardship for other households but not ours, with only our father and me. And I would have gladly given away my ticket, if I had been allowed. I fell asleep at least three times. The speaker began by informing the students that no one would remember who spoke at this graduation and I think he got that right. He joked that they were already celebrities—as freshmen, this future college Class of 1984 had been photographed for a cover story in *Life* magazine; AJ and his friends were front and center in the photo. Then there was that endless roll call of names, drawn out by parents who ignored the edict not to clap or cheer for individual students. AJ got the most applause, but not from my father or me, sticklers that we were for rules.

When it finally ended, we shook AJ's hand and went home with his folded cap and gown. AJ headed out with his gang, a mixed group in every sense of the word—boys and girls, white and black and Asian, theater geeks and jocks. AJ was the glue, the person who had brought them all together—a good athlete, a gifted singer and actor, an outstanding student. Davey and Bash were also big-deal athletes, with Davey exciting the interest of professional baseball scouts, although he was determined to get a college degree first. Lynne could have been an Olympic-caliber gymnast, but she was lazy, content to settle for being the star of the varsity cheerleading squad. Ariel and Noel got the juiciest parts in school plays. Not necessarily the leads, but the roles that allowed them to give the showiest, most memorable performances. AJ was going to Yale, our father's alma mater.

Davey had a scholarship to Stanford. Noel and Ariel were headed to Northwestern, Lynne was bound for Penn State, and Bash had surprised everyone by getting a National Merit scholarship, which he was using to attend Trinity University in San Antonio, where he had no intention of playing a sport. They had so much to celebrate. They popped the tops of their first beers, pleased with themselves, and toasted. "Life is a banquet," Ariel drawled, quoting a line from *Mame,* which had been the school musical. (She had been Agnes Gooch, not Mame, but she upstaged the leads.) "And most poor sons of bitches—"

It was then that the Flood brothers pulled into the parking lot.

"It happened so quickly," AJ would say whenever he had to tell the story. He had to tell it a lot that summer. He and his friends didn't perceive the Flood brothers as a threat, merely out of place in a throng of high school students. The Flood brothers had a reputation for scrapping, but they weren't scary. Only their dad was scary. They weren't that much older than the partying kids at Wilde Lake, and they didn't even look that different. They could have easily passed for members of the school's gentle stoner crowd, with their work boots and Levi's and blue denim shirts. But there was nothing gentle about the Floods, and neither one had known a graduation night. Every Flood boy, seven in all, had dropped out of school after turning sixteen.

These two, the youngest, got out of their beat-up old car, looked sneeringly at the high school students, then homed in on Davey, easy to find in any crowd—six feet five inches and one of the darkest black men I had ever seen in my life. Just that spring, he had played El Gallo in the all-county production of *The Fantasticks.* Beat AJ out for the part, which surprised some people, but not AJ, who was used to losing things to Davey by then. He said before tryouts that he knew Davey was the better, more original choice. There was an air of mystery about Davey, a softness to his husky tenor that made you lean in, as if to hear a secret.

"There he is," one of the Floods said. Separated by only a year, they were almost impossible to tell apart. Tom and Ben. I remember being surprised to learn later that those names were not nicknames, shortened versions of Thomas and Benjamin. When Tom testified at his own trial later that year, that was the name he gave to the court. Tom Flood, just Tom, not even a middle name. They were the youngest of the seven Flood brothers. Maybe their parents didn't have the energy to come up with any more names, not for boys. The baby of the family, the only girl, had been given a much longer handle: Juanita Cordelia Flood. She should have been graduating from Wilde Lake tonight as well, but she had transferred midyear to Centennial.

"This is for Nita," one Flood said, sticking a knife into Davey's back. At first, AJ thought Davey had been punched. Davey barely flinched, just looked surprised and confused, swaying for a second before he fell to the ground. It was only then, as a dark liquid began to spread beneath him, staining his pale lavender polo shirt, that anyone understood what had happened. The Flood who had struck him—it must have been Ben, obviously it was Ben, but in that moment, in the dark, no one knew who was who, could barely register what was happening—raised the knife again. That was when AJ threw himself at him, caring not at all for his own safety. The two wrestled on the ground, and when the older boy—a man, really, already twenty—ran away, AJ gave chase. They disappeared into a dark fringe of trees near the lake's edge.

AJ's determined pursuit of the one Flood brother snapped Bash into action. He ran at the second one, screaming like a warrior. He brought him down with little difficulty. There would have been a lot of confusion now, much screaming, kids running in all directions, yet most of them unaware of what had actually happened. The lake party was lots of little parties, each group keeping to itself. Some girls and boys would have gone off to make out privately. Others would be smoking or drinking in cars or hidden nooks. It's not a big lake. My family lived on the other side, close enough to keep a boat at the dock, if my father had been the kind of man who did things like keep a boat. And if my windows had been open, I might have heard the screams, then the sirens. But it was warm for June and we already had noisy window units rattling ineffectively in our old house.

Nineteen eighty. There was 911, but no cell phones. There was no pay phone near, or if there was, the kids were too rattled to remember its whereabouts. It was Noel who grabbed Ariel's car keys and drove over to the movie theater. He reasoned it would still be open, that someone there could make a call for him. In doing so, he probably did as much to save Davey's life as AJ did. But from the moment AJ emerged from the trees, panting and covered with blood, cradling his left arm, he received all the credit.

———————

The headline in the next day's *Light* was: STATE'S ATTORNEY'S SON SAVES FRIEND'S LIFE IN BRUTAL REVENGE PLOT.

So my brother made news on graduation night, after all.

Credit the Floods points for patience: it had been almost seven months since their sister had claimed Davey had raped her. The story had fallen apart quickly, a vengeful tale told by a spiteful girl. Given that both were under eighteen, the accuser and the falsely accused, my father had tried to be discreet. "For both of their sakes," he said. But it was one thing to shield the facts from the newspapers, another to keep it from the mouths of gossipy teenagers.

Everyone soon learned that this sad, acne-scarred girl had tried to destroy Davey's life. Was AJ also an intended target that night? Tom, charged as an accomplice to attempted murder, insisted not. Ben didn't live long enough to say anything. When AJ tackled him in the woods a second time, his knife thrust upward into his heart. AJ, sobbing, led the EMTs to the body, but they couldn't save Ben Flood.

After a mistrial, Tom pleaded out to a lesser charge and served only four years. As for AJ—they called in a special prosecutor for the grand jury probe, at my father's insistence, and asked a state's attorney from an adjoining county to oversee it. As our father had told AJ, there would be no special treatment for the prosecutor's son. My brother was found to have acted in self-defense, and he left for Yale in September, happy for the anonymity that came with college, especially one where a movie star was in his class, a movie star who would be caught up in an attempted presidential assassination not even six months later. It was common then not to speak of traumatic things, to assume that a firm silence would lead to the fastest healing. So we never spoke about that night, and I assumed AJ's friends also let it go, to the extent that they could. It was harder for some than others. But to my knowledge, the subject never came up. Not with my father and AJ, not with AJ and his friends, and no one would discuss it with me at all. Most of what I know about that night is from reading old court documents and press accounts over the past few months.

I do remember that sometimes, on cold mornings, AJ would complain of pain at the elbow joint. "The frost is on the pumpkin, Lu," he would say to me, and his knobby elbow did look like a puny, discolored squash from certain angles. And if you knew where to look, you could see that his left arm did not hang as straight as his right. He took up yoga, in part, to combat the pain and stiffness. But most people never noticed that, and over time, I forgot as well. But it was there, if you knew where to look. My brother's arm was crooked.

"No hard feelings?" Luisa Brant asks.

"None," says Fred Hollister. Always Fred, Call-me-Fred, except on the nameplate he must have packed over the weekend, on which he had been identified as Frederick C. Hollister III.

Lu assumes her former boss is lying, but considers that a mark in his favor. Lies can be kind, and this one shows more character than Fred demonstrated throughout the fall, when he spoke what he believed to be unvarnished truths. Fred means that he *hopes* there will be no hard feelings eventually, that one day he will be able to forgive her for taking his job. Otherwise, why stop by at all? If he were truly angry, he wouldn't show his face. Maryland politics is rife with stories of ousted state's attorneys who purged computer files or persuaded the remaining deputies to undermine the new boss. Since Election Night Fred has been a class act.

"My family is going to Iron Bridge for dinner," Lu says. "If you want to stop by and have a drink with us."

"Your family?"

"Dad, my kids. AJ's out of town again."

He pretends to consider her offer.

"It would be nice," Lu presses.

"It would look nice," Fred says.

"That, too."

Fred's smile is genuine, if a touch wistful. "We'll raise a glass. Soon, Lu."

"Dad would love to see you. He thinks the world of you." *Even after the crappy things you insinuated about his daughter.*

"And I'd love to see him. Only—not tonight. I'm happy for you. But I reserve the right to be a little unhappier for myself."

"Hell, Fred, you must be awash in offers. I know at least two firms have tried to hire you since November and some of the big lobbyists in Annapolis are probably after you as well."

"I'm not worried about finding work," Fred says. "But, right now, I'm going to take a little time off. To spend time with my family."

It takes her a beat to realize he's consciously wielding that old cliché as a joke, so maybe she laughs a little too hard when she does catch on. Fred is a decent man at heart and an old friend. Lu started out with him in the Baltimore City state's attorney office, was genuinely pleased for him when he moved out here and made the leap to top dog. Five years ago, at the lowest point in her life, he persuaded her to come out to Howard County and work for him, promising the flexibility she needed, a rare thing in the life of a prosecutor. Fred was a good state's attorney, too, conscientious and passionate, and an excellent boss. But something happened in his second term. He did less and less trial work. He fumbled a case against a serial rapist, became gun-shy, refused to take on anything but dunkers. He was the boss, no one would have begrudged him the big trials. But his insistence on doing as little as possible in court—that had been galling to Lu on principle, even if it allowed her to flourish professionally. Fred lost his appetite for trial work. If he had been one of his own assistants, he would have fired himself long ago.

Still, it had been hard, deciding to run against him. Lu did what she did with most tough questions, sought her father's counsel.

"What would you do if he wasn't your friend?" he asked.

"That's easy. I'd run."

"Then not running is the real hypocrisy, isn't it? If you think Fred has done a lousy job, but decline to run against him out of loyalty, then you're saying your friendship with him matters more than the day-to-day criminal issues that come before this county. It's as I've always told you, Lu—the state's attorney's office represents the community. Your obligation should be to the people of Howard County. What's best for them?"

Her father always made everything sound simple. And her brother had agreed with him. "I like Fred, too, Lu. He was good to you at a time when you really needed a friend. But he's had a bad couple of years, with cases reversed on appeal because of mistakes made by his office. I'm just surprised that more people aren't gunning for him. Must be some sort of gentlemen's agreement among the players in the Republican Party."

"Well, as you know, I'm no gentleman," she told AJ, who laughed and said: "No, but you used to dress like one. Remember that outfit you picked out when—"

She doubled up her fists jokingly and he dropped the subject. Almost forty years out, the memory still brought blood to her face, the heat of humiliation.

Running against one's boss is problematic. She had to quit her job for one thing. Can't stay on as a deputy state's attorney once you declare your intention to seek the top job. Lu camped out in her father's sleepy in-name-only private practice for a year, doing a lot of pro bono work, biding her time. She had no competition in the Democratic primary, while Fred had to fight off a challenge from a charismatic plaintiff's attorney. Still, bloodied and weakened as

Fred had been by that ugly primary race, he had the summer to regain his standing as the incumbent and it was a good year to be a Republican in Maryland. He outraised her five to one, ran attack ads.

But all the money in the world couldn't buy a name like Brant.

And now Luisa F. Brant is the first female state's attorney of Howard County, Maryland. Three hundred thousand people, give or take, two hundred fifty square miles, give or take, one of the most prosperous counties in the state, in the nation. She was born here, in Columbia, and is part of the first generation of Columbia kids coming into power. There had been criticism, during the campaign, that Lu leaned a little too hard on her first-family status, along with her "daughter of" prestige, but if that was the best the opposition had, she was golden. Then Fred had stooped lower, brought her kids into it, and that had backfired. Badly. In the end, her father was right: she wouldn't have waffled about entering the race if Fred had not been a friend. The real hypocrisy would have been sitting by, letting him continue in his listless fashion.

"Got a minute before the staff meeting?" Andi Gleason, once her peer, now her deputy, pokes her head through the door, then sails in without waiting for an answer. Is Lu going to have to train people to knock, to remind her former colleagues that she's the boss? Does it matter? Should they knock? Would a man worry about such things? Would he worry about the knock, or would he worry about *telling* people to knock?

"Sure."

Andi sits down and stretches her legs out so they are propped up on the empty-for-now desk. She laughs when she sees the look on Lu's face, plants her feet on the floor. Andi has long, perpetually tanned legs, and she has adopted the strange habit of never wearing hose, even on days as cold as this one. She read somewhere that's what New York women do, go bare-legged no matter the weather. Lu, who prefers black tights and boots with heels as high as she can handle, almost shivers looking at Andi's legs.

"Just testing you," Andi says. Lu doesn't need her closest friend at work to test her. She needs loyalty, support. True, Andi was the one person in the office not to disavow her when she went after Fred's job, although Lu noticed that they met for drinks at Andi's apartment more and more, not out in public. Andi is bold in court, careful in the office. Better than the other way around.

"What's up?"

"This staff meeting at eleven—is there anything I should know?"

"No shake-ups. For now. There's one or two assistant state's attorneys I'll be monitoring closely—"

"John and—who else?"

Lu glides past answering or even confirming Andi's hunch. What was once acceptable gossip between two equals is now off-limits. No personnel discussions with Andi.

"—but your work has always been good and I don't see any reason it would change."

"In 2014, I did all the homicides that went to trial," she says.

Just because Lu wasn't in the office in 2014 doesn't mean she doesn't know the numbers. "All two of them."

"Right. How many of the murders are you going to take for yourself? Do you have a quota in mind?"

"I was going to cover that at the staff meeting."

"You mean, you're going to try them all." Her tone is one of fact-finding. Andi is probably resigned to giving up the homicides for now. But if she confirms this before the meeting, she can nod, unsurprised, saving face with her colleagues.

"Yes, if they're interesting, I'm going to try them," Lu tells her.

"You mean if they get lots of press attention," Andi says. Oh, this is definitely a test. She's probing to see how frank she can be, going forward, where the boundaries are now. Lu has no fear of candor, but she also believes there's a line between candor and rudeness.

"The media and I don't necessarily agree on what's interesting," she says carefully. "You know I'm talking about cases that stimulate me, that intrigue me legally. It's not about attention."

Andi looks dubious. Fair enough, as Lu is totally bullshitting her. Prosecutors tend to like attention. And Lu is more of a showboat than most.

"There will be plenty of work to go around," she promises. She can't, of course, guarantee that Howard County's generally genteel citizens will start killing each other at an accelerated rate. But there are other felonies, other crimes that matter. There's even been some gang activity in Howard County, although most of those cases end up with the feds. "And by the way, I'll tell you first: there's a new protocol. Someone from this office is going to go to all major crime scenes. I'm talking to Biern over at homicide today, telling him to make sure they alert us ASAP when they do catch a case."

"So you'll send one of us, then decide if it's going to be your case?"

"No, it applies to me, too. I'll go, if it sounds like a case I'm going to end up trying. Fred was too checked out. There were some sloppy investigations, which made our jobs harder. Better we be there sooner rather than later, you know?" Lu smiles. "And now you know most of what I'm going to cover today at the staff meeting."

"I'll try to act surprised," Andi promises. She'll do the opposite. Lu knows Andi. She wants people to think she has special access. It always bugged Andi, when Lu first started in the office, that Lu went so far back with Fred. Andi's initial overtures of friendship probably stemmed from her desire to keep her enemy close. Then she realized Lu was, in fact, capable of being a good friend. Loyal and discreet. Extremely discreet.

"Now let me have thirty minutes to unpack a few things, okay?" Lu watches Andi saunter out, notes how streaky her legs look from the back. Self-tanner. If she's going to insist on a year-round glow, maybe she should spring for the kind you get at a spa.

Meow, she thinks, shaking her head and smiling at herself. Cattiness is a waste of good energy. Lu doesn't feel competitive about other women. Lu feels competitive about everybody.

She studies her office, hers for the next four years, maybe beyond. Her father held it for two terms—no, more than that, he was appointed before he ran for office in 1978. Not this physical space, though, a bland, characterless rectangle with a few pieces of cheap furniture and faded squares on the beige wall where Fred's plaques and pictures had hung. Lu takes a small, tissue-wrapped object from her purse and walks over to the bookcase. Lady Justice emerges from the paper, blind as usual, but in the form of a robed skeleton, a Day of the Dead piece that Luisa's husband gave her when she started working as a prosecutor in Baltimore City. It's hard not to wonder what Gabe would think about today. He would have been proud, of course. But Gabe made so much money, first as a founder of a file-sharing company that was acquired by a bigger player in that field, then consulting in tech, that her state job always seemed like a hobby to him, especially after the twins were born.

"Why work?" he asked her.

"How can I not?" she asked back. "I love the law." She did not dare tell the terrible truth that she found straight-up motherhood boring.

"Okay, but it's on you to make it work. Spend whatever it takes and let's hope it's a financial wash, state salaries being what they are."

Gabe had started a second company by then and they had so much money that they were building castles in the air that could be real castles if they could just pick a location. A castle rising in Spain, as their favorite song, "My Romance," had it. They talked about buying or building a second home. Nova Scotia. The Outer Banks. Or the west coast of Ireland, which seemed almost more accessible than the Outer Banks, given that Aer Lingus had daily flights to Shannon out of BWI at the time. The world was their oyster. Better, Gabe said, they were going to sit at that place outside Galway, where the oysters were so fresh that it seemed as if they had been harvested minutes after you placed your order.

And then—he died. Heart attack in a hotel room in San Jose, California. Thirty-nine years old. Penelope and Justin were not quite three. It made sense, as much as anything was ever going to make sense again, to sell the Baltimore house and move back to her father's, accept Fred's offer of a job. Lu needed the work, if not the paycheck. She was strangely, bizarrely, unfathomably rich. She supposed she had been rich all along, but when Gabe was alive, she never really thought about their money. Numb, she stumbled through the days like a zombie, several years before zombies were to become fashionable again. She needed her father. More than that, she needed Teensy, who had worked for her family since before Lu was born. If there was one thing Lu knew for certain, it was that Teensy, although now in her seventies, could care for Lu's children as she had once cared for Lu and AJ. Fiercely, sternly, but with genuine affection.

Lu was less sure that her father, then going on eighty, could adjust to having small children in his home. Yet it was at his insistence that they invaded his quiet, orderly universe. "I'll just turn my hearing aid down when they get too rambunctious," he said.

A joke. He didn't have a hearing aid, still doesn't. Nor does he have a stoop, or memory troubles, or any real sign of aging beyond his gray hair. Again, he made everything seem so simple. Her father is well aware of the world's ambiguities. But when it comes to his family, he is quick and decisive. His daughter became a widow at age forty. She needed her family. She needed to come home. Full circle.

And now she has completed another full circle, earning the office her father once held. Not this very room; the Carroll Building, where she works, was built after her father left office. But she is the second State's Attorney Brant and the first woman elected to the job, although far from the first woman state's attorney in Maryland. She draws herself up to her full height, which, alas, is only five foot two, although today's boots allow her to top five five. Everyone expected her brother to be their father's successor, but she's the one who has the chops for criminal law, the stomach for politics. She practically prances into a courtroom when she has a trial, her small stature and hoydenish quality an advantage. Other lawyers seduce juries. Lu Brant, with her freckles and girlish appearance, widens her eyes and reduces matters to simple issues of black and white. Lifetime—lifetime—she has lost fewer than ten cases and all of those were in Baltimore, where the juries are notoriously tough. She's never lost a case in Howard County.

She doesn't plan to start now.

OH BRAVE NEW WORLD THAT HAS NO TREES IN IT

The Sunday drive was still in fashion the June day in 1969 that my father, mother, AJ, and I made our first trip to Columbia. The "new town" utopia had engaged my father's curiosity. "I want to see the future," he said, which stirred up visions of spaceships in AJ's boyish imagination—and set him up for a huge disappointment. Only a year or two later, AJ would be given a board game called "Ecology," and the idea of setting out for a twenty-mile recreational drive in a car that averaged sixteen miles to the gallon would be considered wasteful. But not on this particular Sunday in 1969. We got into the family's Ford Fairlane station wagon, no one constrained by seat belts, because seat belts were for out-of-state trips only. Daddy driving, mother in front, AJ in the back alone, bouncing from window to window as the view demanded.

I was there in utero, although no one knew, floating in my mother's flat, seatbelt-less belly. My mother, puffing on a Kool, might have suspected my presence, but she didn't quite believe it, not yet. She had had terrible morning sickness with AJ eight years earlier, and there was no nausea at all this time, only a vague rumble of heartburn that came on about 3 P.M. Besides, there had been two miscarriages since AJ's birth and she had been told that she could not have another child.

At the time, my parents lived in Roland Park, a pretty North Baltimore neighborhood that was something of a planned community itself, with a significant swath designed by Frederick Law Olmsted Jr. My mother and father lived with my mother's parents. This was a strange arrangement even in 1969, made stranger still by the fact that my father was not young when he married.

My mother was. A prodigy of sorts, she had met my father on her first day of law school at the University of Baltimore, when she was only nineteen. He was attending on the GI Bill after trying a stint at the local newspaper, the *Beacon*. The life of a newspaperman had not suited him. My father hated what he called the faux objectivity of journalism. On the one hand, on the other hand. He wanted to pick a side, the right side, then persuade, argue. He had been hired by the paper because of his under-graduate degree from Yale; the *Beacon* was snobby that way. But he was not a twenty-two-year-old with nothing but college behind him. He was a thirty-one-year-old Korean War veteran and he thought he should be treated differently from the other young hires. Once he understood that it would be years before he could hope to have a column or a slot on the ed-itorial page, he decided to leave. So after five years of languishing on night cops, he went to law school and met a beautiful young woman named Adele Closter.

"She was like a character in a fairy tale," my father would say later, when I begged him for stories about my mother. Photos established her dark beauty, but my father insisted it was her mind that impressed him. She had graduated from high school at age sixteen, zipped through Goucher in less than three years, then applied to law school. "Not a lot of women went to law school then, so to be a female law student at age nineteen was more astonishing still. Everyone noticed her. I didn't have a chance. I was just some older guy and people made fun of my accent. They thought I was a dumb hick."

My father didn't have to tell me that his accent, long flattened by the years in Maryland, was quite the opposite of a hick's. He was from an old Tidewater, Virginia family, one that could trace its roots to the seventeenth century. My mother's family, while well-to-do, were German Jews, who arrived in the United States more than two hundred years after the Brants. If my father had ever allowed his parents to meet his in-laws, his people would have been appalled. Yet the Closters looked down on my father because he didn't have money. He had broken with his family—and its considerable wealth—because he found their implacable racism infuriating. The Closters didn't care that his poverty was principled. It was still poverty.

But he was one of the few men willing to endure my grandparents' odd ideas about courtship. In a twist worthy of a fairy tale, they kept their daughter under lock and key in a stone house with turrets, twisting staircases, and stained-glass windows. Any man who wanted to date Adele Closter had to pay a call on her parents first. If they approved of the would-be suitor, the dates were chaperoned—by them.

Apparently, this did not appeal to most of the young men Adele met. Only Andrew Jackson Brant was willing to persevere.

And for all her parents' care and oversight, she managed to get pregnant. AJ was born seven months after my parents' wedding day, and everyone pretended he was terribly premature. I think this charade was meant not only to dodge the question of his legitimacy, but also to make sense of the fact that the new family chose to live with Adele's parents. "Just for a year or so," her father said. "Until everyone is on their feet." One year turned into seven. There was always a reason to stay a little longer. *AJ loves his nursery school, it would be a shame to move him. AJ is going to Gilman, practically in our backyard.* I now believe my father steered the family station wagon toward Columbia that day not only out of genuine inquisitiveness, but also desperation. He had to get out of his in-laws' house. The destination was an accident. Or was it?

Columbia itself was the opposite of an accident. One could argue it was inevitable, that this undeveloped land equidistant from Baltimore and Washington, D.C., was destined to be a suburb, but the developer Jim Rouse had something much grander in mind. Visionary is an overused word, but Rouse probably deserved it. Howard County had slightly more than thirty-five thousand people in 1960, but it was expected to boom before the end of the twentieth century. Rouse's company began acquiring farmland privately, to avoid having prices shoot up. People knew the land was being purchased, but for what? There were paranoid, Cold War-fed rumors—Russian spies hoping to get close to NSA, a West German VW plant. Then, in June 1967, Columbia was born, a "town" comprising four villages, with each village defined by a set number of neighborhoods. The early neighborhood and street names—Dorsey, Phelps, Owen Brown, Warfield—drew on the county's history. But the names quickly became more fanciful and literary. Faulkner's Run, Hobbit's Glen, Longfellow. Many of the early buildings in the town's center were designed by Frank Gehry, but the houses themselves were generic split-levels, built to conform to the preferences of buyers at the time. Founder Rouse wanted to challenge a lot of ingrained biases in our culture; taste was not among them. He gave people the ticky-tacky houses they wanted. The only real choices were brick or wood siding, a Baltimore or a D.C. prefix for your phone.

Columbia at the age of two was still raw-looking, with immature trees and unplanted landscapes. According to family legend, my mother hated it on sight.

"It's too cold. Too modern. I hate modern."

"It's the future," my father said. "Breaking down barriers. Here, people of different classes and races will live side by side."

"Soulless," my mother said. "Just because you call something a town doesn't make it one."

"I like it," my father said. "They're trying new things here. Open space education, for example, where kids go at their own pace."

"I hate it," my mother said. "I could never live in one of these cracker boxes."

It was their variation on *Green Acres,* if you know that TV show. Fresh air! No there there. But my father was too fair-minded to use "You are my wife" to clinch an argument.

Instead, he proposed a deal: "If I can find a house that you love, will you live here? I know what you like—something older, preferably made of stone, a house with character." She said yes, probably assuming it couldn't be done. He let the subject drop, and she thought she had triumphed. It was August now. The pregnancy was known, but only to them. They were keeping the news from her parents, whose house, large as it was, could not accommodate another grandchild.

Two weeks before Labor Day, my father took my mother to see a Revolutionary War–era tavern, eight miles north of Columbia on the road once known as the Columbia Pike. My mother had to admit she liked it, especially its tiny windows. She didn't like light, my mother. That's one of the things I know about her. She didn't like light. She had grown up in a dark house, one where sunshine struggled through the amber and violet panes of stained glass. She considered shadows normal.

"The kitchen and bathrooms are hopeless," she pointed out. "Too small, too out-of-date."

"They can be redone," my father promised. "I've found a contractor who has agreed to a rush job. Best of everything, in whatever colors you want. You can keep the wooden floors, which will be nice, I think. You never see wooden floors in a kitchen anymore. Why is that? If they're sealed properly, they're fine."

"But it's not in Columbia. It's practically in Ellicott City." Ellicott City was everything Columbia was not. The county seat, set in a valley alongside a cold, bright stream, filled with stone buildings dating back to the eighteenth century. "If you're open to Ellicott City, why not Oella or Lawyers Hill?" my mother asked, then repeated, hopefully: "This isn't in Columbia."

"It will be," my father said.

"Not on one of those rinky-dink lots. I couldn't bear it." She was grasping now. My mother had the intellect for law school, but no temperament for debate. She took things too personally.

"I found an irregular lot on the lakeside," my father said. "It's essentially a double. Once the plantings are mature, you'll barely be able to see your neighbors."

She was his wife. Good-bye, city life.

Two weeks later, that stone tavern was hoisted onto a flatbed truck and transferred, at a pace of one mile per hour—the journey took much of a Sunday evening into early Monday morning and required multiple permits—to one of the most desirable lots in Columbia, a double on the west shore of Wilde Lake. The move was covered by both the Baltimore and Washington papers. It marked the first time our family had been in the newspaper, literally announcing my father's arrival on the local political scene. "The house will be home to Andrew J. Brant and family. Brant, a Baltimore attorney, hopes to be active in Howard County's Democratic Party . . ."

My mother's parents were angry. It had taken almost a decade, but the prince had gotten around the princess's imperious parents, as the prince always does. They argued. They cajoled. They threatened to cut my parents off without a cent. They offered to pay the tuition to Gilman. But their lobbying campaign to keep them under their roof—my mother and AJ, really; they merely tolerated my father—only signaled to my father the urgency of leaving.

My parents used me as their trump card. As large as my grandparents' house was, there was no bedroom available for another child. I broke the spell. I freed the princess from the castle, brought her to a new palace. I even freed Teensy, who had come to work for the Closter family when AJ was born and insisted on following us to Columbia, despite the fact that it meant an onerous commute for her every day.

Four months later, I was born, Seven days after, my mother died. It was a bitter winter. Everything froze. Wilde Lake froze. The improvements on the house, intended for her, stopped, suspended in time. Again, as in a fairy tale. Or, perhaps, a television show. *I was your wife. Good-bye to my life.*

"Happy birthday." Andi, sailing into Lu's office again. Not knocking. Again. Lu isn't sure what to do about this. "You've got your first murder. If you want it."

"My birthday was Friday. What kind of murder?"

Lu can tell that Andi is struggling with herself. If she makes the murder sound uninteresting, maybe she'll catch it. But if it turns out to be the kind of case that Lu wants to try, all Andi will have achieved is a reputation for disloyalty and dishonesty.

"Middle-aged woman, killed in what appears to be a B and E. Could have been there for up to a week."

"How was she killed?"

"I told you all I know. North Laurel, an apartment complex off Route 1. The Grove. Funny name for a place on Route 1 in North Laurel. I doubt there have been any groves there for a long time."

"When was she found?"

"Call came into 911 a little before three this afternoon. She didn't show up for her shift at the Silver Diner after a week off. Didn't answer her phone or her cell. That was odd enough, her boss says, that he went to check on her."

"Ya me voy," Lu says. *I'm going.* She and Gabe had been in high school Spanish together, although they had barely spoken to each other in any language back then. He hated the fact that his accelerated math skills weren't enough to free him from all of high school; he split his days between grade-appropriate classes in English, history, and Spanish, then was driven to College Park for math and physics. He should have been admired for his double life, but he was a pariah, disliked by almost everyone, especially Lu. He was small, like her, and Lu hated being paired up with small boys by the time she was fifteen. Her own precocity had been burdensome enough, and she had just finally hit her stride socially. She didn't need to be tarred with the brush of another geek.

Ten years later she married him. Twenty-five years later, she had lost him. She regretted, almost every day, ignoring him in high school. *If only I had known,* she would think, even as she mocked her use of the melodramatic phrase. *We could have had ten more years if we really had been high school sweethearts.* If only anyone ever knew anything ever.

———

When they were first built in the mid-twentieth century, the Grove apartments had probably been a place for people—families, even—on the way up. All the little telltales of aspiration are still here, if worse for wear. The curving fieldstone entrance, the swimming pool, the name spelled out in a pretentious, once-fashionable font, although the sign had been reduced to THE G OVE. And there had been an attempt to avoid a cookie-cutter appearance, with two styles of residences—town houses and three-story apartment buildings, done in three different sidings. There is nothing obviously wrong with the Grove, yet Lu senses that the people who live here now are, at best, treading water. Like the Grove, they've seen better days.

Another tell: the cop cars, crime-scene tape don't seem to excite much attention—people pulling out of the parking lot slow a little, but no one gets out, no one is gathered at the tape's edge. It's a bitter-cold Wednesday. Everyone else's life goes on, while Mary McNally's is over, has been for as much as a week.

"Someone left the balcony door ajar and the thermostat was turned way down," says Detective Mike Hunt without preamble, knowing this detail will interest Lu. He is lean, prematurely silver, and absolute trouble when it comes to women, although Lu knows, via Andi, that he tries not to shit where he eats. At least, that's the excuse he gave Andi. Married, kids, trying to maintain a ruthless compartmentalization. Lu approves. Plus, he's a good detective. Smart, confident. He had to be, to survive that name, beloved by prank phone callers everywhere.

"Do you think it was a deliberate attempt to obscure the time of death?"

"Maybe. Or maybe she turned her thermostat down to sixty-two degrees every night to save money and the killer left the door open in his haste to get away. We're taking fingerprints from there and the sliding door where we think he entered."

"The one he left open?"

"No, there are two bedrooms off the balcony, each with its own entrance. Let me show you."

The apartment is nicer, inside, than Lu expected. The Grove's bones are substantial. Superior, in fact, to the apartments and town houses built in Columbia two decades later. The floors are a well-maintained herringbone, and the layout indicates an expectation of gracious living not seen in newer apartments. A large kitchen, separated from a full dining room by a swinging door. Pocket doors between the dining and living rooms. The two bedrooms share a terrace overlooking what was once a garden—and maybe it still will be, come spring. Everything looks desolate this time of year.

"We think he entered here," Mike says, showing Lu the sliding door in the smaller bedroom. "It was locked from the inside, but there are marks. It wouldn't be hard to force it. He comes in, then goes to the master bedroom."

They follow in the intruder's footsteps, down the little hall. The woman who lived here didn't have particularly good taste, but nor was it bad. There's an arid quality to the decor, it's as if she studied catalogs and tried to replicate the rooms exactly, down to the placement of tchotchkes. The hallway, for example, has framed copies of those French liquor ads, obviously reproductions. The decorative items seem impersonal, too, chosen to fill space. Yet it is the home of a house-proud woman, meticulously kept. Any dust that has settled here is subsequent to her death. Lu stops, puts a pin in her feelings, files them away. Faces, names, she forgets. But once she begins to translate a victim's life into a story, it is with her forever. *Mary McNally, a waitress, reliable and well liked, if not well known at her place of work. If it hadn't been for her conscientious reputation, imagine how long she might have remained in her bedroom, staining a carpet she probably never so much as spilled a glass of water on.*

"Is that blood or melted snow in her hair?"

"It's all blood. Although not that much from the blow that actually killed her. She was struck from behind, then choked. That's the cause of death, strangulation. But the body was moved—we're pretty sure of that because she's facedown—and all the damage to the face was done postmortem. I mean, the perp almost took it off. Do you want to see?"

Want? No, she doesn't want to see it. She needs to see. Assuming there is an arrest—and there better be, the good citizens of Howard County will expect justice for one of their own, a nice lady minding her own business—a jury will inspect photographs. She has to feel the revulsion they will feel.

She does. It's one of the more shocking things she's been asked to see in her professional life and—well, what's the line from that stupid song that was on the radio in her teens? "Never Been to Me"? She's seen some things a woman ain't supposed to see.

But Mike Hunt's eyes are on her, so she keeps her voice steady. "Weapon?"

"We haven't found it. We're canvassing the area, hoping he tossed it on his way out."

"Are you using 'he' generically, or because it seems probable that a man did this?"

Hunt shrugs, indifferent to pronouns. Men can afford to be.

"We found a ticket stub in her purse, for the 10 P.M. showing of *The Theory of Everything* at that movie theater at Snowden Square. That was December thirty-first. She had a week off, December thirty-first through yesterday. So we know she was alive December thirty-first. It's possible she was killed that night when she came in. Hung up her coat, headed back to the bedroom, surprised the guy."

"This seems like an unlikely target for a burglary."

"A junkie might have figured the place to be empty because of the holidays, thought it a good opportunity to grab a few things to fence. No tree, no decorations. But nothing was taken except whatever cash she had in her billfold. Assuming she had cash in her billfold. She has a jar of coins in her room—at least $50 to $100 in there, I'm guessing. Heavy to carry, but junkies can be superhuman when it suits them. And you see the iPad next to her bed, on the stand. So if it started as a burglary, the guy got distracted. Let's hope for a hit on the fingerprints."

Lu continues to move through the apartment, trying to absorb every detail she can about the dead woman. The boss at the Silver Diner told Mike Hunt that she was originally from upstate New York, had moved to Maryland for a man, but he had been out of the picture for years. No boyfriend. No real friends, but she seemed content. There was family, back in New York. A mom, sisters. But she didn't visit them at Christmastime because it was so cold. The cold had begun to bother her a lot. She talked about moving to Florida, near Panama City. *There's always a job for a good waitress in resort towns,* she told her boss, *but you got to pick one where there's work year-round. Or where the seasonal work is so good you can survive the slack months.*

Lu will interview the boss herself at some point, nail down more details. Her father once said a murder trial is a biography. The more jurors know about the victim, the more they care about avenging the death. Make the dead live, her father said. He famously did it with no body once, only a shoe. He concocted an entire person from a plaid sandal with one drop of blood on it.

Lu looks at the bedspread, a comforter of khaki and red squares. She can almost imagine the catalog copy, promising that it would bring a hint of Parisian flea markets into a room. It's askew, with one corner flipped up at the foot.

"I think I've seen what I need to see. Call me if you get a hit on the print. And you know what? Grab the bedspread, have that tested."

Mike is too professional to sigh, but she can tell he wants to. "Why, Lu? This shows no signs of being a sex crime. And if she were, um, an active lady, we might end up looking at a lot of DNA that doesn't go anywhere."

"The spread is mussed," Lu says. "As if someone was lying on top of it. And that corner is flipped."

"So?"

"Look at this place. She was a major neat freak. Either she was lying on the bed when the guy came in—or someone else was lying on the bed when *she* came in. Just do it, okay?" She's testing him, making sure he knows who's in charge. She softens her command with a joke. "Respect my authoritah."

"Wouldn't have pegged you as a *South Park* fan. I'll walk you out." That's Mike Hunt, always with the little gentlemanly touches. That's what women love about him. The ones who fall, they think it's just for them, the courtly good manners, but Lu has observed that Mike's gallantry is automatic. He is always, always, thinking about getting laid, and the good manners are an end to that. Sex—conquest—is like breathing for him.

Sure enough, a woman with a bag of groceries is walking up the fieldstone path to the complex and Mike lights up. "Can I get that for you?" The woman is a bit of a butterface, in Lu's estimation, and probably older than Mike realizes because her figure is amazing, set off by a tightly cinched trench coat that's short enough to showcase long legs in spike heels. Lu can't help resenting women with long legs.

"No, I'm fine. I live across the hall from, um, Mary. They said it was okay. That I could leave and come back. It's my day off, I got to do my errands."

"I'll be over to talk to you later," Mike says. Most women would be beside themselves at the prospect, but this one seems leery.

"About what?"

"Anything you might have seen or heard this past week. Even if it didn't seem important at the time."

"I didn't hear anything," she says quickly. Lu knows the type. Just as there are people who never want to serve jury duty, there are citizens who dread being witnesses. "These apartments are well built; they're pretty soundproof. And they're set up so the shared walls are between the kitchen and the dining room. Not much to hear, you know?"

"Look, no right answers," Mike assures her. "I'd still like to talk to you."

"Should I—the people who live here—be nervous? I mean, was it random or a burglary or—what?"

"We'll know more soon," Lu says, hoping it's true. The woman looks at her sharply, in what Lu interprets as a who-asked-you kind of way. Lu reminds herself that she's a public official now, already running for her second term in a sense. She can't afford to be caustic in the face of insults and slights. "I should have introduced myself. I'm Lu Brant, the state's attorney."

"Yeah, I know who you are," the woman says.

"And you are—?"

"Jonnie Forke." Lu, aware that her trouble with names and faces is a liability for a politician, plays her private game of trying to construct a mnemonic trick. *Stick a fork in her, she's Jonnie. Heeeeeeeeeeere's Jonnie—with a Forke for her butterface.* "I mean, no disrespect to Mary and I'm sorry it happened, but I've got to think about myself."

Lu has a reluctant admiration for the woman's bluntness. She's saying what everyone thinks, in almost every situation. *I've got to think about myself.* Most jurors, even the ones who take the job very seriously, think about themselves first. If, when—and it will be *when*, it has to be when, all she needs is a fingerprint to come back, and this perp is no debutante, she's sure of that, no one commits a crime like this his first time out—Lu comes to a jury with the story of how Mary McNally died, they will be judging the victim as much as the defendant. Did she know him? Did she grant him access to her home? Had they met online or in line, at that 10 P.M. showing of *The Theory of Everything*? A truly random case, one in which the victim appears to have been singled out for no reason, would be the best one to try in Lu's experience. An intruder, surprised. He lashes out. The victim turns to run, he hits her from behind, strangles her, then keeps beating her after she's dead, literally defacing her. Any juror can empathize in that case.

But if Mary invited the man into her home—that will complicate things. It will be better in some ways if the bedspread is pristine, as Mike's preliminary scan indicated. With the break-in and presumed burglary, Lu already has a first-degree murder. Sex will just complicate everything. As sex does. Then again, if he *didn't* break in, Lu might have the advantage of witnesses who saw them together somewhere. She catches herself: she, like Mike, is assuming it's a man. The violence at the scene—not a lot of women have that in them. The anger, yes. Just not the strength to act on it. And there is something personal about it. The postmortem beating, the damage to the face. It doesn't get more personal than that. Then again, men can be surprisingly swift when it comes to having expectations from women they barely know. Strange men tell women to smile, they interrupt conversations, they demand female attention in all sorts of ways.

And when they don't get it, they can get very angry.

THE BOY IN THE BUSH

My family moved to Columbia, our future house rolled down the highway on a flatbed trailer, I was born, my mother died—and I remember none of it. These are the stories I was told. The first vivid memory that I trust as my own, in part because AJ agreed on every detail, is the August day in 1976 when we found Noel Baumgarten in our bushes, peering into our kitchen.

Teensy, rinsing the lunch dishes at the sink, shrieked when she realized there was a person in the bushes. His eyes, green as sea glass, might have passed for light-dappled leaves if they had not been moving rapidly back and forth, scanning everything he saw.

"Got-dammit." Teensy belonged to a storefront church in West Baltimore and she never cursed, so this was serious business. She grabbed a broom and headed outside, AJ and I trailing her. We weren't the least bit scared or disturbed by our Peeping Tom. We were excited because something was finally happening and so little happened on those slow summer days, when most of the kids we knew went to camp or the ocean or the mountains. We never went anywhere.

"What are you doing?" Teensy demanded of the boy in the bush.

"Taking photographs," he said cheerfully, showing us the heavy, old-fashioned camera he wore on a cord around his neck.

"Whaaaaaaa—?" Teensy yelled, making futile passes with the broom, the boy ducking and swerving as if it were a dance.

"Of your house. It's wild. What was it, before Columbia was built? Did George Washington sleep here? It's a thousand times nicer than any other house around here, that's for sure."

"Why did you come up to the kitchen window if all you wanted to do was photograph our house?" That was AJ, not Teensy. She was now completely nonplussed, a first in my experience. Maybe it was those eyes. They were so big and green, like something you'd see on a tiny jungle animal in *National Geographic*. Or maybe it was his juicy confidence. Noel, as we would soon learn, was completely without guilt, even when he was doing things for which he should feel guilty. He could stare down any authority figure and proclaim his innocence.

"I bet people take photographs of your house all the time," he said, ignoring the question put to him. "Don't they?"

They did. And, like this boy, they assumed that the house had been there first, that the wood-sided split-levels were the interlopers who had forced themselves on this dignified matron. In that way, the house, although chosen to lure my mother to Columbia, was not unlike my father. A newcomer just six years ago, our father had been appointed to the state's attorney's office in 1975 and already seemed a fixture in the county. People often asked if the Brants went back as far as the Warfields, one of Howard County's oldest, most storied families. That's how my father's brand of confidence worked. He found the place he wanted to be, kept still and poised, and eventually people assumed he had been there all along.

"I didn't mean to scare you," Noel said as he emerged from the bushes, brushing a stray leaf from his hair, blue-black and shiny, like Prince Valiant in the Sunday comics. His hair was all the more striking with those otherworldly green eyes and fair skin. "I just wanted to see if the inside of the house was as old-fashioned as what's outside. I'm Noel Baumgarten."

He offered his hand to AJ. At the time, he was considerably shorter than AJ, although that would change. But he was short enough so that it wasn't crazy of me to hope he might be closer to my age than my brother's, or at least right between the two of us, and therefore a suitable friend to both.

"Where do you live?" AJ asked. "Where are you going to school in the fall?"

"Up on Green Mountain Circle." He hitched a thumb toward the long semicircle of a street that formed the closest thing our neighborhood had to a main drag. "I'll be a freshman at the high school in the fall. It's just me and my mom."

"Did your parents get divorced?" I asked. "Or is your dad dead?"

"Lu!" AJ's tone was reproving. "You don't ask things like that."

Noel laughed. "I do," he said. "I ask questions like that all the time. I ask people how old they are and how much money they have and what kind of cars they drive and my mother says"—here, he put on a high, pained falsetto, cocked a fist on his hip—"my mother says, 'You will be the death of me, Noel Baumgarten.' And, no my parents aren't divorced, but my dad works, like, twenty hours a day. He's at the State Department. And he doesn't want to add to his day by commuting, but my mom thought Wilde Lake would be better for me. I was at Sidwell Friends." Dramatic pause. "I got kicked out."

"For what?" That was AJ, for the record. It seemed far ruder to me than asking if someone's dad was dead.

An enormous shrug, his eyes shining. "Marching to the beat of my own drummer."

Years later, at Noel's funeral service, we would meet the classmate whom Noel was discovered kissing in the boys' bathroom at that exclusive private school. It turned out that neither boy had been expelled, not exactly. School officials conferred with both sets of parents and agreed the boys should be separated. For their own good. Yes, that was something well-intentioned, liberal parents did forty years ago; they tried to nip homosexuality in the bud, hoping it was a bad habit, like smoking. I wouldn't be surprised if some still do it today. Your son is kissing a boy? Chalk it up to confusion, assume that one of them is a bad influence, and separate them, "saving" the one who was led astray. I think it was Noel's mother, already deeply ambivalent about her marriage, who chose to put him in Wilde Lake High School, thinking its progressive open education style was an environment in which her unusual boy might flourish. She was a hard little number, Noel's mother, but she loved her son. In my mind, I see her always in a high, tight ponytail and tennis whites, although that clearly is apocryphal. She would have worn real clothes on at least some occasions. I had a brief period of time hoping that our two single parents would marry, but Noel's mother surprised everyone, even herself I think, by returning to Noel's father when Noel graduated from high school. She had spent four years claiming she moved to Columbia just for Noel. Maybe she came to believe it.

We invited Noel inside, hoping he would pick up on the fact that he must ingratiate himself with Teensy if he wished to have any traction in our household. He started off very smartly by not asking, as so many did, why a six-foot-tall woman was called Teensy. Her nickname was derived, in fact, from her first name, Hortensia. Noel, who had the most finely attuned social antenna I was ever to know, sidestepped that minefield, first apologizing for scaring her, then offering to finish the sink of dishes she had been washing.

"Oh, don't worry about that," Teensy said. "Would you like an ice cream sandwich?"

An ice cream sandwich! Teensy had told us only minutes earlier that we were not entitled to dessert, given our refusal to eat much of the lunch she had "cooked." (Another rule of life with Teensy is that we were not to challenge the lackluster lunches she made, so different from the meals she served in the evening, when our father was present. He came home to pot roasts, lamb chops, whipped potatoes. We got canned soup, bologna sandwiches, carrot sticks. Every day. The only variations were turkey instead of bologna, celery instead of carrots.) Now she opened a box of Eskimo Pies and passed them out to all of us.

And just like that, Noel had the run of our house. When we had finished eating our ice cream on the back porch, he asked for a tour, during which he made approving and knowing comments about the furniture, chosen by our mother and never changed. He liked old things and was appalled that his mother had brought him someplace where everything was new. He told us that his father was old friends with someone in the Rouse Company, Columbia's developer, and that there had been concern, early on, when black home buyers had clustered in certain neighborhoods. The suspicion was that real estate agents were circumventing the explicit plan to make Columbia a heterogeneous utopia, where race and class mingled. But the truth was prosaic and without agenda. Black home buyers, many of them first-time home buyers, wanted brick homes, not wooden-frame ones.

"Like the Three Little Pigs!" I said, pleased to have anything to offer to this fast-talking, fast-moving beautiful boy.

Noel laughed and kept going, not even bothering to ask permission as he opened doors to closets and bathrooms. He sailed into the enormous second-floor bedroom that belonged to my father, picked up the silver frame on his bureau.

"Who's this?"

"My mother," AJ said.

"Our mother," I clarified. It was an odd linguistic habit of AJ's, to use "I" and "my" in situations where "we" and "ours" were more accurate.

"She looks like Norma Talmadge."

Ah, there was Noel's inner drummer again, beating wildly, eager to tell everyone who he was.

Anyway, he was right: our mother did bear a striking resemblance to the actress, with her shortish, curly hair, Cupid's bow lips, and enormous brown eyes. AJ, lucky rat, was a masculine version of her, while I was a petite knockoff of our father, rawboned and sandy-haired. Worse, I was covered with freckles, something my father had been spared. People said I looked like Laura from *Little House on the Prairie*. I disliked the show and did not consider the comparison a compliment.

"She died when Lu was born," AJ said.

"The week after," I said.

"Do you visit her grave?"

Her grave. *Her grave.* Where was my mother's grave? The question captured my imagination. Why had I never thought about her resting place? I had been death obsessed, as children tend to be, and certainly I had specific reasons to think about mortality. My mother's parents had been killed in a car accident within a year of her death. Yet it had never occurred to me that my dead mother was contained somewhere, that I could visit her if I wanted.

"She was cremated," AJ said, dashing my hopes as quickly as they had been raised. "Her ashes are—I don't know where they are, come to think of it. I just know that my dad says she wouldn't have wanted to be kept cooped up anywhere. She was a restless soul. That's what he says."

Noel looked around the room, his eyes catching on a Chinese vase high up on the bookshelves. The vase was out of his reach. He opened my father's desk, an antique planter's desk, one of the few things he had from his own family. I could sense AJ wanted to tell him no, but they were courting each other in the way that new friends do, trying to impress. Girls are more likely to do this, but boys do it, too.

Noel climbed up on the desk and tilted the vase toward him. "No, nothing in here." He was hoisting it back to its place when the desk lid, which had supports that Noel had failed to pull out, gave way under his weight and cracked at its hinges.

Although she was a flight of stairs away, Teensy was in my father's bedroom within seconds.

"What are you doing in Mr. Brant's room?" she asked, huffing and puffing, angry at being forced to rush.

"We're allowed," AJ said. "He's never said we couldn't be."

"But you're not supposed to be around his desk," Teensy said. "You know that. He keeps confidential things in there, work things. And it was closed this morning. You opened it up and climbed on it."

"To be fair," Noel said, scrambling to his feet, still holding the vase. "I did that."

But he was already beloved in Teensy's eyes. He could do no wrong.

"You're a guest," Teensy said. "It was up to them to explain the rules of our house." She surveyed the damage. "It's a clean break. My husband can fix it." Teensy's husband was a mysterious, seldom-seen person, responsible for many edicts that could not be challenged. *My husband likes me home early on Fridays. My husband says you've got to have a little bread at every meal.*

"So Dad won't have to know?" AJ asked hopefully.

She snorted. "You'll tell him first thing when he comes home. No secrets in this house. But I'll pick up the papers that scattered. Because he's particular about those. And while I'm picking up the papers, you can do some of my chores."

I noticed another photograph of my mother, presumably her wedding day photo, saw Teensy sweep that back into a manila envelope marked "Adele." I made a note to myself to come back and inspect the contents of that envelope. When I did, it was only the photograph and a few legal documents of no interest to me. A birth certificate, the marriage certificate, even some of her report cards.

I was assigned the laundry, while AJ and Noel had to mop the kitchen floor. Teensy had a genius for getting us to do things she didn't want to do. At least once a week, we were forced to carry out her work as some kind of punishment. It took her perhaps five minutes to pick up the few papers that had fallen, while our tasks required much of the afternoon. There was no talking back to Teensy, and no appealing her laws.

AJ was her favorite. If it were not for AJ, I doubt she would have decided to work for us, given the twenty-mile drive. You might think—certainly, I thought about it—that she would be even more committed to me, motherless baby girl that I was. But Teensy preferred AJ, always. "Boys need mothers," she would say, rationalizing her bias. "Girls don't need anyone." I think she was speaking for herself. Teensy didn't need anything or anyone. I'm not even sure why she had a husband.

I thought of her as old, always, but she was twenty-three when she came to work for the Closters, which means she was thirty-seven on this August day. When my husband died, Teensy was thrilled to have three new lives to domineer after years of tending to my father. So my children and I moved back into that rambling stone house at the edge of the lake, after my father agreed to add a few rooms and renovate the kitchen and baths, still stuck in the 1970s. My father has supervised this never-ending project and I have since learned that this frugal, careful man can be a libertine with someone else's money. I never knew drawer pulls could cost so much, or that there are bathtubs that will put you back more than a car. But it made him happy and I could never deny him anything that made him happy.

Another full circle in my life, yet my children's lives in my childhood home could not be more different from mine. I can't imagine giving Penelope and Justin the freedom to walk to the 7-Eleven on Green Mountain Circle. Wouldn't matter if I did; it's long gone. The lapping wavelets of Wilde Lake, my onetime lullabye, now whisper to me of their intent to take my children's lives if I ever allow my vigilance to flag. And in my imagination, Columbia's famous walking paths and bike trails are like a Candy Land board game snaking through a forest of potential pedophiles. I don't even send my children to the neighborhood elementary school I attended, a ten-minute walk. They go to private school at the opposite end of the county, which means I still have to have a babysitter, Melissa, just to drive them to and from school every day. Fred tried to make that an issue during the election, even tried to suggest I was a racist because the neighborhood school has a large minority population. That backfired on him when I explained that my children had been enrolled in their current school's pre-K not long after their father died; the school was one of the few constants in their young lives. I was reluctant to remove them from the comfort of a familiar place for what would be shallow, political concerns.

I almost feel sorry for Fred. Almost. It had to be a special kind of hell, running against the unimpeachable Widow Brant. Such a tragic figure, having lost her childhood sweetheart. (Gabe and I didn't start dating until college, but, you know, print the legend.) A respected figure, daughter and sister to two saintly men. And, by the way, a really good trial attorney. He couldn't win, and he didn't. The night of the general election, we were neck and neck the whole evening, but the final precincts delivered the victory to me. A squeaker, 50.5 percent of the vote, but all you need is 50 percent plus one. The gender divide did him in. Women didn't like him going after my kids. The African American women that Fred thought would vote for him in a bloc much preferred me. Even his appearance at Davey Robinson's church didn't help him win those women over.

Besides, if Fred wanted to make it personal, there were better, juicier—truer—rumors to spread. He just didn't know where to look.

They get a hit on the fingerprints quickly, from the door and the thermostat: Rudy Drysdale, a fifty-one-year-old vagrant with a history of loitering, trespassing, breaking and entering. But not a single act of violence, which tempers Lu's excitement. A smart defense attorney could knock this charge down in a heartbeat. With this guy's record, it would be easy to argue that he broke into the apartment after the woman was dead, panicked, and left. That wouldn't answer the mystery of the print on the thermostat, but she's not going to risk charging him on the fingerprint alone. She's not even sure she wants to interrogate him yet, but she also can't afford to leave a killer on the streets. Two detectives are dispatched to the cheap motels along Route 1. Drysdale, on medical disability, apparently stays in motels at the beginning of the month when he's flush with his government money, then resorts to sleeping outdoors if the weather allows. Howard County is not an easy place to be a homeless man. There are no emergency shelters and only a handful of food pantries. How do you survive the winter if you are homeless in Howard County?

You break into a place you believe is empty. Lu thinks back to Mary McNally's apartment. No lights were on. That hadn't registered or seemed important because it was daytime. And, of course, the perp might have turned the lights out so no one would notice the ajar door, assuming he had left the door open on purpose. The thermostat, the door—Lu has to assume the killer wanted to play with the environment, complicate the process of determining the approximate time of death. Did the killer know Mary was on vacation, not expected back at work until January sixth?

One thing's for certain: Mary didn't meet Rudy Drysdale while standing in line for *The Theory of Everything*. Or at a coffee shop, or a wine bar. This was not a man that a woman invited into her home. Unless Mary McNally was the kind of softhearted person who saw a man with a WILL WORK FOR FOOD sign and took him at his word, asked him to do a few small chores for her.

The detectives find Drysdale at the second motel they check. He is docile—so docile, based on what Lu hears, that he might not be competent to stand trial. They attempt to interview him, but he says nothing, asks for nothing, only stares at the ceiling. He's probably happy to spend a night in jail. After a few mild days, Maryland is in the grip of a terrible cold snap, with a low of ten degrees forecast for tonight.

Mike Hunt goes out with Drysdale's mug shot, shows it around the Silver Diner, the apartment complex. Lu's money would have been on the Silver Diner. It seems plausible that Drysdale treated himself to a cup of coffee there, sitting at the counter and nursing it as long as he could on a cold day. Silver Dollar advertises a bottomless cup of coffee. Get an English muffin, eat and drink slowly. As long as he didn't smell and didn't do anything too off-putting to the other customers, he could have spent hours there.

But the Silver Diner comes up empty. It's the neighbor, the one with the long legs, who recognizes Rudy, says she saw him lurking in the parking lot the week before Christmas. Probably saying that just to get closer to Mike Hunt, Lu thinks. But it's enough for a lineup, which Lu attends, and Jonnie Forke is grim, businesslike. Also very definite. "That's the man I saw," she says. "I saw him twice." He was always moving, but there was something about him that didn't seem right, which is why she noticed him.

B-I-N-G-O. With an ID this strong and the prints, Lu will have no problem charging the guy with first-degree murder. She calls home, asks her father if he's comfortable supervising homework and bedtime. When he hears that she wants to stay to observe an interrogation, he says he'll ask Teensy to work late. After all these years, Lu remains too cowed by Teensy to ask her to do anything extra. She still gets nervous helping herself to an ice cream sandwich when Teensy isn't around to give permission.

Lu has takeout at her desk, reads the newspaper online—always strange to see Davey Robinson writing op-ed pieces, stranger still to realize he's an out-and-out conservative—scrolls through the day's e-mail, looks at her telephone messages. Her office still uses the pink "While You Were Out" slips. The last one, logged at 4:45 P.M., is from a Mrs. Eloise Schumann. *Says you will know what this is in reference to,* Della has written on the slip. (Is it wrong that Lu secretly loves having a secretary named Della, as Perry Mason did?) Of course Lu has no idea what it is in reference to. Isn't that always the way? Everyone thinks his or her own drama is so central. She searches her e-mail for "Schumann," searches her mind. Nope, blank, nada.

Mike Hunt calls. "He decided to open his mouth long enough to lawyer up already."

"Fuck."

"Yeah, so we're going to let him spend the night in jail, push the interrogation to tomorrow."

"Why?"

"Think about it, Lu. This guy can't bear to go up to Baltimore, spend a night in a mission. He sleeps outside or breaks into places. Anything to avoid human contact. A night in jail is going to rattle him."

"Is he crazy, Mike? I mean, the kind of crazy that's going to raise competency issues."

"He's got issues, but he's pretty lucid. Lucid enough to lawyer up after being tight as an oyster all day. We played the game with him, told him it would be better not to rush into an official conversation, but he was having none of it. He wants a lawyer. So he'll have one in the morning, the best that the Howard County public defender's office has to offer."

Lu feels let down, almost as if she has been stood up for a date she was anticipating. Twitchy with adrenaline, she considers stopping for a drink on the way home. Or even going to a movie. Who would ever know? Free evenings are rare. She thinks about asking Mike if he wants to have a beer. He's good company and their mutual lack of interest in each other makes it fun to talk to him. But it also makes him dangerous because Lu could imagine confiding in him, if she got enough liquor in her. Better to go home, tuck her kids in as she tries to do every night, have that drink alone. Besides, she'll want to be fresh tomorrow, even if she's only an observer.

"Okay, we can push it until tomorrow. Get your beauty sleep."

"As if I need it," Mike says. How she envies him his confidence. Lu has learned to put on a confident attitude, to wear it like her clothes—and she wears her clothes well, but only after they are tailored. She's built like a short-legged Betty Boop and feels she has to downplay the parts that other women might consider assets. Everything off the rack is too long, baggy below the waist, strained across her chest. Mike is a natural-born winner, and no one understands that better than someone like Lu, who has always had to study, try, fail, try again. It was galling, but as the younger sister of another natural-born winner, she's gotten used to it. What other option did she have?

WE'RE ALL IN COLUMBIA

Summer, usually our dullest season, flew after we met Noel. True, there wasn't much left. But how he breathed life into those last, dreary days of August. He always had plans, which he called escapades. "What sort of escapade should we have today?" he would ask, rubbing his hands together. And although I was not expressly invited on Noel's adventures, AJ wasn't allowed to go anywhere without me. Teensy foisted me on him using the pretext of filial love. I suspect she just didn't want me underfoot, whining about how bored I was. I learned to ride a bike well and fearlessly that summer I was six years old because I was trying to keep up with two fourteen-year-olds.

What did we do? We rode over to Lake Kittamaqundi at what was known as Town Center and rented a rowboat, although that required the boys lying about their ages. Well, AJ claimed to be sixteen; no one believed Noel was even fourteen. We went to the movies and experimented with sneaking into the one we hadn't paid for, a difficult feat at the little two-screen cinema. You had to leave one auditorium, go to the bathroom, then buy something from the concession stand, drop your change, go back to the bathroom, ask for napkins. Noel taught us the valuable lesson that making a spectacle of yourself was sometimes the best way to get people to stop noticing you. Noel lived his life based on that premise, although he would have been heartbroken if he weren't the center of attention when he wanted to be. He was that rare young person who understood exactly who he was and what he needed—and that his parents, his friends, the world at large, were not ready for this information.

We always ended up at the mall, Noel's favorite place. The mall still felt shiny new then, maybe five years old, immortalized by its own television jingle: *We're all in Columbia / At the Mall in Columbia*. Almost everything Noel wanted was in that mall. Noel loved things. Clothes, first and foremost, but, really, everything, anything. He yearned for stuff. He could spend hours browsing. Bix Camera Store, where he was genuinely interested in the lenses and camera bodies. Bun Penny, where he would pretend to be shopping earnestly for a sophisticated event. ("Miss, what kind of cheese would you suggest I take to a Labor Day cookout? Do you have Cinzano? Campari?") At Bailey Banks & Biddle, a jewelry store, he tried on watches, claiming to have a windfall check from his doting grandmother. He liked to get free samples from the "natural" cosmetics place. ("This face cream does smell like almonds! My mother will love it.") We always ended up at Waldenbooks, reading entire novels on the sly, which felt outlaw back then when bookstores did not have easy chairs or coffee bars. We could have ridden our bikes to the library branch in Wilde Lake Village Center, read the same books while sitting comfortably. But it wouldn't have been as much fun.

And, yes, I could read at age six and was already ripping through chapter books. The Hardy Boys, my father's boyhood collection of Tom Swift, Encyclopedia Brown, a series of books about famous people—mostly men—as children. I had been reading since age four. During *that* slow, boring summer, AJ dug out his first-grade primers, which had been boxed up in the attic. Our mother had put them there, I was told, because she had taught AJ to read at a young age and planned to do the same with me. AJ introduced me to Dick, Jane, and Sally. The first word I learned was *Oh*. Sally says Oh. Oh, oh, oh. It seemed an improbable way to learn to read, yet I did. By the time I was five, I could read the newspaper. ("Although only the evening one," my father would say, a joke at the expense of the *Baltimore-Light,* which was considered less intellectual than its morning sister, the somber *Beacon.*) I read my horoscope every day and took it to heart. I was a Capricorn, which grieved me. Who wants to be the goat?

By the time I was six, I was reading newspaper articles about my father, who had been appointed Howard County state's attorney the year before. These articles were generally bland, approving things, but I never got over the thrill of seeing his name—also my name—in print, even if it was usually on the back of the second news section. And in the summer of 1976, he began to appear on Page One almost every day because he was trying a big murder. Murder was rare in Howard County and this case would have been considered sensational in any jurisdiction, in part because there was no body. But there was more to the story than that.

A man had come home drunk in the fall of 1974, blood on his clothes, told his wife he had hit a deer. The damage to the car, an old station wagon, was minimal, but he had tried to move the animal from the road to protect other drivers, he told her. A week later, the wife was using the car when a woman's shoe, a heavy wooden platform, slid out from under the driver's seat. She said she almost got into an accident when the shoe jammed beneath the accelerator, but she managed to kick it free. The shoe was flamboyant, even by the fashions of the day, a cherrywood platform with a cutout between heel and sole, so it looked almost like a fish about to take a bite. The fabric that crossed the foot, leaving the toes bare, was a lovely pink-and-green plaid.

The fabric also had blood on it.

What the woman did next seemed to shock people more than the discovery of the bloody shoe: she went to the state police barracks in Jessup. She told the story of her husband saying he had hit a deer. She produced the shoe. She would have brought the shirt as well, but she had already laundered it. "That's the kind of wife I am," she told police. "I wash my husband's bloody shirts, get every speck out. It took two washings."

The woman returned home, made her husband's favorite dinner, let him have all the beer he wanted. She gave him steak and french fries, despite his cholesterol. She sat at the kitchen table and asked him gentle, probing questions. She told him about the shoe. He demanded to see it. "Oh, I threw it away."

Where? he demanded. *Where? We've got to be careful. If they find that shoe—*

"Honey, what's wrong?" the woman said. "You can trust me."

The story poured out of her husband. He had seen a hitchhiker, given her a ride. It had been the girl's idea to pay him with sex, he swore to this. But the girl had hurt him, bit him. (This part was mysterious to me when I was six. I knew vaguely how babies were made, but I didn't know how someone could bite you during the act. I assume she bit him while they were kissing.) All he did was try to make her stop. Was that so wrong, trying to make a girl stop? When she was hurting him?

They never found the girl's body, but the shoe was used, Cinderella-like, to identify her. Sheila Compson, sixteen, from New Jersey, had decided to hitchhike to a concert in Largo, Maryland, after a fight with her father. I think it was a Styx concert. She never came home. Domo arigato, Mr. Roboto.

The odd thing was that everyone hated the wife. While it is true that spouses cannot be compelled to testify against each other, they have always been free to do so willingly. Yet people treated this woman as if she had violated some natural law. She was cold-blooded, with no real concern for the girl who had died, only anger toward the husband who had betrayed her. My father had to coach her to call Sheila Compson something other than *that slut* or *trollop*.

Meanwhile, the husband became bizarrely pitiable. His defense was that he had told his wife the story he thought she wanted to hear at the time. The truth was that he had a pleasant consensual encounter with the girl at the truck stop near 216, then let her out just north of the Montgomery County line, where he assumed she caught one more ride.

"And she left with only one shoe?" my father asked him when the defendant took the stand.

He held up his hands and shrugged, as if to say *Women!* Under redirect from his own attorney, he said that the shoe had been in a rucksack the girl was carrying, that she was wearing something more substantial on her feet and the shoe had rolled out from her bag while they were in the backseat "enjoying each other."

He would come to regret that turn of phrase. My father used it over and over in his final arguments. "And that blood, on the shoe—I guess, that, too, happened while they were—enjoying each other. A sixteen-year-old girl, trying to get to a concert. A twenty-four-year-old man. He certainly enjoyed himself. Did she?"

Final arguments were held the week before school started. AJ and I were allowed to attend, and Noel tagged along. Standing in front of the jury, my father cradled that shoe in his hand. He told the jurors a story about the girl, who, he reminded them, was not there to speak for herself, whose body was still missing. This shoe was all that was left of her, all we would ever know of her. This shoe and her parents and her room back in New Jersey, where she had a poster of a cat hanging from a chin-up bar and a pink-flowered bedspread and a drawer of T-shirts from national parks, purchased on a trip she had taken cross-country with her family just two years ago. My father had driven up there to meet Sheila's parents, studied her bedroom, learned everything he could about her. Sheila had bought these shoes with money saved up from her job at Baskin-Robbins. He told the jurors how much she made an hour, how hard it was to scoop certain flavors like Jamoca Almond Fudge. But Sheila never complained. The platforms were difficult shoes to walk distances in, but they were her best shoes, and when she decided to go see her favorite band in Largo, they were the obvious ones to wear, even if the chill of autumn had arrived. Those were the kind of decisions a sixteen-year-old girl made. Impractical, heartfelt. She had on overalls, a peasant blouse, and a peacoat when she left school that afternoon. Her parents thought she was going to work, then sleeping over at a friend's house, so they did not worry when she did not return that night. No one mentioned a rucksack. Her parents swore that she carried her books tight to her chest, a small purse slung over her arm. No rucksack.

My father reminded the jury that at least two other men had given Sheila Compson rides that day. They had testified at the trial. They had described a bright, lovely girl, full of excitement. "They enjoyed—her *conversation*," my father said. "Nothing more." Yes, she had quarreled with her parents. Yes, she had defied them, lied to them. She was not a perfect girl by any means. And, yes, she might have chosen to have sex with this man. Here, my father cast an incredulous look at the defendant, who was not particularly attractive.

"She's out there somewhere," he said. "We may never find her. Her parents have been denied the ritual of burial, which is no small thing in our culture. How we treat our dead is central to our humanity. There is no doubt in my mind that Sheila Compson is dead. The defense would have you believe that she is a runaway. But, really, how far could she have run?"

He placed the lone shoe, size seven, on the flat rail of the jury box.

The jury came back in less than two hours. Guilty of murder in the first degree, life in prison. The death penalty in Maryland had been temporarily suspended because of constitutional challenges or this man certainly would have been sentenced to die.

We went out for a celebratory dinner at the Magic Pan—Noel somehow got invited to that, too—and toasted, as was our private tradition, Hamilton Burger, the beleaguered D.A. on *Perry Mason*. Most people rooted for Mason, but my family knew who the real hero was, who stood for justice and the community, not just his client.

"But what about the shoe?" Noel asked.

"What?"

"It was so big, so bulky. He should have noticed, when he buried her—"

"We don't know that he buried her, Noel. There's plenty of undeveloped acreage in Howard County. A body could go years without being discovered."

"Okay, dumped or buried—how could he not notice that she was wearing only one shoe? And if he noticed, then I think he would have looked for it. Maybe he kept it, on purpose. Or maybe—maybe the wife was *there*."

My father reared back, as if from a bad smell. "Don't be silly, Noel."

"I'm just saying maybe they cruised together for girls. I saw a movie like that, where a husband and wife went looking for young girls. Only they were vampires. The husband and wife."

"Vampires," my father said. It was a rhetorical trick of his, repeating a word, then letting it sit, so the silence around it somehow made it ludicrous. *Vampires.* Then: "Who wants dessert?" Everyone did. The Magic Pan had a specialty that was a solid brick of vanilla ice cream in a sweet crepe, covered with chocolate sauce. I thought it was the most sophisticated thing in the world. When I ate it, I felt as if I were sitting high up in the Eiffel Tower with Cary Grant. (Noel had made us watch *Charade* at the Slayton House film series that summer.)

———————

School started the next week. AJ was entering high school, which he considered momentous. And while I had a year of kindergarten behind me, it had been at a private Montessori school, so this would be my first year at the neighborhood school, Bryant Woods Elementary. First grade was the real deal, I decided, the time when the serious business of learning would begin.

Better still, our teacher was brand-new and beautiful, with a cloud of permed hair and peasant-inspired clothing—a loose blouse worn belted, a flowing skirt, high-heeled boots. The moment I saw her, I decided I had to be nothing less than teacher's pet, even if I wasn't exactly sure what that meant. I wanted to bring her home, introduce her to my father, make her my mother. I decided all those things before we had finished saying the Pledge of Allegiance. With a six-year-old's logic, I reasoned that the way to ingratiate myself with Miss Gordon was to show her I was beyond first grade, on a par with her, perhaps better suited to be her assistant. As she began to lead us through the alphabet, I sighed loudly and said to no one in particular. "This old thing."

"What was that?" Miss Gordon asked. She didn't look happy to have been interrupted, so I didn't speak up. The boy across the aisle, Randy Nairn, spoke for me.

"She said, 'This old thing.'" He added a sneer to my tone that I swear wasn't there, spoke in a high voice nothing like mine, screwed up his face in a prissy moue. The class laughed. Miss Gordon didn't.

"Louise Brant? Is that your name?"

"Luisa, but I go by Lu."

"Well, Luisa"—oh, the refusal to use my nickname was hurtful, a rejection of my friendship—"if you're already bored, we can see if you're ready to do second-grade class work. In fact, maybe I could take you to Mrs. Jackson's class right now, just throw you in. Sink or swim."

I sensed a setup. Although I could read, I understood there was more to school than reading. What I didn't understand was Miss Gordon's instinctive dislike, her hostility. Adults always took a shine to me. Adults liked me better than kids did. I was smart. I behaved. I could hold my own in a conversation. And when they found out I was the daughter of Andrew Brant, most adults beamed at me, even Republicans. There was talk, after the trial, that my father could be state's attorney general if he wanted, maybe even a congressman or a senator. I wondered if Miss Gordon knew who my father was, if there was a way I could drop the information casually.

"I'm fine here, ma'am."

"Are you making fun of me?"

"What?"

"That 'ma'am' sounded very sarcastic, Luisa. You are to call me Miss Gordon."

"Yes, ma—yes, Miss Gordon." The ma'am was Teensy's fault. It was as if everyone in my life had set me up to fail—AJ, by teaching me to read, my father for encouraging the habit, Teensy for insisting on manners. Didn't anyone in my family know how the real world worked?

Things never got better that year. They didn't get worse, but they never got better. Even my impeccable classwork did not endear me to Miss Gordon. And when it came to creative work—drawing pictures, using our new words to make simple poems—she was particularly harsh with me. My neat, bland drawings were never placed in the center of the blackboard display. She hated my brown cats and black dogs, my blue skies and yellow suns. She even seemed to dislike my precise rhymes, while she heaped praise on students whose words didn't really go together, insisting they had *imagination*. She stretched out her arms as she stretched out the syllables of that word—EH-MAH-GI-NAY-SHUN! Miss Gordon valued creativity above everything.

Later that fall, when my father went to parent-teacher night, he came home and sat on the edge of my bed to report back, at my insistence. I had told him I wanted to know exactly what Miss Gordon thought of me, word for word. To my father's credit, he agreed to honor this request, although he warned me it might hurt. I imagined a Band-Aid being ripped from my skin. I never cried when that happened. I could handle words.

"I'll be okay," I assured him.

He sighed and began his summation.

He had been told that Miss Gordon was frustrated by my hostility toward creative work. I lacked, yes, EH-MAH-GI-NAY-SHUN. Oh, I could do any task that was based on studying and having facts at hand. In the world of right answers, I was 100 percent. But asked to draw a picture or tell a story, I pestered Miss Gordon with endless questions about the "rules." Did there have to be a person in the story? A tree? Must it have a happy ending? How many words? What do I need to get an A?

"Why is it so hard for you to imagine things, Lu? You read lots of stories."

"I can imagine things fine," I said. "But I want to make sure I get the best grades."

"Why? I've never told you that I cared about your grades. All I ask is that you do your best."

"Yes, being the best is important. Winning is important."

"No, being a good person is important. Caring about others. Being warm and empathetic. Miss Gordon said you make fun of the kids who aren't as smart as you."

"That's not true." I wanted to cry at the unfairness of this accusation. "I try to help them. Some of them can barely print, and I'm the only one who can write cursive. And their rhymes are wrong. Danny put together 'hard' and 'park' and Miss Gordon said his poem was great, while I wrote 'Once I saw a possum / Smelling a blossom,' and she told me that possums don't come out in the daytime, so why would they be smelling flowers. See—when I do have imagination, it doesn't count, I'm making a mistake. But when Randy Nairn draws a dog with smoke coming out of its mouth, he's told he's *wonderful*."

"Your classmates don't want your help, Lu. That's what Miss Gordon says. You finish your work early, then try to insert yourself in the work of others."

I became frustrated, saw that I would never be able to explain the situation to my father. I was battling Miss Gordon for control of the classroom. Losing, but battling. She had rejected me, so I wanted the other kids to see I was as smart as she was. I was at war.

"I just want to win," I said.

"Win what, Lu?"

I shook my head, out of words.

"You're so competitive, Lu. If you make winning everything, you'll never be happy."

"You're happy when you win. You were really happy when you won that case."

"Because justice was done. Because a young woman whose body may never be found wasn't forgotten. When I go to court, Lu, it's never about winning."

But that's what competitive people always say. Have you noticed only another competitive person will ever call you competitive? Yes, I liked to win, but so did my father and my brother. And, oh Lord, how Gabe made everything a competition. *Who's playing the saxophone on this song?* he would ask me when some jazz standard came on a restaurant's sound system. Or, apropos of nothing, *How many Triple Crown winners can you name?* I'm not sure I've ever met anyone who didn't want to win, but I definitely didn't know a Brant who didn't love victory. We played chess, checkers, Botticelli, Geography, "Jimmy has a ball of string." We played Stratego, Life, Operation (and only I could remove that funny bone). Dominoes, gin rummy, a card game called Up the River, Down the River. I was given slight advantages when I was very young, but I was never patronized. When I won, it was real, a true achievement. Winning was everything in my household.

The thing I had gotten wrong was showing how desperately I wanted to win. That was what I had to learn to conceal, what my father and AJ knew from birth: disguise your desire.

Lu watches through the one-way glass as Mike and his partner, Terry Childs, interrogate Rudy Drysdale. Lu expected someone more obviously homeless—matted beard and hair, dirty clothes— but this Drysdale character is fairly neat and well groomed, considering his lifestyle. If one didn't know which was which, he might appear to be the attorney. He has a quiet poise, while the young female public defender is almost aquiver with nerves.

The detectives are pushing for a confession. Seems unlikely with a guy who invoked his right to an attorney so quickly, but Lu is happy to let them try.

To her delight, the inexperienced public defender is allowing her client to speak, almost encouraging him to do so. The whole point of lawyering-up is to shut up, but the public defender seems to believe that Drysdale has an alibi or other information that will lead to his release.

Rudy whispers to his public defender, who then presents his story to the detectives. Lu is reminded of how Penelope and Justin used to confide "secrets" to her in tandem, a hot, damp mouth pressed to each ear, words tumbling out. When had that stopped? They are growing up so quickly and she fears she is missing too much. But then, being twins, they always have each other. Maybe it's natural that they become self-contained at a much younger age than other children.

"The apartment appeared to be empty," says Rose Darling, a lovely name for a woman who is, well, not lovely. Splotchy complexion, overweight, dark frizzy hair. Lu amuses herself by coming up with various tricks to remember the woman's name, which will be useful when they meet again. Public defenders vote, too, and everyone yearns to be remembered. *My public defender is like a red, red rose. Oh my darling, oh my darling, oh my darling defender Rose.* Lu feels bad about the woman's cheap suit. Public defenders make even less than state's attorneys. Lu takes special care to make sure that her expensive clothes do not *look* expensive. Her inherited wealth is one of those ugly topics always just below the surface. During the campaign, Fred called her a dilettante, tried to suggest that she wanted his job so she wouldn't be bored. Has anyone ever suggested that a rich man wanted to work simply because he had nothing else to do?

"When?" Mike asks. "When did you break in?"

Drysdale shakes his head frantically. He looks a little younger than his age, uncommon in a man who spends so much time outside. And he does not appear mentally incapacitated, aside from his aversion to speaking out loud. Once dressed in a suit, he will look presentable at trial. That could work for him or against him, Lu decides. If she were his attorney, she'd try to have him ruled incompetent to stand trial, given his history of hospitalizations. She wouldn't win on those grounds, but she'd at least try. Rose—what was the surname, *oh my darling, oh my darling*—Darling doesn't even seem to realize it's an option. She's the one on the verge of boxing him into a certain set of dates. Drysdale at least seems to realize that the less said about timing, the better.

He leans in to whisper to her again. Rose Darling says: "My

client is not admitting he broke in and he says he cannot be sure of when he was there. He doesn't keep a calendar."

"Did you know Mary McNally, Rudy? Had you seen her at the Silver Diner? Or around the neighborhood?"

He shakes his head no, but only after a long pause.

"Why were you in her apartment?"

He whispers in his lawyer's ear then, and the lawyer says: "He's not admitting that he was in her apartment."

"He already *did*," Mike says.

More whispers. "He can't be sure he was in her apartment because he doesn't know who she is. He doesn't know Mary McNally, has no knowledge of her whatsoever. He entered an apartment in the Grove. He doesn't remember when and he doesn't know who it belongs to. If there was a body in there at the time, he might not have entered that room."

"Buddy, we got fingerprints. You're all over the place. On the door that was open, which was inches from her head, and on the door that was closed. You're on the thermostat. So, what, you climbed up on her balcony, saw the open door, stepped over her body, went to check the thermostat, then left by the other door, which you carefully closed? Is that the story you want to tell?"

Rudy stares at the ceiling as if the conversation has begun to bore him. His affect is like a teenager's, checking out as his parents discuss his failings at the family dinner table. Asked how he got into the apartment, he continues to stare at the ceiling. Asked how Mary McNally died, he makes eye contact only with the light fixture over his head. Asked if he can account for his whereabouts over the past week, he smiles and shakes his head, as if the detectives are being silly. *Fine, don't speak,* Lu thinks. The fingerprints put him at the scene, he's been IDed in a lineup. He's going straight from here to a judge, who will almost certainly order him held without bail.

"I almost feel sorry for that public defender," Lu says to Mike when just that scenario plays out. She has sent Andi to the bail review, an easy bone to toss.

"Yeah, she's a mess. Jury might end up feeling sorry for *her*, too. And him. What a sad sack. Local guy, went to Wilde Lake Middle and High School."

"That's where I went," Lu says. "Also my brother."

"Really?" Mike is too polite to note that the school's reputation is lackluster these days. The original "villages" of Columbia are now called the "inner villages," and the pejorative echo of inner city is not accidental. The money has marched west, and the desirable school districts are in what were cornfields and wilderness in Lu's lifetime. "Still, he has an almost plausible story. All he has to do is claim that the sliding door in the *second* bedroom was unlocked—we can't prove he was the one who pried it open—that he came in that way, noticed it was cold, checked the thermostat, then—"

Lu holds up a hand. She's not a superstitious person, anything but. Yet she has no patience with worst-case scenarios. Bad news will out soon enough, why put it in the universe? When the twins were six weeks old, there were a couple of bad nights with Justin, the smaller of the two, and Gabe kept trying to bring up the possibility of colic. She wouldn't let him say the word out loud and she would hold the screeching baby as if his screams didn't grieve her. Lu believes that you must will yourself not to dwell on all the bad things that can happen, only the good. She imagined herself as state's attorney and here she is. The bad things still find a way to happen.

And if she's honest with herself, there were days when Gabe was forever on planes and corporate jets and traveling to far-flung places that she wondered what life would be like if he just didn't come back. Now she knows. Now she lives it every day. She had thought she was doing everything, that he contributed almost nothing to their children's daily care. But gone is not dead. She had to learn that the hard way.

Gabe's ghost seems to hover at her elbow that evening, as she tries to help Penelope with her math homework. Lu has a firm rule that homework must be done on Friday nights, not Sundays. She is a big believer in getting unpleasant things out of the way, and homework has become particularly unpleasant. In her heart of hearts, she hadn't really believed the dire warnings she heard from other parents about how difficult and demanding homework had become. She never believed any of the dire things people told her about raising children, and yet every stage seemed to arrive as foretold by the Oracle of Delphi. Now multiply that by two children, subtract one spouse—there was a math problem even more daunting than the multiplication tables that Penelope was struggling with long after Justin had breezed through them and earned his hour of screen time.

"It's so unfair," Penelope whines, her hazel eyes filmed with tears, a strand of hair in her mouth. The thing is, it *is* unfair. Lu knows firsthand what it's like to have a brother who's better than you in everything. But at least AJ was eight years older than she was, so she had the consolation of thinking she would catch up to him—in height, in talent, in looks, in social skills. Penelope is six minutes older than Justin and they look so much alike that they could be twins in a Shakespearean comedy, destined to switch identities at some point. They look nothing like Lu, although people claim to see a resemblance. As babies, they were little Gabes, dark and beetle-browed. Now they have that magical combination of olive skin and light eyes, with brown hair that turns golden in the summer sun. They are close, as twins tend to be, and that only aggravates Penelope's frustration.

"Take a deep breath," Lu says, stroking Penelope's hair, even as she yearns to move two hours ahead into the future, when she can sit by herself for a few minutes. She had been a good student and has no idea what to say to a bad one. And how can Gabe's daughter not have an affinity for math? Lu has a brainstorm, tells Penelope that she can put her homework away for now, come back to it tomorrow. "You're tired, I think. That's all. Your brain is fogged." At bedtime, she reads Penelope a chapter from *A Tree Grows in Brooklyn,* the one where Francie conquers arithmetic by turning it into a story. If Penelope did not inherit Gabe's genius for numbers, maybe she can learn Lu's talent for creating narratives. While many prosecutors consider their most violent cases to be their most pivotal, Lu is perversely proud of a theft case she had to try, one that involved a complicated accounting scheme at a city hospital. Any jury can follow a story of murder or rape. Leading them through a thicket of numbers required much more skill.

"Make the numbers live," she says to Penelope, "and they'll make more sense."

"Do they have to be people? Because three makes me think of a bear and eight is a snowman."

"They can be whatever you want them to be," she says, savoring the moment.

———

Her children asleep, her father shut up in his study, Lu goes to AJ's room on the third floor. The linens have been updated, but it is otherwise as he left it, even as the rest of the house has been transformed around it. The transformation continues, in fact, with no end in sight. Her father seems to have become compulsive about renovation the way some women become addicted to plastic surgery. Since Lu's return, he has remade almost every square foot of this old house and built an addition, essentially a new wing, which includes rooms for the twins and Lu. (Her childhood bedroom, which adjoins her father's suite, is now the study to which he retreats at night, sequestering himself from all the noise that accompanies bathtime and bedtime.) But their father wants AJ to decide how his room should be redone, and AJ keeps putting him off. Lu wonders if it's the very fervency of her father's redecorating that keeps AJ from making any decisions. AJ has sworn off material things. Sort of, kind of. But this time capsule of a room is to Lu's advantage to-night. She quickly finds AJ's high school yearbook, the *Glass Hour*, on the shelf above his desk, a modular unit that Lu envied terribly as a kid. She envies it now—this kind of midcentury modern design is back in style and she yearns for a more modern-*looking* house, but her father continues to decorate in the traditional style that her mother preferred. Stout, dark wood, rich, soft fabrics that run to hunter green and burgundy.

Lu flips through the yearbook. As a ten-year-old left behind after her brother's high school graduation, she used to study this book as if it were a sacred text, wondering if she would have as glorious a high school career as her brother. (She did not, although she finally cracked the code of social life and enjoyed the last two years.) There must be at least a dozen photographs of AJ throughout the yearbook. and it is filled with affectionate scrawls of inside jokes from dozens of his classmates. "Ach du lieber, Mrs. Bitterman!" "Still bummed we never made RP room." "AJ Brant for President 2000." How typical that one of AJ's friends would calculate the first year that he could legally run for president.

But the only place she can find Rudy Drysdale is on the mast-head, one of four staff photographers. And in the yearbook staff's group photo, he is listed as absent. He was at least a year behind AJ, maybe two. Still, he almost certainly took some of these photos of AJ—in his soccer uniform, his leg bent at a seemingly impossi-ble angle; as Sancho Panza, looking up worshipfully at Davey's Don

Quixote; surrounded by his group in a candid photo in the cafeteria. Were they a clique? Was that word even used at the time?

Penelope and Justin are only eight, and Lu already has seen so many dynamics she thought wouldn't happen for years—mean girls, bullies, this terrible anxiety about fitting in. And there is so much concern about autism these days. Until the twins turned five or so, the pediatrician was forever asking Lu about laughter and eye contact and whether the twins would tolerate being touched. "Their father died when they were three," Lu said time and again. "They come by their seriousness and anxiety pretty honestly."

She bet her father was never asked these same questions about Lu, although her circumstances were similar. Adele Brant had died in childbirth. Well, not in. She gave birth. She died a week later. As a child, Lu clung to the lie—insisted on the lie—that her mother's heart condition had not been affected by this clearly unplanned pregnancy. Lu was born, a week later her mother died. No connection, no cause and effect, just a series of discrete events. Yep, sure, that makes sense. Even as all the other myths of childhood—Santa, Tooth Fairy, Easter Bunny—fell away, the Brant family maintained this well-intentioned fiction. Her father even insisted that he was the one to blame for his wife's death. Not because Adele Brant got pregnant against her doctor's advice, but because her husband made her move to Columbia, a place to which she could not be reconciled, no matter how hard her husband tried.

And he tried so hard, starting with this very house. If Lu says nothing as the bills come in—Italian tiles, bathtubs that cost as much as small cars, custom rugs, top-of-the-line appliances for the kitchen where Teensy continues to make most of their meals—it's because she realizes her father is trying to make good on a forty-five-year-old promise. He lured his young wife to Columbia, saying he would do anything to make her happy here. He failed. With Lu and the twins, he has a second chance to make someone happy in this house.

But is he happy? Was he ever happy? she wonders. Then she feels guilty, as grown children often do, for how seldom they have bothered to consider a parent's happiness.

THINGS THAT GO BUMP IN THE NIGHT

My January second birthdate seemed tragic when I was young, the cornerstone of all my social failures. If my birthday fell on a school day, it was always the first day back from the holiday, the least happy day of the year. And if it were a Saturday or Sunday, it was still an awkward time. People have no energy for celebrations after January first. Besides, my father didn't know how to throw a party for a girl. With AJ, who had an April birthday, he told him to invite all the boys in his class, and that was that. They played in the yard for three hours, Teensy served a cake, then threw everyone out.

When my father told me I should invite all the girls in my class over for an indoor party for my seventh birthday, I saw the pitfalls. There would be no theme, no organization. If there were games, they would be too baby-ish. The favors would be found wanting. No, there were just too many ways to fail.

"I don't like all the girls," I said. "Some of them are mean to me." That wasn't exactly true. All the girls were mean to me. And most of the boys.

"The Brants don't believe in leaving people out. All or nothing."

"You're leaving the boys out," I said.

"There are twenty-six children in your class," he said. "That is simply too much. But if you don't want to include all the girls, you can have a celebration with AJ and me. You'll have your favorite cake. You can choose an activity. Movie, bowling, ice-skating. And then you can invite your best friend. But if you want to have a party, you must include everyone."

I wondered if my father had noticed that I was seldom invited to parties, that other parents did not observe the Brant standard. He certainly should have been aware that I had no best friend, but then—he did not arrive home until suppertime and I was too proud to speak of my troubles to Teensy or AJ. It made me feel better in a way that my father had no inkling I was friendless. I told him I could not choose just one friend—true enough—and selected ice-skating as my activity. There was a rink on the east side of Columbia and I was good at ice-skating, thanks to AJ's tutelage, and I had my own skates, which provided a tiny bit of cachet. And at a rink, if one moved quickly enough, it was possible to disguise the fact that one was going around and around in circles all alone.

Better still, my father accompanied us and even laced himself into a pair of rental skates, the best gift he could have given me. Our father was not one for playing with us unless it was something brainy. He did not throw a football with AJ or swim with us at the community pool. Other fathers were rare there, too, but when they showed up, they picked up their children and launched them through the air, happy squealing rockets. We sometimes wondered if our father avoided activities because he was klutzy or inept. But when he did do something, he did it well. Still, I doubt he would have put on rented ice skates if it were not for the influence of our new neighbor, Miss Maude.

———

We had thought she was old when she moved into the house closest to ours, just a few weeks before Halloween. Really old, older-than-our-father old. She had silver hair, a lot of it, amplified by a wild curly perm. She never seemed to smile. But she wasn't quite thirty and she came by her sad expression honestly. She was a widow. Her husband had been in Vietnam. "That's probably why her hair turned white," Noel said to AJ. "A bad shock really can do that."

"Oh, that's just nonsense," AJ said.

They were in AJ's room, watching Miss Maude through one of the little dormer windows that ringed the top floor, two to a side. I was in the adjoining room, the one that Teensy used when she slept over, eavesdropping. Two sets of spies. I didn't understand the attraction of watching Maude Lennox preparing her yard and garden for the coming winter. The day was Indian summer hot, but a freeze was forecast for the next week. I glanced out the dormer window in Teensy's room—from the outside, these windows looked like two eyebrows, arched in surprise. Miss Maude was crouching over a rosebush. She wore cherry-red shorts and a gingham halter, her snaky silver hair tamed by a triangle of red bandanna.

Music floated in the air, from AJ's record player. It was a song he liked a lot, something about two people sitting on a hill. The girl apparently had moonlight in her eyes, which sounded interesting to me, like maybe she had moonbeams that shot out like lasers. *Everything was ours, everything was ours.* I imagined a king and a queen, surveying their kingdom, subduing miscreants with lasers.

"I can see her bending over a hot stove," Noel said. "Trouble is, I can't see the stove. Groucho Marx, *Duck Soup.*"

"Shut up," AJ hissed.

"She can't hear us, not with the music blasting. And from this angle, she can't see us. Although it's not her *angles* that interest you, I guess."

"Noel." A slamming sound. The window shutting? The volume on the record player was lowered, because if it were too loud, Teensy might storm upstairs. Whatever they were doing, they didn't want anyone in there. Not Teensy, not me. A smell of smoke, sweet and strange. The sound of the window creaking open.

"Do you think they do it?" That was Noel.

"Who?"

"Kim and Carson."

"Probably. I don't know. I don't care."

"He says they do."

"I don't care."

"Didn't you ask Kim to homecoming?"

"No."

"You said you were going to."

"I said that if I wanted to go to a dance, she'd be okay. Obviously, she's going with Carson."

"I don't think they do it. They're all over each other at school. Between classes—it's like he was going off to war instead of French II. Heh, French II. Based on what I've seen, Kim could teach AP French. She goes for it. Right there in the hall."

"Noel, I don't want to talk about Kim and Carson."

The window closed again.

"What does your dad think?"

Why, I wondered, *would my father care about these people named Kim and Carson, and whether they're going to the dance together?*

"I told you—he doesn't want me to smoke, but he all but said that if I do smoke, do it at home when he's not here. I mean, I'm pretty sure that's what he was saying, between the lines. Can you imagine if Andrew Brant's son got busted for grass?"

I sat there, trying to figure out how one smoked grass. I assumed that Noel and AJ were making fake cigarettes out of grass clippings. Maybe they were watching Miss Maude in hopes of stealing some grass from her yard. Smoking was bad. Smoking killed you. I had nagged my father until he gave up his pipe and now it sounded as if I was going to have to start in on my brother.

"We're not stoners," Noel said. "We can take it or leave it."

My six-year-old brain turned that over, too. Did Noel mean they wouldn't throw rocks at someone? Were they going to throw rocks at Miss Maude? Or was he talking about stonemen, like the ones in the *B.C.* comic?

"We're not really anything," Noel continued. "We're sort of a group unto ourselves. We do the theater stuff and singing, we dominate the productions, but we're not the theater group. That's, you know, Sarah and that boy Mark, the ones who are always drawing attention to themselves, breaking into musical numbers in the hall. We're athletes, but we're not jocks, not even Bash or Lynne. I play tennis and you'll probably make JV for both basketball and baseball this year. You might even be varsity for baseball, as a freshman. We get good grades."

"You have to be pretty lame not to get good grades at a school where there's no failure and they let you retake tests."

"Less and less," Noel said. "Some of the classes are like normal classes anywhere now. Anyway, we're, like, I don't know—the Bloomsbury Group of Wilde Lake High School. I'm going to start calling you Leonard."

"Does that make you Virginia?"

They laughed very hard at this. I guessed Leonard and Virginia were really weird. Then, Noel again: "Come away from the window, you pervert, Lawdy, Miss Maude-y. If I were your dad, I'd be over there with, I don't know, what does the Welcome Wagon actually bring? Is there still a Welcome Wagon?"

"I think that's in *The Music Man*," AJ said. "I hope they put that on when we're juniors or seniors. I want to play Harold Hill."

"No, that's the Wells Fargo wagon, you doofus."

The music stopped and it was evident that AJ was changing records. He put the *Music Man* soundtrack on his stereo, and the two of them sang along to the train rhythms of the opening song. As the record continued, they laughed hysterically at things that didn't seem that funny to me. I could tell from the timbre of their voices that they were lying on the wooden floor, singing to the ceiling. I lay down on the floor in the spare room, wondering what made the ceiling so hilarious. It was plaster, in need of repair, and if you squinted hard enough, you could find shapes in the stains and cracks. But unlike clouds, they were always the same shapes, and I had identified them long ago. A rabbit. A rose. A cow head. *Trouble,* AJ sang, *Trouble.* And Noel sang back: *Right here in Wilde Lake.* The kids in their—what? For years I thought it was their "double backers," not that I knew what a double backer was, but it made as much sense as knickerbockers would have. Then again, it was only this year, listening to Sirius radio in my car, that I found out that I had gone my entire life thinking that the nice man who sang "More I Cannot Wish You," was not, in fact, hoping that the young woman found a man with the "licorice tooth."

————————

A week or two later, our father paid his respects to our new neighbor, taking her a bottle of wine, the kind that had straw on the bottom and, once empty, could be used as a candleholder. He was the one who reported back that she was only thirty, despite the shock of white hair, and really quite friendly, if particular about her lawn and plantings. She was originally from South Carolina, but her husband had been assigned to Fort Meade before he was sent to Vietnam and she came to like Maryland. She wasn't sure why she had bought a three-bedroom house in a suburb. Maybe, she told my father, it was because she still kept thinking she was going to have a family.

My father thought it a kindness to Miss Maude to send me over there on Fridays to keep her company, but he insisted to her that she was doing *him* a favor, that if she looked after me for a couple of hours, Teensy could leave early and avoid the rush-hour traffic. ("My husband wants me home by five on Fridays" was one of her pronouncements.") Miss Maude began stocking her refrigerator and pantry with my favorite treats. She introduced me to the world of soap operas. I seldom got to her house before *The Edge of Night* and I saw only the Friday episodes, but it wasn't that hard to follow. Soap operas moved slowly then, and a lot of the best stuff happened on Fridays. She would walk me home when she saw my father's car in the drive and, often as not, he invited her to share our standing Friday night dinner of Colombo's pizza, which he picked up on the way home. But they never spent any time alone and they certainly never had dates. When we all went ice-skating for my birthday, Miss Maude sat in the stands, stamping her feet and breathing smoke. "I grew up in the South," she said when I asked her to join us. "I never learned to skate. It's a hard thing to pick up when you're older, although your father did, at college. He was on the hockey team."

"He never was," I said, sure that I knew everything about him. But when I asked my father, he agreed that he had played hockey in college, although on an intramural team, not the official one. And he had learned to skate in boarding school, Deerfield. Miss Maude had gotten that part of the story wrong. That made me feel better for some reason.

I remember the winter that followed my seventh birthday as a particularly bitter one. (When it comes to weather, I have not bothered to check if my memory is right. I can't check everything.) Single-digit temperatures, icicles like daggers, yet relatively little snow. For just the second time in my life, Wilde Lake was almost solid enough to walk across, although only the boldest boys risked that. The cold air leaked into our house from every window and faultily hung door. We burned fires in all the fireplaces, even at night, violating our father's long-standing rule about not leaving fires untended.

Yet it wasn't our old house, with fireplaces going around the clock, that went up in flames. It was Miss Maude's.

Now when I was a child, I was famous for being able to sleep through anything, so it wasn't the orange glow outside my windows or even the sirens in the distance that woke me. But then, there were no sirens, not yet.

There was just my father, still in his work clothes at 1 A.M., shaking me and calling my name. "I need to get you outside, Lu. To be safe. We have to go outside. It could jump."

"What jumps?" I asked, rolling away from him and curling up like a potato bug, determined not to leave my wonderfully warm bed, where I had piled three quilts on top of me.

"The fire. Miss Maude's house has caught fire and ours might catch, too. We have to go."

He eased me into my coat and boots. My mind had finally registered the urgency of the situation, but not my limbs, and it was as if I were a toddler, requiring assistance. AJ had dressed himself and was waiting for us by the front door. Once outside, the overwhelming sensation was one of extreme cold and extreme heat. It was so cold that I began to move instinctively toward the flames, only to have my father pull me back. He then crouched low to the ground, holding me between his knees so we could keep each other warm.

The fire trucks seemed to take so long. We heard the sirens first, then saw the lights flashing through the bare trees, visible as the trucks raced down Green Mountain Circle and then turned onto our cul-de-sac. The hoses didn't go on right away.

"Are they frozen?" AJ asked.

"I don't know, son. I just don't know."

The high-powered hoses came on and we almost cheered. But then they shattered the windows on the upper levels of Miss Maude's house, and the water poured in. I thought of her pretty rooms, the pale green sofa where we watched our programs, the freezer full of Good Humor bars.

Yet she seemed almost nonchalant about the damage being done. "I bought this place for the yard," she muttered. "The house can go to hell."

Fine for her, but now our house was under threat. We had always thought of our house as far from its only neighbor, sitting as it did on a double lot, but Miss Maude's house seemed terrifyingly close that night. I understood, then, why people speak of flames licking. That fire had a thousand little tongues that kept darting at our house, eager to taste it, devour it. Sure, it was stone, but there was wood trim and the windows could burst from the heat. My window had been warm to the touch when my father awakened me.

A tree near the rear of Miss Maude's property, right next to the unmarked boundary between our houses, began to go up. It was like watching snakes race up that tree, crimson-orange lines going up, up, up the trunk.

"They might have to train their hoses on our house, just to be safe," our father said. "If that happens—well, water will get in. It can't be helped."

I thought of my room, my beloved stuffed animals, the new toys from my birthday. I had been given a wooden contraption with two long metal arms; the game was to coax a large ball-bearing up those arms until it dropped into one of the circles below. I was better than AJ or my father at this game; I had a delicacy of touch they couldn't match. I could not bear to lose that game, the game at which I always won. Pinned between my father's legs, I started to cry and he tightened his hold on me, as if fearful I would try to run inside. Miss Maude stroked my hair almost absentmindedly.

"It's a sign," she said. "How can it be anything but a sign?"

"Don't be silly," my father said. "And don't blame yourself. Accidents happen."

"Oh, I don't. I don't."

And just like that, the fire seemed to give up, not unlike the witch vanquished by water in *The Wizard of Oz*. It shrank back into Miss Maude's house, or what was left of it. There was a hole in the roof, broken windows, scorch marks. Her house was destroyed. Ours was spared.

"At least I had the presence of mind to grab my purse," Miss Maude said. "I can go stay at the Columbia Inn, I guess."

"You could have the guest room at our house," my father said. "It's always made up for Teensy."

I swear AJ blushed in the firelight, thinking of Miss Maude on the other side of the wall from him, separated by only a tiny powder room. *She'll be able to hear AJ go to the bathroom,* I thought.

"No, no, I wouldn't dare put you out."

She walked over to her car, a VW bug. Although she had on boots, she was bare-legged and the hem of her nightgown showed beneath her coat.

"What happened?" I asked my father. "How did it catch fire?"

"She told the firemen she lit a candle downstairs, then forgot to snuff it out before she went to bed."

It was only when we went back inside that I noticed my father's feet. "You forgot to put on your shoes?"

"I know," he said. "I was in such a hurry to get you out, I didn't think. You know how I fall asleep in my chair at night."

He was walking from fireplace to fireplace, banking the fires we had allowed to burn. I went to his room to get his shoes, assuming he had kicked them off by his reading chair. I couldn't find them, so I brought him his slippers.

"What did Miss Maude mean, saying it was a sign?"

"She's been thinking about moving. I guess this will settle it for her. Although that's a very silly way to be, Lu. To place emphasis on portents. Or horoscopes, or any of that stuff. She left a candle burning and her draperies caught fire."

"I read my horoscope every day," I reminded him.

"I know," he said. "You read it out loud to me."

"That's because it's yours, too."

"Yes, and do you really think that you and I have the same day every day, that what's recommended for you applies to me?"

I did.

Miss Maude never spent another night in that house. It was razed a few months later, and the lot stood empty for years, which delighted AJ and me as it became our unofficial territory. That spring, glorious flowers came to life, peeping through the overgrown grass, the result of Miss Maude's meticulous preparation in her first few weeks, her only weeks, in the house. They never bloomed again.

I was fifteen or sixteen before I realized that my father's shoes were in Miss Maude's house when it started to burn. As was my father. My father was shoeless in Miss Maude's house, and they weren't in the living room when that candle in the old Chianti bottle caught the drapes, or they might have had a chance to put it out. They had gone upstairs. Together.

I called my brother, in law school at the time. I assumed he had figured it out before I did, but I held on to the hope that I might, just once, tell AJ something he didn't already know.

Of course he had pieced together far more than I had.

"It didn't start that night, Lu. He'd been going over there since mid-December, after you were asleep and I was in my room. He'd tell me he was going outside to smoke his pipe—he knew you didn't approve of him smoking and would give him hell if you picked up the scent of his tobacco in the house—but he didn't come back for hours. Then one night I saw him leaving her house, and I knew."

"Eeeeew," I said.

"That's how I felt then." *That's how I felt when I was your age.* I thought, *So infuriating.* "Now I'm happy for him. Although—you know, she wasn't a widow."

"What do you mean? She lied about being married?"

"She lied about her husband being dead. He was at Walter Reed, a double amputee."

"But Daddy didn't know that. He couldn't have."

AJ sighed over the line. It was the mid-1980s. A long-distance call was still something of import, minutes gobbling up money the way the still-novel Pac-Man ate his power pills, although my father never objected to me calling AJ. He wanted us to be close. He had encouraged the ritual of our weekly Sunday call and even allowed me to call before rates dropped if I had important news. However, he probably would have been appalled if he had known what we were discussing on this particular Sunday.

"How do you think I know, Lu? He told me so himself."

"Uh-huh. No way. Daddy never would have been with a married woman. Besides, why would he tell *you*?"

AJ's laugh was raw and sad. "I guess he wanted to warn me that everyone screws up sometime. Even our saintly father. He said she was a de facto widow—wouldn't divorce her husband out of principle, but he was never going to come home, be her husband again."

"So he argued against his adultery on the basis of a technicality?"

"Other way around. He insisted that he was guilty of adultery despite her situation. But he cared about her, in his way, although he was never going to get serious with any woman. At any rate, she saw the fire as a judgment and left." A pause. "Miss Maude wasn't the only one, over the years. There were others. Lu, did you really think our father, who was not quite forty when our mother died, went the rest of his life without female companionship?"

I did. And I still believe that he did not have a single lady friend during the eight-year stretch when it was just the two of us, after AJ left for college. By the time I was in my teens, I was on the alert for love and sex, imagining it everywhere, so how could I not have noticed if it were there?

Then again, how did I not pick up the scent of my father's pipe tobacco?

Perhaps my adolescent self simply balked at that threshold of my father's bedroom, as most teenagers do. I hope so. Now I want to believe that my father found a way to meet his needs, that he had a rich and thrilling secret life.

After all, I did, at least for a time.

"Your first murder," Lu's father says, opening a bottle of wine, one of the better ones in his "cellar"—a corner of the kitchen that now includes two wine refrigerators, one for whites, and one that keeps reds at a steady sixty-four degrees. "Sort of like living in San Francisco," AJ observed on his last visit, which provoked a pedantic observation from his wife, Lauranne, that San Francisco is not, in fact, sixty-four degrees year-round. Lauranne still doesn't have a handle on the Brant sense of humor.

Lu glances at the price tag, which her father has forgotten to scrape off. $39.99, some Australian red with a silly name. And it's just a Saturday night dinner at home, nothing innately special, although they are expecting AJ and that is always a cause to celebrate. AJ lives less than twenty miles away, but his work—his *ministry,* as Lu likes to tease him, knowing that the term provokes him on several levels—means he's on the road, on the go, all the time.

"Not my first murder by a long shot," Lu reminds her father. "My first as state's attorney. I did several as a deputy. You know, not everyone gets appointed to the state's attorney's office. Some of us actually have to *run.*"

He decants the wine, putting out stemless wineglasses for the adults, heavy tumblers for the twins. Andrew Brant, almost forty when Lu was born, had been considered an "old" father and he remains undeniably old-fashioned. He believes that children should learn to negotiate the adult world, that plastic cups with lids only retard their progress. To his credit, he never gets angry over spills or breakage. Teensy is the one who mourns the destruction of the Brants' material possessions. But then—she's the one who has been cleaning them for two generations. When Lu moved back in with her father, she was amazed to realize how little he knows about domestic arrangements. He cannot scramble eggs or make a bed. Or maybe he just *doesn't*. He will buy groceries for special occasions—steaks, homemade ice cream, sushi-grade tuna from Wegman's—but it would never occur to him to go to Giant or Target for everyday things like paper towels and detergent. Teensy does his laundry and ironing. Only his, she made clear to Lu with Teensy-ian logic. "You and the children have so many bright-colored things," she said. "I can't mix them with Mr. Brant's." How many Andrew Brants does it take to screw in a lightbulb? Lu has never been able to nail the precise punch line, but it would probably have to do with him not needing to change the lightbulb. He could just sit in the glow of his own saintly perfection.

The twins helped her finish setting the table, and with only a minimum of nagging. They look forward to their uncle's visits as well. He plays with Justin and is fatherly with Penelope. Lu gazes with satisfaction at the inviting room. Winter is the house's best season. With the trees bare, the lake is in full view from three sides. Hard to remember now the raw, immature landscaping that legend-arily offended Adele Brant more than forty years ago. Lu always thought trees took centuries to reach maturity, yet now they are huge and she is still not old. Forty-five isn't old, right? Especially when one is beginning a new, big job. Lu likes to joke that her midlife crisis was postponed because widowhood was more pressing. What would a midlife crisis even look like for a single mother of two? Some people might point to the one part of her life that she keeps rigidly compartmentalized, but no one knows about it, so no one can cite it.

Which just proves, Lu thinks, how very good she is at compartmentalizing.

AJ—of course—managed to have an original midlife crisis: at age forty-four, he shucked his gorgeous, funny, brilliant wife of ten years, headed out for a *wanderjahr,* returned and fell in love with a mousy yoga teacher. Lu still finds it hard to reconcile herself to this. Lauranne is a drag. A drag on conversation, a drag on meals—a vegan alternative always has to be provided and is never quite right. Yet AJ remains smitten. Lauranne represents the new life he created for himself after walking away from Lehman Brothers. Granted, he walked away in 2006, excellent timing on his part. Two years later and his fortune would have walked away from him. He divested himself of most of his material goods—although only half of his considerable cash—telling his first wife, Helena, that she could have the house in Greenwich, the apartment in New York City, the beach house on Cape Cod. He then made his own *Eat, Pray, Love* pilgrimage around the world, although ascetic AJ skipped the eating part. He found Lauranne in some yoga class along the way and eventually brought her to Baltimore, where they became pioneers in urban gardening, something that Lu and her father privately find hilarious. "AJ didn't even like cutting grass as a boy," her father says. "Now he's practically a farmer."

AJ's embrace of simple living has only made him richer. He wrote a book about his travels that became an unexpected hit in paperback, the sort of thing that book clubs love. The book made him an in-demand speaker, someone hired for $10,000, $20,000 a night. A local radio show on AJ and Lauranne's locavore life ended up being nationally syndicated. Three years ago, he even was named a MacArthur fellow, receiving one of the so-called genius grants. The couple still lives in Southwest Baltimore and AJ is often photographed outside their home, a simple redbrick rowhouse. Photographers and reporters are never allowed inside, however. Luisa suspects this is because AJ and Lauranne actually own *three* rowhouses, reconfigured inside so that there is an open courtyard with a pool bracketed on three sides by the two end rowhouses, a walled garden at the back of the property. Lu has to give AJ his due; it is still a pretty scruffy neighborhood and he is cheerful about the price he pays to live there—graffiti, vandalism, petty larcenies. And he is doing something incontestably good, helping families in Southwest Baltimore grow their own vegetables and learn to cook and eat seasonally. He, in turn, credits Lauranne for much of his success, but Lu cannot bear to ascribe anything positive to her brother's second wife. To her, Lauranne is just a lucky hanger-on.

She misses Helena. Funny, bright, a lawyer. AJ says they broke up over the issue of children, yet AJ and Lauranne don't seem to be interested in having children, either, although she's still just young enough, in her thirties. But Lu can tell, by the way she interacts with Penelope and Justin—which is to say, the way she *doesn't* interact— that Lauranne has no desire to be a mom. Fair enough. Let her eat vegetables and tie her body up in knots and live forever. AJ seems happy, which is all that matters.

Just before 7 P.M., as her father begins to fret on the timing of his meal, AJ and Lauranne arrive in their Subaru Forester. His anti-midlife crisis seems self-conscious to Lu at times, as if AJ thinks everyone is forever paying attention to every choice he makes. At least he hasn't started wearing all hemp. Fit and lean at the age of fifty-three, he favors T-shirts and jeans, which favor him. Balding, he has gone whole hog and shaved his head. Go figure, he looks great. Lu still can't help wondering why he was blessed with their mother's cheekbones and large eyes, while she had to favor the Brant family tree, which runs to freckles. He hugs everyone with great enthusiasm, while Lauranne offers glancing embraces so weak and watery that it amazes Lu those same arms allow her to do headstands.

"Lu has her first murder," their father says as they all sit down. The twins don't even look up.

"Aren't you the least bit curious about your mother's new job?" AJ teases.

Justin shrugs. Penelope takes a long drink of milk that allows her not to answer. She plays it for laughs, holding up one finger to show that she's busy.

"They're so young," Lu says quickly. She cannot bear for anyone to tease her children. And she doesn't want them to dwell too much on what she does. They are prone to nightmares, apocalyptic scenarios in which they lose everyone they love.

"You were, what, five when I tried Sheila Compson's killer?" their father says. "And you begged me for details. Of course, back then, there was a sense of propriety. Newspapers and television stations didn't feel they had to report *every* lurid detail, thank God."

AJ and Lu share a look over their father's use of "back then," a trigger phrase for him, a sign that he might hold forth on the way the world has changed. AJ steps in, trying to keep the conversation from heading down that track.

"I suppose it's an interesting one if you're taking it, not foisting it off on one of your deputies."

"Are you calling me a showboat?"

"More a little prancing pony." Only AJ can get away with that reference to Lu's size. As a child, she sought out books about girls who were short, sturdy, freckled. Laura in the *Little House* books.

(She hated the TV show, but loved the books.) Pippi Longstocking. Later, although not as late as one might suppose, Helen in *The Group*. And although her hair was more sandy than carroty, Lu always had a soft spot for *Anne of Green Gables*. But she never wanted anyone else to note her resemblance to these fictional alter egos.

Lu fills AJ in, sketching out the details of the woman's life, the innate sadness of her situation. Dead for a week and no one noticed, not until she missed a day at work. It's a rehearsal, in a sense, for the opening statement she will make before a jury.

"And the defendant still may request a competency hearing." That's their father. "But Lu doesn't think he has a chance on those grounds."

"No, although he has been institutionalized a time or two. But if he was judged healthy enough to be in a group home, then I don't think they'll have any luck. Not that he would stay in the group homes. He used his SSI to stay in motels, slept outside when it was warm enough. He's probably going to claim he broke into her apartment after she was dead. After or before, coming and going when she wasn't even there. He's been canny enough not to commit to a specific date."

"A lot of people are on the streets who should be in care," AJ says. "Schizophrenics. People with severe mental illnesses."

"And there are a lot of people on the street who aren't schizophrenics. You know that, AJ. A diagnosis of mental illness isn't enough to avoid consequences for one's actions."

"Maybe it should be. He at least could enter a defense of— what's it called?" AJ went to law school, but never bothered to sit for the bar.

"Not criminally responsible," their father answers. He assumes all questions are intended for him.

"God, I hope I don't have anyone like you on my jury, AJ. Anyway—the guy did something very strange, after the woman was dead. He left the little balcony door, near where she was lying, open, then turned her thermostat down. I think he hoped the cold would make it harder to determine exactly when she had died. Does that sound like someone who's mentally ill?"

"That reminds me," Lauranne says. "We've had the most depressing vandalism in some of our community gardens. Can you imagine someone crawling over the fence into a garden just to break things? I mean, it's just empty containers this time of year. What goes on in the mind of someone like *that*?"

Lauranne's interruption signals that she wants Lu to move on from the topic of her first murder case as state's attorney. Lauranne has very strict ideas about sharing conversational time—unless she's the one who's talking. Lu speaks more quickly, not quite ready to yield the floor.

"Anyway, the killer"—she makes it a point to use this word when discussing defendants because it hardens the idea in her mind, crowds out doubt. Rudy Drysdale is not just the defendant, he's the *killer*. "Oh, I forgot. You might know him, AJ."

"I know him?"

"Well, you went to Wilde Lake at the same time, although I guess he was two years behind you. Rudy Drysdale."

"No, no—doesn't ring a bell."

"Yearbook photographer, AV squad, I found him in your yearbook—"

"There were twelve hundred kids in that school, Lu. I didn't know all my classmates, much less some AV geek."

"Anyway," Lauranne says, "we're not sure what we're going to do. Surveillance cameras? AJ hates the idea and people would just steal them, but it's infuriating to see our work undone for no reason. I'd understand if they were junkies—"

"Addicts," AJ corrects softly.

"But it's not like there's metal to steal and fence. It's the worst, this kind of mindless vandalism. It's like they can't stand to see their neighbors doing something positive, they have to drag everyone back to their level."

Lu wants to say *Namaste, Lauranne. Namaste.* Instead, she lets her sister-in-law take the conversational bit into her mouth and run with it. At least she isn't lecturing them on the menu, which happens sometimes. Lauranne claims she's not judgmental about meat eaters, then drones on and on about unappetizing subjects such as GMOs and Big Agriculture. Tonight, the grown-ups (save Lauranne) are having pork tenderloin, while the twins eat macaroni and cheese. Out of a box, but one of the organic brands. Lu doesn't see the point of buying three pounds of cheese to produce some Barefoot Contessa–caliber casserole when this is what her children prefer.

Penelope and Justin, bored by the adults, drift off to watch television—and manage to drift out of hearing range for any chores they might be assigned. Lu's brother and his wife stay late, AJ smoking a cigar with his father on the recently added four-seasons porch, Lauranne offering no help with dishes or bedtime. The only thing she offers is criticism, not for the first time, of the household's failure to compost. Lu would probably have done it by now if it weren't for Lauranne's insufferable nagging.

But AJ loves her so, she reminds herself. And that's enough.

It is 10:30 by the time they leave, 11:30 before Lu is ready to go to bed. Moving through the house, compulsively putting small things in order, she sees light spilling down the stairwell from the third floor. The electric bills are heart-stopping for this inefficient old house, especially in the winter. She fines the children for leaving lights on, and they are generally good about remembering. When she turns the hall light off, she can see more light seeping under the door from AJ's old room. The light is coming from a "modern" study lamp he had in high school, probably purchased at Scan's in the Mall at Columbia. Their father says that it might be of value, that these original Danish modern items are sought after by collectors, and AJ should take it to his home before their father redoes this room. The lamp casts a circle on AJ's desk, but there is nothing in the circle. Lauranne was probably poking around. She has designs on some of Adele's jewelry, and their father has said it's only fair that she have a piece or two, but Lu has dragged her feet about making any decisions. Of course, the jewelry isn't kept in AJ's room, but there are other treasures—a coin collection, a drawer full of photographs, many featuring AJ's high school and college girlfriends. Lauranne has a jealous streak, too.

Lu turns the light off, but she doesn't leave the room right away. Here, in the house's last untouched place, she feels more connected to her past, her family, than anywhere else. She remembers AJ and Noel locked up in here for hours. Smoking pot, she knows now, although she didn't realize it at the time, despite her obsessive eavesdropping. Oh, and almost hanging out the window to get a glimpse of the new neighbor, Miss Maude. "And then there's Maude," they would say, quoting a line from the sitcom's theme song. Then they'd laugh and laugh and laugh, as if it were the funniest thing in the world. Yep, stoned, yet never stoners. She recalls Noel making just that point. "We're not stoners." At the time, she didn't understand what he was talking about, envisioned the characters in the *B.C.* comic. Stoners, stonemen, cavemen. It's amazing how much of life comes into focus years later, how long a memory can drift without context, then suddenly make sense. *B.C.* The comics were her life when she was a child, her frame for understanding everything. She can still see the layout of the morning *Beacon*'s comics page, not even a full page, while the afternoon *Light* had two entire pages. Still, she read the *Beacon* every morning. *Mr. Tweedy, Marmaduke*—those were one-panel cartoons with the horoscope above them. Oh, and that strange little naked couple that was so madly in love. Penelope and Justin don't even look at the newspaper, whereas Lu used to sit next to her father and read the funny pages while he studied the editorials.

Ah, but now she sounds like Andrew Brant, harrumphing about how things have changed. Everything does. Everything but this room. Lu wonders if everyone in the Brant family enjoys this little time capsule. Maybe AJ was the one who was up here tonight.

OPERATOR, CAN YOU HELP ME PLACE THIS CALL?

As spring and AJ's fifteenth birthday approached in 1977, he began to campaign for a new telephone line in our house, a private one, to be installed in his third-floor room. And if not a private one, then an extension. Between sports and his other extracurricular activities, he was almost never home. When he was home, he usually had Noel with him. And if Noel wasn't at our house, AJ needed to talk to him, for hours and hours. We had only two telephones, one in my father's bedroom and one in the kitchen, a fire-engine red one that hung on the wall. The cord was just long enough that AJ could stretch it into the walk-in pantry. I would go into the kitchen after dinner and see this thin scarlet worm taut across the kitchen, hear AJ's mutterings. But even when I could make out the words—and I always lingered as long as I could—they never seemed to be about anything important or interesting.

Yet AJ insisted he needed his own phone.

"I can't see why," our father said. "All you use it for is idle gossip."

"No, we check our math homework. Algorithms are killing me in Algebra two. I don't understand them at all."

"Then I don't think more time on the telephone is the remedy. A tutor, perhaps, if you're really struggling—"

"Also, we could use a Baltimore line, couldn't we? Don't you need to be able to make local calls to both Baltimore and D.C.? That way, I could have a private line. Lots of kids do."

Now in Columbia, at that time, your telephone prefix conveyed an important part of your family's story, its roots. You were given a choice, upon moving in, whether you wanted to be "997," which allowed you to make local calls to D.C., or if you were "730," oriented toward Baltimore. Yet my family, who had moved to Columbia from Baltimore, always had a D.C. prefix. "For my work," our father said, and I guess that made sense. He was in government, government was in D.C. And Annapolis, the state capital. There was nothing left for us in Baltimore. AJ sometimes spoke longingly of the house where he had lived his first eight years—the stained-glass windows, the turret, the fenced backyard. But on our rare trips into the city— usually to eat at Haussner's, the art-crammed German restaurant that my father loved—there was always a reason not to drive by. We were running late, the house was in the wrong direction.

"We don't need a Baltimore line," our father said. "But we can compromise. If your grades are good on your third-quarter report card, I'll install an extension, only in the living room."

The phone that arrived in April was as ordinary as a phone could be: black, squat, unmoving. If you wanted to use it, you had to sit in one of the two wing chairs flanking the round mahogany table where the phone lived. Still, it was a novelty and like all children, I loved novelty. Home alone (except for Teensy) until 4 or 5 P.M., I would sit in a wing chair, the TV muted, and pretend to place calls. The White House, Buckingham Palace, China. I yearned to make prank phone calls, but knew the circumstances would be dire if I were caught. Besides, the only two jokes I knew were about Prince Albert in the can, which I didn't really understand, and "Is your refrigerator running?" (*Then go out and catch it!*) I wasn't even sure to whom someone was meant to place prank calls. Friends? Strangers? I would pick up the black handset, my index finger on the button so the phone was not actually off the hook, and imagine someone calling me. *Lu? Lu? Would you like to come over? Sure, let's make ice cream sundaes and watch* The Big Valley.

I was playing this sad little game when the phone rang one afternoon, vibrating beneath my finger. Startled, I almost dropped the handset. Instead, I lifted my finger and rattled off as I had been instructed, "Brant household-who-may-I-say-is-calling?," even as Teensy was saying the same thing into the kitchen phone, although not quite as swiftly.

"Luisa?" a strange woman's voice asked. "Luisa?"

At that, I did drop the phone with a shriek, let it clatter to the floor, believing a ghost was calling me. From the kitchen, Teensy yelled: "You hang that phone up NOW, Lu. You hear me? You hang up that phone and go outside." I did, but not before I heard Teensy in the kitchen, breathing hard into the receiver. "Please do not call here again. I'm sorry, ma'am, but you know that's how it has to be."

The phone began to ring every day after that, between the hours of three and five. At some point, Teensy decided to stop answering. "Nuisance calls," she said. "Like pranks?" "Yes. Do not pick up the phone. That only encourages them. Just let it ring."

Every afternoon, the phone continued to ring. Five times, eight times, a dozen. We got used to it. As for telling my father—I guess I assumed Teensy had filled him in. Surely this had something to do with his work.

Now, even though Miss Maude was no longer available to look after me, Teensy had come to expect her early leave-taking on Fridays. My father had decided I could stay home alone as long as AJ promised to get there as soon as possible. "As soon as possible," to AJ's way of thinking, was any time that put him through the door ahead of our father, who seldom left the office before 6:30. I kept his secret, enjoying my autonomy and the power it gave me. Then, one Friday, as I was watching a rerun of *The Big Valley,* the phone rang and I was so caught up by the strange things that were happening on the show—the Barkley brothers were threatening a Chinese man, making him swear on a chicken that he didn't know where

Victoria Barkley was, when she was downstairs in his master's basement—that I picked up the receiver almost without thinking.

"Brant-residence-who-may-I-say-is-calling?"

"Luisa? Luisa, is that you?"

The strange woman's voice again. Yet I wasn't scared this time, despite being alone in the house. It was just a prank, after all. Victoria Barkley wasn't scared. She was played by Barbara Stanwyck and on those rare times when AJ was home during *The Big Valley,* Noel would drop into the other wing chair and watch with me, telling me what a great actress she was.

"Yes."

"Don't you know who this is?"

"Miss Maude?"

"It's your grandmother, Luisa. Your mother's mother, Victoria Closter. Your nana."

"I don't have any grandparents," I said, confused. My father's parents might be alive, but I knew he had chosen to live his life without them. My mother's parents were dead. I was quite clear on that. They had died years ago, not long after my mother died. That's why we never saw them. They were dead.

"Oh, that wicked, wicked father of yours, trying to keep us apart. You do have grandparents and we want to see you, darling. I haven't seen you since you were a baby."

"You saw me when I was a baby?" There was no photographic evidence to support this.

"We did. But then your father said we couldn't see you anymore—"

AJ came in then, breathless and red-cheeked; the late April day was unseasonably cold.

"AJ, it's our grandparents! They've alive. It must have been some terrible mistake, like, like"—my mind groped for such a scenario and found it instantly in the soap operas I had watched with Miss Maude—"maybe they just had amnesia!"

He took the phone from me—and hung it up.

"What did she say to you, Lu?"

"That she was my grandmother. But I thought we didn't have any grandparents."

"Did she say anything else?"

"She said our father was wicked."

The phone began to ring again. AJ motioned for me not to touch it. He let it ring ten, fifteen times—phones would do that, then. When the person on the other end finally gave up, AJ called our father's office and spoke to his secretary. "Miss Dolores? This is AJ. We've been having some nuisance calls and I'm taking the phone off the hook for now. I just thought our father should know." Pause. "I'm fine, she's fine. But I know he doesn't want us to have anything to do with these calls."

———————

Our father was home within the hour. He asked AJ to speak to him in his room. For some reason, I accepted this was a private matter. How can this be? Yet my memory is that I sat at the kitchen table, busy at something. What exactly? I had a small loom on which I could make belts, ugly imitations of the Native American styles that were still popular. No, I was getting a head start on Easter, preparing the eggs. Teensy had taught me how to hollow eggs. I couldn't dye them on my own, but I knew how to hollow them. Or thought I did. The kitchen table told a different story, with two destroyed eggs for every one that remained intact, and the intact ones had enormous blow holes. Meanwhile, we had enough eggs to make omelets all weekend. It was almost as if I didn't want my father to summon me to his room, or I hoped he would be so upset with me that he would be distracted. I didn't want to hear what he was going to tell me.

But eventually, he did ask me to talk to him, without any comment about the mess I had made.

In the corner of my father's room that he used as a home office, there was a big leather wing chair, his, and a wooden rocking chair at three-quarters scale, in which I had often read alongside him. I started to climb into the chair, but my father startled me by asking: "Do you want to sit in my lap?"

We were not that kind of family. I sat next to him when we read the paper together; I did not sit on him.

"No, sir, that's okay. We can talk like this." He seemed relieved.

"Lu, there were some things that happened, back when you were born, that I never told you about. Your grandparents—your mother's parents—did not approve of her having a second child."

"Why?"

"They had their reasons—or thought they did. Their reasons didn't matter. Your mother was an adult. Her parents treated her like a child. They wanted her to, um, end the pregnancy. That was not legal at the time."

"They didn't want me?"

"You weren't you yet, Lu They weren't thinking about the possibility of a person, with all your bright promise. All they could think about was your mother. Their daughter. And then when your mother was, well, gone, they said, 'See, we told you this would happen.' They said I had signed her death warrant. They said other things, rude and cruel things. I became very angry. I told them that they were to have nothing to do with us. I didn't trust them to be . . . careful around you, to keep their feelings to themselves. AJ was almost nine at the time. He had lived with his grandparents most of his life. It was very hard on him, but he understood. The three of us had to stick together. Perhaps if they had apologized or acknowledged how hurtful and wrong their words were, things could have been different. I told AJ it was *as if* they had died, that we must live as if they had. I believed they would make you feel responsible for your mother's death, which was not the case at all. I also feared that they would try to do to you, both of you, what they had done to your mother. I couldn't have let that cycle repeat itself."

"What did they do?"

He paused, leaned forward, palms pressed together as if praying, his chin on the thumbs, his nose on the index fingers. "They were too protective. They acted like the parents in Sleeping Beauty. Only it wasn't spindles that needed to disappear—it was *everything*. They would have had her live forever in her childhood bedroom, venturing out only under the most controlled circumstances."

"Why did they start calling after all this time?"

"I don't know. But they won't be calling again. I'm going to get an unlisted number and install a second phone line for just you and AJ to use, although it will be in his bedroom for now."

I wanted to argue that this was unfair, that if the phone were in AJ's room, then it was *his* phone. But then my father might ask how often my friends called and I would have to admit that no one called me, ever.

"What do you say we go out for pizza tonight? I was in such a rush to get home after I heard about the calls that I didn't stop at Colombo's on my way."

There was no such thing as grandparents' rights at this time. But I did not know until recently that my careful father, who was not inclined to leave things to chance, took out a restraining order against his in-laws. Today, I suppose, such a thing would become public. *Did you hear? The state's attorney has a restraining order against his in-laws.* People had more secrets then. Or maybe they were just better about keeping them.

At any rate, the three of us, a team, united, made the short drive to Colombo's, our favorite pizza place. To this day, I find all pizza inferior to the memory of what I ate on Friday nights from Colombo's. As a treat, we ate at the restaurant instead of getting carryout. We even had a whole pitcher of root beer to share. I was beside myself with joy, but AJ's mood seemed grim. I tried to understand. AJ knew our grandparents, had loved them and been loved by them. I wasn't being asked to give anything up. But AJ was, for a second time. Now, I can see it. AJ had lost his grandparents as surely as he had lost his mother. I never had either.

Both the Closters would be dead soon. It turned out that our grand-mother decided to contact us because her husband was dying of pancre-atic cancer. He was gone by that summer, and she followed within a year. There was no inheritance, not for us. When I lived in Mount Washington during the first years of my marriage, I sometimes drove a few miles out of my way to go past the Closters' house. It has been chopped up into apart-ments, and the upkeep is minimal. But the stained-glass windows and the turret are still there. I would have loved to know that house in its glory. And I think I would have liked to have known my grandparents, but if my father thought I needed to be kept away from them, he must have had good rea-sons.

In contrast to AJ's dark mood at Colombo's that night, our father was unusually ebullient. He spoke to strangers, laughed at their jokes no matter how lame, shook hands. I think he even bought pitchers of beer for some tables.

"That was fun," I whispered to AJ in the cozy cover of the dark back-seat. He usually fought to ride in the front, as he was about to get his learn-er's permit and wanted to study our father's driving. "I wish we did things like that more often."

"Like what?"

"I don't know. Go out. Talk to other people, like it was a party."

"Well, sure," AJ said. "The election is only eighteen months away. It's time for Andrew Jackson Brant to pretend he actually likes people."

Our father stiffened in the front seat, and the back of his neck red-dened. Disrespect was a serious offense in our household, perhaps the most serious offense. "Don't sass me," he would say, his Virginia accent suddenly pronounced. Teensy, too, was hell on talking back. But our father said nothing even when AJ added: "Yes, sirree, Andrew Jackson Brant can do a darn good job of pretending to like hoi polloi, the people in whose name he serves. Most people would say *the* hoi polloi, but Andrew Jackson Brant would be the first to tell them that they're wrong, it doesn't require an article. People wonder where I get my acting chops from? Well, look no further. Andrew Jackson Brant could have been the Richard Burton of his day. Although he wouldn't have married Adele Closter twice, I suppose, the way Burton did with Elizabeth Taylor. Andrew Jackson Brant never makes the same mistake twice."

"I would have married your mother over and over again," our father said.

"Isn't that the very definition of *insanity*? Doing the same thing over and over, expecting a different outcome?"

Our father braked sharply, although the light was green. Braked sharply, then turned onto the narrow road that led to the tennis courts behind the Village Center. The lights were on and AJ's face looked even whiter in their eerie glow. He was terrified. As was I. Neither of us had ever pushed our father this far.

But, after a minute of suspenseful silence, our father said, without turning around: "I have no regrets, AJ. I don't expect you to understand that, but it's true."

The next week, we went back to our Friday ritual of having take-out pizza. AJ began taking his slices to his room, talking on the phone while he ate, inserting folded triangles of cheese pizza into his mouth as if he were a sword swallower. I expected our father to reprimand him, but he never did.

JANUARY 12

A knock. *Oh, bless the Lord,* Lu thought, *someone has started knocking on my door.* It's her secretary, Della, but that's a start.

"Fred Hollister wants to know if he can get on your schedule this afternoon," Della says. She's Lu's age, yet looks years older. Plump, matronly. Did people used to age at more or less the same rate when Lu was a child? More and more, aging seems to be a choice. A choice dictated by genetics and disposable income, but still a choice. After all, anyone can dye her hair, pick out wardrobes that won't age her. But Della seems comfortable with her gray hair and cushiony frame.

"To discuss what?"

"He wouldn't tell me, but he says it's important, something he doesn't want you to hear from anyone else."

Intriguing. Lu's mind runs through the various possibilities. She assumes it's some hangover from Fred's tenure, a case that's going to boomerang back on appeal because of shoddy work by this office or the police department. She had plans for this afternoon, but she accepts that this has to take precedence. If Fred thinks she wants to hear it from him first, then she definitely does.

"Put him in for noon. I'll eat at my desk."

Seven days into her new job, Lu is still trying to get a handle on all the bureaucracy that comes with it. She gets up at four and answers e-mail for an hour, but it's like fighting a hydra: for every reply she manages, another three crop up. Meetings, memos, memos about meetings. In the modern age, access cannot be curtailed. Back in the '70s, her father had an office with six lines and no answering machine. No mobile phone, not even when the big clunky models became available in the '80s. Maybe a beeper, she thinks, by his final term. *A beeper*. She feels like some futuristic creature whose every cell is available for sensory input. And it doesn't seem to occur to anyone that his/her message, call, memo is one of many, that what is urgent to them can be of a lower priority to her. To the sender or caller, that message is the *only* one, the crucial one. Lu worked all weekend to justify a long lunch away from the office and now she's lost that reward.

When Fred arrives, he looks much more cheerful than the man who visited Lu only a week ago. More pampered, too. His gray suit is sharp, expensive looking, his graying hair recently trimmed, not that he has a lot of it. New glasses, tortoiseshell frames with a glint of gold at the temples. He's actually whistling, although the first thing he says is: "Whoa—trigger warning. I swear I got a little PTSD walking in here."

"Really? Your step is so *springy*. And that suit. Are you on someone's payroll?"

"I am. Do you know Howard & Howard?"

"Of course I do, Fred. I was an assistant state's attorney in Baltimore. With you. Remember? Howard & Howard is only one of the biggest law firms in the city."

"Right. Of course. Anyway, I'm going to be doing criminal defense work for them. And I thought you should hear it from me: I'm defending Rudy Drysdale. Defending him—and invoking Hicks."

"You want to go to trial within a hundred eighty days?"

"Yes. Jail is hard on Rudy. Every day he's inside is an eternity for him. By the way, I also want a hearing on bond reduction. Rudy's original counsel was, uh, somewhat over her head. I don't know how your office got him locked up with no bail."

"Because he's a homeless man with no fixed address. But, hey, go for it. Even if you can get him bail, it's going to be pretty high. Who's paying for all this? Did you take this on pro bono?"

Fred laughs. "No, Howard & Howard made it quite clear that hiring me as a potential partner did not mean I was free from the burden of contributing to the bottom line, not yet. Maybe down the road I'll have the luxury of cases that don't pay. Rudy Drysdale is paying full freight."

"How?" Lu asks. "He's on SSI, and he can't even stretch his check for a month. That's why he broke into Mary McNally's apartment, right?"

Fred lets that pass. "Arrangements have been made, don't worry."

"Aren't you going to request a competency hearing?"

"I brought it up, but you know and I know he's not going to meet the standard, so it's a waste of time. My client's only concern is that whatever happens needs to happen as soon as possible. Jail is physically painful to him and erodes his mental state. He needs to be outdoors. Do you know he walks, every day, all day, in all kinds of weather?"

Lu has no intention of telling Fred what she knows about Rudy Drysdale. Fred has some kind of ace in the hole. She needs to flush it out.

"Absent a new development," she says, "I don't see a deal on this one. So how fast do you want to go?"

"I can go as fast as you can. This will be the only thing on my plate for a while."

So it's a grudge match, pure and simple. Fred is going to try and show Lu that it wasn't his fault that he pulled away from trials, that the state's attorney has too much other stuff to do and can't focus effectively on trial work. And it's not a bad case for a good defense attorney. She wonders if he will argue that Rudy was in the apartment pre- or postmortem. Which would she argue, as a defense attorney? She runs through the possible scenarios. Premortem. He breaks in, then leaves, never even sees Mary McNally. Then why does he touch the thermostat upon departing? No, he's going to stick to the postmortem discovery. Fred's going to argue that Rudy didn't adjust the thermostat, only that he touched it for some bullshit reason. He's going to introduce a phantom third party, one who didn't leave prints. He can spin whatever fairy tales he wants to spin. That's the advantage of being a defense attorney.

"Fine," she says. "My secretary will be in touch with the schedule. I'm really glad you landed on your feet, Fred. It's nice to see you *enthusiastic* about a case. How did Rudy's parents even know to contact you?"

"I didn't say it was Rudy's parents who contacted me," he says.

"Who else would it be?" Lu asks.

He's determined to have the last word: "By the way, even though I'm not challenging his competency, I am considering a 'not criminally responsible' plea."

"He'll still do time. He might do it at Patuxent"—Maryland's facility with a unit for offenders with psychiatric problems—"but he'll still be inside."

"True. And in the end, I have to do what he wants to do. Rudy says he's innocent. That's good enough for me."

As soon as Fred leaves, Lu goes to her computer and searches the county property database, then finds a reliable website for current real estate values. Rudy's parents live on Rain Dream Hill, less than a mile from the Brants. Their house would have been among the earliest Columbia homes—modern then, stodgy now, with the best on the street valued at less than $500,000. The Drysdale house has no mortgage on it, not as of last week, but it's valued at $375,000, and Google Street View indicates that's a generous assessment. Another reason to invoke Hicks, then. A good defense will run more than $375,000, much more. Howard & Howard will assemble experts, jury selection coaches. They have a big timeline to play with—a lot can happen in a week. Lu has fingerprints and a witness who picked Rudy out of a lineup. She also has a man who has no history of violence, accused of beating a strange woman. *Was she a stranger to him?* Obliterating someone's face is damn personal. They need to lean harder on that. Maybe Mary McNally volunteered somewhere or gave him a ride one day. Heck, she could even be the kind of softie who tried to give a homeless guy some task to do in her house. Lu's going to lean on Mike and her own staff investigator to do more legwork on the victim.

She feels a surge of adrenaline. Lu has always been competitive. All the Brants are. Her father tried to curb this tendency in her, probably because he found it distinctly unfeminine. But this only made Lu more competitive. Fred wants to go all Montague and Capulet, avenge his honor? She won't fall into the trap of thinking it's personal, even if it is for him. She'll win this case because she's right, because a nice middle-aged lady walked into her apartment one night, probably still thinking dreamy thoughts about the leading man in *The Theory of Everything,* only to be strangled and then beaten.

She checks her calendar. She could reschedule her lunch for tomorrow or Wednesday. She calls out to Della, asks if she's right about having that time free.

"It can work," Della says, as she walks into Lu's office and places a phone message slip on her desk. "I'll make it work. Meanwhile, while you were with Fred, that woman who called the other day, Mrs. Schumann, asked that you call her back."

"About what?"

"She still insists you would recognize her name."

Lu doesn't, not at all. And the number on Della's pink memo is a California one, 650 something. She remembers that prefix from Gabe's trips. She will remember that prefix forever. Of course, area codes mean nothing now, just an indication of where you got your first cell phone. She crumples the pink slip into a ball and makes a high, arching shot toward her wastebasket. It hits the rim, but it goes in. Her brother, who deigned to play basketball with her in their driveway on those rare occasions when his friends weren't around, always told her: *It doesn't have to go in pretty, Lu. It just has to go in.*

THE PEOPLE TREE

Columbia turned ten in 1977, the year I turned seven, but its birthday was a much bigger deal than mine, a series of events and concerts and fireworks. My father found what he called the "hoopla" mildly ridiculous, although he was careful not to express this view in public.

"Europe thought our bicentennial was a joke," he said over dinner. It was spring, the sky was bright well into evening, and I stared longingly at the world beyond our supper table. Most evenings, there were just two of us. AJ, as it happens, was at rehearsal for one of the birthday concerts. "And here we are celebrating the tenth anniversary of an unincorporated town. But it would be impolitic for me not to attend all the festivities."

"You're in politics," I said, confused.

"Exactly."

I don't think he minded, really. Much as he disliked celebrations about him, he wanted other people to enjoy themselves. I realized that night that we never had acknowledged my father's birthday, which fell a week after mine. We never did anything to mark the day—at his insistence. Earlier that week, we had been assigned the task of making "spring tradition" cards—no Easter, no Passover in Columbia schools. I had spent my childhood creating holiday cards and Father's Day cards, but never a birthday card, not for my father.

"Why don't you have birthday parties?" I asked.

"It's a week after yours, and yours is eight days after Christmas. The parties have to stop sometime."

"But a birthday—everyone deserves a birthday," I said. "It's your special day, a day of your own day." I had a little book that called it just that.

"I don't think I merit attention for hanging around another year."

"Are all grown-ups like that?" I was nervous that I might be expected to behave this way one day.

"No, not at all. Your mother loved hers. She turned it into a weeklong celebration sometimes."

Later that evening, as I reported the conversation back to AJ, he gave me a scornful look. He had been giving me those looks more and more since he turned fifteen. "It's the day Mom died, Lu. That's why he doesn't celebrate it."

"How did she die, AJ?" I had asked this question before, but I still needed the reassurance that my birth had not killed her.

"Teensy said she just wasn't made for this world and her heart finally gave out."

"But not because of me, right? Not because she had a baby? Is that what our grandparents think? Is that why we don't talk to them?"

"No, not because of you," AJ said. "I think she got some infection or something in the hospital and it ate away at her heart. Because she was already weak. She was in bed most of the time she was pregnant with you."

Still, didn't that make it my fault? I decided to change the subject. "Daddy says it's silly, having a celebration for a city's ten-year-old birthday."

"He can think what he likes," AJ said. "But I was one of only sixty-six kids chosen to sing in the chorus. I think that's a pretty big honor."

The number sixty-six was not arbitrary. Ground for Columbia had been broken in 1966. A year later, the city had dedicated the People Tree, a gleaming metal statue of sixty-six intertwined human figures. Columbia's official symbol, it had been erected near the shore of Lake Kittamaqundi. So when the celebration was planned, it was decided to have a townwide chorus of sixty-six teenagers. AJ wasn't the least bit surprised to be one of them. AJ was never surprised to be picked for anything. Noel and Ariel made the cut, too, and Ariel even had a dance later in the program.

AJ assumed he would be given the big vocal solo. But that went to a boy not in their crowd, a tall, very dark-skinned freshman from Oakland Mills.

Davey.

Looking at Davey, one might have expected a baritone voice, a Paul Robeson kind of voice singing "Old Man River." But perhaps that was just our unacknowledged bigotry, linking tone to color, as if all dark-skinned men were obligated to produce deep, dark notes. As it happened, when Davey showed up at the audition with nothing prepared, the chorus master suggested "Old Man River." Davey didn't know it. After a quick conference with the piano player, he decided to sing a Beatles song, "If I Fell." AJ told me that his voice stunned everyone. He had a glorious tenor, not a baritone, and there was a simplicity to his phrasing that made familiar songs sound new again. He probably could have sung opera if he wanted to. Davey didn't want to sing opera. He didn't even want to be in the birthday concert. A teacher had tricked him into going to the audition, claimed the tryout was required for chorus, which he took only because it was an easy "A" for him. Davey played football and needed to keep his grades up, because his parents had said they would take him off the team if he didn't maintain an A average. His parents' standards were much higher than the school's, which required only passing grades from its athletes. So Davey stood next to the piano, a reluctant star, and sang a Beatles song, assuming he wouldn't be picked.

But if Davey did not understand how magical his voice was, AJ did. So did Noel. They sized him up—a freshman, like them, only a good six inches taller than AJ. Black. Coal black, midnight black. He was obviously going to be the soloist, taking the spot that AJ had assumed would be his. AJ, fiercely proud, probably decided that the only way to prove he couldn't care less was to befriend Davey.

He brought Davey home that very night. Teensy fell all over herself, offering him things to eat and drink. She asked him to stay for dinner. Our father arrived home and also took an interest in Davey, peppering him with far more questions than he had ever asked of anyone else AJ had brought home—Noel, Bash, Ariel. He was excited, I think, that his son had a black friend. That sounds horrible, but in the context of 1977, it was—well, less so. Howard County was, overall, very white. Less than 15 percent of the population was nonwhite at the time; not quite 12 percent was African American. The numbers were different in Columbia proper, but not that different. People who grew up in Columbia during the 1970s remember it as an idyllic, postracial bubble. I don't.

"Do you want to sing professionally?" our father asked Davey over dinner, a quiche Lorraine. ("But I can make you something else," Teensy said, "if you don't like it." She never said that to *me*. Davey said it was all right, his mother made quiche all the time.)

"No, sir," Davey said. "I like to sing, but I'm hoping that I can use football to get a scholarship to Stanford. I want to be a doctor."

"How ambitious," my father said.

"I guess so," Davey said. "My dad's a doctor. A surgeon at Hopkins. Oncology."

My father coughed, gulped some wine. He seemed embarrassed. I wasn't sure why. He wasn't the kind of lawyer who sued doctors for malpractice. He gulped more wine, had another coughing fit.

"And you're at Oakland Mills?"

"Yes, sir. But I'd like to switch to Wilde Lake. Is it true that you can go at your own pace, do courses—I'm not sure what you call it. Independently? I'd like to take extra science and math, and there's no way to do that at my school. But I've got to take calculus in high school and at the rate I'm going, I'll only make it through trig and analyt because I didn't take Algebra two in middle school. My family moved to Columbia after I finished seventh grade and they didn't realize that the math I took in the city was the same as Algebra I. They basically put me back a year in some courses and by the time we figured it out, it was too late to change."

"I believe there are fewer independent courses than there once were," my father said. "Most young people were not well suited to what's called open space education. I remember when the school first opened, the promise was that students could go at their own pace. Now it's more along the lines of—go at your own pace, but there is a minimum speed limit." He chuckled at his own joke.

"Math and science don't have as many self-directed classes," AJ put in. "But if you're supersmart, they make allowances. There are kids who come down from the middle school to take math because they're so advanced. Dad, can't you do something?"

"AJ, it would be unseemly for the state's attorney to intervene in school district policy. However—Davey, have your parents call me. I can certainly give them advice about how to deal with county bureaucracy."

———

Davey became a fixture in our house, the twosome of AJ and Noel easing seamlessly into a threesome. The other friends—Bash, Lynne, Ariel—were more like satellites. AJ, Noel, and Davey were the triumvirate, their group's ruling power. It made sense for Davey to come home with AJ after rehearsals, as they could walk to our house from Merriweather Post Pavilion. The others in AJ's group of freshman superstars approved of him, welcomed him. Bash liked having a guy who wanted to shoot hoops in our driveway. Ariel and Lynne flirted with him, although he didn't flirt back. Davey's parents didn't want him to have a steady girlfriend.

The addition of Davey made their group even more outstanding. He was just so darn noticeable, taller and darker and, maybe, handsomer than the rest. (It's hard to know if one's brother is handsome, especially at age seven. But even Noel's beauty—there's no other word for it—was eclipsed by Davey's good looks.) AJ was the undisputed leader within the group, but Davey was its beacon, drawing attention to them. It was odd when that *Life* magazine article about Wilde Lake High School came out later that year and Davey wasn't in the photo. We had already become accustomed to looking for him. Have you ever tailgated at a big football game? In order to be found in the crowds, some people plant distinctive flags, then say things like: "Find us at the Flying Crawfish." The College Park crowd that Gabe knew flew Testudo, the fighting Terrapin mascot of the University of Maryland. Anyway, Davey was like that. Spot him and you would find the rest.

———————

Merriweather Post Pavilion had been endowed by the cereal heiress of the same name and was intended to be the home of a serious symphony. But by Columbia's tenth year, the Frank Gehry–designed amphitheater was a venue for pop concerts, from Jimi Hendrix to Frank Sinatra. You could sit in seats under the shell or bring a picnic basket and camp out on the surrounding lawn. The night of the birthday concert, my father and I had seats. I was disappointed, but my father was never going to be the picnic-blanket type of father. Even on a warm June night, he insisted on wearing his work clothes, or part of them: seersucker pants, a long-sleeved white shirt, a bow tie, and a hat. At seven, I was still too young to be horrified by a relative's clothing choices. My disastrous fling with fashion would not be for another two years. And I was not embarrassed by my father, not yet. I did not see that he was older than most parents, or that he, like me, had few real friends. Many collegial acquaintances, but no real friends. I did not realize how much of a loner he was, in contrast to AJ. Even then, I sometimes wondered if my brother courted Davey because his talents in music and sports exceeded AJ's. One of the few mean things I ever heard AJ say about anyone, back then, was when Davey was offered a free ride to Stanford three years later: "Well, he plays football. I'd get a lot of scholarship offers, too, if I played football instead of soccer."

Noel had given him a look. "Not to mention that he's black, right?"

"There's not a prejudiced bone in my body," AJ said.

"Of course there isn't."

But that was later. That night, the chorus, sixty-six strong, sang stirring anthems of patriotism and community. One of them, oddly, was the title song from the musical *Milk and Honey,* rewritten to fit the occasion and scrubbed of its Israel-specific lyrics. Davey's voice soared over the rest: *This lovely land is mine. This lovely land is mine. This lovely land is mine.* I officially abandoned my crush on Noel and fixed my affections on Davey. As the song reached its climax, a scrim depicting the Tree of Life fell and somehow it seemed as if the chorus had become a living, breathing Tree of Life.

My father, in his seat next to me, allowed himself a quiet snort, which he masked with his handkerchief as if it were a sneeze.

"Wasn't that great? Didn't you love it?" I asked my father.

"I can't help thinking of another tree of people, another song," he said. "A much darker song, but a truer one, called 'Strange Fruit.' I guess I'm just an old grouch." My father squeezed my shoulder. "Do you want to stop at the 7-Eleven for a Slurpee?"

I did.

———

Sometime over the summer, it was worked out that Davey would attend Wilde Lake. I never knew the circumstances. I think I just assumed AJ made it happen. He had that kind of power. He had decreed that they were to be a group of six now, and so they were. (The truth was more prosaic.

Davey's parents had found a large house in Hobbit's Glen, much more to their taste, and although it was zoned for Centennial High School, the new school was so oversubscribed that they had no trouble getting Davey into Wilde Lake—at Davey's insistence.) The six did everything as a group. When Lynne and Bash started pairing off, AJ didn't approve—not because he was prudish about sex, but because he thought it bad for the group. Luckily, Lynne and Bash didn't really care that much about being boyfriend and girlfriend. They just liked to have sex.

I saw them once, that summer between their freshman and sophomore year of high school. Our father had to go out of town for an annual meeting, something to do with being a state's attorney. Teensy had a wedding in her family and my father decided that AJ, although only fifteen, was old enough to be in charge for a night. No parties, my father said. Of course, AJ said. And had a party. Bash found a burnout college kid who was happy to buy them beer and liquor at the Village Green. They weren't really drinkers, but it was almost obligatory to have booze at a parent-free party. AJ put me in my father's bed with a pound of peanut M&Ms and the remote control for the small black-and-white TV on top of what our father called a chifforobe. He told me that I could do whatever I wanted, but that I must stay in my father's room except to visit the bathroom that connected it to my room. I wasn't sure what they were doing that was so secretive. There was music and conversation, that sweet burning smell I had noticed before. I watched a horror film, one in which *Leave It to Beaver*'s dad ended up underground with the Mole People. I wanted to go to the bathroom, but what if the Mole People were under my father's high, old-fashioned bed? If I climbed down from the bed, they would reach out and grab my ankles and drag me down to that terrible place, where I would be enslaved. But I had consumed almost a gallon of orange soda. There was no way I could make it through the night. I calculated that if I leaped from the bed, I might land out of arm's reach of the Mole person. I jumped, landing on my knees, then made my way to the bathroom without incident. The house was quiet. I assumed everyone had gone home. I decided my own room would be a cozier place to sleep even if it didn't have a television, so I cracked the door, checking carefully for any sign of Mole People.

And then I saw them.

Saw Bash, who was completely naked, which made an impression on me. My father was modest. I had never seen him or even AJ without clothes. I had never seen a man naked, not even his buttocks. Bash was so broad that I couldn't see anything of Lynne's body except her face over his shoulder. Her face looked very serious. Stern, a mean teacher face. She bit her lip, whispered in his ear. "Don't stop, don't stop, don't stop." Yet she looked as if it were hurting, as if she yearned for him to stop. Bash made no noise at all. He barely seemed to be breathing. He tried to kiss her, but Lynne twisted her face to the side. "No, no. Don't stop. Don't stop. Dammit. You—Let me show you—" She made some adjustment in the dark. Whatever they were doing—and I knew, yet I didn't know—she was better at it, I could tell. She had done it before and Bash hadn't. She was like AJ, trying to teach me basketball. I remember the others teasing Lynne about a student teacher who had given her rides home from cheerleader practice and it began to make sense. I was at that age where so much begins making sense, where stray facts and memories lingered in some waiting room of the brain until context came and took them by the hand.

Lynne hissed: "Yes. Yes. That's it. You can do it, Bash. You can do it."

"I am doing it," he said in wonder. He rose up. He looked like a merman, swimming along the tops of the waves.

I backed away, not even trying to close the door. I got into my father's bed and pulled the covers over my head. Now I really couldn't sleep. So that was sex. I knew, but I didn't know. My father had done that with my mother. Had Teensy done it? But she didn't have kids, so, no. Grown-ups everywhere did that thing. Did this make Lynne and Bash grown-ups? Lynne wasn't much taller than I was. She was the cheerleader who was always at the top of the pyramid. But she had looked and sounded like a woman.

Whereas Bash had a grown-up man's body and a boy's face. Would they get married? Would I get to go to the wedding? Would I be their flower girl? I didn't want to be a flower girl. Or maybe I did.

Teensy came over on Sunday afternoon to check on us. The house was immaculate by then, every trace of the party swept away. It was *too* clean and Teensy stalked around, smelling a rat. But all she found was my mess—the empty bag of peanut M&Ms, the jug of soda. Plus, I had a full-on stomachache that I couldn't conceal. I confessed to everything—the bad food, the horror movies, sleeping in my father's bed. I said AJ had no idea what I was up to, that he had stayed in, as instructed, listening to records and watching television.

"What did he have for dinner?" Teensy asked.

I was a lawyer's daughter. I saw how she was trying to box me in.

"I didn't notice."

"Did he offer to fix you anything? There were hot dogs and some frozen pizzas."

"He probably did, but I wasn't hungry."

"After eating a pound of candy? I guess not, you fool." She sat on my bed, felt my forehead. Teensy didn't really believe in illness. Absent a fever or vomit, a child was not allowed to stay in bed on Teensy's watch. But I must have looked ragged that day because she took pity on me, left me in my own bed, even brought in the little b&w television from her room, the one that we watched on a tray on those rare occasions we were allowed to stay home from school.

I dozed off and on in front of the television. I always did. My father did that, too. Still does. He'd rather fall asleep in his chair, the television droning as he reads, than go to bed. It was a Sunday, so a movie was on, but it was just adults talking. People whispered, told secrets. With my eyes closed, I saw Bash and Lynne again. Saw Bash, the freckled merman, riding the waves, his head thrown back as if he were about to sing. Milk and honey, milk and honey, milk and honey.

"Teensy," I croaked from my bed. "Could I have some graham crack-ers?"

"No, but you can have some saltines and flat Coca-Cola." Teensy be-lieved those two things to be medicinal.

I sat up in bed, licking the salt from the Premium saltines. I had seen two people having sex. It was big news, enormous news, but I had no one to tell. Teensy would want to know about the party, and I owed it to AJ not to reveal that. A pound of M&Ms buys a steadfast silence. It didn't occur to me that the others—AJ, Noel, Ariel, Davey—had not seen what I saw, might not know what I know. I had no real friends at school, not the kind that I could share such secrets with. Strangely, the person I wanted to tell was my father. I wondered if he knew that people did it when they weren't trying to have a baby because I'm pretty sure he had told me that was the only reason to have sex. But maybe Lynne and Bash wanted to have a baby. Then again, they couldn't drive yet and I absolutely knew you had to have a driver's license before you had a baby. *My dad had sex twice,* I thought, *once for AJ and once for me.* I bet he was glad he didn't have to have it anymore. It looked messy and painful.

I was a spy. I was every spy that ever was. I was Velma on Scooby-Doo. I was Nancy Drew, Encyclopedia Brown, Trixie Belden, the Hardy Boys. I was Harriet the Spy, although I had not met her yet, but I would, soon enough. They were waiting for me, another member of their clan of spies, snoops, and truth tellers. I opened drawers, searched medicine cabinets and pi-geonholes, pressed my ear to walls, looked through keyholes. I thought I knew everything. I thought I was *entitled* to know everything, that the world was conspiring to keep me in the dark.

JANUARY 13

"Do you like this? Do you?"

Lu tries to make clear exactly how she feels about the fingers digging into her scalp, pulling her hair, but the sensation keeps changing, the pain keeps moving. She is on her stomach and the natural instinct should be to crawl away, futile as that might be, but strong hands grab her waist and flip her, so now she is facing him as he enters her and she gasps—she's lying on a sisal rug, rough on bare flesh under any circumstances.

Then she sees Bash's face and she starts to laugh. After all these years, she can't quite get over the fact that he looks like Huckleberry Finn, with his freckles and chipped tooth and never-quite-combed hair.

"When you laugh like that, it's hard to keep going," Bash says, and he pushes harder.

"Oh—no—it's"—she needs a breath or two for each syllable—"it's—per—fect. Don't. Stop."

"I never do."

He doesn't. Bash at fifty-three is as priapic as a teenager, always ready, inexhaustible. Well, always ready for Lu, whom he sees once or twice a month in this sterile "corporate" apartment in Bethesda. She's not sure he's always ready for his wife of seven years, a hard number who lives in Capitol Hill in what Lu assumes is a drop-dead gorgeous town house. She has never been invited there. AJ, who has, dismissed it as "showy," which told her nothing. *But is it in good taste?* she had yearned to ask her brother. *Or just a little tacky?* She knows the wife is drop-dead gorgeous and not the least bit tacky. Bash brought her to Gabe's funeral, although his flirtation with Lu had begun a few months earlier. It was probably only the timing of Gabe's death that kept Lu from becoming an adulteress; she was well on her way to sleeping with Bash when Gabe died. One might think that a husband's sudden death would shake a woman up, force her to wonder if the universe was sending her a message about the affair she was considering in her head.

One would be wrong. Lu tried to resist Bash, but he had picked up a scent on Lu and pursued her relentlessly. He knew before she did that she was a woman who would revel in a truly secret affair, one that was all about sex, sex that pushed past some boundaries. Lu had been a late bloomer—a virgin until college, married in her twenties to her third-ever real boyfriend. In blue jeans and T-shirt, hair under a baseball cap, she could still pass for a boy from the back. Which explained why she didn't wear such things. It had been a bizarre kind of relief when the flirtation—e-mails, phone calls, odd little gifts left anonymously at her office—finally ended and they settled into a straight sex thing. The flirtation had been the real betrayal of Gabe. The sex—that's merely the betrayal of Lucinda, Bash's wife. But that's not Lu's problem. Is it?

Spent, she makes her way to the bathroom on wobbly legs. She has a large bruise on her buttocks, but who will see it there? She doesn't wash, not yet. He will probably want to go again, given how long it's been since they've seen each other, how hard it is to find time since the election. She has let her secretary infer that she's in therapy in D.C., which would require about three hours with travel time. She has confided something similar to Andi, although indicating she was seeing someone for ob-gyn issues of a vague-but-serious nature. Andi obligingly spread the gossip through the office, then blamed it on Della, who would never betray Lu that way. Thank God she never told Andi the real story, back when they were deputies together. Even then, before Lu had decided to own her real ambition, she understood that this must be a locked room inside her life, a place to which no one can ever be admitted. It scared her at first, the things she wanted to do with Bash, the things she let him do to her. But it thrills her more.

They do not consider what they do to have a name. Not quite an affair, yet more than sex, with a singular appetite for each other, although Lu assumes Bash sees other women. They are rough, but not particularly kinky, sexual soul mates who think it should be sweaty and athletic. Her other lovers, all five of them, were so damn careful with Lu, probably because of her size. Occasionally, she and Bash have sweet, tame sex, although that's usually when one of them is a little under the weather. Last time, way back in November, a week before the general election, Bash had lain beneath her and said, "Fuck this cold right out of me, State's Attorney Brant." And she did.

She had not been drawn to Bash when he was part of her brother's group. She'd had a crush on Noel, then Davey, never Bash. He was a bigger, brawnier version of her, which didn't appeal at all. And she was a child, eight years his junior, precocious of mind, but not body, so he had certainly never noticed her. Their chance meeting in a Whole Foods six years ago had not seemed particularly portentous at the time, not to her. Bash says it was lust at first sight for him.

"Lu?" asked the man in the expensive cashmere coat, who a few minutes before had been staring morosely at the sausages and blocking her access to the good bacon.

She needed a beat to place him. "*Bash.* I'm sorry, you probably don't go by that nickname anymore. AJ tells me you're a lobbyist."

"Is that what I am? Today I am a henpecked husband, trying to find sausages for my wife, who says they can't have so much as a gram of sugar. But I can't find a single sausage that meets her criterion."

Lu flipped through the packages. They were in Baltimore's Mount Washington neighborhood, only blocks from the home she shared with Gabe at the time, but certainly far afield for a Washington lobbyist. "What are you doing here?"

"Trying to buy sausages, obviously. And failing."

"No, I mean in Mount Washington."

"Oh, I have a client who lives in a huge spread not far from here. Claims the house belonged to Napoleon."

"If you mean the house on Lake Avenue, it was Jérôme Bonaparte, and even his connection is tenuous at best. Isn't it owned by some tech billionaire?"

"God, I hope he's a billionaire or I have really wasted my afternoon. You're married to one, too, right?"

"A billionaire? I don't think so."

"But a big tech guy. Gabriel—Schwartz?"

"Swartz. I still go by Brant."

He snapped his fingers. "Right. He gets a lot of ink. You sure he's not a billionaire?"

"Pretty sure." She laughed, but it was to cover her embarrassment at her husband's wealth. He was worth only $20 million. *Only.* "Look, here's one that has less than one gram and it has pineapple, so that's probably why it has any sugar at all. Will that do?"

"I don't dare improvise. My wife gives very explicit instructions and expects them to be followed. I better call herr kommandant."

"I think you mean frau," Lu said icily.

She loathed men who portrayed their wives as nags and terrors. Eight months later, she was in bed with one. Although Lu and Bash don't talk much—there is so much else to do—Bash's wife often features in the conversations they do manage to have. Her special diets, her exacting workouts. She is Bash's second wife, younger than Lu by at least five years. His first wife lives in Columbia with their two children, although in the western part, in the most desirable school district. That once provided cover for Bash to take the occasional room at the Columbia Inn, but it's no longer possible for Lu to come and go there, convenient as it may be. It was risky enough when she was an assistant state's attorney. So they use this corporate apartment he maintains in Bethesda, where he does absolutely no business, not that Lucinda—the non-Lu, the never-Lu, the not-you-Lu Bash calls her—has ever thought to wonder about this. Bash lives larger than Gabe ever dared, and Lu senses it's more of a strain than he lets on. But that's his problem. One of the great charms of Bash is that his problems are his. She's not expected to solve them. She barely even listens to them.

Lu tells herself that she would never have started with Bash if he had children with Lucinda. She also tells herself that every time is the last time. And that their discretion means no one is harmed by what they do, the occasional bruise aside. She even congratulates herself on the concept of an affair as sensible time management for the busy widow with two children. Bash requires so much less attention than a husband or a boyfriend would. Three hours a month. Six, if she's lucky.

"Come back here," he calls. Demands. "I'm not finished."

Ja, Herr Kommandant.

This time, it's almost disappointingly normal at first, Bash on top of her, although his weight alone is enough to create a sensation of discomfort in this position. Then, toward the end, he grips her shoulders, hard.

"No marks," she breathes. "Don't leave marks that someone could see."

He doesn't listen, just continues to press on her shoulders. They don't use safe words. Again, that would mean labeling what they do, when part of the thrill is not organizing it under any banner, belonging to a club with only two members. "Trust me," he says, but his voice is guttural, harsh, not at all conducive to trust. But that's the fun part, says the little piece of her mind that stands back.

Later, as they dress, he produces a distinctive orange box. There is an Hermès scarf inside, a pattern of leaves in muted browns and golds. Perfect for her, Lu thinks, and not at all flattering to Lucinda, who has Snow White coloring. So it can't be a castoff. He really bought this for her.

"This will cover that one place where I gnawed on you a little," he says sheepishly, his manner that of a little boy offering something to a girl he likes.

"So you planned—"

"I never plan anything beyond the time. But I wanted to give you something to commemorate your new job. Is that okay? And then I wanted to take you somewhere you've never gone. I did that, didn't I? Didn't I?"

She kisses him, and it's only a matter of seconds before they begin clawing at each other. It has been three months, after all. But there have been longer gaps over the years they've been meeting each other, so that can't be the sole reason. Something has changed. She is new again, her title excites him. Her clothes are off in seconds, except for the scarf, which he ties around her eyes. The headboard slaps rhythmically against the wall, the sound familiar. It reminds her of the tiny wavelets of Wilde Lake, lapping at the shoreline. "Don't stop," she murmurs. "Don't stop." A vague memory tugs, but the present is stronger than the past. She wants to stay here, in this room, as long as possible. This is the only place where she is allowed just to *be*—no kids, no employees, no pink message slips. It's as if time stops in this room.

Then she goes outside and is surprised to see the sun is already setting. It's an orange sunset today, fiery and rude, a light that makes her glow, brings out the more subtle hues in her new scarf.

KODACHROME

It is possible to anticipate something ferociously, then one day forget that it's happening at all. Part of this is the passage to adulthood; birthdays fade in importance, holidays become something to be endured. I know there are grown-ups who still become excited about Christmas, although I find them suspect. Part of the reason I agreed with Gabe to raise Penelope and Justin as Jews is because I wanted to be done with Christmas. The tree, the stockings, the crash that happens in every household sometime between 11 A.M. and 4 P.M. on December twenty-fifth, when it's all done and the first toy has broken and the kids are frayed from sugar and overstimulation.

Yet Christmas is back in our lives, with a vengeance. I made the mistake of having a holiday open house two years ago, in part to showcase what my father has done with the house, and it became a tradition, just that fast. Even this year, as I prepared to take office, I was still expected to put out platters of smoked salmon and cold turkey, make or procure cheese straws. Inevitably, I feel Gabe looking over my shoulder—not scolding, but disappointed that I would break a promise. However, I made the promise to a living man. His death invalidated all promises as far as I'm concerned. Heck, if I had been the one to abandon him by dying, he would have been married within the year, probably to some happy-to-stay-at-home little lady. His presence was especially strong at this year's Christmas party, but perhaps that was because Bash, much to my annoyance, conned AJ into inviting him. Only Bash, no Lucinda. I'm not sure what he thought he was doing, but I was careful not to go anywhere alone in the house, not to drop my guard for a second.

Where was I? Oh, anticipation. Yes, it's in adult life that we begin to lose track of things that once shaped our years, those little peaks of celebration—birthday, Christmas—and find ourselves living mostly in the valleys, and content to do so. This jadedness begins happening earlier than we might realize. In the fall of 1976, *Life* magazine had come to Wilde Lake High School and posed the then freshmen in the bleachers for what was to be a cover story about the Class of 1984, the year in which AJ and his friends would graduate from college. For weeks, they spoke about it constantly. Would the photo be big enough to show everyone? If so, would they be recognizable? And the accompanying article itself? Would they be interviewed, would they be identified as the best and the brightest? Why wasn't the reporter more interested in them, so clearly the stars of the school?

Magazines worked exceedingly slowly then and by the time the article was published, almost everyone had forgotten it. When it showed up on newsstands in the fall of 1977, it was more like a hangover: bleary, vague, unpleasant.

The first disappointment was that my brother's class was not on the cover. Instead, there was a girl in a sky-blue rugby shirt, caught midcheer under the heading: THE NEW YOUTH. Other words on the cover included TOUGH, CARING, WARY, PRACTICAL, and SUPERCOOL. Even at the time, I was not convinced that these things were particularly "new." To be tough, caring, wary, practical, and supercool was to be an adolescent, then and always. But it was the fashion, then, to keep creating this narrative of innocence and a subsequent fall from grace. People were innocent before the JFK assassination, before Charles Manson, before Vietnam, before Altamont, before

Watergate. It's true, the concept of childhood is relatively modern, but I can't imagine there was ever a time in which people were born anything but innocent. I don't believe in innate evil. On the rare occasion that I've met a true sociopath, the person has been beyond evil. They want what they want and they don't care how they get it. (This always makes me think of *Pinkalicious,* a book beloved by my twins: sociopaths get what they get and they do get upset.) Anyway, I hadn't consciously worked this out when I saw the cover of *Life* magazine, but I think my letdown was more than disappointment that my brother wasn't there. I was, as always, looking for guidance and gurus, information about this strange world that awaited me. Grown-ups were forever saying, "If you're like this now, imagine when you're a teenager." Even my father said it. He and Teensy made my still far-off adolescence sound as if I were on the verge of becoming a werewolf. I was going to be wild, unpredictable, dangerous.

But also: Tough, Caring, Wary, Supercool, and Practical.

Okay, maybe not practical. But AJ was, as were his friends. Now in their sophomore year, they were doing practice runs for the PSAT, in hopes of scoring high enough in their junior year to win National Merit scholarships. They were beginning to game the college application process, ensuring they had a balance of extracurricular interests, visiting the guidance counselor and coming away with glossy brochures. Future generations would be more practical still. They would have to be. Whereas it was considered ambitious to set one's sights on Stanford, as Davey had as a freshman, it verges on impossible dreaming now. Last year, Stanford admitted slightly more than 5 percent of applicants. Harvard was at 5.9 percent. Yale, AJ's alma mater, was 6.26 percent. I used to tell myself that my twins, if they fancied Yale, at least had a sort of double legacy with their father and uncle. But maybe I shouldn't count on that anymore.

At any rate—because AJ and his crew had serious plans for their future, they were dismayed when they read the actual article. A series of unattributed quotes grouped under headings—"Sex," "Alcohol and

Drugs," "The Future," "Clothes"—it coalesced into a portrait of aimless, disaffected youths. ("Pot is, like, everywhere.") AJ was now appalled that he and his friends were so easily identified in the group photo that accompanied the article, front and center in the bleachers. For several days at dinner, he held forth about how the piece had been unfair and slanted. He worried that it could affect his chances at the college of his choice, or cost him the summer job he coveted, as an intern at the *Columbia Flier*. Finally, our father said to him: "Why not write a letter to the editor, making all these arguments? Or, better still, write your own piece, tell the truth as you see it."

The gauntlet thrown, AJ did just that. He wrote an article for the *Flier*, in which he described his friends and their interests. He broke down their days, hour by hour, detailing the life of the overscheduled child long before such a concept was fashionable. (He conveniently left out the information that they did, in fact, smoke pot all the time.) The piece, which appeared under the headline THE CLASS OF '84 HAS ITS SAY, argued that AJ and his friends were making their way in the world, as every generation had, and were entitled to their mistakes and missteps. "The influences that will shape us are unknown at this point," AJ wrote. "We will probably never go to war— it's unlikely there will ever be a war again that involves Western countries." (Yes, people believed that in 1977.) "We will almost certainly enjoy a higher standard of living than our parents, and isn't that what they want for us? But how will we get there? What is the path we will take? Most of us have learned life from the Game of Life, and the only thing we know for certain is that taking the shortcut that allows you to bypass college means you will have less earning power. But, according to the rules, anyone can end up on the Poor Farm with just one bad spin."

A few weeks after his piece appeared, an editor from a New York publishing house contacted our father and asked if AJ could expand his piece into a memoir. A few years earlier, a young woman had enjoyed success with such a book, published when she was only nineteen, and AJ was younger still. A book-length treatment of the same issues could be a sensation.

Our father brought the offer to AJ, advising him: "I don't think you should."

"Why not?" AJ asked. "I might make a lot of money."

"We don't have to worry about money."

"Everyone has to worry about money," AJ said. "Almost all the scholarships are needs-based now. You make just enough that I can't get one, no matter what my grades or SAT scores are."

"You would have to give up your privacy. Can you put a price on that? And"—a significant pause here, the kind he used in closing arguments—"you would have to tell the truth."

We were at the dinner table. It was not a serious conversation. When our father was intent on serious conversations, he took us into his room and closed the door. Yet there was something about his tone that sounded grave to me, as if he were suggesting that AJ did not always tell the truth.

"Of course I would be honest," AJ said.

"Then it's your decision."

For a week, AJ came home and attacked our father's manual typewriter with great focus. But he was in the fall play, *Zoo Story,* and rehearsals began to run later and later. And he was trying to study for the PSATs, while still playing soccer. The memoir was discarded. AJ was a magpie in his youth, saving everything in a file cabinet. But when I went to look for those pages recently, there was no trace of them. I wish he had saved his nascent memoir. I would have loved to read his version of his life, then and now. My brother was achingly sincere. That's the thing that no one understands. I'm not sure even AJ grasped that part of his nature, and what a burden it was to carry into adulthood. People say it's hard to be good. It's harder still to be famous for being good, to find that balance between sincerity and sanctimony. But I believe AJ managed to do it.

JANUARY 14

Lu makes her way carefully up the walk of the shabby house on Rain Dream Hill. There is a fine layer of sleet on the sidewalks this morning, and although some of the homeowners have treated their sidewalks with chemical melts, the walkway in front of the Drysdale house is untouched. Besides, she's always sore the day after a "lunch" with Bash. She may have a gymnast's build, but she doesn't have the elasticity. Lu is that rare modern woman who doesn't exercise, not in any organized way. She doesn't have to. She walks in the morning, sometimes before the sun comes up, but that's more for her mind than her body. There's no compelling reason for her to work out—her weight is steady, all the markers of good health are where they should be. Blood pressure, cholesterol. But the day after an afternoon with Bash, her body reproaches her for not taking better care of herself. A little yoga at the very least, it begs her. But when would she have time?

Both Drysdales meet her at the door, grim and unhappy wraiths, American Gothic without the pitchfork. They are one of those couples who look like brother and sister—small, with fine bones and surprisingly dark hair, only a dusting of white at the temples.

Well into their seventies, they look even older. Their faces are deeply lined and yellow, with a rubbery sheen. Smokers. Lu knows that before she comes across the threshold. The smell is thick on them, hangs in the house like a haze.

"Mr. Hollister says we don't have to talk to you," Mr. Drysdale says, even as he opens the door wider to let her in.

"You don't," she says. "But I'll remind you, you're not his clients. Rudy is. You're just footing the bill. Fred will do what's best for Rudy. That's his job. Eventually, you will have to talk to me—and a grand jury. I thought it a kindness to meet in private—without Rudy's attorney charging you an hourly rate."

There is a formal living room to the right of the front door, but they lead her to the family room at the back of the house, nothing more than an alcove off the kitchen. This throwback to the '70s could never be described as a "great room." The kitchen appears to have been untouched since the house was built. The appliances are what was once called Harvest Gold, and the adjacent sitting area is tiny by the standards of today's McMansions. A sliding glass door leads to a small square of deck; Lu knows there will be another glass door below, leading to the walk-out basement, a feature in almost all Columbia homes of the '70s. But the home's dominant feature are piles. Piles of books, piles of magazines, piles of newspapers. A pile of shirts on hangers, draped across an easy chair. When Lu perches on the plaid sofa, it emits dust and a smell she can't identify, although it seems vaguely animal. Not animal waste, but—something musky, furry, as if a dog once slept here.

"You've lived here how long?" she asked.

"Since 1977. We moved here from the city. Rudy wasn't happy at Southern High School. We thought Wilde Lake High School, being different, might be good for him."

"That wasn't so unusual then. My brother's best friend came here for similar reasons. He had been asked to leave Sidwell Friends in D.C."

She is trying to be polite and friendly, offering this anecdote in the spirit of commiseration, but they seem mystified by her comment, unsure of what to say. They are socially awkward people. Given their own limitations, perhaps they never recognized their son's problems. Oddness used to be more acceptable. Some people were just weird. Now anyone who seems the least bit off has to have a label, a diagnosis, be "on the spectrum."

"How old was Rudy when he was diagnosed?" She intentionally doesn't name a diagnosis and is curious to see if they provide one.

"Nineteen." Mr. Drysdale is the spokesman. Mrs. Drysdale keeps her eyes on his face. Their connection is wordless, almost telepathic. "He was a really good student, but college was hard for him."

"Where did he go?"

"Bennington." Almost thirty-five years after the fact, this still seems to give the parents a little lift. It was probably the highlight of their lives, seeing their son admitted to Bennington. How had they afforded *that*? "He wasn't prepared for the darkness."

"Depression?"

"No, how dark the days were, by the end of that first semester. The sun goes down early in New England. He cared about light. He was a photographer, a good one. He couldn't deal with the dark. Even when he was a teenager, he needed to be outside a lot. He walked everywhere. There was one doctor—this was recent— who thinks he had a vitamin D deficiency. Or maybe SAD, that seasonal thing. Anyway, the doctor says Rudy is self-medicating when he walks. That's why we're worried about him not getting bail."

Cause and effect. Everyone wants there to be a reason, any reason, for the inexplicable things that happen in our world, especially the things our children do. *He's tired. She's hungry. We haven't adhered to the schedule.* And sometimes those reasons apply. But sometimes—how often?—the wheel spins and you get a damaged kid.

"Was he ever violent?"

Mrs. Drysdale runs her tongue around her lips, says nothing. "No," Mr. Drysdale says with as much firmness as he can muster. Then: "We've already decided not to have a competency hearing. Mr. Hollister says it's a waste of our resources. A waste of his time. And money."

"I know. He wants to go very swiftly—he's even invoking Hicks, the rule that says I have to take the case to court within one hundred eighty days. But you know I can challenge that, right? Ask for an exemption if I think it's warranted?"

Their eyes are round, innocent, troubled. "He didn't think you would, though," Mr. Drysdale says.

Fred does know her pretty well. Give him that. He knew she would rise to the challenge of fast-tracking this. Has she fallen into a trap?

"Even if we do have the trial before the hundred-and-eighty-day deadline—you have no idea how much this is going to cost. Your son's defense. And you're not obligated to pay it. I'm sure when Fred came to you—"

"We called him."

Their instant chorus at this convinces Lu that they didn't, but they've been coached to say as much.

"Who suggested Fred?"

"Rudy's public defender. We told her we had—come into some money, that we were going to take a mortgage on the house, said we wanted to hire someone. At least, I think that was the sequence of events. Things have happened—so fast. Ten days ago, we didn't even know Rudy was sleeping rough again."

"Isn't that a British term?"

"It is." Mrs. Drysdale is allowed to speak to this at least. "But Rudy liked it. He said it was more like the way he lived. He wasn't homeless. Our door was always open to him. Always."

"As long as he was willing to abide by a few house rules," Mr. Drysdale mutters.

"Our door was always open to him. *He is our son.*" The second part of Mrs. Drysdale's comment, made under her breath, seems directed more at her husband than at Lu.

"When was the last time you saw him?" No answer. "Christmas? Thanksgiving?" Lu, who feels herself in danger of sinking into the rump-sprung sofa, leans forward. "I mean, when was the last time he *stayed* with you?"

Mrs. Drysdale's eyes dart back and forth. Arthur Drysdale has his arms crossed on his chest. Something happened here. Lu's mind races through the possibilities. Her eyes sweep over Mrs. Drysdale, but it's Mr. Drysdale who has uncrossed his arms and started to rub his right thigh about midway up on the outside, kneading it with his knuckles.

"I'm sorry, I'm so scattered—when was the last time Rudy lived with you," she repeats while standing, so the question will feel tossed off, conversational, something said to fill the silence of departure.

"It was 2013," Mrs. Drysdale says swiftly. "For the summer. He was with us all summer back in 2013."

"Not a single night since then?"

"Not a single night." But it's Mr. Drysdale who says this.

Medical records are private, but some ambulance records are public. It takes much of the afternoon, but by 5 P.M., Lu has found what she needs: a private ambulance transported someone from the house on Rain Dream Hill to Howard County Hospital on August 5, 2013. No 911 call, but the emergency room would have informed the police if they had any suspicions it was a criminal matter. Working backward, Lu finds a police report for the address, made three days later, but no mention of Rudy Drysdale—who, as his mother just told her, lived with them the summer of 2013. Arthur Drysdale had come into the emergency room with a stab wound to his right thigh. He blamed the attack on a mysterious intruder, a home invasion in which nothing was taken. He said he came home to find a strange man in the house and the man grabbed a pair of scissors and jammed them into his leg. No arrest was ever made. Lu, bureaucracy lifer that she is, can decode the flat, seemingly nonjudgmental language of a police report. The police knew Arthur Drysdale was lying and probably wrote it off as a man trying to save pride after a "domestic." If he didn't want to rat his wife out for attacking him with a pair of scissors, what did they care? The incident was listed as an assault. But an attack in a home invasion should have carried a far more serious charge. And why no call to 911? Because the Drysdales were trying to avoid the authorities altogether. Whatever innocuous story they came up with didn't pass muster at the hospital and the cops were called. *OK, fine, would you believe an attack by a stranger?*

Mr. Drysdale walked in, surprising Rudy, and he was attacked. Or maybe they had a quarrel. Whatever. It all works for Lu. That's a violent episode, within the past eighteen months.

Oh, the Drysdales might try to bluster through a grand jury hearing without confirming this, but they won't. They don't have the balls to carry this lie, now that the stakes are so high. True, Lu will have a hard time introducing this information during trial unless Rudy testifies, but it's key. No criminal record for violence? Sure. But Fred can't get away with claiming that Rudy has no *history* of violence, and if that day comes, she'll put Mr. Drysdale on the stand. She should tell Mike and his team to canvass the shelters in the city, just in case Rudy ever had to cave and stay in one when the weather was particularly bitter, as it's been for the past several winters. If he's ever behaved violently or erratically there, the staff might remember. She rubs the bruise from yesterday, thinks of Mr. Drysdale, his hand reaching for the spot where his son stabbed him. He's lucky to be alive.

Luckier than Mary McNally, that's for sure.

Lu had thought that Mr. Drysdale ruled the roost. Now she sees that Mrs. Drysdale does, at least when it comes to Rudy. He was allowed to come home as long as he followed a few rules. *Rudy, stop stabbing your father.* Lu remembers those piles and piles of things in the alcove off the kitchen, the animal scent on the cushions, which also seemed to smell like the outdoors. That's where Rudy slept. Continues to sleep, without his father's knowledge. There was that sliding patio door right there, leading to a deck off the back of the house, another door below. How easy it would be for a mother to leave one of those unlocked, how accustomed a man could become to sliding in late at night and leaving before daybreak. Lu imagines her own Justin as an adult, broken by life or some not-yet-understood brain chemistry. Could she ever turn her back on him? No, no, she couldn't. She, too, would leave a door unlocked, make sure that her son never had to sleep outside, even if he had hurt someone else in the family.

So assuming that option was available to Rudy Drysdale, why was he in Mary McNally's apartment?

PART TWO

INTEMPERANCE

On a snowy evening just before Valentine's Day 1978—I was sitting at the coffee table, dutifully addressing twenty-seven cards to my classmates, knowing I would return home with only four or five cards from the other kids like me, kids whose parents insisted on an all-or-nothing policy—my father arrived home at five o'clock. That was unusual enough. We were lucky to see him at six thirty most evenings, and dinner was often as late as seven. (Teensy grumbled about this a lot, under her breath. "Lincoln freed the slaves, I thought.") Far stranger, our father walked straight to the little butler's bar in our living room and poured himself a half glass of whiskey. He then asked me to leave the living room, as he needed to be on the phone. I didn't dare remind him he had a phone in his room.

I asked Teensy if she knew what was going on.

"Mind your own business," she said, as she improvised in the kitchen, trying to make a dinner that would lift my father's spirits, but it was Thursday and she shopped on Friday. AJ was out, as always. He had basketball practice most afternoons, then rehearsals—school plays, choir, madrigals—in the evenings. He had tried to persuade our father that he should be given a car for his sixteenth birthday in April, but our father was firm that he could not afford such an extravagance, even with the Straight-

A-Student discount offered by auto insurers at the time. AJ had to count on Bash or Ariel, who had early winter birthdays and more generous parents. Bash had a very sharp, bright red Jeep because his family lived so far out. AJ hitchhiked, too, sometimes, another one of his secrets that I banked. I think he hitchhiked home that very night. His shoes squeaked and there were drops of water clinging to his hair when he finally arrived home.

AJ didn't ask our father any questions about his taciturn gloominess. Instead, he did all he could to distract him from his funk, telling stories about practice—Bash had been trying to impress a cheerleader and ran straight into a wall, Davey shot free throws in the way girls are taught, dropping the ball between his legs and arcing it underhand. He had made five baskets in a row that way, AJ said, on a bet. Stories like that, harmless and aimless.

Our father smiled absently, picked at the pork chops that Teensy had tried to defrost in cool water, not entirely successfully. (I'm not sure if most people had microwaves at the time, but I know we didn't. Didn't and still don't. My father loathes them. It's a principle with him, not having a microwave. He says time is not meant to be manipulated that way.) At one point, he almost poured ketchup on his salad, but my warning came just in time. It was odd enough that we even had bottled dressing on the table. On a typical night, my father's salads were an evening ritual, that kind of eccentric family thing that makes a kid proud and embarrassed at the same time. He rolled up his shirtsleeves and dressed the salad at the table in a battered wooden bowl, pouring oil and vinegar, squeezing a lemon wedge. The bowl and the glass cruets were his only family heirlooms, along with the planter's desk in his bedroom. When his grandfather died in the early 1970s, my father had driven down to Virginia and returned with these items, nothing more. He called his salad bowl and cruets his "lares and penates." For years, I thought that was Latin for oil and vinegar.

"What's up?" I asked AJ in a hoarse whisper as we cleaned up. Teensy always left as soon as dinner was on the table, and it fell to us to tidy the kitchen each night. True, this was little more than rinsing things for the dishwasher and putting away leftovers. But given AJ's busy life, I did this alone more often than not and I bridled at the unfairness of it all. There was so much unfairness in life, especially when one was the youngest, and a girl. I planned to change that one day. I was going to be an astronaut or a president, maybe an astronaut and then the president. And here we are, more than thirty-five years later, and we have plenty of female astronauts and we're within spitting distance of a female president. But you know what I consider true progress? The fact that we had a female astronaut disturbed enough to make that famous cross-country trip in adult diapers, intent on killing a romantic rival. When your kind is allowed to be mediocre or crazy—that's true equality.

"There's been an appeal," AJ said. "That man who killed Sheila Compson. He's filed an appeal."

"What do you mean?"

"He says the state withheld information about a key witness, someone who can confirm that he dropped her off alive, just as he testified, and that her shoes were in a rucksack. Dad said something—intemperate to a television reporter."

"Something cold?"

"Not temperature. *Intemperate.*" AJ, still doing PSAT prep, wedged a lot of big words into his sentences for practice. "He lost his temper. And you know he never gets angry, he prides himself on that. But the TV reporters got to him before he heard and he was caught off guard."

"What did he say?"

"He said, he said"—AJ looked around, lowered his voice anyway—"he said 'That son of a bitch is lucky he's not on death row.'"

I know, it sounds quaint now. *Son of a bitch.* Small children probably say it for laughs on cable channels. But it mattered at the time. So many things mattered that don't anymore. Remember, Ed Muskie's presidential hopes had been torpedoed by tears only a few years earlier. "Son of a bitch" at least had the advantage of being masculine, but it was not something a future attorney general or congressman or senator should say. *Intemperate,* as AJ characterized it. Our father had been intemperate.

There was an editorial in the *Beacon,* although it didn't really seem to say much in the end, other than to appeal to all elected officials to uphold the standards for public decency. The real controversy was that our father had been steadfastly against the death penalty, which had only recently come back in to use in Maryland after a series of constitutional challenges. He said he would, of course, uphold the laws of the state, but he was personally opposed to capital punishment. Now here he was, seemingly contradicting himself, wishing a man dead because he had dared to appeal. An unfair interpretation of events, but his political rival was under no obligation to be fair. For the first time in his public life, my father's gracious persona had cracked and he was not beloved.

And he had not, as many realized, addressed the central argument of the man's appeal, which was that there was a witness who would testify that she saw Sheila Compson get out of the man's car near the highway, just as he had said all along. This was a serious charge. Detectives maintained that they had interviewed the witness and found her not credible. My father said he didn't even know about her.

And the witness *was* unreliable. She told a different story from the one she had told three years ago. Back then, she claimed she saw Sheila at the concert, did drugs with her in the bathroom. Now she was trying to say that she was at the rest area where the killer dropped her off, that they hitched the rest of the way together and Sheila Compson definitely had a rucksack. She said she lied before because she did not want her own parents to know that she hitched to the concert. Still, her story should have been made available under *Brady,* the Maryland precedent for prosecutors withholding evidence.

But her story fell apart now, as it had fallen apart then. What about those other drivers who picked up Sheila Compson? They were adamant that she had no rucksack. And the new girl took detectives to the wrong rest area when asked to retrace her steps. She couldn't even tell them what songs were played that night at the concert. The state's attorney's office is not obligated to make false statements part of the discovery process. The guilty man remained in prison for life, and my father, true to his principles, never pursued the death penalty in any capital case, even when that would have been the popular thing to do. He was thrilled when Maryland moved toward a de facto suspension of the death penalty, then vacated it entirely in May 2013. My father was a Quaker, in his own way, a religion he had embraced after leaving military service. But his interest in Quakerism extended only to the occasional—the very, very, very occasional—meeting at the Quaker society in North Baltimore. I don't think he ever attended after the move to Columbia. He left AJ and me to make our own religious decisions, which is to say, we had no religion at all. And I was fine with that, and my children are fine with that now that I've abandoned Gabe's plan to have them bar and bat mitzvahed. When Gabe died, I discovered that religion offered me no comfort, nor was it much use to the twins, so young at the time. When I started researching private schools in Howard County, I didn't even realize that the one I chose had Quaker origins, but it pleased me when that was pointed out at my first visit.

It also was pointed out to me that the school would allow me to have my children board there, when they reached the upper school. I worried that I had somehow transmitted a sense of desperation, of being over my head in those early years of widowhood and authentic single parenting. *Don't worry, we'll take those kids off your hands when they're teenagers.* My father went to boarding school, but he never would have sent us. And I would never send my children away. When they were younger, only four or five, Justin asked if I would go to college with them. I said yes, and meant it. But I won't hold them to that promise, much as I would like to.

The oddest thing to me, about my job, this vocation to which I gave my life, is the ritual oath. Of course, they don't make people put their hands on Bibles anymore, but they might as well, given that more than 80 percent of U.S. citizens identify as Christians. (These are the kind of stats you know when you're in politics.) But I could put my hand on any book and tell you a thousand lies. So you will have to trust me when I tell you my story is true. I guess I could swear on my children's lives—but that strikes me as distasteful. Sometimes, I think we hold the truth in too high an esteem. The truth is a tool, like a kitchen knife. You can use it for its purpose or you can use it—No, that's not quite right. The truth is inert. It has no intrinsic power. Lies have all the power. Would you lie to save your child's life? I would, in a heartbeat, no matter what object I was touching. Besides, what is the whole truth and nothing but the truth? The truth is not a finite commodity that can be contained within identifiable borders. The truth is messy, riotous, overrunning everything. You can never know the whole truth of anything.

And if you could, you would wish you didn't.

"So Fred is going to defend the guy and invoke Hicks? What could he be thinking?"

AJ and Lu are at Petit Louis at the Lake, not far from where the beloved Magic Pan of their youth once sat. AJ probably would prefer to be at the Magic Pan right now, if it still existed. Her brother has come to hate restaurants with cloth napkins and wine lists. He also loathes the locavore places that would seem to embody the philosophy he espouses. Instead, he grumbles that they make food precious, another designer brand, only one to which poor people don't aspire. He's also not that keen on food trucks, for reasons that Lu can't be bothered to remember. It's hard keeping track of AJ's ethics.

But when AJ asked to take Lu to lunch to discuss "something confidential," she couldn't resist picking a restaurant she knew would annoy him. He's taking her away from her Saturday afternoon with the twins, after all, the one carefree day on a weekly calendar that looks more like a battle plan, with babysitters ferrying Justin here, Penelope there.

She can't recall the last time her brother asked to be alone with her. Maybe never? Over the years, they were always good about staying in touch, no matter the distance between them. Their father implemented a weekly call during AJ's college years, then encouraged Lu to choose Bryn Mawr because AJ had embarked on an MBA at Wharton. Nine years of education—four at Yale, three at Columbia, two at Wharton—and now he's basically the world's coolest, richest farmer. At least he's wearing a shirt with a collar to their lunch. Not exactly Brooks Brothers—it's a little sheer, with some hippy-dippy print—but it's fine. For Columbia, on a Saturday afternoon. She wonders if her brother even owns ties anymore. Probably one tie, one suit, and one shirt, suitable for funerals and weddings. They have reached that age when the funerals begin to creep into people's lives. The parents of friends, mostly, but older work colleagues and even the occasional peer.

Then again, AJ and Lu had a big head start on death, first with their mother, then Noel. Almost thirty years after the fact, she still can't believe he's gone. For all the changes her father has made at the house, the kitchen window still faces the lilac bushes where they first saw Noel, spying on them. At night, when the window throws her own reflection back at her, she sometimes thinks it's his eyes she's seeing.

As for death—there's Gabe, too, of course. But that's more like a nightmare from which she can never awaken. *"Mrs. Swartz?"* *"Ms. Brant."* *"But you are married to Gabriel Swartz?"* *"Yes."* Irritable—it was dinnertime, she had twin toddlers, it had been a long day. *"He was found in his hotel room, not breathing."*

To which she asked what seemed like the most logical question in the world. *"But he's started again, right? Breathing?"*

He had probably died almost twelve hours earlier. He missed a meeting, but those things happen, and no one had tried anything but his cell, which had gone unanswered. He was discovered by a housekeeper who assumed the room was empty.

Lu says to her brother: "I'm sure Fred's thinking he has a huge advantage—one case, no administrative duties—and that I can't possibly keep up. But I will. I'm a better lawyer than he is. I proved that time and again when I was his deputy."

She glances out at the lake. It is one of those January days that feels like a hangover. The holidays are past, her birthday is past, even her new job is losing its shiny-new luster despite the challenge of the Drysdale case. The Ravens, as of last weekend, are no longer in contention for the Super Bowl, not that she really cares. She often thinks that's why the Super Bowl was invented—to give people a reason to party into February. The beer companies have been pretty effective at giving people reasons to drink at least once a month—Super Bowl, Mardi Gras, Cinco de Mayo, Memorial Day, Fourth of July, Labor Day, Halloween. She's surprised they haven't figured out a way to make MLK's birthday a bacchanal. Civil rights Jell-O shots for all! This Bud's for you, Dr. King. She remembers when Penelope, age four, came home from school and began telling her there was a man, a very good man, who died too young and he would cry if he saw what life was like today.

For a moment, Lu thought Penelope was talking about Gabe.

"Maybe you should plead this one out, Lu. Take the air out of his tires."

"No."

"And here comes the famous Lu Brant chin action."

It is family lore that Lu, when stubborn, sets her jaw and sticks out her chin. "Bridle" is the correct term. It refers to a horse in bridle, the way the jaw extends when the bit is forced into the mouth. She has never heard the term used to refer to a man. Bridle. Bridal.

Their food comes and she is delighted that AJ has chosen steak frites—it seems a victory over Lauranne—but mystified why he has yet to bring up the confidential matter that this lunch was supposed to feature. They've both had a glass of wine and a leisurely appetizer course—an eggplant Napoleon for Lu, a frisée salad with lardons for AJ. She wonders if Lauranne will be able to smell the meat on him when he comes home, then wonders if AJ cares.

He dips a french fry in mayonnaise, sighs with pleasure. "These are perfect."

"Five Guys are almost as good. That's where I usually go when I need a fix."

"There's not one near me."

"There's one in the Harbor and then one over in that neighborhood they're now calling Brewers Hill. Also, just fifteen minutes down the parkway at Arundel Mills."

"Sounds like you've made quite a study of this. You need better vices, Lu."

She sips her wine, not at all flustered by the fleeting mental vision of her true vice, Bash. Compartmentalization is not a problem for Lu. Bash has a talent for it, too, despite that worrisome appearance at the open house over Christmas. If her fifty-three-year-old brother knew—well, what would he do? Take a swing at his old friend? AJ may be progressive in his politics, his ideas about climate change, and how to feed the planet, but when it comes to his sister, he's stuck in retro big-brother mode. How silly.

"How much longer are you going to stall?" she asks him now.

"Stall?"

"I thought you had something to discuss with me. Are you concerned about Dad?" The second she says that, she realizes that *she* is a little concerned. A line from Wordsworth comes to her: *Getting and spending, we lay waste our powers.* So much getting. So much spending. There's a hint of mania to their father these past few years, and now she wonders if that means there was a depressive phase she missed. No one expects a man widowed at a young age to be the life of the party, but Lu has begun to suspect her father's quiet, contained ways were part of something larger, sadder still.

"Should I be? He seems pretty hale. And sharp as ever. If anything, I'm surprised by how little he changes, and I don't see him day in, day out as you do, so I would be more prone to notice. No, I wanted to talk to you about, um, kids."

"Kids?"

"Having them."

"Well, it all begins when two people love each other very much—"

"No, seriously, Lu. I want to talk to you about surrogacy."

"Oh." She looks into her lap, startled by how personal this feels.

Penelope and Justin were born by gestational surrogacy, a concept that they still don't quite grasp, although she tried to explain it to them on their last birthday. They are bewildered by the fact that the dead parent is the one to whom they are genetically connected, while the living one has no blood relation to them. They have met the woman who carried them, but have little information about the eggs that made them, which is because Lu has almost no information about those purchased ova. A doctor slapped some photos on a desk, accompanied by heartfelt, handwritten essays from women who were willing to "donate" their eggs. "I've chosen ones that look like you," he said. "Why?" she asked. Lu tried not to be sentimental or defensive about her infertility. At the age of twenty-nine, she had to have a hysterectomy for fibroids. It was unfortunate, but it was what it was. What did the doctor think she was going to do, walk around for nine months with a series of larger and larger pillows under her lawyer clothes? She ignored the essays and chose the tallest one.

"Lauranne's still pretty young," Lu says.

"I'm not."

"So what?"

"You've seen the articles, I'm sure. The suggestion that older sperm might be connected to all sorts of things, like autism."

"If it's sperm you're worried about, you don't need a surrogate. A sperm bank will do nicely. And be a lot cheaper."

AJ can no longer meet her gaze. "Lauranne's willing to be a mother. But she's terrified of carrying a child." His words start tumbling out, as if he can hear Lu's unvoiced skepticism, her immediate inference that Lauranne doesn't want to sacrifice her body to pregnancy. "She's genuinely phobic about this. She knows herself well and while she understands that this should be the most natural thing in the world, she believes she'll have problems. Being pregnant. That it will feel as if something alien has taken over her body. Especially if we're not using my sperm. But we might be able to use her eggs."

"Maybe. But the odds of success will be much, much higher with donor eggs. So you'll have donor eggs and donor sperm and a uterus on loan."

"You had two of the three."

"I'm not *criticizing*. Just thinking out loud. Seriously, AJ, if she doesn't want to be pregnant, are you sure she wants to be a mother? Who initiated this?"

"It was mutual."

"Like, one morning, you just both looked at each other and said, 'Let's have a kid!' And then Lauranne says, 'Only I don't want to be pregnant!' And you say, 'And my sperm's too old!' What about adoption?"

"Foreign adoption has gotten much more difficult than most people realize. And with the countries that are still open, I have ethical concerns. I don't want to be accused of buying a baby. Meanwhile, here, most public agencies won't accept us because of my age.

Private adoption—I'm sorry, but that's just a way for people with money to leverage their power."

"You know people will say the same thing about surrogacy. It's getting more and more controversial. There are very real health risks for both the surrogates and the donors. There are people lobbying to ban it outright."

"Says the woman with eight-year-old twins born by surrogacy."

It's as if AJ wants her to say the sanctimonious thing, to remind him of the hysterectomy. About which she does carry some resentment. At the time, her father and brother seemed cavalier in a way that she can't imagine her mother would have been. Lu had no choice—with her fibroids, she would never be able to get pregnant—but it was a difficult thing to endure early in her marriage.

Then again, few fathers or brothers would want to have long heart-to-hearts about a woman's sexual organs. Her father didn't even tell her the facts of life, delegating Teensy to do it when Lu was eleven and had already figured most of it out.

"I'm sorry. I'm being lawyerly, outlining all the positions. It's not often I get to advise you. I want you to know what you're getting into. People can be cruel about it. And when they're not cruel, they're ignorant, which is worse. *Are those your kids? Do they look like their father because they sure don't look like you?*"

"Did you ever regret having kids?"

"No. Never. But I had moments, when they were very young, when I regretted the fact that my career had to take a hit. Maternity leave was not good for me. I stalled out in the city state's attorney's office. Then Fred moved to Howard County and became the boss, so I got a second chance. Even with money and all the child care I could hire, it took a toll. That won't be a problem for you, though."

"Lu, I'm going to be a very hands-on father."

"Uh-huh." Maybe he will be, this ridiculously rich man who has never known a single failure in his life, who can't fail despite himself. Yes, maybe this man, raised in a household in which his widowered father did not know how to do a single domestic task, would be superdad. Lu owes him the benefit of the doubt. She guesses.

"You'll be tired. You can't believe how tired you'll be. And you'll have to fight so hard for those bits of alone time that aren't absolutely essential. Imagine being in the house on a fine spring night. The children are asleep. Finally. The air is soft and it carries the scent of whatever those blooming trees are. And Five Guys is still open at the mall! But you can't go anywhere. Oh, wait—that's my life. Without a partner. You'll have Lauranne."

"You have Dad, Lu."

"Would you leave Dad in charge of young children?"

"He's fine, I'm telling you. Really, have you seen any evidence that his memory or intellect is diminished?"

She thinks about this. "No. But he's not—a caretaker. Never was. He was a loving father, AJ. He did his best by us. I wouldn't trade him for anyone. But did he ever throw a ball with you? Did he even bother to learn how to brush my hair? No, he just took me to the barbershop until I was almost nine." At which point, she grew out her hair and wears it long to this day, despite the advice in women's magazines that the style is aging. Her hair, loose, reaches almost to the small of her back. But it is seldom down in public. She wears it in a French knot, which helps make her look more authoritative. The first thing Bash does when she comes into their room is yank the pins from her hair.

"You know, maybe you should go on match.com. Or one of those places." It's as if AJ is misreading her mind.

"No. Thank. You. I don't have anything leftover to give. When the kids go off to college, I'll start stalking old men."

"When your kids go off to college, you'll be two years older than I am right now."

"Like I said—old men." She smiles at him, pats his hand. They are not touchers. The Brants do not hug upon coming and going. So this is a big gesture on her part. "If you do this, you'll be a great dad. Costs an arm and a leg, but you can afford it."

"Yeah, I can *buy* anything I want."

The self-pity on you, she thinks, but doesn't say.

TO EACH HIS SANCHO PANZA

In the spring of 1978, the all-county musical was *Man of La Mancha*. That is, the show was theoretically open to students throughout the county, yet the leads were taken by Davey, AJ, and Ariel, with Noel snagging one of the key supporting roles. There was some grumbling, but the director had no link to Wilde Lake High School, so the disgruntled parents had no reason to complain. If anyone deserved to be unhappy, it was Noel, who lost the role of Sancho Panza to AJ, who never played the clown. But the director glimpsed an untapped comedic talent in AJ's earnestness and wanted to exploit his chemistry with Davey, the inevitable Quixote, even if he had to be coaxed into trying out. AJ, instead of playing this second banana role with wink-wink self-consciousness, approached Sancho as achingly sincere in his hero worship of Quixote. He did not avail himself of any curlicues of irony, not so much as a raised eyebrow to let the audience know he was in on the joke. He was his master's servant to the end.

If Noel was disappointed not to be given the showy part that everyone assumed would be his, he hid it well. Maybe he enjoyed having a chance to play it straight. And he was wonderful as the padre, especially when he sang the tender ballad, "To Each His Dulcinea." I attended the final performance, a Sunday matinee, and surprised myself by weeping over Davey/

Quixote's death. I then asked my father what, exactly, the muleteers did to Aldonza while singing "Little Bird." They appeared to be beating her. Why were they beating her?

"Let's make sure AJ has a ride to the cast party," my father said. We went backstage and clapped him on the back, told him he was wonderful and that we would see him at the party.

The Sunday afternoon cast party was an attempt to start a new tradition while thwarting an old one. The year before when the county musical had been *South Pacific*—AJ and his friends had skipped this, in order to perform in the anniversary gala—there had been a notorious cast party after the Saturday night performance, which had resulted in a disastrous Sunday matinee. Nellie Forbush could not muster any perkiness; Lieutenant Cable had to leave the stage to vomit in a bucket. The director was adamant that this could never happen again; he would cancel the matinee rather than allow hungover students to perform. It was Davey's parents who stepped forward and offered an alternative: they would have the cast party at their home, *after* the matinee, and the cast's family members could attend as well if they so desired. It would be a catered affair and the students would even be allowed beer and wine—if their parents were there to grant permission. People did that then, allowed underage kids to drink a little, and no one thought much of it.

———————

I was disappointed by my first sight of the Robinsons' house, which AJ had described as luxurious and modern. From the front, it was a boxy one-story cedar bungalow, flat and pugnacious as a bulldog's face. But when you entered, it was as if you were walking into the sky. The builder had taken advantage of the fact that the lot was on a steep slope that backed up to a thickly wooded area, providing optimal privacy even when the trees were bare. With the exception of the walk-out "basement," the rear of the house was almost entirely glass. We were told the architect had been a student of Mies van der Rohe, although perhaps not his best one. Five years ago, the Robinson house, which they unloaded in 1980, was sold as a teardown. A few people protested halfheartedly that it was a historic structure, but the new owner had no problem getting permission to raze it. The replacement is surprisingly modest, a soft-green cottage that also blends into the landscape. I drove past there not long ago, trying to jog my memory of this particular day.

The May afternoon was perfect, the kind of weather that late spring was meant to have. And used to have more often then, I think. The weather was better when I was a child, I swear it, with unbroken strings of these amazing May days—temperatures in the seventies, breezes laden with complicated fragrances. The Robinsons had set out croquet wickets on the tiny level patch of lawn behind the house, and there was a Ping-Pong table inside the rec room. It quickly became apparent that the cast party was, in effect, two parties. The adults remained inside, on the upper floors, while the teenagers chose the rec room at the bottom of the house as their base of operations.

I wasn't sure where I belonged. There were some other younger siblings, but none from my elementary school. Two boys began chucking croquet balls at each other's heads, while I stood apart, pained by their childishness. As the sun disappeared behind the trees, the house seemed to glow. It was like watching a huge ant farm, only these ants were not particularly industrious. They milled about with drinks in their hands, availing themselves of tiny bites of food—miniquiches, quail eggs—passed by waiters. (On the bottom level, there were hamburgers and hot dogs coming nonstop off a grill, a refrigerator full of soda, even a keg of beer.) I realize now how expensive the Robinsons' home must have been, how exquisite their taste. That was the point of the party, to let people observe their superior taste. I saw my father talking to the Robinsons. I wonder if he was remembering the first time Davey had come to our home, how he assumed

Davey would be the first person in his family to attend college, that quiche would be exotic to him.

I could hear the teenagers—they were blasting the soundtrack of *La Mancha* and singing along, laughing as they changed the lyrics to private jokes about various cast members—but I couldn't see them behind the curtained sliding doors of the rec room. They were in high spirits, largely natural ones. You'd have to work hard to get drunk at a party such as this. The one keg, positioned near the man working the grill, made it hard to overindulge, although it was pretty clear that the "rule" about drinking only if a parent were present was being flouted. The cast seemed to feel that the Sunday show was their best yet and were giddy with their sense of achievement. I couldn't say that the matinee was their best, but it was hard for me to imagine something better than what I had seen. I was especially impressed by how Ariel, normally a tiny mouse, had been transformed into a powerful, big-voiced woman. It was strange to see her at the party, reduced to her usual self, not that much bigger than I was. The experience made me yearn to perform, but even then I knew I had no talent for acting or singing. AJ had gotten all those gifts. I sometimes think that was the beginning of wanting to be a lawyer—my desire to be the center of attention, combined with the knowledge that I could not sing, dance, or act. How else does one perform if one has no talent for playacting?

Suddenly, the curtains that hung across the basement entrance flared, as if from a sudden burst of wind, and two boys in polo shirts emerged, running at top speed, Davey and AJ in pursuit, girls screaming. I didn't recognize the running boys. They probably weren't from Wilde Lake High School. Another boy, also a stranger to me, ran out after the others, but headed in the other direction, toward the woods behind the house.

"Assholes!" AJ shouted as he chased the boys up the steep hill to the street. "Why do you have to be such *assholes*?" The incline was so severe that the four boys, the pursued and the pursuers, were all but crawling up on their hands and knees, grabbing at trees and bushes to keep their balance. "Maybe you cow-tipping Howard High farmers act like that, but we don't."

"We're from Glenelg," one called back. "And you Wilde Lake people are white-trash hippies."

Davey didn't say anything. He was focused on the climb, his face grim. He would have no problem overtaking them.

I ran inside the house and climbed to the top floor, where I told my father breathlessly, if somewhat inaccurately, that AJ was in a fight. Alerted by this self-appointed and self-important town crier, all the adults streamed into the front yard, most still holding their drinks. By now, AJ and Davey had the two strangers cornered in an old-fashioned convertible parked along the curb. My brother and Davey stood on the outside, gripping the passenger-side door. The driver could have tried to pull away, I suppose, but the look on Davey's face seemed to suggest that he would hold on to that door until it was wrenched from him.

"Okay, okay, let's calm down, everyone," my father said. "What's going on? Davey, you start."

He didn't want to show favoritism by asking AJ to recount the story; I understood this somehow. Even as a child, I was acutely aware of my father's methods.

"These ass—these guys grabbed some poor kid and pantsed him while he was chugging a beer, pulled his pants down in front of a bunch of girls. The guy's totally humiliated. What did he ever do to you?"

"He's a creepy little faggot, always spying on everyone. We told him to leave us alone and he didn't," the driver yelled.

"He's the cast photographer," AJ said. "That's his job."

"In the *theater,* when we're *performing.* Not at the cast party. Little creep never puts his camera down."

"You're mad because he took a photo of you doing something you didn't want photographed," Davey said. "I saw you light up in my parents' house. That was uncool."

"Oh, who cares, you stupid nigger. You think you're so fancy."

In the deep, shocked silence that fell, I noticed how few black people were in attendance at the party. Davey and his parents, of course. The girl who had been Ariel's understudy, whose skin and eyes were almost amber. Three of the waiters, and the man who had been tending the grill. Of the fifty or so people still at the party, maybe eight were black. Still, I don't think you could have said a more shocking thing in Columbia, not at that time. We were good people. Our choice of Columbia was the ultimate proof of that. We were the people tree, sixty-six strong, indifferent to class and race.

Right. The one thing people are never indifferent to are differences. We may not mind them, we may glory in them, but we notice, don't we? And congratulate ourselves on our tolerance and open-mindedness. But we are never indifferent.

I glimpsed Noel's face in the crowd. I expected him to be beaming with excitement. Noel was always up for a scene, as he called it, the more dramatic the better. But his big green eyes were full of an unreadable emotion. He wasn't enjoying this at all.

My father stepped forward and grasped the driver's side of the car, mirroring Davey's posture. I believed he needed to hold something to restrain himself from hitting the boy. I worried he might do something intemperate.

"You need to apologize to our hosts," he said. "For your behavior, for your words. And then, yes, you need to leave. But not before I have your parents' names. I will be calling them and telling them what transpired here."

"You can't make us tell our names," said the boy in the driver's seat.

"Do you honestly think I won't learn them? Others here know who you are. The director knows. For goodness' sake, son, I'm the state's attorney of this county."

"I can say whatever I want. Haven't you ever heard of the First Amendment? And it's not against the law to pants some faggot. It's what they want, to be bare butt in front of a bunch of guys."

My father seemed, for a moment, at a loss for words. Maybe that's why I channeled the old schoolyard taunt: "Well, takes one to know one."

There was a nervous silence, broken by the booming laugh of the grill man. He laughed much harder, I thought, than was warranted by any eight-year-old's gibe. He bent over, holding himself. He slapped his knees, literally, wiped tears from his eyes. Others began to laugh as well. The two boys in the car blushed furiously. My father stepped away from the car, as did Davey, and the two disgraced boys drove away. They did not race off, as one might expect. They drove the speed limit, even signaled the left turn as they approached the stop sign at the end of the street.

"Our boys are good boys," my father said to Davey's parents. "I'm proud that they stood up for the underdog." I expected the Robinsons to clap him on the back or send up a cheer. But they did nothing more than nod and smile tightly. Their party had been spoiled. People began making their excuses to leave, although there was plenty of light left in the May evening. My father stayed until the end, not something he usually did at social occasions.

At home that night, I asked AJ if I could borrow the *Man of La Mancha* cast album. But it wasn't "The Impossible Dream" that I played over and over that night. I wanted to listen to one of Ariel's songs: "What Does He Want of Me?" Quixote wanted Dulcinea, but not in the way other men did. She thought he was ridiculous, yet she could not laugh at him. The song stirred me in a way I could not explain. I yearned to be wanted. What would that feel like? My father and brother loved me. Even Teensy, in her cranky way, had undeniable affection for me. But what was this feeling that Dulcinea sang about, would I ever experience it? I knew it had something to do with kissing, and yet Quixote's love was better somehow because he did not want to kiss her, which was what all the men on the soap operas wanted to do with the women they said they loved. Yet I wanted to be kissed, too. I thought I did. Maybe.

Also, what was a faggot? I had meant to ask my father on the drive home, but had forgotten in all the excitement.

Lu feels a strange frisson of nerves when she goes before the grand jury to obtain a formal indictment against Rudy Drysdale. As she predicted, Fred had failed in his attempt to obtain a bail reduction for Drysdale at a hearing earlier this week. And he put Arthur Drysdale on the stand, as Lu had hoped, which allowed her to ask if there were any violent episodes in his son's past. The father had stammered and stuttered, even as Fred quickly objected, and Lu happily withdrew her question. They were on notice now, which was all she needed. She knew. Drysdale could take the Fifth if asked about the fake police report, a crime, if a small one. Either way, Fred has to realize now that she has something on Rudy Drysdale.

Still, she is uncharacteristically jittery. She's gilding the lily, going for a grand jury indictment when he's already been charged. What if the grand jury decides it's not a murder one case? Maybe she shouldn't have risked this.

But it's a good trial run for the neighbor, Jonnie Forke, who can place Rudy Drysdale at the scene during the week that Mary Mc-Nally was killed. Lu has to be hard on her because she's sure Fred is going to go after her in court. He'll be right to do so. In her heart of hearts, Lu has trouble with anything that relies on a person's ability to remember another person's face. Maybe that's her own personal bias, born of her particular inability to remember names and faces. But as the science on memory advances, she wonders how it will affect the future of criminal trials that rely on eyewitnesses. What if criminal attorneys start to use "memory experts," the way, say, medical trials present experts on both sides of malpractice cases? Then again, the average person is reluctant to admit to a less-than-stellar memory until a certain age, although Lu knows lots of women who will cop to "mom brain" during pregnancy and menopause. The fear of dementia is part of this culture of denial, Lu believes, but she also thinks memory is part of the holy trinity of self. Ask anyone and they'll tell you: they have a good memory, good taste, and a good sense of humor. Oh, make it the holy quartet: everyone, everyone Lu has ever met, considers themselves superb judges of character.

Jonnie Forke hangs tough on the stand, though. Too tough. They need to sand down her edges a little bit before the trial. She looks fine—in fact, she's more attractive than Lu realized—but her personality is spiky. She's sort of the looking-glass version of the victim, according to Lu's investigator. A waitress at a late-night restaurant at the casino at Arundel Mills, extremely outgoing, divorced, but with grown kids and a lot of family. The night Mary McNally was killed—assuming it was December thirty-first—Jonnie Forke was at her daughter's house for a family party, seeing in the New Year with three generations. This woman's death would never go undiscovered for a week.

Lu asks her: "The man you saw that week—was he clean-shaven?"

Trick question. Lu knows Drysdale did not have a beard at the time. But does Jonnie?

"He didn't have a beard, if that's what you mean," she says. "I didn't get close enough to see how recent his shave was, but he didn't have a full beard."

Oh, she's good.

"How close did you get?"

"Maybe ten feet. He was on the edge of the parking lot, just standing there. I noticed him because he had a big puffy coat. And it wasn't that kind of cold that day, it was in the forties."

"So you noticed his coat?"

"And his face. He didn't have the hood up. So I saw his face and his hair." A pause. "His hair was longer then."

She's *really* good. Credit Andi, who helped prepare her. Rudy Drysdale does have a fresh haircut, although the suit he's wearing is almost greenish with age. Fred probably told his parents they didn't need to splurge on a new suit for a grand jury proceeding.

"Still, he's not an unusual-looking man, right? Brown hair, brown eyes. It would be easy to confuse him with someone else."

"Not for me. People in my job, you pay attention to faces, make eye contact. It's the difference between a decent tip and a good one."

"And where do you work, Ms. Forke?"

"Luk Fu." She grimaces. "It's not like I named it. It's a noodle bar. It's pretty good, for the price. Those critics on Yelp can—" Lu's eyes beseech the witness to get back on message. "They can go somewhere else if they don't like it."

Lu toys with her a little longer, but she's rock-solid. Then she lets the jurors ask her questions. They, too, are curious about how she can be so certain of the ID. She's almost too adamant, a person who never admits to being wrong. She's certain that she never forgets a face. An unflattering thought flits through Lu's mind: *probably better with men's faces than women's.* She just gives off that vibe to Lu. But then, Lu always feels as if she has to overtip extravagantly to make up for people's biases about women.

Drysdale takes the Fifth, of course. Fred has instructed him not
to lock in his testimony. Anything he says here can't be contradicted
in court and who knows what discovery still might bring?

They're done by midmorning, and the grand jury hands up its
indictment before lunch. Murder one.

———

The courthouse is theoretically within walking distance from the
office—but not in January and never in four-inch heels. It's a two-
lane road with no shoulder, risky enough in daytime, dangerous at
dusk. Lu drives the scant mile back to the office, parking in the
permit spaces. She has no designated space here or at the courthouse, a security measure for the judges and other officers of the
court. Back inside the Carroll Building, she shuts herself up in her
office. This isn't the kind of situation in which one does a victory
lap. She has to act as if she never doubted she would win. Grand
juries are supposed to be slam dunks for prosecutors.

She spends the afternoon attacking the usual raft of phone messages, then tries to put a dent in the e-mail. She tells Della she's
available for media calls, but there are no media calls. Mary McNally's murder received maybe four paragraphs in the big newspapers,
while Rudy Drysdale's arrest and initial charge were considered only
slightly more newsworthy. The *Howard County Times,* now owned
by the *Beacon-Light,* is content to use the press release put out on
the HoCoGov's Twitter feed and Facebook page.

It is almost seven before Lu leaves, which means Teensy has fed
the twins and her father, technically Teensy's job, but something
that Teensy seems to resent terribly. It has become Brant family
legend that Teensy is *their* boss, that she's the one who gets to pick
what she does and doesn't do, and all because she chose them
over the Closters forty-five years ago. The myth is self-serving.

Teensy is probably underpaid and overworked by almost any legal standard. Still, it's a little frustrating having a housekeeper who resents any housekeeping duties that do not serve the man-of-the-house. Does Teensy consider herself Mrs. Brant, in a sense? It's not the first time that Lu has allowed herself to consider this. It's a tantalizing and impossible idea, one she has tried to discuss with AJ, who finds it merely impossible. It's not that Lu thinks they have sex, her father and Teensy. Even when she came to accept that her father was a sexual being, having discreet dalliances with Miss Maude and others, she could not imagine him with Teensy. Tidewater Virginian that he once was, he resisted, for a time, the new information about Thomas Jefferson and Sally Hemings. But when he came to accept the scholarship, he turned on his former idol. During a family outing to Monticello last summer, the docents begged Andrew Brant to withhold his side lectures about Jefferson and Hemings—whom her father, rightly, calls by her real name, Sarah—until the tour was over. And yet—there is a sense that Teensy, still married to the seldom-seen Ron, considers herself the Brant matriarch. On nights such as this, she won't even leave a plate for Lu.

It has been a bitter winter so far. The cold, when Lu pushes through the employees-only door at the rear of the building, invades her sinuses like some spiky parasite. She gasps at the shock of it, then gasps a second time, startled by a woman emerging from the shadows, moving too quickly, her speed almost menacing, yet her stature so petite that it's hard to see her as a threat. Unnerving, but not threatening. Lu readies herself for a citizen encounter.

"Lu Brant? Eloise Schumann. I really need to talk to you."

"I'm headed home," Lu says automatically. "Monday, perhaps. If you call my secretary—"

"I have been calling your secretary. You never call me back."

"Well, yes." Might as well tell the truth. "You never say why you're calling and I'm afraid I have no idea why you're calling because I don't know who you are, despite what you think."

For a moment, the woman looks angry, insulted. She balls her hands, bare despite the subfreezing temperatures.

"How can you forget Ryan Schumann? It was one of your father's most famous cases."

"Schumann?" And finally Lu remembers. Schumann. Shoe. Man. That was his surname, not a nickname bestowed on him by Noel, but an inevitable pun: Shoe Man, Sheila Compson's killer. The victim's name is burned into her faulty memory, as is the image of that sandal, balanced on the jury box railing. That was her father's genius, his intent. To make people remember the girl, even if this was all she had left behind. Humanize the victim, demonize the perp. Ryan Schumann.

"But you're not his wife," Lu says, her voice rising with uncertainty. She has a mental image of that woman on the stand, grim and angry. This woman seems too young, no more than ten years older than Lu, which would have made her barely twenty at the time. "How old are you?"

"I'm fifty-five. And I'm his second wife. I married him while he was serving his sentence."

"While—has he been released?"

"No. He died in prison late last year. Just like your father wanted. Even though he was so sick at the end. He should have been given compassionate leave."

Lu has no compassion to spare for Ryan Schumann, who not only killed and probably raped a young girl, but refused to tell her parents where they might find her body. Life in prison seems right to her.

"How can I help you?"

"I want a posthumous pardon for him."

"That seems unlikely."

"What if I can convince you he was innocent?"

"Even less likely."

"Maybe you should talk to your father before you make up your mind."

"My fa—"

"He knew me as Ellie Cabot. Ask him. Ask your father what he knows that he never told anyone. Ask him why he railroaded an innocent man, a good man who never did anything wrong."

She turns, walking swiftly, but not toward the public side of the parking lot. She heads for the dark, two-lane road that leads to the courthouse, the road that Lu won't walk even in the daytime. Had she gone there first, in search of Lu, thinking to catch her after the hearing, then walked here, not realizing what a dark, dangerous trudge it was in the winter dusk? Although the woman has done her no harm—seems scarcely capable of doing harm—Lu clutches her coat at the throat. She didn't think it was possible to feel colder than she did a minute ago, and yet she does.

THE AGE OF REASON

The first time I saw Nita Flood—really saw her, noticed her, who knows how many times I had walked past her before—was on my back-to-school shopping trip to the Columbia Mall in 1978. That is, I was supposed to be shopping for new clothes, which my father would come back and pay for, an arrangement reached after a summer devoted to wheedling and arguing. It was a ridiculous thing to grant an eight-year-old girl, but I think even my head-in-the-clouds father had come to understand it was unfair to entrust Teensy with the oversight of my wardrobe, and *he* certainly wasn't up to the job. Witness my hair, worn quite short, cut by a barber, so it had no elfin, gamine quality. If my nickname hadn't already been Lu, it would have been Lou.

Yet when my triumphant shopping day finally arrived, I was in no hurry to get started. Instead, I trailed AJ and his friends through the mall. They roamed in a pack, their agenda clear only to them. They seldom stopped moving and they never went into stores. There was a conceit at the time, a *sub*urban legend if you will, that Wilde Lake students, whose high school was a two-story, windowless octagon built around the hub of a "media center," had been trained to walk in a circle. When AJ and his friends stopped moving, they leaned on the metal railings along the mall's second floor, just as they leaned on the railings at school between classes. There was a photograph in AJ's yearbook, the *Glass Hour,* showing them doing just that in the fall of 1978. Let the freshmen and sophomores hurry to class. They were juniors now, sure of their power.

On this particular August day, AJ and his group lingered long enough at the Hickory Farms kiosk to grab samples of summer sausage from a girl with stringy hair, a face sodden with acne, and a Barbie-doll figure. If the term "butterface" had been in vogue then, someone might have made that cruel assessment, but I don't think that crass term existed.

Cruelty did, however. We had plenty of cruelty in 1978. AJ's friends didn't even bother to walk out of earshot before they began making fun of the girl.

"If anyone knows sausage," Lynne said, "it's Nita Flood."

Everyone laughed at this, except Ariel, who blushed and looked at the floor. Nita Flood stared stonily in the other direction, as if fascinated by the small camera store tucked into the corner of the mall just opposite her. I didn't get the joke, but I knew better than to ask. That would only draw attention to my not quite legitimate presence. My arrangement with AJ was that I could follow him when he was with his friends, but I couldn't interact with them. I was like Casper the Friendly Ghost, condemned to scare off the very people I wanted to befriend. AJ posed this as a win-win—we both got out of the house and away from Teensy, who always found chores to fill our idle summer days. But it was more of a win for AJ. My brother was generally a good big brother. And like our father, he disdained overt unkindness. I was astonished that he didn't reprimand Lynne for mocking someone, just as he and Davey had come to the defense of that kid at the cast party. But the girl selling sausage apparently wasn't worthy of his protection.

We were almost to Friendly's when Lynne whispered something in Bash's ear and he, with a backward glance at me, whispered in turn to AJ.

My brother stopped and walked back toward me, hands in pockets, eyes fixed at some point behind me. "Lu, don't you have any friends your own age to hang out with?"

That was cruel. AJ knew I didn't. Although I did have a plan to take care of that, a strategy for transformation that would make me the most popular girl in the third grade. All summer, I had been reading magazines like *Young Miss* and *Seventeen,* trying to figure out the formula for popularity. Clothes were the secret. Clothes and hair and clear skin, but skin was not my problem, unless one counted freckles. Over the summer, I had started growing my hair out, having persuaded our father that I could take care of it. And after studying the magazines, I had decided on a particular back-to-school outfit, which I found later that day in the girls section at Woodward & Lothrop. My father, as promised, came back to the mall with me that evening and paid for the outfit on hold there, along with some other basics—jeans, T-shirts. I wasn't a tomboy, but I had grown up in a household of men. (Apologies to Teensy, but she never fussed over me. It was easier for her if I wore clothes like my brother's, even his hand-me-downs in some cases.) I could score a baseball game, but I couldn't find the business end of a lipstick. I suppose that made my upbringing progressive in a sense, but it was mainly careless and it left me vulnerable to missteps. The outfit I chose that day was disastrous, but no one in my household seemed to recognize that, not even AJ, who always wore the right thing, said the right thing, did the right thing.

Why did he allow me to make such a horrible mistake when it came to my third-grade back-to-school outfit?

Maybe he simply realized it was too late to intervene when I showed up for breakfast a week later in plaid gauchos, a long-sleeved white blouse, a newsboy cap, and a ring-tab-festooned vest I had crocheted that summer under Teensy's supervision. Had the Annie Hall fad finally trickled down to the junior set? My father immortalized the first day of school with photos, so I don't have to rely on my memory: I looked like a caddy, circa 1920.

"I've heard of high-waters," one of my classmates said as I took my seat in the second row. (The front row was for brownnosers. I had made that mistake last year.) "But I hope the water never gets knee-high."

"These are gauchos," I said. Then, always quick to go on the offensive—if the other kids didn't appreciate my superiority, I would simply rub their noses in my grandness—"And they cost seventeen dollars."

To be fair, I don't think *Young Miss* or *Seventeen* had encouraged me to brag about the price of things to gain popularity.

"Isn't that a kind of a cookie? Gauchos?"

"Or that old guy with a mustache who died last year?"

Randy Nairn bent over at the waist, walked up and down the aisle, pretending to puff a cigar. For the rest of the day, whenever the teacher's back was turned, kids would point to me and waggle their eyebrows, smoke pretend cigars. Randy, ever bold, even jumped into the aisle a time or two when the teacher's back was turned and did the loping Groucho walk.

I was dangerously near tears. And I never cried, never. That was one of the things I was famous for as a baby, according to my father. *I never cried.* Thinking back on this from the vantage point of having had two children, I now have to wonder: Did I really never cry or did my father just not hear me? I'm not saying fathers don't hear their children cry, only that they may not remember it as a mother would. And he would have been pretty shell-shocked at the time, trying to care for a new baby, alone except for Teensy and AJ.

At any rate, I didn't cry, not that day. I seethed, intent on revenge. I made sure to leave school the split second the bell rang and went storming down the bike path in the opposite direction of my house. Columbia was full of such trails, and I knew the one Randy had to take home, which led to the town houses near the high school. The ones where poor kids lived, but you weren't supposed to say that. The town houses were on the other side of a busy street, Twin Rivers Road, so here the path became a tunnel, a culvert under the street. To this day, I marvel that my eight-year-old self had figured out what all those new town planners could not, how predator-friendly those bike paths were. I cut through the culvert then climbed the hill on the other side, scrambling to the top where I would be able to see Randy approaching. I dragged a dead branch up the hill with me—it was heavy enough to strike a blow, sharp enough to scratch or take out an eye.

Was that what I had intended to do? I have thought so often about that day, my intentions, the lengths to which I was willing to go. When do children understand right and wrong? Some people think that Catholics have established seven as the age of reason, but that is a simplification of the church's rules. Jews established the age of majority at thirteen for boys. (It used to be twelve for girls, which I find interesting, a stray fact discovered when I was still keeping my promise to raise the twins as Jews.) And in the law, *my* law as I used to think of it—ah, the law. When I first started studying criminal law, there were ironclad rules about juveniles who committed crimes, almost uniform standards throughout the United States. Young offenders were granted anonymity. They were deemed worthy of a second chance. Those days are over. Now younger and younger people are being tried as adults, sent to regular prisons in some cases.

But in 1978, an eight-year-old girl who beat a nine-year-old boy with a stick—Randy had been held back a year in first grade—what would be the consequences? Factor in the not irrelevant information that I was the daughter of the county's state's attorney. This would not have been in my favor, by the way. If I had accomplished what I now believe I wanted to do that day, no one would have come down harder on me than my own father. He would have made sure that I faced the full censure of the law.

I watched Randy approach. He was alone. I was going to let him cross under the tunnel, then attack him from behind. I was not only murderous, but cowardly. He disappeared into the tunnel. I estimated it would take him about thirty seconds to pass through. *One one thousand, two one thousand . . .*

I crawled down the embankment, stick in hand—

And there was my brother with Noel, approaching from the other direction. The high school students were released earlier than the elementary-school students. They should have been long gone by now, or in practice for something, although AJ did not play a fall sport that year and there would be no rehearsals on the first day of school. AJ and Noel were speaking to each other in arch British voices and doing odd staggering, skipping walks. Noel, whose house had better television reception than ours, watched Monty Python on the D.C. channel on Sunday nights, then acted out the entire show for his friends, who eagerly picked up the most memorable lines and sang the song about the lumberjack, which I didn't get at all.

But they were not so lost in their silliness that they didn't see me on the hillside, holding my branch with two hands.

"Lu, what do you think you're doing?" AJ asked. He didn't sound particularly urgent or concerned. Randy emerged from the tunnel and looked up, following AJ's gaze. As soon as he saw me, he laughed and pointed, began walking his Groucho walk. He probably thought I wouldn't try to do anything with two high schoolers present.

He didn't know me very well.

I threw my stick down and jumped him. He was a runty kid, probably one reason he picked on me. And he wore the same clothes almost every day, come to think of it, which was worse than wearing new clothes that people thought silly. I kneed him between the legs, pretending I was Angie Dickinson on *Police Woman,* which had been my favorite show before it went off the air, although I had to watch it on the sly if Teensy was around. (Our father didn't believe in censoring anything we watched or read.) Randy collapsed, whimpering, and I jumped on top of him, landing blows and kicks wherever I could, pulling his hair.

"Luisa Frida Brant." AJ was shouting now, trying to pull me off Randy. I could hear Noel laughing, which made me madder, as did the use of my full name, which I had managed to keep secret so far. I began fighting AJ, a losing battle, but I gave it my all, windmilling my arms into his stomach and chest.

"He deserves it. He made fun of my clothes. And him with only two shirts that he alternates and even then, he always smells by Friday. Who is he to make fun of anyone?" There was the true source of my rage. Not that I had been mocked, but that I had been mocked by *Randy,* that he had been sly enough to exploit my weaknesses so his wouldn't be noticed. And now he knew my horrible middle name, chosen by my mother for some stupid Mexican artist that no one had ever heard of, not when I was a kid. My fists thrummed on my brother's chest as if it were a taut drum. "What business is it of yours, anyway, Ajax Homer Brant?"

Randy, no dummy, had fled as soon as my attention was diverted, slowed by his limp. My Pepper Anderson kick had been effective. But no one cared about Randy anymore. Noel had stopped laughing and was looking at AJ, his unearthly green eyes round with wonder and mischief.

"Ajax Homer Brant? I thought you were Andrew Jackson Brant, like your father. How can you be AJ Brant Jr. if you don't have the same name?"

"I was supposed to be," AJ said. "It was a mistake, at the hospital. Some stupid nurse who filled in my birth certificate—she got it wrong. I'm going to change it legally, when I'm an adult. Plus, it's not so bad. Ajax is a hero in the *Iliad.* That's where the Homer comes in."

Noel did not seem to pick up on the inconsistency in AJ's story. He was probably too busy mulling the possibilities of knowing AJ's true name. A chink in the armor of AJ the Perfect. Their friends would delight in this information if he shared it with them. Noel was not unlike me, I realized, stockpiling secrets about AJ, unsure how or when they might be used. Yet we never ended up exploiting any knowledge we gained because we both loved him so.

"Couldn't your parents have changed it right away? I mean, your dad is a lawyer—"

"It's hard to change a birth certificate. And my mom—"

"Our mom," I corrected, sniffling.

"Our mom, she thought it was bad luck. To change a baby's name. Dad said I had to wait until I was eighteen."

"Even after she died? What did it matter then?"

The answer was obvious to AJ and me, if not to Noel. It mattered more than ever. After our mother was gone, nothing she touched could be changed. And she had named AJ, not some nurse. The house stayed as it had been, despite the fact that she had lived there less than a year. There was still a small pile of books on our mother's side of the bed, and on the nights when I had bad dreams and went to sleep with my father, he was always far to one side, as if he were still sharing the bed with someone.

AJ, meanwhile, would not speak of her at all. Although not generally selfish, he hoarded his memories of our mother as if they might evaporate in the open air. I envied him, but the truth was, I didn't want AJ's stories. I wanted my own and I could never have them. AJ had a mother for eight years. I had one for eight days. That was an injustice that could never be righted. There are a lot of challenges about having twins, but at least one never has that imbalance of time. Penelope can't begrudge Justin for having had a father longer than she did; Justin will lose his mother at the same time Penelope does.

Our mother had named her son Ajax Homer, her daughter Luisa Frida. That was no error and those names could never be changed. Our names were her legacy, one of the few things she left behind. They were burdensome when we were young, but not horribly so. As an adult, my only regret was that I had allowed myself to be "Lu" for so long that I couldn't return to the fuller, sweeter name she had given me.

As far as I know, Noel kept the secret of AJ's name. But in college, AJ was dismayed to discover that there were *two* warriors named Ajax—Ajax the Great, the son of Telamon, and Ajax the Lesser, who survived so many attempts on his life that he ended up boasting that not even the gods could kill him.

The gods promptly did just that.

"Maybe I was named for Ajax the Lesser," my brother said to me the last time we spoke.

It is Sunday night before Lu has a chance to ask her father about Eloise Schumann/Ellie Cabot. She is not avoiding the topic. She is simply too busy trying to survive the weekend. Her kids are far from overscheduled. In fact, they have had to accept the hard truth that a single mom with a demanding job cannot be on call to take them to every practice, game, rehearsal, and activity. (Justin has his uncle's flare for singing and dramatics, while Penelope loves soccer.) That's what Melissa the babysitter is for. Lu does what she can and she manages to make the truly important stuff—pageants and "championships." But she grew up without a parent attending most of her milestone moments, and she doesn't feel she was harmed by this.

Even if Gabe had lived, Lu doubts the two of them would have been able to handle life with the twins without multiple babysitters, not as long as she insisted on working. And Gabe was too evolved to admit that he wanted her to be a stay-at-home mom. A SAHM. The very acronym looks like some dreary department within the Social Security Administration, or a form that one has to fill out for benefits. SAHM. Say it out loud and it's just one letter away from "Om," the chant of peace and contentment and centeredness. But the SAHM, in Lu's opinion, sacrifices her center, hollows herself out by caring for others. Before Gabe's death, they were probably on a collision course over this issue, although he was the person far more suited to staying at home. Is there such a thing as a SAHD? Say *that* out loud and it sounds like a toddler trying to describe her feelings. *I'm so sahd.*

But, having checked out of her kids' after-school lives, Lu does cater to them on weekends as much as possible. They go to movies. They go to the place with the climbing wall. They go make pottery together. They *go*. And they are good company, her kids. For one thing, they have exquisite manners, thanks to Teensy and their grandfather. They also eat everything. Lu tries hard not to be Ms. Smug McSmugginton when the topic of fussy eaters comes up because she knows she didn't really *do* anything to instill good eating habits in her kids. She was just too lazy to make two dinners from scratch every night and Teensy, bless her heart, is lazier still. This weekend, the twins asked to try a Korean restaurant in D.C. and they both ate kimchi.

Then Sunday evening comes and it's like a bad storm front sweeping through. Much of this is due to Penelope's anxiety over school, which reminds Lu of her own struggles with math, although she was in high school before she hit the wall. Still, she develops a sympathy stomachache as Penelope heads tearfully to bed. Penelope continues to rail at the unfairness of it all. Why does she struggle in math when Justin doesn't? Yet Justin is not bothered by his problems in spelling, while Penelope excels in anything to do with language. They are, more than one person has noted, very much like their parents. People even think they see Lu in Penelope's features. It's funny how suggestible people are. They see a woman with two children and they begin to see resemblances that are not there, can never be there. And yet—Lu does see herself in Penelope's temperament. She is competitive, more competitive than Justin. She loves to argue. Even in math, she wants to debate. The answers seem arbitrary to her. Lu understands, although she is baffled by her daughter's resistance to geometry. Lu loved geometry, with its clear-cut rules and elegant proofs.

Penelope and Justin have adjoining rooms in the new wing of the house, upstairs from Lu's. Until recently, she would find one of them in the other's bed most mornings. They are still close. But they are turning out so differently. Penelope is that odd combination of baby-girl and forty-year-old divorcée, while Justin seems to live happily at the bull's-eye of eight-year-old boyhood. Penelope often reminds Lu of Noel's mother, that hard little number in her tennis whites. But tonight, Penelope is her baby self and she needs to be rocked to sleep. Lu almost falls asleep at the same time, but catches herself, snatching up her head in a whiplash of awareness. Almost nine o'clock. She should talk to her father.

He is in his study, enjoying one last glass of wine, not yet drowsing as he often is at this hour. This room feels like a time capsule for a time that never was, a false memory of genteel contemplation—the globe of red wine, opera on the stereo. Her father, like Lu, used to fall asleep while putting his children to sleep. The days are long, but the years are short, that old cliché. The years are long, too. Will her father even remember the events of forty years ago?

"A woman came to see me," Lu says without preamble. "Eloise Schumann. She said you'd know her as Ellie Cabot."

"So that's why you've seemed so distracted all weekend," he says. "Or abstracted, as Teensy likes to say."

Has she been distant? She thought she had just been enjoying her time with the twins, fully present. Sure, sometimes her mind wandered, but it was to the McNally case, not that woman outside the courthouse.

"She was waiting for me, in the parking lot at work Friday. She thinks Ryan Schumann deserves a posthumous pardon."

"She never stops. She's like that"—he pauses, one of those pauses that grip Lu's heart. Her father's pauses are more suspenseful than any horror movie with a racing soundtrack. His pauses, to paraphrase Whitman, contain multitudes. When does groping for a word become the first signpost on the road to dementia? She thinks, bizarrely, of the sign on Interstate 70, the one that shows the mileage to Columbus, St. Louis, and Denver for no reason she can fathom. How far out are they? When will they get there?

But he finishes strong: "Pink bunny, the Energizer. She goes on and on and on. Although she's always beating a slightly different drum. What is it this time?"

"*This* time?"

"What's her latest reason for claiming Ryan Schumann is innocent?"

"She—oh, she . . . Wait, is she the witness? The one who came forward in 1978 and accused you of violating *Brady*?"

"Yes, and she did talk to me back during the original case. But she didn't say she was a witness." He chuckles. "She claimed she did it."

"*What?*"

"After her second story was shot down, she told yet another one. She said she was at the rest stop where Sheila Compson was dropped off. She said she told Sheila Compson it would be safer if they hitchhiked together as darkness was coming on. According to her, Sheila had pot—in a rucksack, just like the rucksack Schumann kept claiming the girl was carrying—and they hiked into the woods to smoke. And, according to Miss Cabot, Sheila Compson became violent and tried to attack her. She jumped on her and she pushed

her off. Sheila Compson hit her head on a rock and died. According
to this young woman. Who was, by the way, eight inches shorter
and thirty pounds lighter than Sheila Compson. But we humored
her. We told her to take us into the woods and show us the body.
She couldn't do it. She didn't even pick the right rest stop. So, no,
our office did not provide her testimony during the discovery phase
because it was false. I was doing a professional kindness not sending
them down that rabbit hole."

"Why would she do this?"

"Women fall in love with killers all the time. Girls still love bad
boys, that's never going away. And she was very young. Nineteen, I
think? Eighteen? Saw his photo in the paper, I guess, and decided
she loved him. And you say she's calling herself Eloise Schumann
now. Did she really marry him or is that another fiction?"

Lu is ashamed to tell her father that she didn't even think to
check for a marriage license. He wouldn't have made the same mistake. "I probably should."

"So he's dead," her father continues. "He was only . . ."—that
pause again. "He was only twenty-six when he was on trial. So
born 1950. Lived to almost sixty-five, then. Spent more than half
his life in prison. Yet he never told us where the body was. I asked
him. I asked him every year until I retired. He always said, 'I can't
say.' *Won't,* I would correct him. *You won't say.* Oh, I understood he
didn't know exactly. The woods near that rest stop were vast. *Where
is she, Mr. Schumann?* Sheila Compson's parents died, denied the
ritual of burial. Now he's dead. Well, I'm sorry, but I can't really feel
anything for him."

"Hashtag sorrynotsorry," Lu jokes. Her father looks utterly mystified. He uses a computer but has drawn a line at all forms of social
media. He was horrified to learn that the state's attorney's office
puts out press releases using the Twitter handle HoCoGov, while

Lu was miffed that her office, unlike the library and the cops, didn't merit a unique Twitter feed.

Intemperate. She remembered her father's rage when the appeal was announced, his ill-considered words. The mild profanity he used would never inflame people today. Or would it? Even as standards for behavior seem to fall, it also seems easier, quicker, to end a career forever with one verbal transgression. An intemperate moment, a wrong choice of words, can go viral if it is captured on video, or in a screen grab.

Forever. One photograph. Girls still love bad boys. If Lu's secret life were ever to become known—but, no, it won't. She has built it that way. Certainly, there are no photographs. She seldom texts Bash and their phone conversations are matter-of-fact arrangements of when they might meet, no where or when stipulated. No records, except for the occasional bruise, scratch, or bite mark. She is careful. She will continue to be careful.

But it would be fascinating if a female public servant had to defend her legal-but-not-exactly mainstream love life. Fascinating as long as it happened to another female public official. Can't you take that hit for the team, Hillary Rodham Clinton? Step on down, Ruth Bader Ginsburg. Now that would be true equality, a female politician coming back after an ignominious sex scandal.

There is the fact that Bash is married. That alone could be enough to torpedo Lu's career—unless they pretend to be IN LOVE and are therefore given dispensation to break with common decency. Why are people allowed to hurt others in the name of love? Why is love given so much credit, as if it is always a power for good? Does Eloise Schumann love Ryan Schumann, a man she can't possibly know, a man she never knew, not sexually. Only six states allow conjugal visits and Maryland is not one of them. Even if Maryland were to permit it, an inmate such as Ryan Schumann, sentenced to life in prison for a capital crime, might have a hard time earning the privilege. How had any woman managed to become attracted to him? Lu remembers him as weaselly and small, even to her six-year-old eyes. As a small woman, she is always careful to avoid small men because she doesn't want anyone to think the man had settled, choosing her for stature alone. Gabe was slender as a reed, but a respectable five foot eleven. Bash is shockingly broad—but, no, Bash doesn't count because no one has ever seen them together. No one will ever see them together.

Maybe when Penelope and Justin are out of the house, she will go on match.com. For now, this is the best solution she can fashion.

She sips her glass of wine, enjoying the companionable silence, the strains of—ah, it's *Carmen*. Old age looks pretty good from here. And she will be all of fifty-five when the twins leave for college, far from old despite the joke she made to AJ. Some women are just getting started at fifty-five. Again, look at Clinton and Ginsburg. In Lu's third act, whatever that proves to be, she might finally eclipse her brother *and* her father professionally.

Not that she's competitive or anything like that.

K-I-S-S-I-N-G

By the time fourth grade rolled around in 1979, I had a best friend. Because he was a boy, my classmates tried to tease us, say he was my boyfriend, I was his girlfriend. We didn't care. Two people can brave the taunts that one person finds intolerable. We left school every afternoon, their silly words bouncing off our backs.

Lu and Randy / Sitting in a tree / K I S S I N G / First comes love / then comes marriage / Lu and Randy with a baby carriage.

Yes, my new best friend was the boy I had wanted to kill a year earlier. It happens. For us, it happened this way.

When AJ told our father about the fight on the first day of third grade—a rare betrayal on my brother's part; I think he was mad about me giving up his real name to Noel—our father drove me to Randy's house the next day and insisted I apologize.

Randy's house was like a funhouse mirror version of my own—a distorted, disturbing mirror version. A motherless household, where the boy was the youngest. Chaotic and cramped and messy, with far too many people, whereas my house always felt as if it didn't really have enough people to justify all its rooms. Randy's father worked as a night watchman, although I think that was his second job. He was getting ready to go to work when we arrived. He looked surprised, yet not surprised.

The moment my father introduced himself, Mr. Nairn seemed to assume that Randy was in the wrong. Why else would the state's attorney be in this postage stamp of a living room, trying to be heard above the blasting television that no one thought to turn off?

"Randy," he screamed. "You get down here right now." He wore a gray uniform. The living room wall had a hole in the Sheetrock, and there were what seemed like a hundred teenage girls milling about, although there were only three, Randy's sisters.

Randy came downstairs, cowering like a pup. My father said swiftly, "I think you misunderstood, sir—it was Lu who started the fight, Lu who needs to apologize to Randy."

I wanted to explain myself, tell the full story, how Randy had provoked the attack. But I also wanted to get out of that strange house, away from its smells and damage and the sensation that a fight might start at any minute, over anything. Staring at a point over Randy's shoulder, which happened to be the hole in the wall, I mumbled. "I'm-sorry-I-hit-you-it-was-wrong-I-won't-do-it-again."

My father had told me I had to shake Randy's hand, so I stuck out my hand, feeling ridiculous. Randy looked around as if he thought an enormous joke was being played on him, but he took my hand in his smaller, sweatier one, giving it the fastest shake ever.

Still, I doubted he was finished with me. He knew my middle name. I assumed he would use the information to seal my fate, move me from the category of someone who was merely friendless to being a true goat, the butt of every classroom joke, a walking punch line. It might not seem much, my odd middle name, but I could not bear to have it dragged out into the open and mocked. It had been my mother's gift to me and, as much as I disliked it, my distaste for it was private.

I went to school the next day, resigned to the beginning of the end. Inside my desk, I found an eraser shaped like a giraffe and a pack of Now and Laters, lime ones. Lime Now and Laters were my favorite. I was not likely to put an unopened pack in my desk and forget about it. I looked around, wondering if there was a new kid who had gotten confused, tried to take my desk. I was careful not to let the candy be seen; it was contraband and would be seized. But the eraser—I held it up, examined it. I caught Randy looking at me, but his eyes scooted away. I was still thinking about my middle name.

During recess, it was my habit to take a book and sit by myself. The book was usually something chosen to impress, even though I knew by then that nothing I did could impress my classmates. On that particular day, I was reading *Jason and the Golden Fleece*. A simplified version of the myth, but a real book, with chapters.

"Why do you read so much?" Randy. It wasn't the first time he had asked me that question. But it was the first time it hadn't been a taunt, for an audience. He was alone, standing at the edge of the playground as if he didn't dare touch the grass where I sat.

"Well, I like it," I said. "You can do it everywhere, so you're never bored. In a car, at night before you go to bed. In the bathtub."

"Not the shower, though."

My temper almost flared. I hated being contradicted, topped. But then I realized that Randy was only trying to build on what I said. He was trying to have a *conversation*.

"Yeah, but I don't take showers."

"I do. There are five of us and only one bathroom with a tub. We each get three minutes, in and out. Even then, the hot water is kind of weak." He was explaining to me, I think, the faint odor he carried. Randy didn't stink, exactly. But he had a particular smell about him, sort of like fall, only not as pleasant.

"I'd like having a lot of brothers and sisters."

"No, you wouldn't. Not my sisters. They're horrible. It's better just to have one good one. Like AJ."

I knew then that Randy had fallen for AJ, that the friend he really craved was that golden high school boy who had saved him. But he would settle for me. It was an oddly satisfactory friendship, conducted in secret at first. At school, we kept our distance, trying to look out for each other, but not too obviously. At the end of the day, we walked off in different directions, with Randy circling back to my house. Teensy did not approve of him. He did not receive the kind of extra attention that she had lavished on Noel and Davey. Teensy was the biggest snob in our household, which is saying a lot.

"He lives in those town houses by the high school," she said one day when I asked if he could stay for dinner.

"Well, Daddy can drive him home," I said. "If he's here. Or AJ could. AJ could drive him home in the family car. He loves to drive."

She rolled her eyes. "It's not about the drive. It's about—" Teensy didn't finish the sentence.

By fourth grade, we no longer cared if the other kids knew we were friends. We felt superior to them.

"Don't pay them any mind," I told Randy as we headed out together. "They're jealous because they know we're having fun. More fun than anyone else has."

Which was to say, we were the two least supervised kids in our class. Did that make us neglected? Maybe so. But it was a benign kind of neglect. No, more than that, it was constructive. Other kids went home to inquisitive, nosy moms. Randy, like me, had no mom. We were stronger, tougher than our classmates. If we did not know what it was like to come home to a cold glass of milk, a plate of cookies—Teensy was up for the milk, not the cookies—we had learned other things. We knew every inch of open space in our neighborhood. The bike paths on which I had tried to kill Randy the first day of third grade were now battle maps to us. We named them things that revealed our complete ignorance of history—Mason-Dixon Line, Maginot Line. We ran raids, hid in bushes. The only thing we knew about war for certain was that the United States had never lost one. We were winners.

One November afternoon, a Friday, we were lying on our bellies in a patch of overgrown grass near that culvert tunnel that led to Randy's house, waiting for a German tank to roll by. We held sticks like rifles, pretending to "sight" through the points of the twigs. The game was to pretend to shoot any cyclist who came into view. But the first person we saw was on foot, a familiar figure, at least to me, tall and dark, moving with lanky grace.

"Davey!" I cried, jumping up. I might have been eager to show off a little. Davey was such a natural star. Even if Randy knew nothing about Davey and his accomplishments, he would see that, be impressed that I knew such an amazing person.

"Little . . . Lu," Davey said with a distracted, almost sleepy tone, as if he had just awakened from a nap. I frowned at the "Little"—and the pause. Did he not know me? He and AJ had been friends for more than two years at this point. "Who's your buddy?"

"Randy Nairn," I said. Davey shook hands with him, very solemn, as if greeting an important dignitary. "Nice to know you, dude." It was like Zeus leaning out of the heavens and introducing himself to a mere mortal. Yet Randy did not seem particularly awed.

"What are you doing around here?" I asked. "Are you coming to our house?"

"Your house? No, I just—I just sometimes like to . . . perambulate," Davey said. "Nice day like this. I like to wander. No practice today, tomorrow is a bye week, so I decided to kill some time before taking the bus home. You think my parents might give me a car, they have the dough, but no, no, no. That might be a distraction. *You'll get a car when you graduate, young man.*" The last said in a prissy voice, only deep, so I guess he was quoting his father. "But what am I going to do with a car when I go to college, especially if I get into Stanford? I need wheels *now*."

It was hard enough to talk to Davey when he was just hanging with my brother. One-on-one, him in this odd state, it was almost impossible. But I kept trying.

"Yeah, AJ wants a car, too."

"We all want so much," Davey said. "Everybody, whatever they have, it's never enough. You know what? Not only can you not get what you want, you can't always get what you need. No matter how hard you try."

"Uh-huh." I had no idea what he was talking about.

"Yeah, well—I thought I might hit the McDonald's at the mall. See ya, Little Lu."

That name again. I winced. Davey went weaving down the path.

"I see that guy all the time," Randy said.

"Where?"

"Near where I live. Like, at least once a week."

"What would he be doing—over there?" I did not want to say: *You live in those town houses where poor people live. Davey lives in Hobbit's Glen, miles away, near the golf course, in a really nice house.*

"Buying pot, I guess."

"Davey doesn't buy pot," I said.

"Then I guess someone gives it to him because he was H-I-G-H high just then. My sisters get high all the time. I know what it looks like."

"Davey's an athlete," I said. "And a good student. You can't do those things if you get high."

"Ah, who cares? Let's play something new. You know I have to go home by dark and that's getting earlier and earlier. Next week is Thanksgiving already."

"I know. Four whole days without school."

"Yeah."

"You sound like you don't like days off." Even this year, when I finally had a friend and a teacher who seemed to like me, I was happy to have two extra days off. I would watch the parades on Thursday morning, then watch my father and brother watch football in the afternoon. Our dinner wouldn't be anything much—Teensy made most of the sides a day ahead, and they weren't very good reheated. My dad roasted the smallest turkey that Butterball sold. But he couldn't make gravy, and he never remembered to put the Parker House rolls in the oven. There was a part of me that felt as if I should take over in the kitchen, learn how to do some things. Certainly, Teensy was pushing me in that direction. But there was also a part of me that never wanted to be that person, someone I thought of, dismissively, as the *girl*. No cooking, no sewing, especially not after the crocheted vest debacle. Once, when I was particularly unhappy at school, my father asked if I wanted to go to a private one. It turned out he had in mind some all-female place up near Baltimore, which horrified me. I'd have rather gone to an all-boy school. And not because I disliked females. I'm not one of those women. But if you weren't competing with boys, it seemed to me, the bar had been lowered. I ran against boys, played their games on their terms, ceded no ground to them in schoolwork. I don't think it's an accident that I married the smartest person I've ever known, the only person who was unequivocally smarter than I am. Except for my father, of course. My father and AJ.

"We don't really do Thanksgiving at my house," Randy said. "My dad almost always has to work, and my sisters just want to eat Chef Boyardee out of the can."

"Maybe you could come to our house," I said. "I can ask."

I think he had been hinting for just this invitation, but he kept his reaction simple: "Okay, you ask, and if your dad says okay, I'll ask my dad. It would be better if your dad called my dad, though. I don't think my dad can say no to your dad."

The sun was down, the light fading rapidly. It was time for us to part, but it was hard to say good-bye for some reason. The days were growing shorter, and our time outside would be coming to an end soon. Where would we go, as the days grew dark and cold? It doesn't seem a stretch to say that we felt a little like Adam and Eve, about to be thrust out of Eden.

Maybe Randy felt this, too, judging by what he said next.

"Should we kiss?" Randy asked me.

The question threw me.

"I don't think so."

"Why not?"

"I'm just not—a kisser. I'm not a girl who goes around kissing."

"Have you tried it?"

"Have you?"

"No, but my sisters sure do seem to like it. Their boyfriends come over, after dinner, when my dad has left for work. I think that's all they do. I stay in my room. If I didn't stay in my room, one of them would take it and do her kissing in there and I don't want anyone kissing in my bed. Except me, I guess. They're mad that they have to share a room; they think I should sleep with my dad if there are only three bedrooms. It's not my fault I'm the only boy. Amanda, that's the next one up—she tells me I wasn't planned, that I'm not supposed to even be here and that's why our mom left. She said I was the last straw. What does that even mean?"

"Your mom left?" I knew moms died. I had no idea they *left*.

"Yeah. She got a job in Ohio or something. Don't forget to ask your dad about Thanksgiving, okay?"

He insisted on walking me back to my street, as far as the communal mailboxes. That was another Columbia concept—the mail didn't come to your house, it was delivered to a locked compartment in a large box that served the entire cul-de-sac. This was supposed to foster community spirit. In my house, it meant that AJ or I had to get the mail because the last thing my father wanted at the end of a long day of serving the community was to talk to actual members of the community.

I watched Randy walk away. He walked like a grown-up, an old one, his narrow shoulders rounded, his feet shuffling like the characters in the animated Peanuts cartoons. He walked as if he hoped he never got to where he was going. Why had he brought that thing up about kissing? Was it because of what the other kids said, planting the idea in his head that we should be kissing? I wanted none of that. Now I was going to have to watch him all the time, make sure he didn't try it on the sly. Kissing ruined everything.

FEBRUARY 11

Lu looks at her plate. She has seen this plate of food many times. It is the meal inevitably served at such luncheons, luncheons that make up too much of her life. There is a salad with iceberg lettuce, two slices of cucumber, edges crimped, carrot shavings, and one—always one—cherry tomato. The salad is always served with a choice of ranch or raspberry vinaigrette dressing, both of which she declines. Always. The salad will be followed by string beans and one's choice of beef, salmon, or chicken. Lu has learned over the years that the salmon, counterintuitively, is always the safest choice. Dessert, which looks fantastic—a fudgy brownie with ice cream on top—is served at the exact moment she is called to the podium. She knows the harried waitstaff will have cleared her brownie before she returns.

Today's luncheon is for a professional women's group in Howard County and Lu is the keynote speaker. More insultingly, she is the *fill-in* speaker. They wanted the state's attorney of Baltimore City. She is younger, an African American woman whose election last fall was considered big news, overshadowing Lu's election as the first female state's attorney in the history of Howard County. (Baltimore has not only had a female state's attorney before, but she was African American, too, so the only notable thing about the new attorney's election was that she defeated a well-financed incumbent. But Lu did that, too.) Now, listening to her introduction, she has a sinking feeling that it may not have been updated, that the woman at the lectern might be describing the originally scheduled speaker. No, wait, there it is, the telltale phrase—

"And, not incidentally, the daughter of one of the most beloved men in Howard County, the former state's attorney Andrew J. Brant."

Former state's attorney. Why did he stop there? Strangely, Lu has never reopened that topic with her father, not since 1986 when he stepped down, amid speculation that he would run for Congress. Yet he never did. He said, at the time, that he felt he was out of step with the county and the country. Reagan was still president. Lu suspects her father's real problem is that he preferred the Senate to the Congress; her father's temperament was better suited to that more sedate, formal body. But Barbara Mikulski was elected to the Senate that year and it was believed it would be a long time before there would be a vacancy in the Maryland seats. The belief was true. Sarbanes, elected in '76, didn't leave until the 2007; Mikulski is still in office, although speculation is rife that she might announce this is her last term. Now Lu wonders if her father worried that moving up through the political ranks would cost him that adjective, *beloved*. Certainly, almost no politician is described that way anymore. Even the people who vote for you didn't seem to like you that much.

In front of an audience such as this, she can go on autopilot. Lu never prepares her speeches ahead of time but works from a menu of discrete topics, which she can arrange in endless forms depending on her audience. This group wants heartwarming empowerment, so she talks about work-life balance, the challenges of being a woman in public office, especially a single parent. *That went well*, she thinks, as she tries to rush out without seeming to rush out. (Sure enough, her brownie was gone. So it goes.)

But as she moves through the kind, smiling, congratulatory women, a younger one blocks her way. Lu, still on autopilot, extends her hand, but the woman, whose suit looks like a cheap knockoff of the rag & bone suit that Lu is wearing, keeps her arms crossed on her chest, a bad sign unless she's chilly—and it's not cold in this room. Overheated if anything.

"That's a bit disingenuous, isn't it? Describing yourself as a single mother."

"I don't know what else you would call me," Lu says. "I am a single mother. My husband died."

She chooses to speak bluntly as a rebuke to the young woman's borderline rudeness. In another situation, she might have used the more genteel "widow" or said that Gabe had "passed away."

"And left you millions, right? So you can afford to send your children to private schools and you have help."

"My husband's money was left primarily in trust for our children and I administer those trusts. I live with my father and the housekeeper who cared for me when I was young. In the village of Wilde Lake, in my childhood home. I have a babysitter, a college student, who takes my children to school and picks them up in the afternoon because I work at least twelve hours a day. It's not a particularly high-flying lifestyle."

"But you don't *have* to work, right? So are we returning to that model in which public service is only for those people who don't need the salary? What am I supposed to take away from your story? I'm thirty, I have a three-year-old and so much college debt that I can't ever see getting out from under. Your earrings probably cost more than I make in a week."

Alas, they did, although they're not showy in that way. They are vintage rose gold, from a flash-shopping site. On Saturday nights, Lu likes to have an extra glass of wine and shop the no-return sales on certain websites for the thrill of it. Yes, she's crazy that way. Buzzed shopping is her biggest vice. Second biggest.

"They're used," Lu says. "And I bought them at 50 percent off. I'm sorry if my personal experience doesn't speak to you. But I think the point is that women, whatever their challenges, benefit from networking and support. I'm so sorry—I really do have to go. Thank you for having me."

"Does your office have an on-site child-care facility?" the woman calls after her.

———

Back in the office, trying to catch up on all the things she might have done while she was sharing cheery anecdotes about work-life balance, she sighs and says to Della: "I guess the day can only go up from here."

"Don't be so sure," Della says. "You have that meeting with a community watch group tonight, the one that's worried about cemetery vandalism."

"Maybe there will be cookies." She thinks of the strident young woman who seemed so angered by the fact that Lu did not "have to" work. Yet Lu feels she must. And while she would never say the words *noblesse oblige* out loud, is it the worst thing in the world when a public official doesn't need the paycheck? The building in which Lu works, the Carroll Building is—she assumes, she has never thought to question it—named for one of Maryland's first U.S. senators, Charles Carroll of Carrollton, a signer of the Declaration of Independence, an immensely wealthy man.

Also a slaveholder who disapproved of slavery in principle—yet never freed his own slaves. A man of his times, as they say. But aren't we all? Lincoln freed the slaves—but he believed they should go back to Africa. And the Emancipation Proclamation didn't free the slaves in Maryland because the Old Line State fought, however reluctantly, for the Union. *The despot's heel is on thy shore,* the state song begins, and everyone tries to pretend they don't know the despot is Lincoln. Then again, almost no one sings the state song, whose tune was stolen from "Oh, Tannenbaum."

Oh, Maryland.

Lu sighs, resigns herself to an afternoon of e-mail and phone calls, then heads out to the community meeting. There are no cookies. There is nothing to eat at all. *I should have stopped at Five Guys,* she thinks. Then a bad accident on I-95 leaves her stuck in traffic, listening to the rebroadcast of a local NPR show, where Davey Robinson is one of the panelists. He's still talking about marriage equality, more than two years after Maryland voters approved it overwhelmingly. Hey, if Ben Carson can toy with the idea of running for president, why can't Davey Robinson dabble in politics? It is almost 9:30 when she arrives home and begins foraging in the refrigerator for something she can pretend is a reasonable facsimile of a meal. She has lost five pounds since taking office. She has missed too many dinners, attended too many luncheons with iceberg lettuce salads, thin slivers of salmon, one cherry tomato, a dessert that is always whisked away before she eats it. She checks her cell, on mute since she walked into the meeting at the synagogue. Mike Hunt has called. Three times.

"Took you long enough," he says. "You allergic to good news or something? At least—I think it's good news."

"What?"

"The Rudy Drysdale case? Remind me to heed your hunches. They found his DNA on that spread. His and nobody else's. Down near a corner, like he, um, cleaned himself off after. Or maybe just a few drips—"

"I'm *eating*, Mike." Or about to be, if she can find something edible. Whatever Teensy has prepared—pork, chicken?—has aged poorly, congealing on the plate in an unappetizing sauce.

"This late? That's a bad habit. Anyway, it's something to throw into the mix."

"Yeah, but it doesn't necessarily *help*. I mean, there's definitely no sign of sexual assault. His DNA could confuse jurors."

"I think she walks in on him. While he's—taking care of himself. He freaks."

"You mean he broke into her place to masturbate?"

"Or he breaks in, thinking's he found a vacant place to spend a night. It's the holidays. She's got no trees, no lights. Looks like a safe bet. Maybe that's why he's lurking, sizing the place up. But he screws up, picks a place where someone's not away. She comes home and he's got, you know, one hand full. She screams, he freaks out. She's between him and the door. He panics. What's the defense going to argue, that she brought him home for consensual sex? That he broke in to sleep there, found her dead body, then stayed to jerk off? That he broke in before she died, jerked off and left, then reset the thermostat on his way out because he's worried about climate change?"

"I'll worry about the defense's case," Lu says, a little curt. Her mind is racing. A jury will love the DNA because juries love DNA. But they might get stuck on it, too. The presence of semen doesn't make it a sex crime, and there's no need to alter the charge, anyway. She's already got murder one. But she should go ahead and tell Fred now, not make him wait for discovery. Because if Drysdale wants to confess *now*, she's fine with it. She told the cops to test the bedspread, it's her legit victory. Oh, yes, she'll welcome a confession, but not to a lesser charge. It will be murder one or nothing; the only negotiation will be on the length of his sentence. Under those circumstances, the win goes into her column, no asterisk.

This makes the day a winner in her book. Then she finds a pint of raspberry chocolate chip in the freezer. And while she's eating it from the carton, her phone buzzes, a text from a familiar number, although it is one that she has never entered into her Contacts.

NEXT WEEK?

Her first instinct is to say yes, but then she thinks about the timing. The week after Valentine's Day. Ugh. So she types back only:

Maybe

Who's she kidding? It's probably going to be yes.

I'M DREAMING OF A WHITE (TRASH) THANKSGIVING

Our fathers spoke and Randy was granted permission to attend our Thanksgiving dinner. He arrived at 1 P.M., bearing a bottle of crème de menthe in a paper bag; the seal was broken and the bottle appeared to be about three-quarters full. My father thanked him with grave courtesy and placed it on the butler's bar alongside his cut-glass bottles of clear and amber liquors.

"Won't you get in trouble?" I asked Randy while we played checkers in my room. "For taking that bottle?"

"I didn't take it," he said.

"Randy—it's not even full."

"Okay, I took it, but my dad will never know. He'll think one of my sisters took it and they'll blame one another, or even their boyfriends. I'll be fine."

Randy had a cunning streak. Was it always there or was he coming into it now that he was almost eleven? I just hoped he wouldn't use his cleverness to try to kiss me. I made sure the door to my room stayed open, and I tried not to turn my back to him at any point. But he seemed far more interested in my stuff than he was in me, pulling board games off my shelves, exclaiming over such ordinary things as playing cards and Trouble, which I considered way too babyish for fourth graders.

At dinner, he was polite about my father's dryish turkey, the cold Parker House rolls, the reheated cornbread dressing. That is, I assumed at the time he was trying to showcase his good manners. I realize now that our lackluster meal seemed like a feast to Randy. Dinner done, Randy, as our guest, was exempt from cleaning, not that he objected with even token protests. While AJ and I washed the good china and silver by hand, Randy sat with my father in front of the football game, a plate with a slice of (store-bought) pumpkin pie on his lap. He looked terrified, too terrified to eat. He perched on the edge of the wing chair and balanced that plate of pie on his lap, unsure what to do. Eventually, he began to pick at it with his fingers, one crumb at a time, careful not to let any crumbs fall from his plate. His fingers inched closer and closer to the glop of Reddi-wip I had added to his slice.

"Use a fork, Randy," I said, coming out to the living room with my own piece of pie.

"That's not good manners, Lu," my father said.

"Eating with your fingers isn't good manners—" I started. My father stood and summoned me back to the kitchen, where I received what can only be described as a tongue lashing. *Manners,* my father said in a low, hard whisper, *are about making one's guest feel comfortable.* When someone who didn't have the privilege of my upbringing came into our home, it was my duty to demonstrate good manners without calling the guest out. This lecture went on and on.

"But how's he going to learn?" I asked. "Maybe he doesn't notice what he's doing wrong. And other people won't be nice. They'll laugh at him. At least I'm nice. But, Jesus, Dad, he's just white trash."

And that's how I ended up in my room on Thanksgiving Day. I'm not sure if it was the "Jesus" or "white trash." Possibly the combination. Or maybe it was because I was carelessly loud and Randy overheard what I said. My father urged him to stay, but once I was exiled, I don't think Randy could get out of there fast enough. He had come to our house for a respite from fighting.

Ah, well, holidays always end badly, don't they? Anticipation builds up; anticlimax is inevitable. Confined to my room, I found the deadness of the day especially acute. It didn't help that AJ was pacing the halls like a tiger, unused to being at home. Toward early evening, "his" phone rang and he pounced on it.

"That was Bash," he told our father. "He wants to come by and pick me up, go out for the evening."

"And do what?" Our father had an intense loathing for "just hanging." He allowed AJ to roam the mall because AJ always claimed to have an errand, a purpose. But the mall would be closed on Thanksgiving night.

"Well, nothing's really open, except the movies, and we've seen what's playing. We just thought we'd drive, maybe go to Roy Rogers or the Double T Diner."

"You can't possibly be hungry," our father said. "And if you are, go make yourself a turkey sandwich. Driving around, with no plans—that's how young people get in trouble. Young people and not-so-young people. I see it all the time. I'm not a churchgoing man, but the Bible got it right, about idle hands."

"Honestly, Dad—"

"Not tonight, AJ. You can go out tomorrow and Saturday, if you have concrete plans. But not tonight. Your friends, however, are free to come here if their parents agree."

"There's nothing to do *here*." AJ, usually so amiable, stormed into his room and didn't emerge again except to slice another piece of pie.

Over dinner the next evening, AJ told my father that his group had worked up a definite plan for the evening: "The girls want to go bowling, up on Route 40. And they always want to go get ice cream after, even when it's cold out."

Our father was not the kind of man to gloat in victory. He was so glad AJ was doing things his way that he gave him twenty dollars. But when AJ asked if he could have the family car, he demurred. "Can't Bash come get you?" he said. "It's practically on his way."

"In what universe? He could go straight out 108 to 29 if he didn't have to come down here first."

"I just hate that turn," our father said. "That left onto 29 from Governor Warfield Parkway, with no lights and that enormous blind spot—I worry when I know you're headed that way."

"But if Bash picks me up, he has to make the turn. What difference does it make?"

"I'm not always rational," our father said, smiling at his own inconsistency. "Sometimes, I'm a father first and a lawyer second. But, okay, you make a good point. Take the car. All I ask is that you be home by midnight."

"Midnight," AJ groaned.

"How late are bowling alleys open?"

"I *said* the girls wanted to go out after and they'll want ice cream, but the guys will want sandwiches or burgers, so we'll probably choose the Double T because you can get everything there, and it's open all night."

"Twelve thirty."

AJ was home by 12:25. Could I have been awake? Is that how I remember hearing him, then checking his arrival against my digital clock, a gift at Christmas a year ago? A digital clock. I am old enough to remember when they seemed magical. Or do I know the time AJ returned home because he would have to repeat the fact again and again over the next few months, and our father would confirm it? He arrived home at 12:25 A.M. and went straight to bed.

Eleven hours later, the Howard County chief of police called and said my brother might be a material witness to a felony.

Lu waits a week before sending the DNA report to Fred. In her heart of hearts, she has come to believe that Rudy Drysdale did not set out that evening to kill someone. But that is not how the law defines intent, which can be formed in an instant. He broke into Mary McNally's apartment. He was probably masturbating when she walked in. Imagine the moment for both of them—she finds a strange man seated on her bed in midstroke or perhaps just finishing up, tidying himself with a corner of her pretty red-and-khaki bedspread. She screams. Maybe they both scream. It's New Year's Eve. Her nearest neighbor is out, and a hoarse shout or two, even a scream, might not attract attention. He can't let her scream again. She has to stop screaming. Maybe he panics because she's between him and the door. He hits her in the back of the head, knocks her down, chokes her. He has to stop the screaming. Then, when she's dead, he takes whatever he has used to hit her—what, they still don't know, and Lu is resigned to the fact that the weapon will never be discovered—and hits her again and again and again. Is it his humiliation that accounts for the ferocity of the attack? Is he trying to blind her?

But, also—if his pants are down, how does he move so quickly? Or is he pleasuring himself through the fly? God, it's almost comic. Until the moment he strikes Mary McNally on the back of the head. Blood must have been everywhere—on his face, his coat. Yet his clothing was clean when he was picked up. She thinks again of the walk-out basement below the deck of the Drysdales' home—would he have been bold enough to sneak in there and do his laundry? He had time, although he couldn't have known it would be a week before the body was found. How far would Mrs. Drysdale go to protect her son? How far would Lu go to protect her son and daughter? She hopes never to find out.

At any rate, she can't accept a plea to anything but first-degree murder. The only thing she's willing to negotiate are the terms: a minimum of twenty years, no parole. It's a capital crime, with or without a semen stain on the bedspread. What if he sat down and masturbated after killing her? What if the act of violence was what got him off? He would have to be pretty cold-blooded, but then—he was cool and collected enough to adjust the thermostat, open the sliding door. That's the story she'll tell, and if he wants to tell another one, he'll have to get on the stand. If he doesn't take the stand, then Fred has to convince the jury that Rudy Drysdale entered the apartment after Mary McNally was dead, then sat down within arm's reach of her body and masturbated. Or that he has been in the apartment twice, returning for another date with himself and finding the body.

Twenty years is generous. He's a time bomb, the kind of guy who could go crazy in the Columbia Mall, attacking kids on the carousel, running around the fountain with a machete.

Of course, twenty years is also tantamount to life in prison for him. Prison shortens a man's life. She thinks of Eloise Schumann, realizes she never bothered to check the clerk's office to see if she was legit married or just appropriated Ryan Schumann's name. The woman never came back, never called again, so chances are she's every inch the nutcase her father says she is, programmed to go off at staggered intervals.

———

"Murder two," Fred says. It's practically the first thing he says after arriving at her office. How odd it must be for him to sit on the other side of the desk, to see how quickly she has made this space hers. The walls have been painted white with the tiniest hint of teal—one has to look closely to realize they are not white-white. Lu painted them herself over the MLK long weekend, using a Farrow & Ball shade called "Borrowed Light." (Her father's newfound snobbery about decor must be contagious. He's been adamant about using that pricey brand for all their remodeled rooms.) The three chairs in the office are strictly government issue; it seemed in bad taste to have chairs different from those her staff uses. But she has created a sitting area, with a small blue love seat and a low coffee table fashioned from an antique door. She found the latter piece in a store on Ellicott City's Main Street; the seller claimed the door was from the original jail, which makes no sense, but it's a good story. The overall vibe is of a serious room with subtle feminine touches. Of course, for a meeting such as this, she would never use the love seat, or ask Della to bring them coffee. Fred can sit in a wooden chair and get his own damn coffee.

"How do you make the case for second-degree? He broke into her apartment. He jacked off." Using the vulgarity to establish dominance, to make him uncomfortable. "He beat himself off, then he beat her face off."

"I can make the case for second-degree because nothing you have actually proves he killed her. A homeless guy sneaks into an empty apartment, spends the night, leaves. Just because you have his prints on the thermostat and the door doesn't make him a killer. For all you know, she turned it down whenever she went out. His thumbprint doesn't prove he set the temperature."

"I hope you've pulled her utility bills and established that pattern, of her turning down her thermostat to save money. Oh, wait—utilities are paid by the apartment complex, so that makes no sense. Not her money, so why does she care?"

Lu doesn't know if this is actually true. Then again, Fred probably doesn't either.

"Okay, middle-aged lady having night sweats, so she turns her thermostat down every night as soon as she comes in. Rudy left the patio door open, another guy came in and is lying in wait. He kills her."

Fred can't possibly believe he can sell this story to a jury. Not with the DNA on a bedspread.

"What does your client want to do, Fred?"

Fred's eyes slide to the right, toward the triptych of pen-and-ink drawings by Aaron Sopher, city scenes that Lu and Gabe once had in their dining room. They don't really fit in her father's house—*our* house, she reminds herself—and she likes having them in her workplace. There's an energy in Sopher's economical line drawings that gives her a lift. She's a city person at heart, like her mother. Her life in the suburbs is an accident of birth. And death.

"My client wants to go to trial. Because he intends to walk."

"I hope you've told him that changing to a plea of not criminally responsible doesn't mean he won't do serious time."

"He understands that. And you know, for all his, uh, issues, he's actually kind of brilliant. But between his learning disabilities and his claustrophobia—"

"Learning disabilities—please. He got into Bennington, Fred."

"Which didn't require standardized tests. And he dropped out freshman year because of depression. But no, he's not crazy *enough*, cuckoo Froot Loops crazy. In fact, he's looked at his case pretty rationally and he believes he has an excellent chance for an acquittal."

"And what advice do you, as a lawyer, give your client, Fred? I have to think that your legal acumen is better than his, no matter how smart or rational he might be."

Sitting opposite her former boss, in what was his office less than two months ago—it's like a perverse job evaluation. *Do you think you can beat me, Fred? On this case, with these facts? What would you have done, Fred?* He offered murder two because that's what *he* would have taken. Fred wouldn't have gone to the scene. Fred wouldn't have told the cops to make sure to grab the bedspread because it was mussed.

"I would be willing to tell him that murder two and ten years would be a pretty good deal."

"No way."

"Then we've got a trial."

"Yes, we do. Still intent on invoking Hicks?"

"My client wants to get in there as soon as possible. Really, it's almost inhuman to keep him confined."

It's inhuman to beat a woman to death for no crime greater than walking into her own bedroom.

"Let me ask you this, Fred—what makes Drysdale so confident that I can't win this case?"

"The obvious answer, Lu, is that he didn't do it, so he believes justice will be done."

"I guess I'm asking you why your client would think there's any likelihood that I can't get a conviction, based on these facts?"

"You know, you're good, Lu. But you're not as good as you think you are. Few people are, when it comes down to it. There's been one great Howard County state's attorney—and that was your dad."

It has the whiff of something he has long planned to say, an insult held back for the most perfect, hurtful moment. And it does hurt, but Lu won't give Fred the satisfaction of seeing that.

"One great Howard County state's attorney *so far*. I've been in office less than two months. Let's see where I am in four years. Who knows, Fred? One day, maybe you'll be arguing a case before the Court of Appeals—and I'll be sitting above you in one of those crimson robes."

"Court of Appeals—oh, I'm sure your ambitions go much higher than that, Lu. After all, there are plenty of women who have risen to that position. I assume you've set your cap for attorney general, or maybe even governor. Hasn't been a woman alone in the governor's mansion since Bootsie Mandel kicked Marvin out for having a mistress."

"See you in court, Fred. Can't wait to see how you spin this. Don't forget to ask Drysdale what he used to take her face off. You know how jurors get obsessed with those little details, let their imaginations take them to the darkest places. Oh, and although you don't represent them, you might ask which of Rudy's parents wants to take the stand to testify about the time he attacked his father."

Fred may have devolved into a timid prosecutor, but he was never a dumb one. "You can't introduce past crimes unless Rudy takes the stand. Besides, there are no records of any violent behavior on his part."

"True. But you also can't claim he has no history of violence. There is a history, Fred, and it's a very troubling one. But let's move forward, get everything on the schedule, assuming there's no chance for a murder one plea."

"No chance. He's rolling the dice, all or nothing."

"Well, then, I'm going to have to assume probability is not one of the things at which Mr. Drysdale is brilliant."

THE GAME OF LIFE

Even on a Saturday during a long holiday weekend, our father went to the office. We were used to his workaholism. Complaining about it would be like complaining about cold weather in winter, humidity in summer. AJ was still asleep when he left. AJ seldom rose before noon on holidays and weekends, a pattern established early in his teens. I could not believe how much he slept, my brother. My father said I would sleep like that one day, too, that the enormous physical changes of adolescence would exhaust me. He was wrong about that, as it turned out. But I grew very slowly and not very much, maybe only six inches in all from age twelve to age eighteen.

So I was doubly surprised when our father returned home two hours later and expressed annoyance at AJ still being in bed at 11:00. He walked upstairs to AJ's room, his voice loud, almost yelling. Our father never yelled.

"AJ, get up. I need to talk to you."

Inaudible mutters, moans.

"*Now,* AJ. Don't get dressed. Don't brush your teeth. Come straight to my room."

More muttering.

"Then go to the bathroom, for sweet Christ's sake, but get moving."

My room shared part of a wall with my father's. Intensely curious about what AJ had done to be in such trouble, I decided I would clean my room, as I was supposed to do on the weekends, although I usually waited until Sunday evening.

"Where did you go last night?" our father asked AJ. Then, before he could answer: "The truth. You need to tell the truth."

The whole truth and nothing but the truth, I silently amended.

A long pause. I could almost feel AJ sifting through the consequences of his answer. Clearly, he had not gone bowling. But what could he have done to make our father sound like this? Angry, yet scared, too, a slight tremble in his voice. He didn't know the answers to the questions he asked. That was rare for our father.

"The girls did go bowling. But Bash and Lynne are in a fight, he didn't want to go. And Davey was stuck at home. So we went over there."

"Were his parents there?"

Soft, barely audible. "No, sir. They drove up to Harrisburg to see Davey's grandmother. They let Davey stay home because he said he wanted to work on a report for AP European History, but they said he couldn't go out."

"Who else was there?"

"Only Bash, Noel, and I were invited. It wasn't a party. We just wanted to hang out, listen to Mr. Robinson's stereo."

"AJ, stop trying to skirt the truth by the way you phrase things. Okay, Davey invited you, Noel, and Bash. Was anyone else there, invited or no?"

"A girl named Nita Flood showed up."

"Who is Nita Flood?"

I almost spoke out loud, excited to know the answer. *Nita Flood. She sells sausage at the mall.*

"A girl in our class. Not a friend of ours, not really."

"Just showed up?"

"Yes, sir."

"How did she get there?"

"Someone dropped her off. She hitched, I think. She said she had been working and she bummed a ride. But she lives near the high school, not Hobbit's Glen."

"Why did she come to Davey's house?"

"She was mad at him."

"Why?"

"Because he took a girl from Glenelg to our homecoming dance. She thought he should have taken her."

"Why?"

My father was in attorney mode. He wanted AJ to tell the story, line by line, fact by fact. He was trying very hard not to put words in AJ's mouth, I could tell, not to lead him in any way.

"Because—because they've been having sex." The embarrassment in AJ's voice was palpable. My face burned with mortification and I wasn't in the room. "Off and on for more than a year, only in secret. Davey never takes her anywhere, doesn't talk to her in front of other people. He goes over to where she lives, after school, and they have sex. Nobody knew. Bash, Noel, and I didn't suspect a thing. She said she was his girlfriend and Davey said she wasn't, that his parents don't want him to go steady with anyone. They had a big fight, in the Robinsons' bedroom. We could hear them all the way down in the rec room. But then they, um, made up."

"What do you mean?"

An interminable silence.

"AJ? What do you mean by 'they made up'?"

"They had sex." I knew AJ was not looking at our father when he said those words. "They had sex and they came downstairs and we played a drinking game. We played Life and you had to take a drink every time you had a kid. She got wasted, really fast, because she drank vodka and the rest of us were having beer. Bash and Noel drove her home. She threw up

inside Bash's car. He came back to Davey's house and we helped him clean
it up. I also helped Davey clean up the house."

"What do you mean by clean up?"

He was almost whispering now. "We added water to the vodka so his
parents wouldn't know someone drank a bunch. And we bagged up the
beer cans, took them to the Dumpster behind Jack in the Box." A beat. "I
was home on time. I'm sorry I let you think I was going bowling. I *thought* I
was going bowling. It was only when I went to Davey's house that they told
me there was a change in plan."

"Is there any more to the story?"

"No, sir."

"Think hard. Is that the whole story?"

"Yes, sir."

"Fine, because you're going to tell it to a police detective."

AJ's gasp was loud enough that it provided cover for my stifled one.

"Why, sir? I mean, I know I was wrong to drink and that I lied to you
about where I was going last night, but are you really going to turn me in to
the police? I promise I won't do it again, I really do. I mean—"

"Juanita Flood was admitted to Howard County General this morning.
She has been beaten. And she says that she was raped by Davey Robinson
last night."

"Raped, beaten—no sir!—"

"Don't speak any further, AJ. A lawyer is going to meet you at head-
quarters. I have advised Bash's and Noel's parents to bring attorneys as
well, if possible. But they, at least, can sit in on their sons' interviews. I have
to recuse myself from yours. This is all—this is very complicated. You may
go get dressed now."

"Sir?"

"Yes?"

"Just now, when you talked to me—were you speaking as my father or
the state's attorney?"

AJ had hit on the same question I had, even if I hadn't been able to articulate it. What was our father's role in this? What was AJ's role? Would his story help or hurt Davey? I didn't know because I wasn't sure what rape was. Something bad, but how bad?

"I am always your father, AJ. Always. If this goes forward—I'm not sure how it will work. My deputy will be there, monitoring all the interviews. Just tell the truth, tell them what you told me. Don't lie. Don't try to outthink this. Tell the truth and everyone will be fine."

AJ left our father's room. Quicker than I thought possible, my father entered my room through the hallway. He looked at me thoughtfully. I was sitting on my bed, but it had not occurred to me to pick up a book or make myself look busy. I probably looked as suspicious as any nine-year-old ever had, sitting on her freshly made bed, hands folded in her lap.

"I have to go out, Lu. AJ and I—we have to go out."

"Okay," I said, then wanted to kick myself. I should have said "Where?" or asked to accompany them. My ready acquiescence was even more suspicious. But my father didn't seem to notice.

"I really shouldn't leave you here alone, but—you're big enough, I think. You'll be ten in less than two months." He seemed to be trying to think of the single most important warning he could give me. "Stay inside, don't open the door to strangers. Don't touch the stove."

"I've been making my own hot dogs and soup since I was in second grade," I reminded him.

"Not today," he said. "There's still plenty of leftovers. Eat those if you get hungry."

"Even pie?" I asked. I always liked to spell out all the terms. "With Reddi-wip and ice cream if I want?"

"Sure."

He called upstairs to AJ: "What's taking you so long?"

"Ariel and I were supposed to meet to rehearse our duet for madrigals. I just wanted her to know I couldn't make it."

"Well, get a move on."

I assumed they would be gone for maybe an hour at the most. After all, the conversation in my father's room had taken very little time. But it would be almost 5 P.M. before they returned.

As soon as they left the house, I climbed the stairs to AJ's room and looked up the word *rape* in the dictionary on his desk. It was defined as an assault. I looked up assault, which was defined as an attack. Stymied by the circular nature of these definitions, I headed to our father's room, where he kept a big, old-fashioned dictionary on a stand. This was a marvelous book, with full-color plates that I loved to study—butterflies, flowers, the internal organs of the human body—but I ignored those today. I had only one thing on my mind: rape.

The act of seizing and carrying off by force. That was the first definition.

But Nita Flood had not been seized or carried off. This made no sense. She had been taken home after she drank too much.

It was the second definition that specified: *To force a woman to have sexual intercourse.*

But how could you force someone to do that? I honestly could not fathom this. I went into the bathroom and examined my own private parts. It seemed impossible to me that they could be accessed without my co-operation. Was that why she had bruises? Because someone had tried to force her body to have sex? My mind reeled. Soap operas, hours of *The Big Valley*—nothing had prepared me for this. A body would close itself to such an attack. It would have to.

Dinner was a silent meal that night, although not in an unhappy way. If anything, my brother and father seemed relieved, as if they had faced down something difficult and put it behind them. My father even opened a bottle of red wine and offered small glasses to AJ and me. I thought it would taste velvety and rich, like a deeper, sweeter grape juice. But it was vile and I ran to the sink, spitting out my mouthful. AJ didn't like it much more, I could tell, but he swallowed his sip by sip, as if it were medicine.

"I don't really care for alcohol that much," he said.

"Yet you drink, sometimes," our father said. "Why is that?"

"I—I don't know."

"Don't be a sheep, AJ. Don't do things just because others do them."

"I'm not. I don't."

"Good."

Davey was at school Monday morning. Nita Flood was not. No charges were filed. There probably would not have been a grand jury hearing if not for my father's insistence. He wrestled with this decision. Given that he was sure of the outcome, he worried it was unkind to Nita Flood to make her tell her story again—and to be exposed, again, as a liar. But his son's best friend had been accused, his son was a witness. He wanted to be as transparent as possible, to avoid any accusations of favoritism. He recused himself from the case, asking his deputy to convene the grand jury, which listened to the boys who were there, the ER attendants, Nita Flood herself. Ultimately, they no-billed Davey Robinson on the charge of rape. Because it was a matter for the grand jury, it remained private. Besides, the accuser and accused were minors, deserving of protection even in open court. Not a word about the case appeared in newspapers.

Of course, those records are available to a state's attorney, so I have read them. The testimony of Davey, AJ, Bash, and Noel is consistent. They were having a party. Nita Flood came by, uninvited. She quarreled with Davey, but they made up, apparently having sex in Davey's room. She insisted on playing a drinking game with them, a version of Monopoly in which people could choose to pay fines or drink, although the amount of the drink was relative to the size of the fine. AJ had told our father it was the game of Life, but I guess he realized later he misspoke, as he and the other boys all agreed it was Monopoly. Nita became woozy, they took her home.

No one hit her. They were, according to them, exceedingly gentle with her. Their only failure, as gentlemen, was to leave her on the doorstep, terrified to come face-to-face with the fearsome Mr. Flood.

Nita's testimony is, of course, different. She says she hitched to Davey's house, bumming a ride from another mall worker whose name she didn't know. She said she had not been drinking before she arrived. Yes, she went upstairs with Davey but she had told him she would never have sex with him again if he didn't treat her like a girlfriend. He held her down—those were the bruises on both her shoulders—and forced her to have sex.

"Did you scream?" she was asked by the assistant state's attorney, the closest thing she had to an advocate in the court.

No, she was too embarrassed. If she screamed, the other boys might come upstairs and she was naked below the waist. She wouldn't want anyone to see that. But that's why she began drinking, during the board game. Because she was embarrassed and she just wanted to forget what had happened. She remembered drinking—then waking up on her own front steps, vomit crusted on her top, in the corners of her mouth.

"What about the bruises on your face?"

"I guess they happened while I was passed out."

"You think Davey—or the other boys—beat you for fun while you were unconscious?"

"I don't know."

The medical record from the ER was entered into evidence.

"There are marks on both shoulders, but the bruises were only on the right side of your face. Does that sound right to you?"

"Yeah."

The boys were asked if they were right-handed or left-handed. Each one said he was right-handed.

Nita's father was left-handed. Her father, Al Flood, who was the reason that Bash and Noel had left Nita on her steps and fled, not even bothering to ring the bell. If the Flood brothers were famous for being raucous, their father was more so. Randy had told me he was the one who had punched a hole in the Nairns' living room wall, during a particularly rowdy poker game.

Boiled down to the testimony before the grand jury, it all seems so obvious, even thirty-five years later. A jealous girl felt she had been spurned. She wanted revenge. Or she feared the wrath of her father, who probably did beat her when he discovered her drunk on the door-step. She said she had been raped. It was easier than telling the truth. The kindest interpretation was that she had lied to end the beating, that she hadn't set out to punish Davey at all. Or that she was confused, the next day, unclear on the events of the night before. She didn't re-member vomiting in Bash's car, didn't even remember getting into Bash's car.

It was possible, in 1979, for such things to happen and not make the news. If we're honest, I think we know it's possible today, as long as no one pulls out a phone and begins taking photos or video. Again, they were all minors. Under any circumstances, Nita Flood's name would have been protected. But the initial police report, taken at the Howard County ER, was never made public. The accused was seventeen. It could—and should—have remained confidential.

Yet it didn't. The story got out, traveling through that octagon of a school with such speed and ferocity, it was as if lightning had struck the metal railings that circled the hallways. Within a week, all the students seemed to know the story and they favored the vengeance version. Nita Flood had lied. She had tried to ruin Davey's life, torpedo his chances for Stanford and medical school. I heard about the stories from Randy, whose sisters brought home the high school gossip. Nita lived just three houses down from them.

"They said she pulled a train," Randy reported to me, his eyes wide.

"What does that mean?" I asked.

"I can't tell you."

"You don't know."

"I do."

"Then tell me."

"It's embarrassing."

"You don't know."

We were walking around the lake. It was a blustery January day, but we couldn't figure out anything else to do. Teensy was waxing the floors and said we couldn't stay inside unless we wanted to help.

"It's when you do a bunch of guys, one after another."

"That's not possible," I said. "You can only have sex when you're in love. Besides, my brother was there and he's never had sex."

"Are you sure?"

"Pretty sure."

And I couldn't imagine Noel, either, doing such a thing. It was hard enough to imagine Davey had done it. Bash, of course, I could envision. But only with Lynne.

Lynne, it turned out, was the source of the stories. She and Bash had broken up again and she was angry with him. She told people that Bash and Nita had sex that night when he took her home, which seems unlikely, given the vomit. Yet the rumor grew and grew. Four boys, eight boys, sixteen boys. Her brothers, her father. Nita Flood would have sex with anyone.

At the end of the semester, Nita Flood transferred to Centennial High School, where she finished her senior year, the first Flood to earn a real high school diploma, as opposed to a GED. But she didn't show up on graduation night. She took a bottle of pills the week before and ended up in the ER again, this time needing her stomach pumped.

And that's when her brothers decided to go looking for Davey Robinson and his friends. Did they intend to kill them? Did they understand what it meant to take a knife and shove it into another person? Were they any wiser than I was the day I stood next to the culvert, ready to hit Randy Nairn across the back of his head with a stick? Certainly, Ben Flood never anticipated falling on his own knife when AJ tackled him from behind. Perhaps AJ did save Davey's life that night. But Ben Flood lost his. As I understand AJ's quite personal definition of karma, he broke even at best.

Jury selection is a misnomer. It is more properly jury *elimination*: the lawyers, prosecution and defense alike, meet in circuit court to select the people they *don't* want to serve. For a first-degree murder charge, Lu will have a large pool from which to choose, including a good number of recidivists in the bunch, as she thinks of them, people who have served before. Her staff investigator has already pored over the list of citizens called today, checking to see who had experience in the jury pool—and what that experience was.

Howard County is a good place to be a prosecutor. Law-abiding citizens, concerned with their quality of life, with warm fuzzies for the people paid to protect and serve them. Murder is shocking here, and the federal investigation into possible gang activity distressed some old-timers, who never thought "urban" problems could find their way to Howard County. Advantage: Lu.

But one determined contrarian can infect eleven law-and-order types. Lu will pay particular attention to anyone who brings a book to jury duty, which indicates someone who expects to spend at least a day in court. If it's a crime novel, so much the better. But there are outliers, respectable citizens happy to serve, who end up being enormous pains in the ass. Lu distrusts early Columbia "settlers," despite the fact that her family was among them. That first generation of Columbia homeowners, now in their seventies and eighties, skew bleeding-heart liberal. Rudy's status as one of them, along with his mental health issues, could win him sympathy with that crowd. And there are crotchety libertarians scattered throughout the county, people who think that North Laurel doesn't belong in Howard County, that Prince George's County should be forced to annex it. If people "down there" want to kill one another—that's *their* problem.

I'm so happy this is a white-on-white crime, Lu thinks, and not for the first time. No race issues, not in the crime itself. It still factors into jury selection, however. Although it is strictly forbidden to consider race as an issue when striking a juror, almost every attorney has theories about how race affects an individual's behavior on the panel. African Americans tend to hold police in a lower regard than do white citizens. It's an earned contempt, but a troubling one for prosecutors. In a case where cop testimony is crucial, Lu will try to find a legit reason to keep her jury as white as possible.

The judge reads the standard boilerplate questions to the jury. Fred has requested—and Lu has acquiesced, happily—to add a question about whether potential jurors have any ingrained ideas about mental illness. She understands that Fred is going to try to use Drysdale's mental issues as a kind of a subtext, hoping to find the sweet spot between sympathy and hostility. Most citizens dislike insanity pleas and have no problem sending mentally ill people to prison. Whatever it takes to get them off the streets, they reason.

She sits at her table, her back to the jury pool, and even as potential jurors move in and out of the box throughout the morning, she tries not to make too much eye contact. People don't like it. Men in particular can take it the wrong way. Lu is just pretty enough that she has to be careful in her courtroom interactions with the opposite sex. It's amazing what men can infer from a woman's direct gaze. Romantic interest, often, but also arrogance, which will not work for her in this situation. She needs the men on the jury to take her seriously *enough,* but she can't come across as aggressive or angry. She wants the women to respect her, but not resent her. These are her private ideas, culled from years of trial experience. There are thousands of theories about jury selection, but the science is far from perfect. Lu goes with her gut. Fred, backed by the deep pockets of Howard & Howard, has access to the services of jury consultants, but that costs extra. She's sure that the Drysdales have eliminated any frills they can.

Lu has dressed with particular care today as this will be the potential jury's first impression of her. A suit, tailored as all her clothes must be, in a flattering shade of loden green. Luckily, it is unseasonably cool for early April. By tomorrow, if the forecast holds, she will be in a blouse and a pencil skirt, which means she will have to forgo her beloved boots for regular heels.

Fred calls a middle-aged man for voir dire. Plaid shirt, horn-rims, short salt-and-pepper hair. During the boilerplate, he raised his hand on two questions—the one about law enforcement and the one about mental illness. Interrogated by the judge, he reveals that he has a son in the military and he's an MP.

"Do you think you can be a fair and impartial juror in this trial?" the judge asks.

"No," the man says like a shot. Probably lying, but if he doesn't want to be here, Lu doesn't want him. She hates using one of her strikes on him, but it's probably worth it. She wants women on this jury. Preferably middle-aged women who can imagine themselves alone and vulnerable, being beaten to death for the simple fact of arriving home after a movie.

After voir dire, they start seating the potential jury, moving people in and out of the seats in the box, alternating their strikes. It's going pretty smoothly. How long has it been since Fred tried a case? Lu can't even remember. She thought he would be more puffed up and cock-of-the-walk, but he's keeping it low-key.

Rudy Drysdale is restless, shifting in his chair, sometimes making little grunts. Is he trying to create the impression of a man more unstable than he is? Lu thinks his brief exposure to his beloved outdoors might have riled him up this morning. He is clean-shaven and his suit, while cheap looking, is new, not the greenish one she remembers from the grand jury hearing. Another expense for Ma and Pa Drysdale. What would it be like to be Rudy's parents, to be responsible for a manchild who never found his place in the world? She can't imagine it. Rudy is almost AJ's age, yet he seems trapped in late adolescence. Petulant, moody, incapable of taking any responsibility for his actions. He wanted a place to sleep and a woman ended up dead.

He had a place to sleep, she thinks. But maybe he didn't feel comfortable masturbating under his parents' roof. Could it be that simple? This forever teenager needed a place where he could experience relief. Not his childhood home and definitely not in a shelter.

By lunchtime, they are so close—eight jurors have been seated, several returned to the jury room to see if they are called for another trial. Lu wishes they could keep going, but the meal break is sacred. Sure enough, all momentum is lost an hour later when they reconvene. Everyone is logy, irritable. Especially Judge Sampson, who is generally friendly to prosecutors. Even Lu, who has eaten sensibly—some roast chicken, a banana—feels her energy flagging.

And her boots hurt even while sitting. It is almost 4 P.M. by the time they have a full jury—four women, eight men, with two women as alternates. Overall, Lu is pleased. But two of the women are African American, which gives Lu some concern. They might have sons who have had run-ins with cops, even if they didn't raise their hands when asked if they had any ingrained biases about law enforcement. Sadly, the odds for young black men having bad experiences with cops are almost 100 percent. Luckily, the case against Rudy is more about science than police work—fingerprints at the scene, the DNA. That helps a little, Lu thinks, glancing at her watch. No time for even opening arguments today. The judge gives the jury its instructions—don't talk to anyone about the case, and that includes social media; don't research the case; be back at the courthouse by 8:30 tomorrow, ready to go. The trial is expected to last only two to three days. Lu hopes she can wrap it up before the weekend. Juries are very prosecutor friendly on Friday afternoons, in her experience.

"Everybody rise," the clerk says.

Later, Lu will describe what happens as a whoosh, more a sensation of noise than movement, then almost blinding pain as she hits the floor on her left side. She then hears gasps and screams, but all she knows is that her left arm hurts like a son of a bitch, as does her head, which is now being pounded on the floor—by Rudy Drysdale. It's as if he flew from where he was standing, not quite ten feet away. He bangs her head once, twice, three times, then stands and races for the door, marshals in pursuit. Lu, dizzy and disoriented, struggles to sit up, and it seems, in her blurred vision, that Drysdale is surrounded by a halo of light, shimmering, almost suspended before the closed courtroom doors, so close to freedom. Yet the bailiff, who is old and rotund, has no problem grabbing him and throwing him to the ground, where he is quickly cuffed.

"Motion for a mistrial," Fred screams at the judge. "Motion for a mistrial, Your Honor."

His timing is a little disconcerting—he could at least pretend to care about Lu, who is feeling her head, her wrist, shocked that there's no blood, nothing actually broken. But, hell, if Fred didn't ask for a mistrial, she might. She doesn't want to try a case in front of a jury that has just seen her flung to the floor like a rag doll, even if it does establish Rudy's predilection for violence. Maybe this guy *is* mentally ill. What the hell was he trying to do? Fred's been saying all along that Rudy's desperate to get to trial as soon as possible, in hopes that he might be released. Yet he's just delayed his own case by days, possibly weeks. And if the attack is reported in the press—luckily, there are no reporters here; the local reporter went home when it was clear there would be no opening statements—Fred might even demand a change of venue. With shaky fingertips, Lu traces the goose egg rising above her left ear. Rudy really could have killed her if he wanted. Had he come at Mary McNally this way? Did he intend to hurt Lu more seriously? No, he was focused on escape.

She hears a woman crying, saying his name over and over. *Rudy, Rudy, Rudy.* For some reason, Lu thinks of Cary Grant and almost starts to laugh. Is inappropriate laughter a symptom of concussion? Someone—the judge?—crouches down next to her and tells her not to move, to wait for paramedics. She shakes her head impatiently, then realizes it really hurts to shake her head.

"Lu," a familiar voice says. "Lu. Can you hear me?"

Shit, her father is here. He must have sneaked in toward the end or she would have seen him before now.

"Lu," he says. "Lu." Mrs. Drysdale says *Rudy, Rudy, Rudy.* Lu senses that her father wants to hold her but is restraining himself, in part because he's not a very huggy guy, but also because he doesn't want to undermine her authority.

"How do you feel, child?" She should be angry at that word, *child*, but it makes her happy.

"I'm fine. It probably looked worse than it was. It was the first blow—when he jumped me and knocked me down—that really hurt. After that, it was more like he was trying to shake me and my head kept hitting the floor because he didn't have a good hold on my shoulders."

Having said it, she realizes it's true. The impact of his body hitting hers, knocking her to the ground—that hurt like hell. But his hands on her throat, her shoulders—well, she's known rougher, for sure.

Saying that to her father right now would probably not be all that comforting.

————

The EMT guys decide to let her go home, although with muttered imprecations about concussions, and while Lu scoffs at them, she finds herself unaccountably nervous as bedtime nears. She drinks cognac, knowing it's a terrible idea—it will knock her out, only to have her wide-eyed at 3 A.M. Then it doesn't knock her out anyway. She simply cannot sleep. It's not that she experiences the attack when she closes her eyes. Instead, she has the strangest sense of déjà vu. That whooshing noise. A man running. Rudy at the door of the courtroom, so close to the outdoors for which he longed. Yes, the attack on her was a diversion, an attempt to throw the court into chaos. So why didn't he then break for daylight, as the saying goes?

Because he's crazy. But not crazy in the way that counts. Not crazy in the way that allows you not to be legally culpable for another person's death. Lu is sure of one thing now—Rudy Drysdale knows how to blindside a person, can move fast when he wants to.

And he had the strength to kill her if that's what he wanted. Rudy Drysdale *has* killed.

But it wasn't what he wanted, not today.

She checks the Internet, winces at the light of her laptop in the dark room. The story of the attack has made it to the news, but with no video, the TV stations can't do much with it, and even the newspapers are hard-pressed to flesh it out. Her office has been asked what charges Drysdale will face. The answer, so far, issued through Andi, has been that Lu cares more about the charges he already faces for the murder of Mary McNally. What happened to her is unfortunate, but it cannot distract from the matter at hand: murder in the first, of a citizen, a woman who never harmed anyone.

Lu and her father agreed before he drove her home to spare Justin and Penelope the story for now. Easy enough for twelve hours. It's not like they watch the news. Delightfully self-centered, they didn't notice how slowly she was moving, like someone with potential whiplash. (Maybe she does have whiplash. It was, after all, a collision of sorts.) But she will have to tell them before school tomorrow, or risk a well-intentioned teacher asking them about it. She will downplay the incident as much as possible. It's not as if she had a brush with death. There wasn't even time for fear.

The phone rings before breakfast, before there's time to tell the twins anything. Lu does not, despite her out-of-body feeling at the courthouse, actually believe in déjà vu. She has read that such sensations are simply a neurological blip in which the brain processes a new experience or image so quickly that one believes it has been seen before.

Yet she will come to believe that she knows, when her cell phone rings at 6:45, what has happened. It's a county number. What kind of news comes in at 6:45 A.M.? Death. Only death calls this early. Someone is dead and almost everyone she knows and loves is accounted for, sleeping under this very roof. She is going to answer the phone and find out that Rudy Drysdale is dead.

He is.

THE BOY WITH MOONLIGHT IN HIS EYES

And then there were none.

When AJ and his friends left for school that September, I was star-tled by the intense, lonely silence that overtook our house. I had never realized how much buzzy excitement AJ had generated just by coming and going. Noel, Davey, Bash, and Ariel had felt like *my* friends. (I never cared for Lynne, who in an unguarded moment told me I could be a cheerleader if I took gymnastics, as I had the right size and build. "But you'll have to be really good because if you're not cute, you have to do all the moves perfectly.")

My father, sensing my melancholy, tried to help. He established the ritual of our weekly call with AJ, one that I maintained even after I went away to college. He signed me up for a gymnastics camp, where I did excel, although I decided never to try out for cheerleading. I knew I was good enough that I could make the team on merit—and then I would never know if I was cute. And I was intensely curious about whether I was cute, or going to be, when I was a teenager. Of course, I could have tanked the tryout, muddled a leg on a cartwheel, to see what would happen. But even as a ten-year-old, imagining my life as a fourteen-year-old, I could not envision failing on purpose, ever.

My father also gave me a book about two children whose older brothers and sister went off to boarding schools, their left-behind siblings desolate. We read it together at night, although I was long past the age of needing to read with him. And the book didn't really make me feel better. First of all, someone created a scavenger hunt of sorts to amuse and distract the pair in their loneliness. I hoped this was a hint, checked the mail every day, but no one sent me on a quest. Besides they were *two*. I was one. Randy and I were still friends, but he had a growth spurt over the summer and now towered over me, which made me wary of him. I was worried he would bring up that kissing thing again. I was worried he wouldn't. He found a girl named Amanda, who had no ambivalence about kissing, and they started going together, which meant we couldn't hang out anymore. Even in fifth grade, that rule was clear.

Finally it was Thanksgiving. AJ came home, as did Noel and Ariel, but San Antonio was too far for Bash to return. As for Davey—he had never left. He had deferred his admission to Stanford because he needed a long time to recuperate from the Flood brothers' attack. When he was finally well enough to attend school, it had seemed formidable, traveling cross-country in a wheelchair.

Ben Flood's knife may have struck only once, but that was enough. He had sliced Davey's vertebrae, leaving him a paraplegic. Davey never walked again. His parents bought him a car as they had promised, but it was a van equipped with hand pedals, and he used it to commute to the University of Maryland, which at the time took almost any in-state kid with a high school diploma.

"Are you going to see Davey?" my father asked AJ that Thanksgiving weekend, which felt as if it were a decade later than the previous one, given how much had happened. Our father was issuing an instruction, not asking a question: AJ *was* going to see Davey, whether he wanted to or not. Dutifully, he drove to Hobbit's Glen, spent an hour in the company of his friend, Sancho Panza visiting Quixote on his deathbed, mind, body, and spirit shattered.

I was more curious about when Noel would stop by. Only he didn't. It was a hectic three days, with AJ constantly on the move, going from party to party. Nor did we see Noel at Christmas break, but by then his mother had returned to D.C. and his father, more or less in that order. It was a hassle for Noel to get to Columbia from D.C. Summer came, but Noel didn't come back. He landed a summer theater gig, interning in Chicago. He was paid nothing, but they liked him, invited him back the next summer, began to use him as an actor. By the age of twenty, Noel was a member of Steppenwolf. At twenty-two, he moved to New York, began landing small parts. He was six foot four then, very slender. Some say that one's eyes appear large as a child because eyes never grow while our heads do. But the photographs I saw of Noel—the *Columbia Flier* was quite proprietary about his success—made them look as large as ever. And as green as ever, I assume, but the photos were black and white. Remember that, when newspapers were black and white and read all over?

And then, at age twenty-six, Noel was dead. AIDS. Remember when young men didn't die from "viruses" at the age of twenty-six?

Noel had come out in college. Was that even the phrase used then? I'm not sure. I don't even remember if I was ever told that Noel was gay, much less if I would have understood what that word meant. What I remember is a Christmas party at our house, one not attended by Noel—the distance from D.C., again, the lack of a car—where Ariel, his classmate at Northwestern, spoke almost exclusively about his life, not hers. "He's just so happy," she said over and over again. Which seemed odd to me, because I thought Noel had always been happy. Happiness had seemed to be one of Noel's many talents.

The discussion of Noel—and happiness, come to think of it—ended when Davey arrived. Our old house was not well suited to a wheelchair, even an electric one. He needed help over the threshold, then had trouble coming down the skittery rug in the hallway that led to our living room. And while his friends had seen him in the chair before, his appearance seemed to throw them, as if they kept thinking this was a play that would eventually end, Davey standing up, announcing himself healed. Don Quixote is not dead, Dulcinea tells Sancho. Some man she never knew has died. Then the man rises from his deathbed, reverts to his true self, Miguel de Cervantes, and goes to face the Inquisition, manuscript in hand. Seeing Davey for the first time, it was all I could do not to say something stupid about *Ironside,* which was my only frame of reference for anyone in a wheelchair. People gathered around him, trying to pretend that they were interested in his stories about rehabilitation, that his autumn had been like theirs. Davey played along. Maybe it wasn't playing, come to think of it. This was a time when everyone had gone off and crafted a new persona. Hadn't Davey in effect done the same thing, to a greater extent? Everyone was starting over.

The sextet of AJ, Davey, Noel, Bash, Ariel, and Lynne would never be together again, unless one counts Noel's funeral in May 1988. I'm not even sure the surviving five wanted to be together then. But Ariel had prevailed on all of them to come, no matter how difficult. (AJ, having finished law school at Yale, was now getting an MBA at Wharton, which was a factor in my decision to apply to Bryn Mawr. As was the realization that I would totally dominate everything at a girls-only school. Unfair, but I wanted to go to law school and I felt I needed not only top marks, but a résumé that showed me as president of the student body, or something equally impressive.) Ariel even asked Davey, who was active in his church choir, to sing at the service. It seemed to me his voice was more beautiful than ever, with richer, deeper tones. He sang a ballad, one requested by Noel, the song AJ had played on his record player so many years ago while they spied on Miss Maude, the one about the girl with moonlight in her eyes.

AJ, sitting next to me, coughed at the word *girl.* Liberace had died only a year before. Rock Hudson, whom I knew as McMillan of *McMillan and Wife*—television cops were basically my window on the world, if that's not clear by now—had been dead three years. People, real people, people we knew, did not die this way. Yet Noel had.

The funeral was in D.C., Georgetown. The church was exceedingly pretty. In fact, I think it was chosen for its prettiness. There was no sense that the Episcopal priest who spoke had ever known Noel or his parents. An impressive number of Noel's new friends came—from New York, even from Chicago. In fact, they quite outnumbered the family and the high school gang. The old friends—AJ, Bash, Davey, Ariel, Lynne—did not sit together in the church, but they gravitated toward one another at the reception, which was terrifyingly fancy, with an open bar and passed hors d'oeuvres. I was reminded of the party at Davey's house, his gleaming glass house with all those levels; no wonder his parents had sold it. And I remembered Noel's face when those boys screamed "faggot" and no one took offense. Had it really been almost ten years ago?

"Did Noel pick the song you sang?" AJ asked Davey. I sensed he wanted to ask: *Why were you picked to sing, not me? Noel and I were closer.*

Ariel answered for him. "He did. Noel accepted he was dying. He began making plans a year ago. All of this—the church, this restaurant, the service—was his idea. He outlined his plans to his mother and me months ago. He knew what was happening. It was the rest of us who were in denial, even when he went into hospice."

"So you two were still close," Bash said.

"Why wouldn't we be?" Ariel, mild and quiet as a teenager, had become flamboyant. Her hair was full on one side, almost shaved on the other. She wore only one enormous earring, on the shaved side; her black dress had a bubble skirt, which I knew to be very fashionable. (It had taken years, but I had cracked the code of popularity. I dressed well, was cute verging on pretty, and was even considered somewhat cool. Too bad it had taken me until junior year in high school to get there.) Lynne, by contrast, wore a red "power" suit with padded shoulders. She was getting a little thick, I noticed, filing that information away. Petite women such as us had to stay petite as we aged or we would look like fireplugs. Maybe I could offer Lynne that helpful advice, as she had once advised me on my gymnastics career.

"Settle down," Bash said. "I didn't mean anything by it."

"It just would have been nice," Ariel said, "if other people had visited him. He knew, even when he couldn't really talk anymore. He knew when people came to see him."

"Noel stopped talking to *me*," AJ said. "Not the other way around. I just assumed he didn't want to see me. Those are his friends." Using his chin, he indicated the men who had come from New York and Chicago. And they were almost all men. Extremely somber, haunted-looking men, wearing red ribbons in their lapels. Looking back, I realize these men were just beginning to understand that their lives had become a horror film. They were being stalked. Their ranks would be decimated. How many of them would die within a decade? The conventional wisdom is that people my age, who came into their sexuality in a post-HIV world, were denied something. But I never felt that way. Maybe it came down to the old adage of not being able to miss what you never had. Noel had a few giddy years of finding his place in the world, of being his authentic self. It had killed him. Even at the age of eighteen, I could see how horribly unfair that was.

"The phone works both ways, AJ," Ariel said. "You could have picked it up any time."

"And said what? 'Hey, it's your old friend you cut off without a word of explanation'?"

"Really? Without a word?"

AJ had grown dangerously fond of arguing. That was my father's observation, issued just yesterday, when AJ had arrived home for the funeral. "You have grown dangerously fond of arguing. You need to watch out for that. You don't have to win all the time. Not even with me."

AJ said now: "Is there something you're trying to suggest, Ariel? Did Noel ever tell you why he stopped talking to me?"

Ariel considered, started to say something, changed her mind. "No," she said. "We really didn't talk that much about you, AJ. Believe it or not. You were no longer the center of our universe."

Davey, using the mild tone of someone hoping to derail an argument, said: "It doesn't matter now, does it? I just hope he had a chance to renounce his sins and make a clean breast of things with God."

"What?" Ariel and AJ were united in their dismay at least.

"I'm sorry, but it's a sin. Homosexuality. Why do you think they're being punished this way? It goes against God's will."

"If Noel knew you felt this way, he never would have asked you—I wouldn't have asked you—" In her distress, Ariel could not put a sentence together.

"Look, I was punished, too. For my sins."

"What sin?" AJ asked. "You didn't do anything."

"Sex outside marriage is a sin, too. I almost died and maybe I should have. Noel helped to save my life that night, getting the paramedics there." I noticed that Davey did not credit AJ. "I'll never forget that, and that's why I was happy to sing here today. I owed him that much. But my church, my calling, considers homosexuality a sin. I'm sorry, Ariel. There aren't exceptions for friends when it comes to God's law. No loopholes."

"I think I'll go check with Noel's mom to see if there's anything she needs," Ariel muttered. Bash and Lynne, who seemed to be getting back together yet again, went to the bar, his arm around her waist. (I did not understand then that funerals, as much as weddings, could lead to hookups.)

"You didn't do anything wrong, Davey," AJ repeated.

"I didn't break the law. But the law, as written, allows a lot of sin. You went to law school. I'm going to seminary. We're not going to see things the same way."

"Do you really believe premarital sex between consenting adults is a sin?"

"I believe in God's word. Laws are made by men. Sin has been defined by God."

"I feel like I don't even know you anymore, Davey."

"I've changed. I'm sorry if that threatens you—"

"Why would it threaten me?"

"It threatens everyone. A change like this, a big change. It's like when a person stops drinking or doing drugs. A lot of people in their lives don't support them. I've found meaning. I understand things now. You know, it's never too late to start being good, AJ."

After a long silence, AJ said: "Speaking of drink, I need one."

Now I was left alone with Davey. That had never happened before, just the two of us, one-on-one. Had we ever spoken other than the day on the path, when I was with Randy? *He must have been coming from Nita Flood's house that day,* I realized. Randy thought he was high, but maybe he was just a young man besotted with a young woman. Were his parents the only reason that Davey hid his relationship with Nita? Or was it her reputation, her acne-scarred face? *Nita Flood knows her sausage.* God, Lynne had always been a bitch.

"You've gotten very pretty, Lu," Davey said.

"Not really," I protested, although I was pleased he had registered the change in me. Then, because I had no idea what else to say: "Are you really going to be a minister?"

"I hope so. People need God. It was a mistake, I think, not having real churches in Columbia when we were kids. Or synagogues or mosques or whatever. An Interfaith Center. What's that? It sounds like a good idea. Everyone equal, everyone welcome. That's a lie. So much about where we lived—it was a lie."

I was flattered that he was speaking to me as if I were a peer, but I had no idea how to respond. I had been raised to think that religion was, if not an opiate, then something for lesser minds. My father, the son of Methodists, had been appalled that his parents, who considered themselves religious, saw no contradiction in being hateful racists. He had disliked his in-laws' Judaism, too, because it did not make them kind or ease their materialism. His affiliation with the Quakers was more political than religious.

Out of conversation, I asked Davey: "Can I get you something to eat?"

"No, thank you. I'm being careful."

"Careful?"

"To tell you the truth, I was a little scared to come here today. No one really knows how you catch this thing. But I prayed on it and realized it was the right thing to do. Noel wanted me to sing, so I sang. And the song was okay. I would have preferred a hymn, but it was a respectful song."

"Why did Noel want you to sing if you—" I wanted to say, *thought he was a sinner,* but settled for: "Didn't really see him or talk to him?"

"I have theories, but they're only theories. You should ask your brother."

"AJ?"

"He's your only brother, isn't he?" And with that Davey glided away.

Left alone, surveying the room of gorgeous men and Noel's friends and family, I realized Davey was the only black man. Not even Noel's actor friends, from New York and Chicago, included anyone dark-skinned. Again, I thought of the party in the glass house, the sense of an ant farm, but so many white ants, so few black ones. African American, I guess I should say here. In just my lifetime—from 1970 to now—the accepted term has kept evolving. Negro. Black. African American. And now politicians such as myself are trying to learn the minefields around gender-identity issues. Not that long ago, two prostitutes from Baltimore stole a car, drove into the National Security Agency campus, got shot, one of them fatally. They were originally identified as "cross-dressers," men in women's clothing. But they were trans women. "Had they had the surgery?" my father asked and I tried to explain that the question is no longer allowed, that we accept people as they see themselves. "Then they're transvestites!" "No, Dad, no." I tried to explain "trans" and "cis," which, it turns out, I didn't completely understand myself. He waved his hand in front of his face, as if I were an ignorant child again, frustrating in my stupidity. Only my father never treated me that way when I was a child. It is only quite recently that he has become impatient, crotchety. Well, he has cause. I remember Gabe's father, on his deathbed when we tried to explain how we were going to have children, the nice lady in Texas who was carrying our twins. Gabe knelt by his father's bed, saying, "So the first thing you do, is you find a Texas lesbian—" His father waved his hand, said "Pah!" Or was it "Pa"? He was lucid, but down to words of one syllable. He probably thought we did not know how babies were made. Ten days before he died, the twins were born. He saw their photos, but it was never clear if he understood he finally had grandchildren, thanks to some cheerleader's donor eggs, a Texas lesbian and a suave Egyptian doctor who had blended our baby cocktail and then inserted it into our beloved surrogate. On Yom Kippur of all days. So while Gabe was in synagogue, praying and fasting and atoning for whatever, I was roaming the sterile suburbs of Northern Virginia, trying to find a Five Guys for our ravenous savior, a woman who could do the one thing that had eluded me: hold two fertilized eggs in the lining of her uterus. She was the one who introduced me, in fact, to the wonder that is Five Guys.

Thirty-five years ago, I would have had no chance to have children with a biological link to their father; Penelope and Justin would not exist. How can I long for that world? Thirty-five years ago, people I loved made disastrous decisions that made perfect sense within the context of the world they knew, the moment in which they had to act. They were men of their times. How can I fault them?

Then again, people died, people were hurt, however indirectly, because of those decisions.

You can argue people died because of my decisions. Some people blame me for Rudy Drysdale's death. But I regret his death only because I will never know exactly what happened, despite my best efforts. To be clear: Rudy Drysdale was guilty of murder and he killed himself. He hit his head against the wall of his cell over and over again. Do you know how determined you have to be to kill yourself that way? Determined and stoic. And stealthy. He beat his own brains out with a steady, persistent drumming on the wall. If he had miscalculated, he might have ended up in a coma. Maybe he wouldn't have minded that. And maybe you're a step ahead of me, or have been all along, but I understood, when I got that phone call, why Rudy had attacked me in court. He was counting on being shot. Suicide by cop is a glib term, but it's real, it happens. That's why Rudy hesitated at the courthouse doors. It wasn't my imagination or a case of blurred vision brought on by being slammed to the floor. He wanted to be shot. Yearned to be shot. It was April 2015. Police were obligingly shooting young men everywhere. Four weeks later, Baltimore would burn in the wake of Freddie Gray's death, his body broken on a classic Baltimore bounce, an unsecured rough ride in a police van.

But Howard County is not Baltimore. Or Ferguson or North Charleston or Cleveland or—you get the point. Rudy Drysdale was a middle-aged white man in a suit that his mother had bought from JCPenney only a week earlier. Now she would bury him in it. Did that mean I got the win, even if I never made it to opening statements? I decided it did.

It was a victory that cost me almost everything I hold dear.

PART THREE

Lu debates visiting the funeral home where Rudy Drysdale's body was taken after the autopsy. Pro: She will appear magnanimous. Con: She will seem calculated and insincere. It is hard to know how such a move will play and she is—at heart, in her marrow, in her DNA—a politician. If you don't care about what people think about you, then don't run for public office.

So far, the media attention has helped her more than harmed her, raising her profile considerably. One *Beacon-Light* columnist tried to make hay out of Drysdale's mental illness, harping on the absence of a competency hearing. "I think that's for his attorney to speak to," Lu demurred. "My office was open to discussing a plea of not criminally responsible."

She then sat back and gritted her teeth as the columnist spun his story out of the most convenient details, whipping up something with about as much structural integrity as cotton candy. The piece, published two days ago, allowed Fred to suggest that Rudy's suicide was a desperate reaction to his severe claustrophobia. So what would the columnist do with claustrophobic killers? Construct prisons with vast parks, like the fake savannahs of more progressive zoos? *Seriously,* Lu harrumphs to herself. But only to herself. Her father would commiserate, maybe even AJ, who is more upset about the attack than anyone. In this case, she does get a kick out of his protective big-brother side. Plus, he seems to feel a retroactive guilt about ever suggesting that Drysdale deserved more compassionate treatment.

But the column makes her feel it's obligatory to visit the funeral home. "Paying one's respects" is the correct and felicitous phrase. *I have victim status, too,* Lu reminds herself. She is still sore from that initial hit. Strange—that night, when Drysdale was still alive as far as she knew, she wasn't particularly traumatized by the incident. It is only since his death that she sees his face whenever she closes her eyes. Expressionless, utterly impersonal. Did she really see him or is the memory manufactured, the usual attempt to project meaning backward onto a moment that made no sense at the time? And even if she did see his face, did it really tell her anything? No, he was impassive. He was doing what he had to do to achieve an end. It was about as detached as an attack could be.

Why me? But she knows why he chose her. Because she was the smallest, because he wanted to trigger the protective impulses of the armed men who might then shoot him. In that room, it had to be her or the judge, and the judge was too far away. Rudy Drysdale was trying to commit suicide by cop. When he failed, he did the job himself.

————————

The funeral home is in Baltimore, on the long avenue that dead-ends at Fort McHenry, the military installation that was under attack when Francis Scott Key dubbed a still young country as the home of the free and the land of the brave. Twenty years ago, this was a working-class neighborhood, but now Under Armour crouches near one end of Fort Avenue, while a luxury high-rise to be known as Anthem House is under construction a few blocks to the west. AJ keeps telling Lu that Baltimore has become a magnet for millennials, spiking rents in the neighborhoods around the harbor. In this part of Baltimore, artisanal cocktails and new spins on softshell crabs are in demand, while in the "other" Baltimore an estimated one to four people live in food deserts. These are AJ's facts, AJ's stats, AJ's rhetoric. Lu likes a good cocktail.

But while Lu realizes it is a markedly different city from the one she left only five years ago, she feels its working-class character is as intractable as kudzu. Parking her car, she notices a man with his T-shirt rolled up to his armpits—the better to expose his remarkably tanned barrel of a belly—kneel and pray before a shrine of Mary outside the local parish. The temperature will barely top seventy today, but in Baltimore, that's a reason to dig out your shorts and flip-flops. There aren't enough high-rises or Starbucks or Chipotles to eradicate Baltimore's eccentrics.

There is only one visitor in the room assigned to Rudy's wake— Fred, in a hushed, urgent conversation with the Drysdales.

"I'm truly sorry for your loss," Lu says, offering her hand to both parents. Neither one takes it. "This is not what anyone wanted."

Mr. Drysdale all but rolls his eyes: "Guess he saved the state some money, didn't he?"

Oh, the words, the taunts that spring to mind. *Saved* you *some money, I guess. Your son was well on his way to being the state's paid guest for the rest of his life.* But a politician must be politic, even in a room with three people who are guaranteed never to vote for her.

"I'll always regret that he didn't have his day in court. That doesn't mean I don't think he was guilty. But I also believe he was entitled to a fair trial. And that Mary McNally's family deserved answers, a sense that justice had prevailed."

She leans hard on the victim's name, just as her father taught her. *Another family lost someone. I won't let you forget that.*

"They didn't even bother to show up for the trial," Mrs. Drysdale says.

"It would have been expensive for them to be here throughout the trial. We talked about it and decided that they should save their money, come to court for the sentencing phase, when they would have been allowed to give impact statements." In an attempt to appear modest, she adds: "Assuming, of course, there was a sentencing phase."

"Oh, we know he did it," Mr. Drysdale says. "But your kid is your kid. Even when he's in his fifties. For better or worse. It's funny that you say those words when you make your wedding vows. They should make you recite that oath the day your kid is born."

"Arthur." Mrs. Drysdale almost squeaks in her fury. "We do not know that Rudy did any such thing. We will never know."

Sure, Lu thinks. If, by knowing, you mean you require some unimpeachable primary source—a video demonstrating the deed, a confession. But, by those standards, we would know almost nothing. What happened on 9/11? How do you *know*?

She says nothing. No one says anything. The silence should be uncomfortable, but it's not, not for Lu. The casket is closed, inevitable given the circumstances of his death. She isn't faking her sympathy. She's genuinely sorry for the Drysdales' loss. This is not where a parent's journey should end, ever. *Did you wash his clothes, Mrs. Drysdale? Did he come to you that night, tell you he was in trouble? What do you "know"?*

"A lot of our family still lives around here, so we came back to the neighborhood to bury him," Mrs. Drysdale says, offering an explanation for a question Lu hasn't asked. "They'll probably come later."

"Oh."

"They told us we were crazy." The unfortunate word hangs in the air. "When we moved to Columbia. They said it was for hippies and—well, they said it was for hippies."

"Almost forty years ago? I suppose a lot of people did think that about Columbia."

"We did it for Rudy. He was smart, but he wasn't the right kind of smart, not for a regular high school. We thought Wilde Lake could help him. And he did really well there and then he got into Bennington. But, even there, people were mean to him. College, high school. Almost everyone was mean to him. Columbia was supposed to be all *kumbaya*, or whatever, but kids are kids. We tried to do what we could to help him fit in. We let him work at the mall. We bought him a car. He thought it would make him popular, if he had a car."

"I'm sorry," Lu says for the second time. What else is there to say? Despite what people think, "I'm sorry" is more than adequate. When Gabe died, that's all Lu wanted to hear. *I'm sorry.* She didn't want to be told that God wouldn't give her anything harder than she could handle. That she would be happy one day. Or that Gabe wanted her to be happy. She certainly didn't want to answer any questions. *What exactly happened? Who found his body? What was the cause of death? Were there any warning signs?* Given the other choices, "I'm sorry" is really underrated.

She stands to go. Fred does, too. "I'll walk you to your car." She starts to protest that it's early, the neighborhood perfectly safe, but maybe Fred needs an excuse to go. Or maybe he wants to reproach her for the passive-aggressive jab in the column.

"I liked him," he says once on the sidewalk.

"Who?" she asks, her mind still on the *Beacon-Light.*

"Rudy. I offered to pay for the funeral, but his parents said a good Samaritan had stepped forward. They're pretty strapped. I don't know how they were going to afford the trial. I guess I didn't want to think too hard about how they were managing this."

Well, the trial did get cut short and there won't be any appeals.

Fred seems to pick up on her unspoken snark.

"As I got to know Rudy, I would have been happy to do this case pro bono, not that it was my choice. Once he trusted a person—he could be good company. Funny, self-deprecating, smart. You know, he did pretty well, getting as far as he did in the world, given that no one figured out he was depressive and dyslexic until after he dropped out of college."

Dyslexia? This is the first Lu has heard of it and her office pored over reams of medical documents about Drysdale, all provided by Fred.

"How could no one have noticed that?" Lu asks.

"It was never an official diagnosis, but it's so clear to me that was part of his problem. People had these very narrow ideas about dyslexia a generation ago. They thought it meant you couldn't read at all, and Rudy's good grades helped mask his problems. Rudy had this genius for coping. He had this—not exactly photographic memory, but his memory was very visual. He taught himself to see the page, whole, and somehow, that allowed him to fake it. He was a good listener—I mean, really good, in a way almost no one is. Plus, at that crazy high school you all attended, you could take tests over, right? Rudy told me that. If you flunked, you were allowed to take the test again. And it was the same test. He could memorize the answers, the second time. I'm not describing it right, his condition. But you get what I'm saying."

"I was years behind him at Wilde Lake. And by then, it was a totally conventional school. A good one, too." Lu has always been a little defensive about her high school, which now has a less-than-stellar reputation. "You know, you didn't provide any of this information. In discovery. Was dyslexia going to be a part of his defense?"

"I don't want to talk about what might have been."

She yearns to ask Fred if he thinks Rudy did it. Not because she has doubts. She doesn't. She just wants Fred to admit she would have beaten him like a drum in that courtroom.

"People think dyslexia is all about reading," he repeats. Lu tries to hide her impatience. *Lord, once a man goes to the trouble of acquiring new information, he can't let it go. What's the point of learning something if you can't bore others to death with the subject.* "And that's the core. But there are other issues. For Rudy, the biggest problem was spatial. He got so confused, about left and right. I thought that was why he hesitated at the courtroom door, at first. He was trying to remember which way he would have to turn when he ran out."

So, no, she hadn't imagined Rudy stopping at the door.

"I think it was an attempted suicide by cop."

"Yeah, I think that, too. Now. But left and right was a huge problem for him. Sometimes, he wrote the letters on his wrist. L, R, so he would remember. I thought you should know."

"Why?"

"It wasn't part of my case. I'm not breaching privilege here. I observed this on my own, and then his mom filled me in. I could still see the 'R' and 'L' on his wrists, the day I visited him in lockup. I thought the 'R' was for Rudy. But the letters were fresh that day."

"Fred, what the hell are you talking about?"

He smiles. There's a sense of payback here, as if he needs to tear her down because she didn't win fair. *Gee, Fred, sorry your client attacked me and committed suicide. I'm sorry, too, I didn't get my day in court. Because I would have destroyed you.*

"See you, Lu. Who knows when our paths will cross again?"

She stews all the way back to Columbia, mired in rush-hour traffic, an unpleasant novelty for her, given how early and late her days run. What the hell was Fred talking about? Right, left, who cares? She goes back to the office, cursing the Drysdales for the three hours her kindness has cost her, resigned to working late. No good deed, etc. etc.

———

Dusk has fallen by the time Lu thinks to glance out the window. She sees her reflection in the glass. The glass makes her think of sliding doors, a woman walking into her bedroom, discovering a strange man.

Then she thinks of the man, standing outside the apartment in the dark, choosing his point of entry.

He didn't know right from left. He didn't know right from left.

If Rudy had gone to the other apartment, his victim would have been Jonnie Forke, the state's witness, the woman who saw him lurking around the complex the week before Mary McNally was killed.

Okay, so what? What difference did it make if Drysdale killed the woman behind door number 1 or the woman behind door number 2? If Jonnie Forke had any connection to Rudy Drysdale, she would have mentioned it to Mike Hunt or Andi. They would have told her over and over again to be candid, to reveal anything that might come up in court. If she knew him, recognized him from somewhere, it only would have *strengthened* the ID.

Lu Googles "Jonnie Forke"—nothing. Literally, nothing, which is bizarrely impressive. She plugs "Jonnie Forke" in Facebook, finds an entry for Juanita Forke. Graduated Centennial High School. No overlap with Drysdale there. Relationship status, single. She has only seventy-four friends, so she's one of those people who actually uses Facebook for friends, yet doesn't think to opt for the highest-security settings. To be fair, the site changes its privacy policy so often, some well-intentioned people don't realize their fences are down. Lu can even look at all of Jonnie Forke's friends.

Nine of whom have the surname Flood.

Jonnie Forke.

Juanita Forke.

Jonnie Flood Forke.

Juanita Flood Forke.

Had she given her full name at the grand jury proceeding, the syllables sliding past Lu's ear because she was so full of adrenaline she couldn't be bothered to note that a witness's legal name was different from the one she used? But "Juanita" didn't mean anything to Lu, and there was no reason for Jonnie Forke to use her maiden name.

Juanita Flood Forke.

Juanita Flood.

Nita Flood.

The apartment doors at the Grove—still THE G OVE on the sign, perhaps forever THE G OVE now—have fisheyes. Did they always, or were they an add-on, a concession to the modern age and the changing nature of the people who lived here? Not that a fisheye would have saved anyone from Rudy Drysdale, no matter which door he chose. Lu stands in front of Jonnie Forke's door for one, two, three minutes, waiting to be examined and deemed worthy of entrance. She definitely heard footsteps in the apartment after she knocked. Didn't she? She takes a few steps backward, just in case the person on the other side of the door can't see her. Can't blame the woman for being extra careful. After all, a tenant was killed here not that long ago.

Killed by someone who might have been looking for the woman across the hall.

Go figure, Fred finally went the extra mile. But he didn't share the information about Drysdale's dyslexia with the state's attorney's office because there was no gain for him to advance the theory that Rudy Drysdale meant to kill Jonnie Forke. That's ethical. Fred is not obligated to help the prosecution do its job. And it's possible

that Fred knows only that the intended victim was one of the prosecution's key witnesses. He may not have figured out that she has a
complicated history with the Brant family.

"Hi" is all Jonnie—*Nita*—says when she finally opens the
door. Of course Lu has seen her several times since Mary Mc-
Nally's body was discovered, but only now is she seeing Nita
Flood, the teenage girl she glimpsed perhaps two or three times.
If anyone knows sausage, it's Nita Flood. That was Lynne, throwing shade long before the term existed. Lu never cared for Lynne.
She remembers Ariel, flushing bright red, embarrassed by her
friends. The others had laughed. Had Davey laughed? Lu has
never thought to connect that scrap of memory to what happened
later that fall and then on graduation night. Or the time she and
Randy—what was his last name?—saw Davey on the path near
where Randy lived, but also where the Floods lived. *I see him
around all the time,* Randy said. Suddenly, a bright line is shining
in her mind, connecting so many isolated events. What else will
be connected before she's through?

"You don't seem surprised to see me," Lu says.

"I'm more surprised how long it took you to figure it out. Everyone's always saying how smart you are."

Lu doesn't recall any time the newspapers have given her credit
for being extraordinarily intelligent, but who knows what Jonnie
Forke reads between the lines.

She follows her into the apartment, noting Jonnie Forke's skin,
which has the orangey glow of a year-round tanner. *Self-tanner or
tanning salons,* Lu thinks, then wonders why her mind is stuck on
such a trivial track.

Possibly because she'd rather contemplate Jonnie's grooming
routines than the questions that have brought her here.

Still, she gets right to it once she is seated on the green sofa in

Jonnie's living room, no formalities: "When did you realize that you were Rudy Drysdale's intended victim?"

"Who says I was?"

"His own lawyer." Okay, so it's a lie. It's not like this is an official proceeding. Lu can say whatever she wants to shake the truth loose. And Fred all but said it. Maybe he, too, is trying to figure out just how smart Lu is.

"I didn't know until the newspaper published his name. I honestly didn't recognize him when I saw him hanging around here. He's put on weight since high school. He was just another creepy homeless guy. But I did feel as if he were watching me. Then I saw his name and I remembered I knew him, but—well, I was glad it wasn't me. Sorry, I was."

Definitely a case of hashtag sorrynotsorry.

"How well did you know him? Back in high school?"

"We both worked at the mall. Sometimes he gave me a ride. That was about the extent of it."

"Then why would he want to kill you?"

"No idea." Jonnie's eyes flick right, toward the patio doors off her living room, the sliding doors that Rudy meant to come through almost four months ago.

"It's against the law to lie to an officer of the court," Lu lies. She's not on official business. Jonnie can lie her head off.

"I'm *not* lying. I never did anything to him. I haven't spoken to him for thirty-five years. I don't know. Who says he wanted to kill me, or anyone? Maybe he had a crush on me, all those years ago. He was always doing favors for me. Then again, lots of guys did favors for me."

"And you did favors for lots of guys." It just slips out. Lu wishes she could take the words back. It's as if she's channeling bitchy Lynne. But the woman's confidence is annoying for reasons she can't pinpoint.

Jonnie shrugs it off. "What? You don't think guys would like me unless I had sex with them. Because I had acne? Guys always liked me. Because I was *fun*. And I'm not talking about sex. I liked to laugh and I drank beer and I wasn't a drag like the prissy girls. I didn't sleep with anybody I didn't want to sleep with. Until the night that Davey Robinson raped me."

Lu cannot believe she is still clinging to that story, after all these years.

"Davey Robinson did not rape you. A grand jury heard your testimony and decided not to indict him. Wasn't it obvious that your father was the one who beat you? That you lied to protect him?"

"I told the truth to get my father to stop beating me for being a slut. Sure, I had sex with Davey before that night. We'd been having sex for a year. I liked him. But not that night. He held me down, he raped me, then acted as if everything was normal. So I did, too. I wasn't going to break down in front of his friends. But I was upset, I drank too much, and those stupid shits just dumped me on my doorstep. They could have walked me around, cleaned me up. Even with the vomit caked on my clothes, I smelled like sex. My father beat me because I wouldn't tell him, at first, who it was. Me saying I was raped—telling the truth—probably saved Davey's life because the police got to him before my dad did. If I had told my father we'd been together a bunch of times before that night, he would have just driven to Davey's house and straight up killed him then."

Over a year. Again, Lu hears Lynne's cruel taunt, realizes that Davey is already sleeping with the girl that his friends are mocking. Maybe he blushed, too, that day, but his dark skin concealed the blood rushing to his face.

"You were mad at him keeping the relationship a secret. You can't deny that. The other boys all said they heard you fighting."

"We both wanted it to be a secret. My dad wasn't going to let me have a black boyfriend. Davey's parents didn't want him to have any girlfriend at all. So he took different girls to dances and I was okay with that. But he took that Sarah chick to homecoming, then went to homecoming at her school, and that wasn't part of the deal. That's why I got mad. We were in love, we really were. I never knew anyone like him. And, yeah, maybe at first, he liked me because I was cool with sex. But that's not why he stayed. That's not what he said to me. He said he loved me."

Before or after orgasm, Lu wants to ask, but manages to keep this to herself. Why do people put so much stock in that word, *love*? As if no one ever uses it falsely, as if it's always true. Love can be the biggest lie of all.

"Your brothers did their best to finish the job your father didn't have a chance to do."

"And one of my brothers died," Jonnie says softly. "Everyone seems to forget that. Just because you have seven brothers doesn't mean you don't mind losing one. My dad was never the same. My mom, either. It tore my family apart, what happened to Ben. Tom ended up dying in a car accident a few years later, drunk and high. Both my parents were dead before I was thirty-five. That left the six of us. But we're really tight. We have to be."

"Ben died because he tried to kill another person—and ended up maiming him. A person who did not, by law, rape you."

"Yeah, that's what the law said. But who was there, who was in that room? Me and Davey. Who held who down? Who had bruises? He weighed, I don't know, probably about two hundred pounds? I weighed a hundred and ten and wore size 3 jeans. You see, I knew what sex was like. I didn't have any confusion about how it was supposed to go. What happened that night was rape. The fact that he was my boyfriend, that he kissed me when he was done—that didn't change it."

"Of course that's what you'd say now. But the law—"

"The law? You mean your father? Well, *fuck* him. Big, hand-some, rich Davey Robinson held down a stupid little acne-scarred slut, forced her to have sex, but no one believed her. Turns out there were all these tests, all these rules I didn't know. 'Did you scream?' Sorry, I didn't know I had to scream for it to be a crime. Next time, I'll make sure I scream. 'Did you struggle?' Yeah, I struggled, for all the good it did me. I said no. But because I had said yes all the other times, no didn't count."

Lu believes her. *Almost*. Which is to say, she thinks Jonnie is telling what is now the truth in her head, but it's a story born of thirty-five years of hindsight. Davey, the gentle giant, would never have done such a thing. Lu can see, however, that Jonnie absolutely believes what she's saying. She has conveniently forgotten that she had a motive to lie back in 1979. She was angry at Davey. She was trying to protect her father, who had beaten her severely enough to require an ER visit. Her refusal to tell the truth about the beating benefited him.

"Davey Robinson ended up with a life sentence that the law never would have given him—paralyzed from the waist down. Didn't that satisfy you?"

"For a while," she says, then looks startled by her own unvar-nished honesty.

Silence, a dead end. Lu, not sure what to say, asks: "What hap-pened to Mr. Forke?"

"Oh, him. I don't know. I was almost twenty-seven when I got married, which seemed late to me, old enough to make good choices. We had three kids, boom, boom, boom. He took off after the third one. But I raised good kids. I'm a grandma now and proud to be one. That's Joni Rose."

She indicates a set of three photographs in a triptych on the table next to the bright orange armchair where she sits. A baby, a toddler, a little girl, maybe four or so. All the same kid, Lu assumes. Bald as a doorknob as a baby, with one of those ridiculous headbands that proclaims, *I am a girl, dammit*. Still pretty wispy haired as a toddler and kid. Too bad she didn't get Jonnie's genes. The woman's hair is impressive, thick and glossy.

"Did you ever see Davey again?"

"Why would I do that?"

Nonresponsive. *The witness is directed to answer the question.*

"Heck, you might have run into him somewhere. He still lives here." Davey and AJ lost contact years ago. But Lu knows—anyone who reads a newspaper knows—that Davey is a minister, one of the leading opponents of Maryland's move toward marriage equality two years ago. "He's at the big, new superchurch in far west Howard County."

"Well, I'm not much for churchgoing," Nita says with a harsh laugh. "God hasn't done too well by me and my family."

Lu gives up, bids the woman good evening. She leaves believing that Jonnie-Nita Flood-Forke has her suspicions about why Rudy Drysdale targeted her—and has no intention of sharing them. Lu can't force her to talk. Rudy is dead, his intent no longer important. And it would not be particularly comforting to Mary McNally's family to learn that she was an even more random target than anyone ever dreamed.

Back in her car, Lu picks the Sinatra station on Sirius, hoping to quiet her mind, roiling with nervous energy. She catches the end of "You Couldn't Be Cuter."

"Ella Fitzgerald," she says out loud, as if Gabe were still there, quizzing her. "Written by Jerome Kern." She could almost always identify the vocalists, even if she couldn't tell Django Reinhardt from . . . well, whoever else was famous for playing jazz guitar. Gabe would have considered Reinhardt too well-known for his pop quizzes. This song is on the *Jerome Kern Songbook* album and Lu is old enough to remember albums, the days when one listened to a record in order. When the song dies out, she half expects to hear what would have followed on the album or CD: "She Didn't Say Yes." Now, there was a politically incorrect song if ever there was one. And yet a wise one because it realized that people, most people, could not get outside their own heads. *So what did she do? . . . She did just what you'd do too.* Translated: People behave as you would. And if they don't? They're probably wrong.

Nita Flood didn't say yes, she didn't say no. Nita Flood, caught in a lie about being raped, came to believe it. Our minds shape our memories to be something we can bear. Happens all the time. What if Nita decided that her story, more credible now because of the way times had changed, was something she should go public with, despite the potential embarrassment for a very public, very righteous pastor? There was no record; Davey had been no-billed by the grand jury, everyone involved was a minor. Ben Flood's attack on Davey was always reported as provoked by unfounded rumors. At the insistence of Lu's father—again, he had always been thinking of Nita, the way her lies could destroy *her* future. The Wilde Lake students who had once gossiped about the story probably had dim memories now: Nita Flood was a slut who got drunk, had sex with her boyfriend, then accused him of rape because he wouldn't take her out in public. Yet over the past year, more and more women had come forward with stories about being drugged and molested by a famous comedian. What would happen if Nita Flood tried to do the same thing to Davey Robinson? Would people still be so quick to ignore her?

Lu can't imagine the young man she knew hiring a homeless drifter to kill his former girlfriend. But then—she can't imagine

Davey opposing marriage equality and supporting the death penalty. Davey has power; he has been in the media a lot over the past few years. He doesn't even believe in sex out of wedlock. What would he do if his former girlfriend threatened to speak publicly about what happened between them?

The only thing to do is to ask.

"What are you thinking about?"

Lu wakes with a start, confused and disoriented. What is she thinking about? *Where is she?* The dim room, the neutral "art" on the walls, the heavy, humid presence of another body—she has fallen asleep in Bash's place, something she has never done before. He catnaps sometimes, but she never does.

"I—I must have dozed off."

"Guess I'm losing a step."

"No"—yawn—"no, lover, no. I'm . . . just . . . so . . . tired. Insomnia."

Lu is used to being tired. She's been tired since her kids were born. But as of late, she's tired in a new way. Twice in the past week, she has fallen asleep on the sofa while watching television and it felt as if she were pinned to the cushions by invisible hands. She would open her eyes at 2 or 3 a.m., surprised and disoriented, the very act of rising and stumbling into her bed seemingly impossible. Yet once in bed, she can't sleep at all. She has always slept well. What is happening?

"Ah, it's your age, I guess."

"My age? I'm eight years younger than you."

"It's a female thing. Insomnia at midlife."

This may be her least favorite conversation ever with Bash. Not that there have been that many conversations to begin with. She doesn't waste a lot of time talking to him. Bash was the "dumb" one in AJ's group, and even when it turned out that he had been stealthily intelligent all along—making National Merit Scholar, getting a full ride to Trinity—his reputation was more or less sealed within the group. Old friends, like family, have a hard time letting personae change. You are what you were. That's why Lu can't stand to have anyone refer to her stature. It reminds her, always, of "Little Lu."

"Your wife is even younger than I am, Bash. What do you know about women at midlife?" She's trying to make a joke, but an edge slips into her voice, a little pocketknife showing its blade.

"I've got a pharmaceutical client who's trying to break ground in menopause, perimenopause. It's promising stuff, if we can just get the FDA out of our way. I hope it gets online in time to help women your age."

Okay, this is *officially* her least favorite conversation, ever. The last thing she wants to do is tell Bash she went through early menopause because of fibroids. Although Bash's tone couldn't be more impersonal, she feels as if—her mind searches for the source of her unease, finds it—as if she is being set up for a disappointing job evaluation, something that has happened to her exactly once. It was her first year in the city's state's attorney's office and she was disheartened not to receive the highest evaluation. They claimed it was a policy not to give first-year employees top marks, but she later found out that the other newbie, a man, was given the best possible rating. Anyway, it feels like that. Is she about to be fired as—what is she? She's not a mistress or a girlfriend. Her mind rejects the crude pop culture term that would seem to best describe what they do. She's not Bash's "buddy." And although she calls him "lover," she's not fond of that word either, given its root. If she thought she were capable of loving Bash, she wouldn't be with him. She would never claim to love another woman's man. That's the true betrayal.

Yet she remains curious about his other life, his "real" life. She senses that, say, should a truck mow down Mrs. Arnold "Bash" Bastrop on Capitol Hill tomorrow, Lu would not be a candidate for being his public companion, although Bash is clearly one of those men who cannot live without a mate. But he requires a *decorous* one, a woman who would be delighted to consider her husband and household her "job." How interesting, Lu thinks, that Bash and her brother have chosen such retro wives. Because Lauranne, for all her blather about her "partnership" with AJ, is very much a junior partner, tolerated at AJ's side because he insists on it. He's the brand. And it's a cinch Davey has a dutiful, passive wife.

Davey.

Lu has not been able to summon the—strength, moxie, chutzpah?—to go visit him. How do you show up in the life of someone you haven't seen for almost thirty years and try to figure out if he ordered a hit on his old girlfriend? There's no evidence that Davey even knew Rudy Drysdale. After all, her brother didn't. A little Internet sleuthing quickly determined that Davey's church does give out bag lunches every week, in a parking lot near North Laurel. Still, it's hard to imagine Davey himself handing out lunch bags, looking for a killer to recruit. None of this makes sense.

Jesus, Rudy, why didn't you just confess before you killed yourself? Would that have been so hard?

She sits up, stretches, and Bash pushes her back down, covers her with himself. She is starfished on the bed, arms pinned. Again, she thinks of those waking moments on the sofa, the sense that she is being weighed down by something she cannot see and cannot overcome. But she can see and feel what is holding her in place and she likes it. So Bash has pharmaceutical clients. She had always assumed his ability to go more than one round was simply the result of pent-up lust, but there probably is some sort of pill involved, come to think of it. *Come to think of it.* She is on the verge of doing just that when Nita Flood's voice hisses in her ear: *He weighed, what, almost two hundred pounds? And I was a hundred and ten, wore a size 3 jeans. How could anyone tell if I struggled?*

Her pleasure is dimmed. Still, she manages to finish. Bash notices that she is distracted, but he probably assumes she is making that inevitable transition into real life, the life that has no place for a healthy, harmless lust. Would Bash's wife find this so harmless? As much as Lu wonders about her, she has no desire to know anything. *This is civilized,* she tells herself. *I'm a forty-five-year-old woman, I need a sexual outlet, but I don't need a boyfriend or a partner, and I definitely don't need a husband. I am taking care of enough people.* The term "high maintenance" always seems to be applied to women, but Lu has never known any woman who needs as much care as a man. Heck, her father has had an ersatz wife in Teensy all these years.

Lu drives home, wondering if it's time to let go of Bash, but only because she wants to be the one who ends it. If he calls it quits, she fears it will arouse old feelings, that intense desire to win, no matter the cost. As a young woman, she got a little crazy in the face of rejection. She was only in her twenties. But she can still be embarrassed by some of the things she did. Lu, as a young woman, preferred being direct and confrontational. She could not believe that there were men who would simply walk away, cut off communication—and make you feel gauche for thinking the game should be played any other way. She was the opposite of cool, in those early love affairs. Then she reconnected with Gabe, and his heart was so open, his sense of self forever informed by the short geeky boy he had been, that she felt she had, in fact, found her soul mate. "We were imprinted early on each other, like ducks," she once told him.

She didn't tell him that she had stolen that line from a book.

He was two hundred pounds . . . . Why is Jonnie in her head, when Jonnie clearly had no desire to help Lu figure out why she was targeted by Rudy Drysdale? Maybe it's not really Jonnie at all, but Blind Lady Justice, the omnipresent conscience that insists on what is right and wrong, a conscience whose voice sounds strangely like Lu's father's. *Fuck him.* There was Nita again. How can she not realize that Lu's father was one of the few people who had her best interests at heart, all those years ago?

It's a coincidence, Rudy going into the wrong apartment, Lu tells herself. She'll go see Davey, ask him a few questions, and they'll have a good laugh. He'll tell her that he never knew Rudy Drysdale and he doesn't fear his old girlfriend because he *didn't* rape her. A grand jury made that determination thirty-five years ago. Davy's alleged crime was not hidden or hushed up. Juanita Flood Forke's complaint was heard—and rejected.

When Lu pulls up in front of the Triadelphia Community Church, the first thing she notices is the long, graceful ramp that snakes up to its front doors. Of course, all churches—all public buildings— are obligated to be accessible in this day and age, but this particular ramp is clearly the aesthetic focus of an otherwise unremarkable beige rectangle. The ramp is centered, flanked by two staircases. Sheep to the right, goats to the left, Pastor Robinson front and center.

Inside, the accommodations continue. The center aisle seems particularly wide, and there are gently sloping ramps on either side of the nave. In contrast to the blah beige outside, the woodwork is dark, the lighting dim. This is Davey's church in every sense. Davey's fiefdom. Pastors are prohibited from endorsing candidates, but they are instrumental in getting out the vote and they have ways to indicate which candidates they favor. Lu did not ask to appear here during her campaign because she could not align herself with some- one as conservative as Davey. But nor could she afford to alienate him. Davey may not have been able to stop marriage equality, but he was part of a coalition that helped derail the legislation the first

time it came before the Maryland legislature a few years ago. Safe
on the sidelines then, Lu was fascinated by the debate, the anger
expressed over the idea that gay marriage was a civil rights issue.
Davey, in particular, was one of those who framed race as a given,
homosexuality a choice. He was never strident; that wasn't his style.
He still had that husky, resonant voice that made you want to lean
in, lest you miss a single word.

Davey has been a public figure for almost a decade. Lu remembers when the church was built, not quite five years ago. Because it was a so-called megachurch—almost thirty-five hundred
members—the community worried about the impact on traffic.
There were contentious meetings, Davey presiding as the benign
Buddha he has become in middle age. He managed to suggest,
subtly, that it was not the *number* of people that had the residents
worried, but the color of his congregants' skin. The locals were
horrified, of course. An agreement was reached quickly. Since
then, as far as Lu knows, the church and the nearby residents have
coexisted peacefully, except for an incident three years ago when a
sixty-six-year-old man got on his riding mower and began ramming
cars leaving the church after Sunday's service. No charges were
filed, and Lu supported that one bit of inaction on Fred's part. The
man was in the early stages of dementia, beyond any agenda other
than his own confusion. Fred made it clear that his office would
not bring charges if the man's wife and adult children agreed to
find care for him.

"May I help you?"

A woman has entered the church from behind the nave. She is
young and shapely, dressed so stylishly that Lu can't help feeling like
a dowdy little bird. *Would I dress in bright, tight clothing if I weren't a
public official?* Lu has been a civil servant for so long—civil *servant*,
her mind snags for a moment on that second word—that she no

longer knows if she's following the dictates of her taste or the dictates of the job. You lose a little bit of yourself in public life.

"I'm here to see Davey Robinson."

"Is *Pastor* Robinson expecting you?"

"Yes." Lu had not wanted to visit without some warning. She delayed the meeting for one reason or another—work, the tax-filing deadline. Finally, she called yesterday, said she wanted to talk to him about the events of 1980. Those were her exact words. "The events of 1980." She chose 1980 and not 1979 because Davey would assume she meant the night he was attacked. But, of course, everything goes back to 1979. Citing 1980 was simply less adversarial.

"Follow me," the woman says, moving quickly on her long legs, admirably swift in her stiletto heels. Lu feels ridiculous, trying to match the woman's stride without appearing like a clumsy little puppy. She's pretty sure that's the point.

Davey's office does nothing to diminish Lu's first impression, that this church is a castle he has built for himself. His desk is huge. Across from him, she feels like a child, called to the principal's office, not that Lu was ever called to the principal's office as a child. She has to perch on the edge of the chair so her feet are flat on the floor. She is Gulliver among the Brobdingnagians, dwarfed by the scale of everything here. And Davey is larger than ever, broad in his chair. She wonders how hard it was for him, an athlete gifted enough to be considered for a college team, to adapt to a body that could no longer move as it once had. But he has spent almost twice as long in this body as he did in his previous one.

"Look at Little Lu," he says. His tone is affectionate, so she tries not to bristle at the use of "little." "Who knew you were going to grow up to be such a player, the most powerful woman in the county right now?" *But not as powerful as you, right, Davey?* "I read about what happened earlier this month."

He almost certainly means the attack, and Lu would feel sanctimonious, telling him that Rudy's suicide has affected her far more than the assault.

She says only: "I'm fine. But something, well, weird has come up, in the wake of that. I have reason to believe that Rudy Drysdale intended to kill someone else, that he broke into the wrong woman's apartment that night."

Davey cocks his head as if interested, but confused. *Why am I listening to this story?*

Lu takes a deep breath. "He had a kind of dyslexia that resulted in spatial confusion, literally couldn't tell right from left. If the events of December thirty-first were premeditated, then he might have entered the wrong apartment. The woman who lived across from the victim was Nita Flood. She thinks Rudy was sent to kill her, but she won't tell me by whom."

Davey's eyes narrow, all friendliness gone. It was a fake friendliness to begin with, Lu realizes. He may have hoped this was not to be the topic today, but he's not particularly surprised.

"What are you suggesting?"

"I'm not suggesting anything. But when I spoke to Nita—Jonnie, she's known as Jonnie now—she still maintains, after all these years, that you raped her." Quickly adding: "I know that's not true. If you had, you would have been charged. My father did everything he could to make sure that no one was given special treatment. But *she* believes this to be true. Or has come to believe it. It's probably sheer revisionism on her part, thirty-five years later. But if she had threatened to go public—"

"Thou shalt not kill," Davey says. "I'm a minister, Lu. I preach the Lord's words. Do you think I could so easily violate one of his most basic commandments?"

The fact is—she can't. The moment she began to speak, she

felt ludicrous. "No, no, I don't. But I do believe that Rudy Drysdale targeted her and I can't figure out why."

"He always liked her," Davey says. "She barely paid him any mind, but he had a crush on her."

"You *knew* him?"

"Just to nod hello. He worked in the camera store in the mall, the one near Nita's cart. He was always hanging around her, doing things for her. I noticed because I would hang around, when I could. I'm not even sure she knew his name. I used to tease her about Rudy. I sure as hell wasn't jealous of him. I was surprised when I read about him being arrested, but—well, he seemed to be pretty far around the bend. He was always an odd duck. Some people thought he didn't like girls at all, but I never got that vibe from him. He definitely liked Nita."

She feels almost deflated by the banality of it all. Man sees woman he once had a crush on, breaks into her house—believes himself to have broken into her house—ends up killing the wrong woman in sheer panic. That could even explain the DNA: he became excited, in advance. Rudy was a violent man. He stabbed his father. He attacked her. It fits together. Never disdain the obvious answer. That's an article of faith for police and prosecutors. The defense attorneys are the ones who have to manufacture conspiracy theories and alibis and alternative killers. Even before Facebook, people were inclined to look up old crushes. Rudy Drysdale, a deeply disturbed individual, saw his old high school crush and decided to kill her. Or something. It's not as if he were known for making rational decisions.

Davey laughs softly, as if privy to her whirring mind. "Not so mysterious now, is it? If I had known—but, of course, I didn't know. Well, I guess Nita was due some good luck."

"Due?"

"I hear she has a sick grandchild."

"Hear? How did you 'hear'?"

"It was on some listserv, I think. The Howard County Interfaith community. The girl needs an experimental treatment, but the insurance company won't cover it. Her pastor said they were going to do a fund-raiser, donate the Sunday collections to her."

"I remember when you thought 'interfaith' was Columbia's problem."

Davey laughed, a rumble almost as beautiful as his singing voice. Does he still sing? "This is just an e-mail digest that allows various religious leaders to share our concerns. My problem with the Interfaith Center was that it pretended we were all the same."

"Nita goes by the name Jonnie Forke now."

"Does she?" Polite, uninterested. Not getting it.

Lu stands to go. "I feel silly to have bothered you. Davey—do you still sing?"

"I sing with my congregation. But, no, I don't perform. It appealed too much to my vanity. We have to be careful of our weaknesses, Lu. I was so proud of my body, the things it could do. We know how that turned out."

"Do we?" Lu asks.

"What?"

"Nothing."

———

Andi is almost pathetically grateful when Lu asks her if she wants to catch a late bite, although surprised by the suggested location.

"The casino?" she says. "Why would you want to go there?"

"I just have this yen to play a few hands of blackjack, have a few drinks. All work and no play—"

Andi does not bother to assure Lu she isn't dull. She's too con-

cerned with nailing down which one of them will be the designated
driver.

"We have to be careful. Wouldn't look good if one of us were
flagged at a sobriety checkpoint."

"I'm happy to pick you up at your place. And if you get lucky—"

"I'm not that kind of girl," Andi says, feigning mock outrage. "I'm
a *lady*."

"The kind of lady who takes his number and calls him the next
day."

"As I said, a lady." Lu laughs. Outside of work, Andi can be good
company.

And, for an evening that began as a ruse, it is surprisingly fun.
Lu sets her limit for losing at $200 and blows through it even faster
than she hoped. Andi is having an unusually good night—winning
hands and winning the attention of a perfectly nice looking man in
a suit. She barely seems to notice when Lu says she's going to grab a
bite in the noodle bar.

Jonnie Forke does a double take when she sees Lu, tries to disguise it.

"I'm not your waitress," she says. "I'll tell someone you're waiting."

"Jonnie Forke of Luk Fu," Lu says. "Unlucky Jonnie Forke of
Luk Fu."

"What?"

"It's this thing I do. It helps me remember names, faces. I'm sorry
to hear about your grandchild—what was her name? Joni Rose. I
didn't realize—the other day when we were talking—that she was
sick. That sucks."

She shrugs. "Yeah, well, what are you going to do?"

"It's good, at a time like this, to have the comfort of religion. I'm
not a believer, and it makes it harder to get through certain things."

"I don't go to church. Your waitress will be with you in a moment. But I'll put your drink order in if you're anxious."

"Just club soda with lime. But I can wait."

Andi and her new friend join Lu then, flush with possibility if not actual cash. "I'd say winner buys," Andi says, "but then we'd have to kite the check and how would that look if two prosecutors walked out on a bill? This guy was up five hundred dollars, then totally blew his wad."

"You two good-looking ladies could not possibly be prosecutors, unless you play them on *Law & Order*," says Andi's admirer, who close up is about ten years north of fifty, where Lu had originally pegged him. Still, he has all his hair.

"Dinner's on me," Lu says, putting down two $100 bills. "Andi— you use Uber or call a car service when it's time to go home. *Promise* me. We have a meeting tomorrow morning, you can't be late."

"She'll be fine," Andi's new friend says, sounding like the perfect gentleman. Lu sizes him up, then says: "Text me when you get in, Andi. I won't sleep a wink until you do."

Of course, she's not going to sleep anyway. She had been skeptical, when talking to Davey—he spoke of Nita, not Jonnie Forke. But if she didn't go to church, then she had no pastor to share the story about her sick grandchild on a listserv. Davey was lying about that, Lu is sure.

In her car, Lu instructs the Bluetooth panel: "Call my brother, please." She cannot break the habit of saying "please," even to the nonperson who lives inside her car's dashboard. She is her father's daughter.

AJ's voice, on another machine, replied: "Hi, you have reached AJ Brant. I will be traveling until May twenty-fourth and may be slow returning calls. But leave a message or e-mail me in care of the foundation and I'll—"

She disconnects. A sister shouldn't have to queue on a brother's answering machine, another supplicant yearning for his time, money, attention. How can he be away for a month? Oh, it's almost Earth Day, a big date in AJ's world. No problem. May twenty-fourth is the Sunday of Memorial Day weekend. They'll have a barbecue. She'll buy vegan hot dogs for Lauranne if that's what it takes to get a little time alone with her brother in order to broach the unbroachable subject, that Friday night after Thanksgiving 1979. Did he lie to protect his friend? Would he continue to lie to protect his friend?

The bigger question for Lu is whether she will be speaking as a sister, or the county state's attorney.

MAY 25

"I guess this day is for you, dear Father."

AJ raises a beer—a local one that he brought to the barbecue, presumably brewed from ethical hops. Whatever those are. But their father shakes his head. "Memorial Day is for those who died. I merely served. You can toast me in November."

"Of course," AJ says. "Of course. My bad. It's not like I wish you were dead."

He seems a little loopy to Lu, but it's probably jet-lag. AJ was at the Sydney Writers Festival and he arrived at BWI only yesterday afternoon. Although his memoir about his wanderjahr is several years old, it was a bit of a sleeper hit in Australia and a big publisher there has just brought out a new edition, with an introduction by some hot-shit novelist that Lu has never heard of and a new afterword by AJ *and* Lauranne, all about how individuals matter, small changes, blah, blah, blah.

Lu scrapes the leftover baked beans and corn from her plate into the trash and endures two withering glances from Lauranne— one for the paper plate, the other for the lack of composting. She glares back, unhappy they are dining on the screen porch. The day is shockingly hot, a misery, especially coming as it does after two perfectly pleasant spring days. But AJ and Lauranne said they preferred to be outside in "real air," and they were the "guests," so the family has congregated here. At least her father had the good sense to install ceiling fans on the porch. And the twins keep leaving the porch doors open, so the house's downstairs AC unit—one of three required to cool the house—whirrs and groans, sending puffs of cool air toward them. Lu is simultaneously grateful for every artificial breeze and despairing of the utility bill. She keeps thinking the heat will back off when the sun goes down, that the planet has simply not absorbed enough of the sun's warmth to torture them into the evening. But, so far, there is no respite.

There is, however, that deeply layered fecund smell of the suburbs. The light grassy scent of lawns, the darker fragrances from the trees. Lu may want to believe she's a city person, but she is, at heart, a child of the suburbs, a child of *this* suburb, and she can't live without yards and trees and flowers. Their first two years as a married couple, she and Gabe had lived in the treeless yuppie playground that was Federal Hill in the 1990s and she was secretly miserable, then ashamed of herself for being miserable. But she missed these smells.

"You want to take a walk with me?" she asks AJ, as the sun—finally—begins to set. "Around the lake?"

"I'm sooooooo tired, Lu. I'm still on Australian time. My body's living in tomorrow."

"That's the price of being a visionary," she jokes. Then, in a lower tone of voice: "*Please.* I want to hear about the status of your, um, project. The one we discussed all those months ago."

A lie, but it will take at least forty-five minutes to stroll around the lake in this heat. She figures that they will have exhausted the topic of AJ's fatherhood by the time they reach the dam—only yards away from the events of Graduation Night 1980.

It turns out that AJ doesn't want to talk about fatherhood or IVF or rented wombs. He is full of Australia, practically a travelogue on the topic, and a pedantic one at that. "As we head into summer, Australia is on the cusp of winter . . ." *Oh, really, dear brother is that how the Southern Hemisphere works?* He speaks of how expensive it is, pontificates on its island-country-continent status, praises its food, its sense of ecological responsibility, its rich cultural life.

"The primary cultural export I remember from Australia is the Wiggles," Lu says. "Although they were fading by the time the twins were born. The Wiggles and Mel Gibson. And now there's a new Mad Max movie. Nothing ever changes—until it does. What's happening with your baby plans?"

"Not much. We thought we had a surrogate, but it didn't work out. Ridiculous falling-out over the silliest thing. I don't know. She didn't like us, that's the bottom line."

Oh, so she met Lauranne, then? But Lu holds her tongue.

"I saw Davey Robinson the other day," she says.

"Where?"

"At his church. I went to see him. Something very weird came up." She fills AJ in, as briskly and neutrally as possible. Somehow, she knows he will argue with her. And he does.

"Life is full of coincidences, Lu. For all you know, Fred could just be fucking with you."

"True. But Davey lied to me. He told me that Nita's pastor shared information about her sick grandchild. She—Nita, Jonnie as she's known now—doesn't even have a pastor. I think she tried to shake Davey down last fall, threatened to go public with the story of the events of Thanksgiving 1979, and he did whatever was necessary to keep that from happening. It's the only thing that makes sense."

"It makes sense because *you've* decided to link these facts. Rudy Drysdale killed a woman. That woman lived across the hall from

Nita Flood. His intended victim might have been Nita Flood. It might not have been. You're imposing a pattern on events because that's what our minds are trained to do. Nita didn't tell you anything. Davey didn't tell you anything. Rudy is dead."

"Davey told me that Rudy had a crush on Nita, in high school."

"Have you talked to Dad about this, Lu?"

"No."

"I didn't think so. Because he'd tear you apart for this kind of shabby thinking. Heck, it almost sounds as if you're Rudy's defense attorney. *He did it. He had cause. He didn't have cause. He was hired.* I mean, what is it? Pick one."

"I think Davey hired Rudy to kill Nita Flood."

"As you said, they barely knew each other."

"His church does a brown-bag giveaway. Every Sunday in North Laurel."

They are nearing the grove of trees where Ben Flood died. Lu wouldn't be surprised if AJ decided to pick up the pace, but he slows down, takes in his surroundings. "Things are supposed to get smaller as you get older. But the trees get bigger. Our family home is literally bigger. Everything about our family just gets bigger and bigger. I tried to make my life simpler, and it's more complicated than ever."

"Have you even been here, since—"

He stares at the trees, gray green in the dusk. "I don't really remember any of it. I remember the story, but not the actual event. Does that make sense? I had to tell it so many times, it's like something I read in a book. I hate that Ben Flood died that night. But it wasn't my fault."

"I know." Lu touches his arm, the one he broke, the one that never quite hangs straight, although he says his years of yoga have helped him regain almost all his flexibility.

"Except—I ran after him. I tackled him—or tried to. I barely grazed his calves with my hand before I fell on the rocks and broke my arm. But he turned—he turned his head to look at me. I'm seeing it now, Lu. I don't want to see it. It took me so long to stop seeing it—"

"Let's keep walking."

It seems cruel now to keep talking about Nita and Davey. They walk another ten minutes in silence. They reach the halfway point, the spot from where they can see their own house across the water, full of light.

"Damn, it really is huge," AJ says.

"Good thing he bought a double lot all those years ago. AJ—did our mother like the house?"

"I thought so. I mean, when you're eight, you can't really tell if your parents are happy or sad. But I think she liked it. Why do you ask?"

"I don't know. It seems so very much *his* dream house now, tailored to his tastes."

"Three massive HVAC units," AJ says. "That's quite a carbon footprint you're leaving."

"Says the man who just flew to Australia, the man with three rowhouses, disguised to look as if he lives in just one."

"We try never to use the AC."

This is true, Lu knows. It's why they don't visit her brother June through August.

"Was she sad? Our mother?"

"Lu, she was very ill."

"I know, I know—the heart thing."

He is rubbing his left arm now. A long plane trip has probably aggravated the stiffness there. "No, Lu. She was mentally ill. She was a depressive. I'm sorry. I assumed that dad had finally told you everything."

She stops on the path. "What 'everything'?"

"I always promised—and I thought by now he would have—look, you have to talk to him. He has to tell you the rest. Because there are questions only he can answer."

Hadn't AJ said the same thing about sex almost forty years ago? *There are questions only he can answer.* Lu was eight and still trying to piece together what really happened when babies were made. But it turned out there were a lot of questions their father could not, would not answer. Most particularly—Why would anyone do that? "Well, we have to have babies," her father said then. And she knew, the way children always know when they are being lied to, that he was withholding something important. That's why she had ended up talking to Teensy about the whole messy affair.

But had she really never guessed that their mother's sadness, which now seems obvious in every anecdote she knows about her, was something more than mere moodiness? That Adele's parents had guarded her not from the dragons outside their Roland Park castle, but from demons within? Lu cannot wait to get home, send AJ and Lauranne back to Baltimore with the leftover cherry pie, deposit the children in their beds, and confront her father. She wishes she could leave her brother standing here, plunge into the lake, and swim a straight hard line toward the large, light-filled house on the other side.

But life doesn't work that way when one is an adult. There are Penelope and Justin, who need to go to bed at a decent hour because there's school tomorrow, a kitchen to clean. Life goes on. Life is relentless. And when the house is finally quiet, Lu discovers her father dozing in his usual chair. She cannot bear to wake him, much less start peppering him with questions.

Instead, she goes to his desk, the planter's desk that Noel broke all those years ago, scattering her father's papers, and finds the slender file that loomed so large in her imagination, one that she used to sneak peeks at when she was a child. It is a plain manila envelope with her mother's name on it. There are photos, a birth certificate, a marriage certificate.

A death certificate, too, which Lu doesn't remember ever seeing in this envelope before.

Maybe that's because it's dated 1985.

"Nineteen eighty-five," Lu says, not for the first time, waving the death certificate as if it were an exhibit in a trial. She is standing over her father, who sits at their dining room table, his eyes downcast, but his demeanor defiant. "She lived for fifteen years after I was born. How could you keep this from me?"

She has called work and said she will be late because of an "urgent family situation" and were truer words ever spoken? The *situation* goes to the heart of her family, and if the *situation* doesn't seem urgent to anyone else—her mother has been dead for thirty years, her father has been lying to her for forty-five—she cannot imagine doing anything until she has this conversation. It took great resolve last night not to shake her father awake and demand to speak to him then and there. She has not slept at all, and she snapped at the twins throughout the morning routine, then snapped at their babysitter for being all of five minutes late.

And yet her father, the true object of her wrath, is unrepentant, even if he cannot meet her gaze.

"Lu, you were never going to have a mother. Adele was not capable of taking care of anyone, including herself. She wasn't fit to live outside an institution."

"But to lie to your children and say that she was dead—"

"She was, in a sense. She attempted suicide several times. In 1985, she managed to slit her wrists with a knife she conned a staff person to smuggle in. If you want to berate me for something, then focus on the eight years that I lived in denial of the fact that my wife was severely mentally ill, the terror that her disorder visited on your brother. The day after you were born, she had a full-blown psychotic episode and attempted to kill herself for the fourth or fifth time. She was admitted to the psychiatric wing at Johns Hopkins. And, as far as I knew, she was to spend the rest of her life there. I tried to visit her once or twice, but she was truly a hopeless case. It did no good. For either of us."

"But—the death certificate says she died in Spring Grove? How did she end up there?" Spring Grove was the state psychiatric hospital in Catonsville. Her mother had been perhaps ten miles from her family through much of Lu's childhood.

"I don't know. I gave your grandparents power of attorney. They were responsible for her care."

"They blackmailed you," says Lu. True, she has blackmail on the brain, but that doesn't mean she's wrong. Her father was and is a circumspect man. He would have agreed to any condition if it meant keeping this secret.

"It was never that—coarse. But we did reach an agreement. They would keep her in the hospital if they could have power of attorney. They were wealthy people, better able to care for her than I was. Our insurance was running out—And, as far as I knew, she was being cared for. I think she may have been switched to Spring Grove after their deaths. I don't know."

"Why did you tell AJ and not me?"

"I didn't. He also thought she was dead. Then he became very depressed while at college. I thought I owed it to him to know about the family history. The children of suicides are so much more likely to commit suicide."

"Only she didn't succeed until AJ was a year out of college," Lu points out. "And she was—what was her diagnosis?"

"When she was first diagnosed, in her teens, they said it was schizophrenia. I've come to believe it was probably what we'd call bipolar disorder now. She had stunning mood swings, but she also was delusional at times. We had no hope that she could ever live outside a hospital setting. She was beset by paranoia, incapable of recognizing those who loved her and cared for her. You have to remember, Lu. Your brother knew her, lived with her for eight years. Eight fraught, difficult years. I owed him the truth because it helped him make sense of his childhood."

Isolated events are connecting in Lu's memory. This is why AJ was worried about having a child. It's why he didn't want to use his own sperm. And it was why her father and brother didn't seem overly concerned when she had to have a hysterectomy in her late twenties. To their way of thinking, she dodged a bullet.

"What about me? Why wasn't I owed the truth?"

"I suppose you were."

His ready agreement deflates her. Nothing defangs a good rage quite like the other person admitting that you've been wronged. "I rationalized, as people do. One, you never knew her. Why not let you have a mother you could mourn. Two—I didn't sense any of that melancholy in you. You're tough, grounded, my little pragmatist. But as AJ got older, he was prone to depression. He was in a very dark place for a while there, during college. I kept it from you at the time, but he almost dropped out of Yale freshman year. So I told him everything—that his mother was still alive, but quite ill. When she finally killed herself five years later, I wondered if I had made the right choice after all."

"Did you ask AJ not to tell me?"

"No. I told him only that I preferred to share the story with you when the time seemed right, and he agreed. Then I kept putting it off."

All the family legends are unraveling in her head. What was true? Fact: Her mother was beautiful; Lu has seen the pictures. Fact: Her mother died. Everything else is now up for review. She thinks about her mother in this very house, her alleged hatred of light, which now streams into their home from all angles. Who was Adele Closter Brant?

"Did she ever hold me?" Lu asks her father. "Even once?"

"I'm sure she must have," he says. His words are less than persuasive.

Fifteen years. Her mother lived for fifteen years after Lu was born. Yet—she was not inclined to be Lu's mother. Her father gave his children a myth in place of a parent. Two different myths. For young AJ, the story, eventually, was that the woman who had become increasingly unreliable around him had gone into a hospital and never come home. For Lu, it was even simpler. *This beautiful woman gave birth to you and now she's gone.* If this is grief, it's an odd kind of grief, mourning the loss of a lie, the end of a fantasy. Lu might as well cry for Santa Claus, the Easter Bunny, and the Tooth Fairy.

She wondered if AJ ever confided in Noel. The boy with the absent father had zeroed in on their missing mother that very first day. *Norma Talmadge,* he had said right before he broke the desk. *Where is she buried?* What had come between Noel and AJ? *He stopped talking to me,* AJ said at his funeral. Did the others know what happened?

But Lu has no more time for her family's mysteries. Work calls, literally. Della is trying to put out any number of fires, and Lu needs to be there, *now*. She goes to get dressed, frustrated. Her father's apology was too ready, too easily given. He doesn't believe he was in the wrong. She's glad she knows, but it makes her feel odd about her father. Lots of people like to proclaim melodramatically that so-and-so is dead to them. Her father carried through, killing loved ones who became problematic. First he cut his ties to his own parents, then his wife, his in-laws. Why did he find it preferable to end relationships so definitively? What would happen if Lu or AJ ever disappointed him profoundly?

The revelations about her mother blindside Lu, throw a long shadow over a scorching, relentless June that, after a brief retreat into jacket weather, doubles down on heat and humidity. *These are vicious days,* Lu thinks, *in every sense.* Baltimore is experiencing homicide numbers that haven't been seen since the early days of the crack epidemic. Even Howard County's homicides for 2015 double—to two.

Lu decides, after much back-and-forth, to take the new case, but only because she doesn't want anyone to think she is gun-shy after the Rudy "incident." This one is a domestic, a term she hates. *Domestic violence* may not be an oxymoron exactly, but the term mitigates murder, as if death at the hands of a former loved one is gentler. It's hard to imagine a stranger doing something worse to this woman: her ex-husband, returning their nine-month-old after his weekend visit, shot the baby's mother in the forehead when she asked for her support check. He now claims he was driven to the act by her divorce attorney's demands. The case against him is so easy that Lu worries it is beneath her, a dunker she ought to hand off to Andi or another deputy. She would be happy to plead it out. Ah, but a man who has the ego to think he can end a person's life because he doesn't like the terms of their divorce also has the ego to demand "my day in court." This phrase, *my day in court*, comes up so often that Lu feels as if she's dealing with a demented bride. *My day, my day, my day, my day.* He believes that he is the wronged party, that all he needs is a venue to tell his story and everyone will agree he had no choice. Okay, sir, you shall have your day. In fact you might have as many as four days in court and then you will have many, many, many days in prison to think about your *day*.

At least the case offers a distraction, something on which to focus. Something to think about other than her mother, alive in a hospital one county over for fifteen years. Fifteen years. Fifteen years. It's a dirge that plays in her head.

Lu's father and the twins don't even seem to notice the undercurrent of sadness in her, whereas AJ is unusually affectionate. He calls constantly, no matter where his travels take him. He has called almost every day since he has directed her toward this discovery. He has apologized over and over again for not telling her as soon as he knew, back in college. He also has apologized for telling her at all. According to AJ, whatever he did would have been the wrong thing at the wrong time.

"I don't know why it came out then, when we were walking," he says at one point. "I guess I was—overwhelmed."

"Heck, AJ, it was probably jet lag more than anything else. You were loopy."

She's glad he told her. And she can't decide what she thinks her father should have done. Obviously, she couldn't be told when it happened. She was a newborn. At what age would she have been able to absorb the information? And what could her father have told her that wasn't a lie? She is not a stranger to such issues: there are articles and books written for parents such as herself who have to explain the facts of life to their children, then explain why those facts don't apply to them. When the twins were five, she began to drop hints: "You know, you weren't in Mama's belly." How they laughed, thinking her droll. *Of course they were in her belly.* Then, last year, when they asked where babies came from, she had given them the full information, adding that they had been in another woman's belly.

"So we had a different mama?"

"No," she said. "I was always your mama. But my body couldn't make a baby, so we found someone to help us."

So far, this version has satisfied them. But the books warn to expect flare-ups later. They may ask to meet their surrogate. (They have met her, in fact, and would see her more often if she lived nearby. They know her as Miss Michelle.) If they want to meet the donor—well, good luck with that. All Lu knows about her is that she looked a lot like Adele Closter Brant, because Lu chose a light-eyed, dark-haired donor who had more in common with AJ than her. No matter—the kids came out looking like miniature Gabes. Dark hair, dark eyes, olive skin.

Because AJ is being so kind and big brotherly, Lu finds herself feeling solicitous of him. It's obvious to her why he told her when he did. The trauma of standing there, near the site where Ben Flood died, probably kicked up some tough memories and those were a springboard to his memories of their mother. They are not, he has finally admitted, memories to envy. "I mean she loved me—loved us—but it was impossible to know what mom you were going to get. It was like I had three moms. There was sweet mom, mean mom and sick mom."

Sweet mom read him books and played games with him, delighting in make-believe. She sang songs—AJ's voice is her legacy. Sick mom shut herself in her room for days at a time, sobbing and refusing to come out.

"Mean mom," AJ said, "told me that I had ruined her life, that she wished I had never been born."

"Oh, lots of mothers say that," Lu assured him, knowing it was a lie. She hoped, more than ever, that AJ would become a father. Motherless, Lu had no one to teach her how to be a mother and she thought, in the main, that she was a good one. AJ would be a good dad, and that would make him see that his mother's legacy was not a damaging one.

───────────

On the last Saturday morning in June, Lu is amazed by a fleeting thought: *I'm happy*. It's a beautiful day, hot but not wretchedly humid, the sky so blue and bright that the world feels as if it's in a picture frame. Penelope has an all-day swim date with another family, a family generous enough to drop Justin at his sailing camp. (Lu tries to separate them, to the extent that they will allow themselves to be separated.) Her father has gone for his morning walk around the lake. She has a moment alone in the house, something that almost never happens. The silence is delicious. She makes a second cup of coffee in her father's high-tech espresso machine, froths some milk. Lu notices, as she often does, that the kitchen now bears no resemblance to the original—every footprint has changed—but the sink still faces a window in the side yard. She looks into the lilac bush, its blossoms long past, and remembers the day she and AJ saw a pair of green eyes in there, staring back.

Impulsively, she picks up the phone and calls her brother, wanting him to hear that her voice is lighter, happier, than it has been in weeks.

Wonderfully, his is, too. "Lu!"

"Where are you?" she asks.

"In Italy," he says. "Just finishing lunch before I go tour this bio-dynamic vineyard."

"Nice life," Lu says, ungrudging. If AJ and Lauranne go ahead and have kids, things will be less freewheeling. Yet he might be happier. That's the paradox. Life is harder with kids, yet somehow better.

"Well, we can't all spend summer in Columbia, Maryland."

"You know what I was thinking of just now? Noel, the day we met him. And I've always wondered—what came between the two of you? Why did you stop talking to each other?"

"Oh, Lu, it was so long ago. I'm not sure exactly what happened. Noel was a drama queen. He got mad at me, I got mad at him for being mad at me. He got madder at me for being mad at him for being mad at me. Frankly, I always thought he was a little in love with me and that was a problem. Because I was never going to have those feelings for Noel. Never." AJ sighs, less happy now, and she feels a twinge of guilt. "I don't want to talk about Noel. It hurts. I regret so much not going to see him when he was sick. But I was scared."

"Of contracting HIV?"

He pauses for so long she begins to think the connection is lost. "Yes," he says at last. "It was early days, Lu. No one knew anything. I'm ashamed to say that, but it's true." He yawns. Loudly, showily. "I'm going to need a nap. Lunch was amazing. You cannot believe the food here. You should come here. Let's do it as a family next summer. I'll book a villa for a month."

"I'm a public servant, AJ. I don't get to go to Italy for a month. I'll spend one week in Rehoboth this August and I'll be tethered to my e-mail. I used to think Dad was mean, never taking us anywhere. Now I get it."

Another showy yawn. "It's just so *beautiful*. It makes you wonder—what are we doing, running, running, running, working,

working, working? Such busy little bees. Or ants. Whichever one works harder. I thought I simplified my life, but all I did was find another way to be busy, telling other people to simplify their lives. Why am I touring a biodynamic vineyard, except for the fact that I want to have material for a podcast? Or an op-ed for the *Times*? Then I can deduct my trip, as if I need to worry about tax deductions. Drinking wine, eating good food is reason enough to come to Italy. I had a lovely white wine at lunch. Vermentino. I have no fucking clue if it's biodynamic. But it made me happy."

"Sounds like you're working on a sequel."

"No," he says adamantly. "No more polemics disguised as memoirs. Or memoirs disguised as polemics. I've said everything I have to say. I'm going to learn to *be*."

"You sound really happy," she says.

"I think I am. I leave in two days. Can't miss Fourth of July with the family, fireworks over Kittamaqundi."

She hangs up, delighted AJ is finally learning to enjoy himself. Then, out loud in the kitchen, although no one is there to hear. "I do believe my big brother was a little tipsy just now. Good for him."

And if AJ can let loose—she calls a familiar number, one she has not used for many weeks, one whose messages she has ignored or fended off with pleas of busyness, another ant with her head down, working, working, working. Maybe she can't have Vermentino with lunch, but there are other earthly pleasures to pursue.

"Stay," Bash says.

"What?" They have been together for almost four hours and she has showered, dressed. In her mind, Lu is already on the road, going through her parallel tracks of to-do lists, work and home.

"It's a federal holiday. I know that even if my wife doesn't. And, yeah, I'm sure you have a ton of work to do, blah, blah, blah, but— c'mon. We'll get a pizza, have some wine. Or we could even go out for an early dinner. Bethesda has lots of good places. There's this one, with tacos and good tequila—"

"*No,*" she says. "Not out." Never out. The demarcation between here and everywhere else is thick, defined, never to be breached. She experiences Bash only inside, in rooms where no one else visits, with the exception of cleaning ladies who arrive long after they have gone.

"Then we'll have delivery. Or I'll go out and get something, bring it back, whatever you want. If you run back to your office, you're going to end up eating at your desk. Just *stay.*"

She is being lobbied by a lobbyist, one of the best. Still, it's worrisome, a reminder of that surprise visit to her Christmas open house. She thought they were safely past that. Really, a Bash who talks about pharmaceutical solutions to menopause is preferable to one who wants to take her to a restaurant.

"Something fast," she says. "Pizza."

They sit at the granite counter in the never-used kitchen, eating pizza straight from the box, drinking a ridiculously expensive red wine from water glasses. Lu studies the label, wonders if her father would like it. Good wine is a nice gift for the man who has everything, even if much of it is paid for by his daughter.

"I feel bad," Bash says. "About the last time I saw you."

Oh. "Oh. That's okay. I'm sensitive about any discussion of menopause because—" Still, she hesitates to tell him that she went through menopause after her hysterectomy. She feels it de-sexes her. "I guess all women are."

"No, not about that. I—I didn't even mention what happened to you. That crazy Rudy Drysdale jumping you in court that way."

Maybe it's the recent revelation about her mother, but the word *crazy* hits her ear hard.

"He really did have severe mental issues," she says, with frosty sanctimony. "You have to be pretty disturbed to do what he did."

"Oh, I know. Sorry. Force of habit."

"Habit?"

"That's what we called him in high school, Crazy Rudy. He was like our mascot for a while there. Always hanging around. Finally, he took the hint and left us alone."

Davey knew him, Lu reminds herself. But he said he saw him at the mall, hanging around Nita. And Davey was alone whenever he was with Nita Flood.

"A mascot—you mean, one of the teams you played on? Was he Willie the Wildcat?"

"No, he was always mooning over Davey and AJ. There was some party or something at Davey's house—I wasn't there, but I heard about it—and these guys embarrassed him, but Davey and AJ took up for him. End of sophomore year, junior year? We could not shake him after that. He was worse than you. He showed up everywhere. AJ and Davey were nice to him. I mean we all were. I think AJ finally had a talk with him. At any rate, he stopped hanging around."

"AJ said he didn't know him in high school. We discussed that when he was arrested." She is seeing a yearbook, the *Glass Hour*, a circle of lamplight. AJ pulled his own yearbook out that night, but remembered to put it back on the shelf. Why? He either knew Rudy or he didn't. Did he think a picture would jog his memory?

"Maybe AJ didn't remember him. I didn't, not right away. Then it clicked—and I was, like—oh, yeah, Crazy Rudy. I always thought he was harmless. But isn't that the cliché? Watch out for the quiet types."

The *Glass Hour*. The glass house. Lu tries to remember everything she can about that afternoon at the cast party—the humiliated boy who darted from that walk-out basement and into the woods behind the house, the trees that allowed the Robinsons to live in a house where their lives were on display. Where did he go? Everyone's attention had been focused on AJ and Davey, the nasty boys they had chased. No one thought to go looking for the boy they had taunted.

"Bash, was Rudy there that—that night Nita Flood crashed your party? The one at Davey's house, where everything . . . happened."

"*No.*" He seems irritated that they're still talking about this. "I told you, he followed us around, but we didn't invite him to stuff. That was just me, Davey, Noel, and AJ. We were the only ones."

"And Nita."

"She was shitfaced. Even then, I'm pretty sure she couldn't remember much."

"But not when she was with Davey. She got drunk playing the game, right?"

"Monopoly," Bash says promptly. Promptly. As if *prompted*.

"That's some memory you have," she says. "Monopoly, Rudy Drysdale."

"It's hit and miss. Like I said, I didn't remember Rudy, not right away. AJ probably forgot him, too."

"I have to go," she says, sliding down from the stool.

"Really? You've barely finished your one slice." He grabs her wrist. She looks at his hand circling her arm. His hand looks enormous. He's so much stronger than she is. Who isn't? If he decided to force her to stay, if he decided to force her to do anything, he could. And if she dared to complain or suggest his behavior criminal, what would he say? *You always liked it before. I've sent you home with bruises and you were fine with it. I thought it was what you wanted.*

She removes his hand. "I have to go. It's Friday. Teensy doesn't like to stay late on Fridays."

———

The highway is clogged despite the fact that the holiday weekend should be in full swing, everyone released from their obligations yesterday. Some of Lu's people tried to find a way to take Thursday off as well, but she put her foot down. Weekend creep has to end somewhere. She passes the exit to Columbia, continuing north another twenty miles. Teensy's not even working today. The twins are with their babysitter, Melissa, who is happy for a few extra hours.

Lu says grimly to her phone, via the dashboard: "Find funeral homes, Locust Point, Baltimore, MD." It takes a while, with the phone offering almost comic alternatives, but she is finally connected to Charles L. Stevens Funeral Home.

"Hi, I'm calling about the funeral costs for Rudy Drysdale, whose wake and burial you arranged back in April. I'm his cousin and the family never received the invoice. Could you tell me if it was sent and what address you used?"

Sure enough, the bill went to the very address toward which she is speeding.

––––––––––

"Lu," AJ says, opening his door to her, the center one. Door number 2, as Lu thinks of it. The other two doors are nonfunctional, one bright blue, the other bright red, their street addresses still visible, all part of AJ's attempt to disguise his wealth. His attempt to disguise who he really is.

He's not surprised to see her on his doorstep, unannounced. She wishes he were.

"Is Lauranne here?" she asks.

"She's teaching a hot yoga class at Charm City's Midtown location," he says. "She'll be home about six or so." Then: "Do you want to stay for dinner?"

She doesn't and doubts that he will want her to, in the end. But all she says is: "If things aren't too crazy at home. Melissa's with the kids."

"I'm sure, Dad can—"

"AJ, why did you lie to me about not knowing Rudy Drysdale?"

He doesn't answer right away. He walks to the kitchen, Lu on his heels; he gets a bottle of wine from his retro refrigerator, a bulbous thing in orange, the kind of appliance that looks cheekily affordable, but costs a lot.

"I brought five bottles of this back from Italy," he says. "I wish I could have imported cases of it. Costs maybe six dollars a bottle and it's just the perfect summer wine. Want a glass?"

"No, thanks."

"I'll bring the rest tomorrow, for the party. Have to fight these hoarding instincts." He is in no hurry to have this conversation. He pours himself a glass of wine, fixes a plate with slices of cured meats and cheeses, despite Lu's assurances that she's not hungry. "Smuggled all this in. Don't tell Dad. You know he's a stickler. I guess I shouldn't tell you, either, officer of the court."

"Not my jurisdiction," Lu says. "However, Rudy Drysdale was."

"Let's sit by the pool," he says. "It's nice in the shade."

"Nice" is a bit of a reach, but it's pleasant enough. AJ really does have a green thumb and the U-shaped courtyard is full of containers. Mostly plants and herbs, but there are some pots of impatiens.

"How much have you figured out?" he asks.

"Enough," Lu lies. Everyone knows the old canard that an attorney never asks a question to which she doesn't know the answer, but that's for court, after investigations, depositions, discovery. Right now, Lu doesn't have the luxury of knowing the answers. She has to bluff.

"But not everything," AJ surmises. "You can't. No one can. Only Rudy, and he's dead."

"You knew him in high school. You can't have forgotten him. Davey remembers him. Even Bash remembers him. He's the kid you were trying to protect, at the cast party. For months, he hung around you, tried to get in with your crowd. That's not someone you'd forget. Why would you lie about that?"

"He's a disturbed individual, Lu. I didn't want to be linked to him."

"Davey didn't have a problem admitting he knew him."

"Good for Davey."

"Of course, Davey didn't pay his funeral expenses." She decides to risk a guess. "Or his legal bills."

AJ nods. "You're a good investigator, Lu. The Drysdales don't even know who helped them out. I used an intermediary."

"Bash?"

"No, why would you think that? I mean, once a bag man, always a bag man, but I didn't want him involved. He had as much to lose as anyone, I guess, but I couldn't trust him either. And no one had more to lose than Rudy. It was his idea, he acted on his own, no one knew he would do anything like that. I wanted no part of it. *Settle down*, I told Rudy. It's just talk. No one's going to listen to her. No one's looking for you. But then Davey had to go and pay her. Worst thing you can do with a blackmailer. For one thing, it only convinced her that she was right, after all these years. Why would Davey pay her if he didn't rape her? Forget the statute of limitations—who wants to deal with this kind of scandal in midlife, when you've finally got things figured out. Who wants to be accountable for his seventeen-year-old self? Even Bash couldn't afford to have something like this being batted around. It's one of the few times I've been glad Noel is dead. He was spared this stupidity, at least."

His voice trails off. From somewhere in his house, a phone begins to ring. It rings twice, stops, goes to voice mail, presumably. Lu remembers another ringing phone, the black squat phone in their living room, how it rang and rang that winter their grandmother was trying to get through to them. Their father changed their home number, then AJ got a phone in his room. *Anything to keep the secrets at bay, right, Dad?* AJ had a phone in his room, and Lu was so jealous. He was on it all the time. All the time.

"You all talked that morning and agreed on a story. You worked out all the details about what you were going to say." *Right down to the board game you played.*

"Everything we said was true, so what was the harm in making sure we said the same thing? I was a lawyer's son. The key was to protect Davey. I knew what could happen if we opened the door to any doubt. Davey's future was hanging in the balance. She showed up, uninvited. She and Davey had a big loud argument in his room, but then they were quiet as anything. We did play a drinking game. She passed out, we put her in the Robinsons' bed to sleep it off, then Bash and Noel took her home. True, it was kind of chickenshit to leave her on the doorstep, but no one wanted to come into contact with her old man under the best of circumstances."

Lu's memory for faces and names isn't good. She's long been aware of that weakness and done what she can to correct it. She read somewhere that it's bullshit to say, *Oh, I don't remember names or faces.* But she tries. She knows she tries. What she does remember are stories, especially family ones. She could have recited every detail about the short life of Adele Closter Brant, as it was told to her. She can taste the Eskimo pie she ate the day they met Noel, remember the feel of the air on that June night she saw AJ sing in the Tree of Life chorus, count almost every freckle on Bash's back as he rose and fell on top of Lynne in Lu's childhood bed. She remembers that Thanksgiving weekend, her father pulling details out of AJ, telling him to stop toying with language about who was *invited,* who wasn't *invited.* And not two hours ago, Bash said of Rudy: *He wasn't invited.*

She says: "Rudy Drysdale was there. That night. How—"

AJ stands, walks to the edge of his pool. *A lap pool,* he defended to Lu when she mocked this expense by ascetic AJ. He and Lauranne needed to swim to counterbalance their vigorous yoga practices. If the kids of his Southwest Baltimore neighborhood ever learned about this hidden oasis, no one could stop them from scaling the fence behind the property. But as much as AJ had given to the community, he had walled off this part of himself. Walled off the pool, the sustainable lawn furniture. AJ didn't want the world to know what he had, what he desired.

"Not exactly," AJ says to his lap pool. "He offered Nita a ride home from work. Turns out that when he realized she was going to Davey's house, he parked his car up the street and sneaked around to the back. Isn't it ironic—I'm pretty sure it's irony, at any rate. Davey and I defended him, at that very house, from being a little Peeping Tom pervert, skulking around with his camera. And there he was, in the woods, watching *us*."

Lu feels as if she's approaching a woodland creature, something timid and prone to bolt. She lets him keep his back to her, doesn't move. "And what did he see, AJ?"

"What we *said*," he replies, irritably. "Davey and Nita, having sex. Willingly on her part, best he could tell. When Rudy got wind of the investigation, a week or two later, he was dying to be the hero, begged me to let him talk to the grand jury. He wanted to repay the favor. He said he owed Davey and me everything. I told him to cool it, that it was better to let things lie. Nita barely knew his name, did you know that? When asked who drove her to Davey's house, she always said: 'Some guy from the mall.' That's all Rudy was to her. Some guy from the mall."

Lu reaches for a piece of salami from AJ's platter, although she's not really hungry. The city sounds are so different from what she's used to. Traffic, a police siren in the distance, a helicopter whirring overhead. AJ glances up. "That's a police chopper," he says. "They're looking for someone. You learn to tell the difference, living here, between the police copters and the traffic ones. God, this year."

She is not going to be distracted by idle talk. "What else did Rudy see? That night. You could see everything from the back of that house, if the lights were on."

"I don't know, Lu. Four teenage boys, living the life he wished he could live, pitiable as that sounds. Funny, isn't it? Rudy got teased for being a 'faggot.' Yet Noel never did."

"Why not let him speak to the grand jury, then? What part of your rehearsed story was he going to contradict?"

"I told you, everything we said was the truth."

There it is again, the carefully parsed argument. *Everything we said*—what had gone unsaid? What had Rudy seen that AJ didn't want entered into the record?

"What parts are you leaving out? What did you leave out then? This is your sister, AJ, not the state's attorney. I need to know."

AJ's shoulders sag, weighed down by a secret that four boys, now three men, have carried for thirty-five years. "She passed out. During the game. We carried her upstairs to let her sleep it off. And we started giving Davey shit that she was his girlfriend. Because she was, you know, and that was embarrassing. Nita Flood wasn't supposed to be anyone's girlfriend. Davey got angry. He said he didn't care for her at all. He said he cared for her so little that we could all take turns, if we wanted. So—" He shrugs, his back still to her.

"You raped her," Lu says.

"I *didn't*. I went into the room and just—looked at her. I was still a virgin. I didn't want my first time to be like that. Noel made the same decision, although he pretended he made mad passionate love to her. That was his phrase, of course. What's that from? Some movie, I guess. 'Mad passionate love. Oh, yes, I made mad passionate love to her.' Later, he took it back and I told him I hadn't done anything either. He didn't believe me. I didn't believe him. That was what ended our friendship. Realizing that each of us thought the other was a liar. I thought Noel would have sex with her, just to see if he was gay. He thought I'd have sex with a dead-drunk girl because she would never know."

"What about Bash?" Lu asks, wishing that her interest was dispassionate, only a matter of fact-finding.

AJ turns back, able to face her now. "Oh, I'm sure Bash had

no compunction. He's a Neanderthal, Lu. He'd do it with a knot-hole."

She feels the urge to defend him, but maybe it's herself she wants to defend.

"Then she was raped that night. No matter what happened between her and Davey, even if you and Noel declined. She was raped. Bash raped her. Probably Davey, too, but I get why you didn't make that distinction."

"Yes, if the facts of that night were to be examined today, it was rape. But—that's not how people thought then, Lu. I'm sorry, but it's true. And remember, she wasn't saying anyone else had sex with her. She also was lying her head off, claiming Davey beat her up. Don't forget that part. *She* lied. We just left out the stuff that would have detracted from the lies she was telling to protect her rotten bastard of a father."

Only the lies didn't end with Nita. Where did the lies end?

"So last fall, Nita asked everyone for money. But only Davey paid up."

AJ kneels in front of Lu and clasps his hands around hers, as earnest and sincere a man as anyone Lu has ever known. "It was your election, you know. That and her granddaughter being sick. If it weren't for you running for office, Nita wouldn't have had any traction. She contacted Davey last fall, said she was going to 'make some noise' if we didn't pay her. Davey gave her a week's worth of collections from his church, but all that did was make her greedy. She started calling me. Over the years, I had kept tabs on Rudy. Well, truth be told, he kept tabs on me. As soon as I landed back in Baltimore, he started finding ways to make contact with me. It was like high school all over again, Rudy showing up on the fringes of events, watching me. I had to tell Rudy. He was involved, too."

"Why would Rudy care? Nita never knew what he saw. She didn't even know he was there. He wasn't going to be drawn into this."

The question clearly flummoxes AJ. Her brother, who makes a point of living without air-conditioning as much as possible, pops a sweat so sudden and noticeable that she wants to offer him one of Bash's magical pills for menopause. His eyes shift right and left—toward the perfect little lap pool, then back toward this trompe l'oeil of a house, designed to look like three discrete rowhouses from the front, revealing its true nature only from the back, behind this high fence, which protects him from not only the neighborhood kids' petty larcenies, but their prying eyes. What do people find when they spy on people who think no one can see them? What did Rudy see at Davey's house that night? Why would Rudy care what Nita decided to say? What did Rudy, of all people, have to lose? Rudy hid in the woods, watching other boys have fun, but he didn't participate. Rudy followed AJ's crowd around, keeping his distance. Watching, forever watching.

Like high school all over again, showing up on the fringes of events.

Lu sees her brother, studying a copse of trees on their Memorial Day walk, becoming overwhelmed. He becomes so overwhelmed that he tells her the secret of their mother, a story he was comfortable keeping for almost thirty-five years. She sees now that he was desperate to change the subject, end the conversations about Nita and Davey, shut down his inquisitive sister, who was at once so close and so far away from the truth.

"Graduation night," she says. "Rudy was there."

AJ nods, his expression a combination of misery and respect. His smart little sister has figured it all out.

"He was fast, Rudy was. I was chasing Ben and, all of a sudden, there was Rudy, passing me, catching up to Ben. I was trying to tackle Rudy when I fell and broke my arm. He killed Ben, Lu. In cold blood. That thing about Ben falling on his knife—that's not how it happened."

"But you were down, you didn't see, and the investigation cleared you—"

"The fix was in, Lu. As long as everyone thought it was Andrew Jackson Brant's boy who was the hero, no questions would be asked, no difficult questions about how the story didn't exactly match the evidence. I always told Rudy that it was better that way. Ben Flood had reason to attack Davey and me. I'd be forgiven for chasing him, for fighting him. Rudy wouldn't. It wasn't his fight. Again, he was always there, watching, wanting to 'repay' us. You know what? If I could live my whole life over again, I would just let those sad fucks from Glenelg High School have their fun with him and be done. I've paid a thousand times over for doing the right thing. I wasn't going to let Nita Flood punish me for something I didn't even do."

"You asked Rudy—"

"No. *No.* I told him what was happening. That's all."

"But, AJ, you had to know what he would do—I mean, the fact that you paid for his defense—"

"I knew he needed a good attorney who would plead him out to not criminally responsible. I chose Howard & Howard because it's one of the best law firms in the state. I couldn't know that Fred had landed there or that this stupid case would become some fucking battle between the two of you. Your stupid, stupid pride, Lu. Why couldn't you just settle?"

"*My* pride, AJ? You're going to blame this on my pride?"

He drops his head into his hands, still in a crouch before her. Some part of Lu's mind detaches, wonders at her brother's knees, his ability to hold this pose so long. "What are we going to do, sis? What are we going to do?"

She wraps her arms around his neck, an atypical display of filial affection. "It's a long weekend. Let's just get through it, and then we'll sift through all the implications of what you've told me come Monday, OK? Rudy is dead and if you tell me he acted on his own, without anyone encouraging him to go after Nita Flood, I have to believe you. Come to the house tomorrow, watch the fireworks, eat some barbecue. We don't have to solve it *now*."

"It's going to kill Dad. If any part of this comes out. He's always tried so hard to do the right thing. Even when he was wrong, he never knew it. Whatever he's had to live with, he's never been in doubt. Whereas I've lived my whole life, knowing I'm a fake and nothing I've done—nothing—can make up for that. When I told Rudy about Nita, I never dreamed—I guess I am Ajax the lesser."

"Shhh," she says "Shhh." She can't bear to know anymore.

———————

That night, about an hour after paramedics are called to AJ's home—there is a hideous comedy involving the address, with the EMTs trying to gain access through the wrong doors as Lauranne wails inside, not that it matters in the end—Lu and her father receive the courtesy of a personal visit from Mike Hunt, who has been informed by a detective he knows in the Southwestern District that AJ is dead. He waited until Lauranne went to bed, then apparently drank two more bottles of his nice Italian wine, chased it with a handful of pills, and walked into his own swimming pool, tying a metal drum of tomato plants to his ankle to ensure he could not change his mind.

Lu sees her father's knees buckle—the phrase makes sense to Lu for the first time, and the next image that comes to her mind, crazily, is one of the towers on 9/11, that seeming moment of hesitation as it swayed, then collapsed—and she realizes that her own pain and anger and sorrow will have to wait, possibly forever, certainly for the rest of her father's life.

She grabs him by his elbow, pilots him to a chair with Mike Hunt's help.

"Why?" Andrew Jackson Brant keeps asking. "Why?"

But that is the one thing she must never tell him.

MIGUEL DE CERVANTES IS CALLED TO THE INQUISITION, OR THE FINAL SHOE DROPS

My father became old overnight. Maybe he was old all along and I willed myself not to notice it. Other friends have told me that they watched their parents sail through their eighties, only to age suddenly at ninety, and my father was getting close to that milestone. At any rate, he is increasingly frail. He doesn't eat enough, subsists on cold cereal and bananas. He no longer walks around the lake. His hearing seems to be going, or maybe he just doesn't want to answer the questions put to him, simple as they are. His practice had been a charade for years, albeit a charade that seemed to keep him alert, active, happy. Now I barely trust him to drive a car to the grocery store. He has stopped reading books and it takes him much of a day to make his way through the *Beacon-Light,* slender as it is. The television is on almost all day. MSNBC and, much to my amusement, endless repeats of *Law & Order.* It is the one thing that seems to get a rise out of him, those *Law & Order* episodes. He finds all the lawyers wanting, in acumen and strategy. But, come the end of the hour, at least you know everything. That's one luxury I will never have.

Suicides take their secrets with them. Was Rudy wily enough to kill Mary McNally as a warning to Nita Flood, or did he make a mistake that night? Fred said he saw the faded "R" and "L" on his wrists a week after he was arrested. A mistake might explain that trace of DNA. Was he excited about what he was about to do? Or was he sitting on the bed he presumed to be Nita Flood's, thinking about another cold night, in which he hid in the trees and watched boys come and go in a room where a girl appeared to be sleeping. *What did you see, Rudy? What do you know?* But his loyalty, to the very end, was to AJ; and if my brother were my client, I would have no problem presenting a plausible case in which he had no knowledge of what Rudy intended to do. And paying for someone's attorney does not prove conspiracy. Nor does telling your sister a life-changing secret at the very moment she is closing in on this fact. Give AJ this: he was very good at derailing me. That lovely Saturday lunch we had to discuss surrogacy—he was milking me about the case, trying to figure out what I knew, realizing that Rudy would need a better attorney.

As for his break with Noel—only Noel and AJ know what happened between them. I remain convinced that AJ left out some essential details, as was his wont. Never lying, but frequently omitting. Maybe Bash knows, but I don't see Bash anymore, and I never really *talked* to him. He assumes our breakup has something to do with my grief over AJ, but I don't want to be with a man who would screw a knothole. Or a blacked-out girl. I have no reason to doubt AJ on this part of the story, as he didn't know I would care. Now when I think about Bash showing up at my open house last Christmas, I wonder where he and AJ were that night. Was Nita Flood still making noise, threatening them? Had they met with Davey, discussed strategy? Almost every detail in my life is up for grabs now, full of new meanings.

I resigned from my office on August 1. I said I needed to spend time with my family. No one questioned this excuse or put it in ironic quotation marks. After all, I was considered a success as state's attorney. And there was my father, suddenly in need of so much care. I am trying to keep him home as long as possible, but—irony of ironies—the dream house that my father oversaw is not suitable for a man in his increasingly frail condition. For now, we are making it work. For now. But I'm not sure how much longer I can keep him at home. And once he leaves, why would the twins and I stay here? We can live anywhere we want, only—what do we want? I realize it's a luxury to be able to ask that question. But it's a luxury for which I have paid dearly. I think I want to go somewhere far away, or at least far enough away that our name, Brant, means nothing except to birdwatchers.

Anyway, once I had resigned and was an ordinary citizen again, there was nothing to prevent me from calling Eloise Schumann and asking her to take me for a walk in the woods.

———————

"There was this big piece of concrete, the remains of an old amphitheater, or something," she said. Her stride was purposeful and strong. I found myself thinking: *She's a tiny thing.* Then: *Wow, I never get to think that about anyone; do people think that about me?* Until recently, I never really felt tiny. Now I feel as if the wind could pick me up and carry me away.

She spoke incessantly as we walked, always about Ryan Schumann. She was girlish on the topic, as silly and giggly as the teenage girl she was when she met him at age fourteen. "I was short, but I had a good figure, I didn't look like a kid. And he wasn't all that tall, so he liked my height. He said I was like a little doll. He was in love with me, but, of course, we had to wait. For him to get divorced, for me to finish high school. I would have done anything for him, *anything*. So when he said, 'Let's pick up that girl hitchhiker,' I said sure. And when he asked her if she wanted to go party with us in the woods, I was okay with that, too. But she got flirty when she got high. Real flirty."

I asked: "Did you tell my father this?"

"Yeah, the second time. But because I lied the first time, no one believed me. After Ryan had been away two years, I couldn't take it anymore. I told your father that she had died, but it was an accident. That she sassed me and I pushed her and she grabbed me and we were fighting and then I pushed her off me and she hit her head on a rock."

"But that wasn't true, was it?" My father had told me that Sheila Compson was much taller than Eloise, and at least thirty pounds heavier. He had reason to doubt her.

Now Eloise was not so talkative. She walked a little farther. "I swear there was an amphitheater. But it was more than forty years ago. I guess it's amazing the woods are still here. One day, I bet there won't be any trees left between Baltimore and Washington. When I was growing up here, it was country, real country. We hated Columbia, with its tacky houses and all those circular streets that don't really go anywhere."

"Cul-de-sacs," I said. It was, admittedly, an inane thing to say. But Eloise Cabot Schumann was born in 1959 and she was acting as if she was the original owner of the colonial tavern that had become my family home. She was all of seven years old when ground was broken for Columbia. These words, these memories, these complaints belonged to someone else. Possibly Ryan Schumann.

"How did you meet Ryan?" I asked, knowing this would get her talking again. This was the story she wanted to tell. A love story.

"At the mall," she said. "I was at McDonald's. I thought I had enough money for french fries, but I didn't. I was seven cents short. There were all these people behind me in line and they were so mean when I was looking for that seven cents because I was sure I had it. One man began yelling and the girl at the cash register, she could have just let it go, but she wouldn't. I was about to cry—I wanted those french fries so bad, I had hitched up to the mall to get them—and Ryan came up and he gave me the change and then some, bought me a Big Mac, and we started talking and that was that."

"When was this?"

"September 17, 1973."

"You were fourteen."

"And only fifteen when he was arrested. That's why he didn't want me to testify. He was trying to protect me."

"And himself, I guess? From statutory rape charges?"

She hesitated, then said, "Yes, that, too. But, really, he did what he did out of love for me."

We had been walking for forty-five minutes now. I didn't really expect she could lead me to Sheila Compson's grave, and I wasn't sure what I would do if she did. She hadn't been able to do it thirty-some years ago, when her memory was fresher, the landscape virtually unchanged. But what else is there to do on a long walk but to talk and talk?

"He told the truth. He didn't kill her. And there *was* a rucksack, and the sandals were in there. One must have rolled out, in the car."

"What happened to the rucksack?"

"We threw it away."

"Why? Why didn't you just leave it with her body?"

"It was a long time ago," Eloise Schumann said. "I can't remember it all." She stopped at a dying tree. "It might have been here. I don't know. We probably should have marked it. But, you know, it was an accident and we panicked because no one was going to believe that. Ryan was trying to protect me. So he buried her and we threw the rucksack in a Dumpster behind the Giant in Laurel. If that one shoe hadn't rolled out in his car, if his wife wasn't so mean—"

Eloise is a middle-aged woman and while she looks younger than her age, she still looks like a middle-aged woman. She was wearing what I think of as a Chico's ensemble—a striped T-shirt dress, a little too long on her tiny frame, bright red Toms, which are not the most practical walking shoes for this terrain. But as she spoke about Ryan, her voice was as light and high as a teenager's. She had held these memories close for so long.

"There was blood on the sandal," I reminded Eloise.

"Well, like I said, she hit her head. But it was an accident."

"But the sandals were in her rucksack. She was wearing a different pair of shoes. That's what frustrated you and Ryan so much. The things he told the truth about, no one believed. You hit her, didn't you, Eloise? You hit her from behind, with her own shoe, and you thought it was back in the rucksack you tossed later. You killed her and Ryan covered it up for you and then neither of you knew how to make it stop. He was an accomplice, once he hid that body, so the only thing he would gain if you came forward was a reduced sentence for testifying against you. You tried to do the right thing, I guess. You told my father that you saw her at the concert, then you told the story about the accident, claimed he had withheld it from Ryan's defense counsel. You kept trying to figure out how to get Ryan a new trial without incriminating yourself. That's why you want a posthumous pardon. He spent his life in prison because of you, for you. The pardon isn't for Ryan. It's for you."

Eloise Schumann shrugged, blithe as a teenager discovered in a minor lie.

"Like you said, if we told the truth, we both would have ended up in prison. He always said, 'What's the point in that?' But those other truck drivers, they said there wasn't a rucksack and there was. They didn't tell the truth, the whole truth, and nothing but the truth. He deserved a new trial. Because there was a rucksack and the shoe did roll out. All those things were *true*."

Ah, the rucksack. How had two witnesses gotten the rucksack wrong, made the mistake about her shoes? Could be the cops, could be someone in my father's office. They might have been led during the interviews. But I don't think my father suborned perjury, not over so trivial a thing. He was a good lawyer. He could have knocked the rucksack down six different ways. No, I think my father repeatedly spoke to a young woman who was giving him every reason to believe she had been involved in a murder—and his mind rejected the notion. My father, the great protector. He married a fragile woman who needed him, tried to save her. In his mind, he also was saving

Nita Flood from her own impossible story. A girl could not be raped by a boy with whom she had been having sex for more than a year. He was not that different from Don Quixote—Don Quexana, actually. The translations vary, as does the spelling of Quexana's name, but they all agree on one thing: after Don Quexana spent all those years of reading courtly tales, about knights and the fair maidens they saved, his mind dried up.

"I want that posthumous pardon," Eloise said. "It's the least you can do."

"You can't get that unless you tell the truth. And there's no statute of limitations for murder. The new state's attorney would be happy to take your confession." *Boy, would she,* I thought. Andi had been appointed to the top job, at my recommendation, after I stepped down. "But if that's what you want, I can make it happen."

I was lying, of course. Already in my mind, I was imagining my father's obituary. His triumph in the Compson case, his victory in obtaining a conviction with no body, no evidence but that damn shoe—how could I take that away from him? It was one of the singular triumphs of his legal career and he believed it, always. Whatever mistakes my father made, as AJ said, he never lacked conviction. If his mind balked at the idea of a tiny teenage girl killing another girl, if he did not believe that a young woman could be raped by her boyfriend—well, those were the things he believed. He was a man of a certain generation, a man of his time. We always want our heroes to be better than their times, to hold the enlightened views we have achieved one hundred, fifty, ten years later. We want Jefferson to free his slaves and not to father children with any of them. We want Lindbergh to keep his Nazi sympathies to himself. We want Bill Clinton to keep it in his pants. Martin Luther King Jr., too. And that's just what we expect of the *men*. The present is swollen with self-regard for itself, but soon enough the present becomes the past. This present, this day, this very moment we inhabit—it all will be held accountable for the things it didn't know, didn't understand.

The things *we* don't know, the things *we* don't understand.

I did the only thing I could do. I got out my checkbook and wrote one more check for my father's refurbishment project. I even wrote "interior design consultation" in the memo line on the check. I told Eloise Schumann that she had to report the income, but that's between her and the IRS. My only job now is to take care of my family. I'm a SAHM *and* a SAHD—stay-at-home daughter.

Oh, there's nothing to keep me from practicing law again one day, aside from my willingness to indulge in that little bit of implicit extortion. I assume that's why AJ killed himself, so I wouldn't have to figure out if my brother needed to be charged for soliciting Nita Flood's murder. He was trying to save my career. Or maybe he was trying to save his reputation. He died—oh that word—beloved.

At any rate, I've lost my taste for the legal profession. It is too serious to be treated as a competition, too flawed to be a calling. Even with the twins now in fourth grade, days are easier to fill than one might think. From sunup to well past sundown, I go and I go and I go. I could have sent Teensy off into a well-remunerated retirement, but neither she nor my father would have liked that. If the fates are kind, he'll be giving her a ride somewhere and they'll overshoot the driveway and plow into Wilde Lake together. Of course, Teensy being Teensy—that is, endlessly perverse—the more I do around the house, the more she does; even the spacious kitchen is not enough to keep us from bumping into each other as we battle for housekeeping supremacy. *Homemade rolls? I'll see that and top you with pasta made from scratch, not even using a machine.* The more dishes we dirty, the more time I have to spend cleaning the kitchen at night, my form of meditation.

When the house is clean, the voice of my father's television finally silenced, I sit in the living room and drink a glass of wine or three. On windy nights, the fake lake is stirred into action and I can hear its wavelets smacking the shore. *AJ,* the lake says. *Noel. Rudy. Mary McNally. Ben Flood. Adele*

Closter Brant. Gabe. How many deaths can one family hold in its ledger? It's as if death begets death. It was practically the family business. My only hope is to free my children from its legacy. That's why this investigation, donated to the Howard County Historical Society, is to be sealed for one hundred years—not unlike the papers of H. L. Mencken, to cite another man who shocked future generations by being a man of his times. Let strangers pore over them one day, piecing together my family's history. My children don't need to know any of this. They, at least, are blameless. How long can I keep them that way? Does anyone get through life blameless?

They certainly don't need to know their father was with another woman when he died. A woman who called me several weeks later, apologizing profusely as she sobbed, begging me to understand that they were IN LOVE, but they never wanted to hurt anyone. A woman who says she was with him earlier that night, but swears he was alive when she left. Who knows? *Love,* she kept sobbing to me. They were in love. She never would have hurt anyone; she and Gabe spoke often of how much they loved their partners, but—love. Love, love, love. I offer this story only because I think it provides context for some choices I have made since then and for the scant information I have offered about Penelope and Justin. This is not their story. This is not their legacy.

I told that woman never to call me again. On good days, I think she was a liar, a troublemaker, someone who thought she would be offered money to go away. On bad days—well, at any rate, *she* didn't get any money from me.

I tell the story here so I may never tell it again. My childhood was made up of stories and so many of them were false. Is that because the true stories were unendurable?

Just last week, I ran into my childhood friend, Randy Nairn, at Wegman's. We were both buying sushi-grade tuna. He owns a wholesale liquor distributor and he has the look of a marathoner: lean, almost too lean, as his face is a little weathered, ten years older than his body, but then—his body looks great. He's married, happily I assume, because he didn't flirt at all and I might have given him an opening, mentioning the time he asked to kiss me. I might have touched his elbow. He glided right past that, instead recalling Thanksgiving dinner at my house, that opened bottle of crème de menthe he brought as a gift. He laughed at himself with the ease of someone who knows he has transcended the foibles of his past, a trick I'll never master. I still get mad when people tell the story about my golf caddy back-to-school outfit. That is, I would get mad, if there were anyone left to tell it. Maybe I will tell Penelope and Justin, and they can tell it back to me. The Brants have a few stories left that can still be told.

"Your house was like a castle to me," Randy said. "It was like you were living in some palace, high above everybody else. I thought you were royalty."

We did, too, Randy. We did, too.

AFTERWORD

Where to begin? I am indebted to Alison Chaplin and Molli Simonsen, who did everything in their power to help me get things right. Alafair Burke, Calvert County State's Attorney Laura L. Martin, and Jane Tolar provided much-needed expertise on legal matters. *New City Upon a Hill: A Brief History of Columbia* and the "You Knew You Grew Up In Columbia" Facebook page filled in the gaps in my knowledge about the place where I lived and attended high school, 1974–1977. I appreciate the support of everyone at William Morrow, particularly my editor of twenty (!) years, Carrie Feron. Also with me for twenty years, my agent Vicky Bijur.

Those who know Howard County politics will know that Lu Brant is not, in fact, the first female state's attorney, but I gave her that distinction for the purposes of the novel; Marna L. McLendon served back in the 1990s.

I am lucky to have a spouse, David Simon, who can answer stray questions about homicide investigation. My daughter, Georgia Rae, is eager to contribute illustrations to my books, but says that must wait until she finishes school in twelve years. The FLs keep me sane even as they encourage my worst impulses.

But in the end, all errors are my own—and some are deliberate.

About the author

Read On

Insights,
Interviews
& More . . .

Meet Laura Lippman

Lesley Unruh

Since Laura Lippman's debut in 1997, she has been heralded for thoughtful, timely crime novels set in her beloved hometown of Baltimore, Maryland. She has been nominated for more than fifty awards for crime fiction and won almost twenty, including the Edgar, and her books have been translated into more than twenty languages. Now a perennial *New York Times* bestselling author, Laura lives in Baltimore and New Orleans, Louisiana, with her family. ❧

An Introduction to "Five Fires"

THE TERM "RAPE CULTURE" may seem fairly recent or avant-garde, but reliable sources—OK, Google—date its coinage to a 1975 documentary and trace its origins back to the Greek mythology I have loved since I was a child. (Like Lu Brant in *Wilde Lake*, I liked reading about Jason and the Golden Fleece.) Of course I knew that Zeus raped Leda, while in the form of a swan, but—well, gods will be gods. Somehow, it escaped my attention that Medusa had been raped by Poseidon in Athena's temple. Athena is so upset by this sacrilege that she transforms Medusa into that famous monster, with her snakes for hair and a face that turns anyone who sees it to stone. Yes, when your uncle rapes someone, clearly the victim is to blame.

I know I first learned the word "rape" while watching a television show in the 1960s, *Judd for the Defense*. A girl was found, crying. "He raped me." Cut to commercial. I spent the break—again, not unlike Lu Brant—looking up rape in the dictionary, learning nothing. My dictionary hid behind words like "assault" and "attack."

But the term "rape culture" did not cross my mental threshold until October 2013. There had been the horrific rape of a teen in Ohio, posted to social media. And then I learned of a lesser-known case in Kansas, documented by a stunning piece of journalism in the *Kansas City Star* newspaper that received a lot of attention in social media. A girl in the small town of Maryville said she was raped by a football ▶

3

star; criminal charges were never brought. She was named Daisy, the accused was Matt. Ultimately, Daisy's family left the small town where they had hoped to make a second start; soon after, their house was burned down. One small detail in the article leaped out at me: Daisy's mother told the reporter that a girl had attended a dance wearing a shirt that read: Matt 1, Daisy 0.

I couldn't let go of that detail. *Who does that?* Yes, it was a small town, emotions ran high, sides were taken. But how does any girl or woman mock another one who says she was raped?

At the time, I hadn't even conceived the book *Wilde Lake*. But, offered the opportunity to write an original short story for a digital-only outlet, I wrote the piece you'll find included here, "Five Fires." It's a different kind of story for me, but to explain more would be a huge spoiler. It's also set in a fictional small Delaware town, Belleville, which will be the setting for my next novel, due out in early 2018.

I don't think *Wilde Lake* would exist if it were not for this story. Because, even after writing "Five Fires," I found I could not stop thinking about rape and the way laws and attitudes about rape had changed in my lifetime. I thought, wincing, about a rape joke I once told. (Just one, but that's enough.) I decided to stop using the terms "acquaintance rape" and "date rape." Rape is rape; those modifiers seek to minimize its horror. And, unfortunately, rape is a problem that our culture continues to respond to anecdotally, case by case. We persist in assessing victims, whether we realize it or not. Do we still live in a rape culture? It's hard for me to say because I think that term has evolved as our understanding of rape has evolved.

But I know we still live in a world where people mock rape victims and judge them. And I wish that weren't so.

Laura Lippman
March 2016
Baltimore, Maryland ❧

"Five Fires"

"There was another fire last night." That's the first woman. Tennis skirt, Lacoste polo, gold chain with a diamond on it, like a drop of water.

The other woman—I don't know either of them, you can't, even in a town as small as ours, know everybody—says: "That makes three this month, doesn't it?"

"Two. The one at the vacant—you know that place. And now behind Langley's."

And the playhouse, I want to say. *The first one was that playhouse.* But I don't say it, because, again, I don't know them. But three is right. There have been three since August 1, and it's only August 10.

"Do they know the cause?"

"Lightning."

"There wasn't a storm last night. There's barely been a drop of rain since Memorial Day. Good for the beach towns, but nobody else."

"I know, but there was heat lighting. You could see it in the sky."

"Heat lightning doesn't cause fires."

"Why not? It's still lightning."

"But it doesn't strike the ground, does it?"

"It must strike somewhere. There's no other explanation. No evidence of arson. I suppose, at Langley's, someone could have thrown a cigarette in the dumpster, but there's nothing that can make a vacant lot catch fire, except lighting."

But the playhouse had electricity. Or did it? I'd never been in it, of course, but I'd heard about it. The two-story house that Horace Stone had built for his only daughter, Becca. It had a kitchen and a bedroom and real furniture and, I think, running water. But no electricity. Or maybe it had electricity but not running water? It definitely had a bed. But everyone in town knew that. About the bed.

Now that I think about it, I'm pretty sure it had running water. And maybe a little mini-fridge with ice. There had to be ice. Not that I ever knew Becca Stone to play with. She's a lot older than I am, four years ahead of me in school, going into her senior year at Princeton. She may want to be my friend, all things considered. But right now, I'm going into my senior year at Belleville High School, and it's hard to imagine a day when I'll be friends with people so much older. Even people who are inclined to like me, like Becca Stone. At least I *think* she likes me. Or would, if we get to know each other. ▶

The women take their sandwiches and go. They never said a thing to me the entire time they were in the store, except: "Wheat bread." "No mayonnaise." And: "Do you have any other chips?" It was like I wasn't there. So I don't say goodbye. I don't know them, although I might know their kids, if they have any. Kids don't come to the deli. It's not cool. Most of the kids go to Subway or McDonald's, maybe the Sonic, although only to get food to go, not to stay and eat in their cars, despite the fact that it's a drive-in. That would be uncool, too. I've made a study of what's cool and what's not, but it's harder than it looks. Why is it cool to get Sonic food to go, but not eat there in your car? I don't know. I just know that's how it is.

* * *

It's almost four, when I get to leave, if Wendi, who works the next shift, is on time. Big if. Wendi's boyfriend, Jordan, is working as a lifeguard at the community pool this summer, but she's not sure of him, so she goes to the pool and stays until the last possible minute, then comes here, smelling of lotion and chlorine and french fries. I think she's silly. He's not going to do anything while she's around, and watching him until the last minute isn't going to make Jordan behave. I don't know, if some girl were watching me that way, I think I might feel obligated to do something.

And when Wendi finally gets to work, she wants me to stay and listen to her complaints and suspicions about Jordan, even though I've punched out. Wendi is one of those people who doesn't seem to exist when she's alone. But she never talks to me anywhere else, so I don't see why I have to linger past the time I'm on the clock to listen to her talk about Jordan. True, I used to like it. Back when she was happier with him, when I could be a positive influence. Back last fall, when people said some nasty stuff about Jordan, I told Wendi she should trust him. She seemed to appreciate it.

"And then Caitlin—she's such a slut—"

"I've got to go, Wendi."

"Why?" she asks. Meaning: *You don't have anywhere to go.* Wendi knows how to do that, put a lot of meanness into words that aren't necessarily mean.

"Actually," I say, "someone's waiting for me."

"Who?" She thinks I'm lying, I can tell. Won't she be surprised when she finds out who's back. But that's a secret, for now. I've promised not to tell. So I just smile. Enigmatically. That's one of my vocabulary words. En-ig-mat-i-cal-ly. I'm not going to take the SAT, but if I did, I bet I would get a pretty good score.

There are exactly seven ways for me to walk home from the deli. I worked it out. It's sort of like an algebra problem. I've always tried to vary it, even before this summer, because I like some variety.

"More like geometry," Tara says, falling into place beside me at the corner of Tulip and Elm. The north–south streets are named for trees, the cross streets for flowers.

"No," I say, conscious that she's smart, that she got into a good college, even if she decided not to go there in the end. Her decision, no one else's. But that doesn't mean she's always right. "It's not about the shapes. It's about the variables. If I go straight on Elm, then there are three possible places to turn right—so those would be X, Y, or Z. But if I choose to go right here, on Tulip, there are still two more possibilities. So that makes Tulip 'X,' or—"

"BOR-ing," she says, the way she used to in class sometimes, in a light, high voice, almost like singing, that all the boys seemed to think was funny. "Is there anything more boring than figuring out how many ways you can walk between your job and your house? Except this town."

"Well," I say, "you didn't have to come back to Belleville if you think it's so boring. And you don't have to stay."

"Of course I have to stay," she says. "At least for a little while."

"Why? Your family moved away last spring. Why did you come back?"

"You know why," she says. I don't know why she thinks that. I mean, I know she's here, staying with a friend, I guess. But she hasn't explained everything to me, and it's not like we were close in school.

* * *

No one's home at my house, 333 Rose. My mom's working four to eleven this week. "I can't have people in when my mom's not home," I tell Tara. "You know that."

"Like you've never broken that rule."

"I haven't."

"Only because no one's ever wanted to come over to your house."

That's not true. Okay, it's true, but it's not nice. But Tara was never that nice, despite what some people think. She wasn't mean—it wasn't like the movies, where the girls are so nasty you can't quite believe it. She just ▶

made it really clear that she thought she was up there and other people weren't. True, she was pretty and a cheerleader, but her family didn't even move to Belleville until she was a junior. And, sure, she made varsity cheerleader without ever being on JV, but so what? It's not like she was the only girl who ever did that. Becca Stone made varsity as a freshman and also graduated at the top of her class, then went to Princeton. There's a world of difference between someone like Tara Greene and Becca Stone, and Tara never seemed to get that. Mama always said that the Greenes just didn't understand Belleville, that you don't move to a place and try to make it be like you. *You* have to learn to be like *it.*

I guess Tara came back because she's a few credits shy of her diploma. But if she's not in college, she has no one to blame but herself.

I shut the door, leaving her on the walk. "See you tomorrow, Beth!" she says, but I'm already thinking if maybe there's a new way to walk home from the deli, a way that will keep Tara from waiting for me. It was interesting at first, having her seek me out, determined to be my friend. Now I'm not so sure. She's sneaky. I don't know what she wants from me, but I don't owe her anything.

I don't mind coming home to an empty house, although I feel bad for my mom, who hates the night shift. But if she's here when I get home, she's on me. Even when school is out and there's no homework to do. She tells me to take a shower because I smell like salami and sweat. She tells me to put my clothes in the hamper, then says, "Can't you see that hamper's full, Bethie? Start a wash." She stands nearby when I count my tips—at the end of your shift, if you've worked alone, you get everything in the tip jar, although there's a tradition that you leave a dollar for the next girl. I don't know why, but I do it. Wendi doesn't, though. She's not . . . honorable. It's silly not to do it. It's not as if you lose out. Because, of course, if everyone does it, no one loses a dollar.

I still hide my tip money from my mom, although she's okay now. I can't imagine her going through my room again, looking for my savings. Well, I can, but if it happened, I would know what to do. I'd tell her to call Bill, the guy responsible for getting her through the rough patches, and if she wouldn't, then I would. That's happened only once, and if you ask me, it was kind of Tara's fault. I mean, things got so crazy there for a while and it was hard on my mom. People said mean things. I was okay with it, but she was fragile, taking it one day at a time, like they say, and she had a bad day. One. Only one. I'm really proud of her.

Thinking about my mom, and how she loves me and wants the best for me, makes me want to be good to her. So I do all the things she would tell me to do. I take a shower. I start a wash, gathering all the dark clothes, except that one bright red T-shirt at the bottom of the hamper. It's not that I'm ashamed of it, not at all, it's just that I won't know what to do with it once it's clean. Plus, once it's clean, then, I don't know, it's as if everything will be over, and I really don't want things to be over. I keep thinking that maybe it's just summer, that life will be exciting when school starts again, but I'm not sure. Daniel Stone graduated, and he's going to Johns Hopkins on a lacrosse scholarship. Some people say it's wrong, Daniel Stone getting money he doesn't need, but I don't see why he shouldn't get a scholarship. I mean, it's for being a good athlete, and if having a poor family shouldn't keep you out of college, then having a rich one shouldn't keep you from being recognized for your genuine talents.

I wanted to go away to college, but my mom says it's community college for me unless the sky rains money sometime between now and next spring. I'm a good student, but I don't have any kind of special talent that gets you scholarships. It's not that I wouldn't get *some* aid, but my mom is dead-set against loans and says it has to be a free ride or nothing if I want to go away.

Last fall, I talked to a recruiter from Delaware State University, but my mom just got this look on her face and said, "Over my dead body." I told her that it wasn't an all-black school anymore, hadn't been for a long time, that it's ranked very high on some lists and a U.S. congressman went there. I kept in touch with that recruiter, telling her of my situation, and she seemed really encouraging until this winter, when she suddenly said she didn't think the school would be a good fit for me. I figure my mom went behind my back and said something. What can I say? My mom is prejudiced. Lots of older people are.

Also, my dad left her for someone from Dover, and I think she just has a grudge against Dover. She's lived in Belleville all her life. Me, too. My dad didn't move here until he was in first grade, and he stayed here until he met that schoolteacher from Dover. She got a flat tire on the way to the beach. This would have been the summer I was three years old, but I remember it. Well, I remember him packing up, moving out. My mother told me about the schoolteacher, her red Miata, how she rode in the truck with the tow truck driver, wearing a shift that was barely a shirt over her bikini. *Slut,* my mother said. *Nice example for a third-grade teacher to set.* ▶

9

"Five Fires" *(continued)*

The teacher had a summer share over at Dewey Beach with a bunch of other schoolteachers. My father started taking weekend shifts at the garage, coming home on Saturday nights with a two-tone tan—dark brown on his forearms and face, a paler brown on his torso and legs. And he smelled of beer and the sea, without a speck of grease on him. He would try to get into the shower fast, he'd be a blur moving toward that bathroom, but my mother knew and she threw him out, expecting him to come crawling back. (She's told me this story more than once.) So he packed up and moved up to Dover, and next thing we know he's sending Christmas cards, addressed only to me, with one baby boy, then two, then three. His new wife encouraged him to push himself, and he switched to selling cars. He pays child support, and he used to visit, but it wasn't fun for either of us, so we let it go when I was twelve or so. "You have your own life now," my father said. "You'll be too busy on the weekends to see your old man. You'll go out for cheerleading, start dating." I thought he knew something I didn't, that those things happened when you were a teenager, almost by law. I was a little puzzled at first, when my life turned out differently, but I didn't mind.

"Your father never knew what the hell he was talking about," my mother said. "Besides, he's got those other kids now. He's too busy driving them to soccer and baseball and whatever else they do. Well, he always wanted a son, and now he has three. I hope he's happy."

I don't think she does.

My dad kept up his support payments, though. And he says he'll help, if I get into a school, but he can't pay the full freight or even put up enough to bridge the difference between what I've saved and the full cost.

Del Tech, here I come.

Luckily, the Georgetown campus offers an associate degree in criminal justice, and it's only twenty miles away. I just have to make sure that I don't take Friday afternoon classes during the summer term, because the beach traffic will make even that short drive hellish. People who don't live here can't understand what it's like, in the summer, to live in the kind of town that people are forever driving through, how you have to put everything on hold for much of Friday-Sunday and it's annoying. Today is Thursday and everyone is running around like a storm is coming—going to the grocery store, getting gas, whatever— because by noon tomorrow you won't be able to cross the highway. My mom and I are lucky that we live in town, but even that gets crazy, as there are a bunch of people who think they're so slick, skipping the bypass and going through town. Why do you think they built the bypass? They come roaring through in their big SUVs, bicycles strapped on the back, kayaks and canoes on the roof, the cargo space filled with beach toys. Belleville comes at the point in the journey when most of them have been on the road long enough to be impatient, but there's still more than an hour of driving ahead of them. You can almost feel how cranky the kids are, even from behind the deli counter.

"They don't use half that stuff they pack," my mother says. "The boats and the bikes. You just know they don't even get it off the car. It's only a week, two at the most, and they pack like they're going to Siberia."

I've lived thirty miles from the beach my entire life, and I go only once a year, at most. Not even that anymore. It's a hassle, and my mom always says, "For what? To get a sunburn and a pound of sand in your underwear." Besides, you can break your neck bodysurfing. She read about a guy in the newspaper who did just that.

I don't even know how to swim. That's one reason I don't go to the community pool, where Wendi keeps watch over her boyfriend.

I hang the laundry. We have a dryer, but we try not to use it in the summer unless there's rain, because it heats up the house so and you have to run the A/C even higher and my mother says she doesn't work all the hours she works to keep the wives of Delmarva Power executives in fur coats.

I make a bowl of microwave popcorn for my dinner—it's a diet I've been trying: normal breakfast and lunch, but microwave popcorn for dinner, and I'm down six pounds—and fall asleep in front of the TV. The next thing I know, I'm dreaming and there's the bonfire, but it's the weird kind of dream where I stand outside myself, I see myself in my red T-shirt and I don't care what anyone says, I think I look pretty, but then there is a pounding, pounding, pounding sound and these women in fur coats start looking around and Daniel Stone puts his arm around me and says, "Thank you, Beth," and it's not clear if he's protecting me or I'm protecting him, and the pounding keeps coming and I think it's Tara, at the front door, ignoring my mother's rules, but—

Shit. It's raining, a hard, intense rain pounding the roof. I grab the laundry from the line and put it in the dryer, hoping the cycle runs before my mom gets home. I don't know why I'm so tired. But it was ▶

"Five Fires" *(continued)*

busy at the deli, it being Thursday and all, and I was on my feet for five hours. ("Now you know how I feel," Mama says when I talk about my feet hurting. "I do it for eight, and I'm twenty-five years older than you.) And wouldn't you know, the rain stops almost as fast as it started and the sky looks clear, although there are flashes of heat lightning to the east.

Sure enough, before my mother comes home, I hear the sirens of the Belleville Volunteer Fire Department heading out into the night.

Fire number four.

This one's at the snack bar of the community pool, and they just decide to close the place for the rest of the summer, seeing that summer's almost over anyway.

* * *

"Arson," Wendi says. "There's yellow tape up and everything."

It's been a slow day—a Friday in August, so the main highway is clogged and people are in their hives, as I think of it, just staying put. Like in the high school cafeteria. Did you know that queen bees are determined before they're born? The potential queen eggs are laid in queen cups, and the queen develops differently because she gets more royal jelly, the name for a protein that's secreted by the worker bees' glands. There can be only one queen bee. Tara was one of the wannabes. Wannabees? Anyway, I guess she learned her lesson. She wanted royal jelly and she got it.

That's pretty funny. I wish I'd thought of it at the time. I'd have told Daniel Stone and he would have laughed, I bet.

"Why are they so sure it was arson?" I ask.

"They found something. Unlike the others. It looked like the person tried to set it in the trash can, but everything was wet after the rain. So someone broke the lock on the gate they pull over the snack bar at night, turned on the gas. It blew up like a fireball."

"That could be an accident," I said. "I mean, the man who works there—he's from that place for grown-ups that need help. He might have left it on. Plus someone would have to climb the fence."

"Boys climb that fence all the time," Wendi says. "The lock on the gate had been broken, and gas doesn't just *ignite*." She's excited. Jordan won't be at the pool anymore, so she won't have to hang around there, watching him behind her sunglasses. Wendi is a redhead. Having to keep tabs on her lifeguard boyfriend hasn't been good for her looks.

She has fair skin, set off by her bright red hair and green eyes. Did you know that only 2 percent of the population has green eyes? I didn't, until Wendi told me. I checked it out: turns out she's right, although 20 percent of Hungarians have green eyes. I asked Wendi if she was Hungarian and she said no, they were Lutheran.

I leave, taking my tips, leaving behind a dollar in the jar for Wendi, knowing she won't do the same at the end of her shift because she's closing. Wendi doesn't understand that there's a psychology to the tip jar, that you want at least a dollar in there all the time, because it gives people the *idea* to tip. It sets the tone. My mom hates tip jars. "If anyone's going to have a tip jar, it should be me, on my feet at the cash register at Happy Harry's for seven hours." She's not wrong, but there's nothing I can do about it except rub her feet, bring her coffee in bed the weeks she works the night shift. I did that this morning. She was awake, staring at the ceiling.

"Did you hear the sirens last night?" she asked me while sipping coffee from a mug I made for her when I was ten. Well, I didn't make it, but I decorated it. She was the one who told me the fire was at the community pool. She saw the trucks on her way home. I decide to go by there, too, after work. I plan to take law enforcement classes at Del Tech, although I doubt I'll be an arson investigator. Arson is scary. You have to be crazy to set fire to something. I mean, something that's not supposed to be set fire to. Every fall, just before Halloween, there's a big bonfire in Belleville, a pep rally for the game against our big rivals from Christiana. Everyone goes. It's my favorite night of fall. It makes up for not having trick-or-treat anymore, now that I'm too old for it, for the cold, gray days that come rushing in once it's November. Winter usually isn't a big deal here. Schools close more often for fog than they do for sleet or snow. But last year, we missed eight days for snow and had to make up five of those days. Except for the seniors, which didn't seem fair. They graduated, and the rest of us still had another week. There's a yellow-crime-tape scene at the pool, just as Wendi said, a state trooper's car. Not the first time I've seen that in Belleville, but it's real rare. Tara's standing off to the side, watching them. I'd thought I'd avoid her, coming by here, and I make a point not to catch her eye. But when I start walking home, she falls in step beside me.

"What do you think?" she says.

I look down at her feet. "About your new sandals? It's a shame how muddy they are." ▶

"Five Fires" *(continued)*

"They're not new. They're the same sandals I wear every day. No, I meant what do you think about this fire?"

"None of my business, I guess."

"That didn't stop you. Before."

My mom taught me that when you don't like what someone's saying, just don't say anything.

"I was a Brownie," Tara says. "And a Girl Scout, before I moved here. I bet you think that's corny. But I was disappointed that they didn't have a troop here. I had so many badges and insignias, the most of anyone in my troop back home in Philadelphia."

Back home in Philadelphia. *Exactly,* I think. *That's your home. Go back there.*

"I was really good at camping. I can start a fire by rubbing two sticks together. Honest," she adds, as if I won't believe her. But I believe her. About that, at least.

"Big deal," I say. "I suppose anyone who watches *Survivor* knows how to do that. Or who has YouTube."

"Yeah, but can you do it?"

"I don't want to do it. And I don't want to talk about it."

"I had so many badges. So many insignias. You could barely see my uniform for all of them. And that was in—"

"Philadelphia, I know. You were forever talking about Philadelphia." I'm tired of Tara, tired enough to be rude. "Nobody liked it. How much you talked about Philadelphia, how everything was better there. You kept saying all you wanted to do was go back there, and you did. So why are you here?"

"Believe me," she says, "it wasn't my idea. But I've got to finish up."

"You mean you have to get your credits before you can go to college."

"Something like that."

We walk a few blocks or so and she doesn't talk for a while. We're almost to my house when she says: "Did everyone really hate it?"

"What?"

"When I talked about Philadelphia? I did it only because I was homesick. And new."

"Well, 'hate' is strong. But you did talk about it. A lot."

"Daniel seemed interested," she says. "He asked me lots of questions. He said he was considering Penn."

"Oh, I know you thought Daniel was interested."

"You're mean, Beth."

"No. No, I'm not. I was never mean. You were. You never talked to anyone. You never talked to me, and you only talk to me now, because I'm one of the few people in town who wouldn't run away from you. You were stuck-up."

"I wasn't." She looks close to crying, and I admit I feel something I haven't felt in a while. It's powerful yet scary, making someone like Tara cry.

Today she doesn't even ask to come in, just stands on the front walk for a while, staring at my house. It frightens me, the way she looks at our house. I don't sleep at all that night, not even after Mama comes home, because I can't tell her what I'm scared of, what I suspect.

The sirens sound at 1 a.m.

This time it's only a few blocks away, but on the other side of Alamo, which makes a world of difference. I bet you're thinking: *But you said the streets are named for trees and flowers.* Well, *alamo* means "cottonwood." Belleville was settled by a group of priests, including one who was Spanish. The houses on the other side of Alamo are the grandest ones in town. The Stone family lived at the dead end of Iris; their land backs up to the river. The sirens keep going and going and I can't help myself. I sneak out my bedroom window. It's not something I've ever had to do, but I've practiced a couple of times, in case my life takes a turn and I become the kind of girl who sneaks out of windows at night and goes to meet other kids. Wendi does that. Tara did, too, as everybody found out. I bet even Becca Stone did it.

I follow the sounds and the smells and the lights and find myself standing across the street from Tara's old house at the corner of Iris and Oak. She's out front, alone, hugging her arms as if it were cold. But the night is warm, and the fire makes it warmer still. *Step back, step back,* the firemen say. I've never seen someone fight a fire before. It's amazing how fire moves, how quick it is. I watch a flame race up a tree. "It's going to jump, it's going to jump," someone shouts, and the firefighters aim their hoses at the house next door, trying to wet it down. The paint is bubbling on the place next door, and the windows give way from the pressure. I feel bad for the people there, but the fire is strangely beautiful. There are people in town who say they want to end the bonfire, in part because it's dangerous, especially after this summer of drought. They say it's irresponsible, bad for the environment. But it's a tradition; it's what we do in Belleville. Traditions are important.

"I'm sorry," I say to Tara.

"No, you're not," she says. "I'm not, either. It's not as if my family ▶

were ever coming back here, you know. And they can't sell it. Whoever did this, did them a kindness."

"But where will you stay now?"

"With you?"

"Our house is pretty small, just the two bedrooms, and my mom—"

She laughs in my face. "As if I would ever live with you, Beth. You know the house was empty, that I've been staying somewhere else. Is it true your real name is Bethesda, that your mom saw it somewhere and thought it was pretty?"

"It is pretty."

"Then why don't you use it? Why didn't you use it when reporters took your photograph and asked your name? Were you ashamed?"

"There's no talking to you," I say. "I said I was sorry, and you just turn it on me. You're the mean one. And you're named for a plantation, so who are you to talk?"

I walk home. Belleville is a safe place. A girl can walk home at 1 a.m. in Belleville, knowing nothing would ever happen here. And if it happened, it would be because of a stranger, someone passing through, one of those long-haul truckers. A long time ago, before I was even born, a magazine put us on the list of the ten best small towns in America. I never read the article, but I heard about it. Last fall, everyone kept saying that. "One of the best small towns in America in which to live . . ." Although they never mentioned that was twenty years ago and Belleville never made the list again. But I guess we still are, despite what happened. Despite these fires. I bet it is heat lightning. That's the only explanation. Even at the pool. Lightning could have sparked the fire if the gas had been left on, right? And heat lightning must travel to the ground, and I don't believe Tara was a Girl Scout, much less that she knows how to rub two sticks together. She was the kind of girl who acted as if she needed protection from the silliest things—insects and dogs and puddles. Everyone remembers the story of how Daniel Stone lay down in a puddle—didn't just put his jacket on it, but lay down in the puddle, the way Sir Walter Raleigh supposedly did, and let Tara walk across him. Sir Walter Raleigh never did that, actually, but Daniel Stone did, and half the school saw it. She traipsed across his back, giggling, as if it were her due.

The trees seemed to be whispering as I climbed back through the window. A breeze is kicking up. It never fails, no matter how the weather changes: every August, before school, before Labor Day, a front moves through. It drops temperatures for just a few hours. The next day it's hot again. But it's not the same kind of hot. It's like someone has knocked summer down in a fight and it gets back up, but it's staggering, weaker. It's going to get knocked down again. Again and again and again, until it no longer gets up.

Then fall will come, my favorite season. In the fall, anything is possible. I'm going to buy some new clothes at Kohl's up in Dover. I might go all the way to Wilmington, or even Baltimore, to get my hair cut. I'm going to be a senior. It probably won't be as exciting as last year, but it might be. Last fall was the best fall of my life.

* * *

Everything began at the bonfire, the first one. The cool kids had a plan to go drinking afterwards. I don't drink, so I couldn't have gone even if they asked me. But I love the bonfire. I stood at the far edge of the circle, listened to the speeches, watched the cheerleaders flip so close to the flames. Their shadows were huge. *We've got spirit, yes we do.* Tara, the lightest, was hurled to the top of the pyramid. She had entered school the winter before, but we still thought of her as the new girl because no one newer had come along. New people are rare in our high school. I guess most families wouldn't move when their kids were halfway through their junior year. Why did Tara's family move here? They said it was because they wanted a simpler life, as if Belleville was simpler than Philadelphia. Smaller, sure. But not simpler. Still, Tara would not shut up about how amazing Philadelphia was. God, how tired everyone got hearing Tara hold forth on Philly cheese steaks, as if that skinny twig ever ate anything. You know how some people yell "Eat a cheeseburger" at skinny girls? I always wanted to yell, "Eat a cheese steak." I didn't, but it would have been funny if I had. I bet Daniel Stone would have laughed.

The crowd dispersed, the boys leading the way. Daniel didn't play football. He didn't have the build for it. He played lacrosse, which in some ways was a bigger deal, because our lacrosse players went on to good college teams and our football players almost never did. Tara and her friend Chelsey scampered after him. Scampered like puppies trying to keep up with a big dog.

"Where are we going?" I heard Tara ask.

"Stone Manor," Daniel said.

"Stoner Manor," put in his best friend, Charley Boyd. ▶

"Five Fires" (*continued*)

They giggled. I heard them. They giggled.

Stone Manor was what Daniel called his sister's playhouse. It wasn't like any playhouse you've ever seen. For one thing, it was two stories, a replica of the Stone house, painted the same soft green color, the paint freshened every few years. The front door locked, not that it ever was. Most people in Belleville don't lock the front doors to their houses—another detail that the reporters seized on. Did the Stones know what went on in the little house? They said they didn't, but I guess they did. Look, kids drink and get high. I mean, I don't, because of my mom, I have to be careful, but it's not a big deal. Kids drink, and it's up to girls to police themselves. Sorry, but that's just how it is, even in a place like Belleville, where you can walk home at night without a worry. Tara was from Philadelphia, as she reminded us every day. She was smart. As she reminded us every day. She went to Becca Stone's playhouse with Chelsey and four boys.

Do the math. What did you think was going to happen?

She knew. She knew.

And the video: what did it prove? For one thing, it proved it was only Daniel and Charley, not the other two boys, Wendi's Jordan and a guy named Bobby Wright. Nothing happened to Chelsey. No one forced Tara to drink all that punch. Sure, she looks groggy and out of it, but she doesn't say no. She never says no. It's weird that Charley filmed it, but—I know this sounds odd—it looks kind of romantic. The bed even had a canopy, and Daniel whispered in Tara's ear as he moved on top of her, slow and careful. "Are you okay?" he says over and over. "Are you okay?" He cared about her. I mean, he wasn't in love with her, and that's probably why she got mad, but in that moment it looked like he was being real sweet.

And it was only after everyone started sharing the video that Tara filed charges. Said she didn't remember. How could she not remember? Her eyes were open; she was with Daniel Stone. I'd remember every minute. She said Charley raped her, too, but there's no video of that. Conveniently. She's just a slut. And that's why I wore the T-shirt to the second bonfire, the one where we stood up for Daniel and Charley and our town, Belleville. My T-shirt said:

SKANKVILLE

POPULATION: 1

18

The letters were white. Red and white are the school colors. Go Cardinals! There was a photo of Tara under the letters. And for once, I didn't stand at the edge of the circle around the bonfire. I went straight up to it. I led the cheer. *Slut, slut, slut, slut* . . . And everyone yelled with me. I can't imagine it feels any better, flying to the top of a pyramid.

The Wilmington paper ran my photo. It went everywhere. People around the world saw me. Some people said I was angry in the photo, but I wasn't angry. I was righteous. Our town, our boys. That's what the signs said. We love our town. We love our boys.

On the Internet, people wrote some nasty things about me under that photo. I learned to stop reading those comments, though. And while I'm on Facebook, I keep it tight, just my real friends or Candy Crush, so I didn't see the things people said there. Daniel Stone told me personally that he was grateful for my support. He said it just that way: "I'm grateful for your support. That girl tried to ruin my life."

And Charley's, too, I guess, but he complicated everything by agreeing he had done it. But, again, it wasn't what you think. The police told him he could be put in jail because he was eighteen—he has a late-summer birthday, his parents held him back a year so he'd be more competitive at football—and Tara was only sixteen, but that wasn't even true. They put him in a room by himself and said all sorts of things that weren't true, that Daniel was blaming him, said it was his idea, that he was having consensual sex with Tara but Charley sneaked up on them, taking that video with his phone, then said he deserved a turn. Later, Daniel said Charley admitted that not a word of it was true. Who knows what really happened? Tara had no bruises, no marks. They couldn't do a rape kit, because she didn't even tell anyone for almost a week.

She looks fine in the video. If she threw up and they carried her home, left her in her yard, well—they did ring the bell. They thought her parents were there. She had sneaked out before, several times. How could they know her parents had gone away for the weekend, that she wouldn't be found until the morning? She just made up that story to keep from getting in more trouble with her parents.

"Don't drink around boys," my mom told me. "You'll get what you deserve." This whole thing upset her. My mom is third-generation Belleville, used to lord it over my dad, who wasn't born here. We didn't like seeing our town in the news, seeing a good boy from its best family accused of a horrible crime. It's not that we don't understand date rape. We're not stupid or unsophisticated. We watch the same TV shows ▶

you do, go to the same movies. We have Facebook and smartphones and DVRs and computers and Internet. Just because there's cornfields and Kiwanis barbecue and produce stands along the highway, just because you drive through at sixty-five miles an hour—the speed limit is 50, by the way—with your windows up and your kayaks and your bicycles, you don't know us. You don't know anything about us. The Stones are good people. Their name is on the old theater and the scoreboard and the snack bar at the community pool, which hires mentally slow people and contributes its proceeds to the booster club. They own a grocery store and a seafood restaurant, and they're not the least bit stuck-up. My mom would love to work for them instead of Happy Harry's, but chains are buying up everything now.

When my photo appeared in the Wilmington paper, it wasn't a big deal. I mean, it was on page 1, and a lot of kids said, "Go, you," and not at all sarcastic. A week later it was online, in a newspaper all the way in London, England, and it said: THE FACE OF BELLEVILLE. Well, I'm not, but I would be proud to be that. And the part underneath, "A Town Unites in Hate Against Rape Victim," wasn't true. Because Tara wasn't raped. No charges were filed; her lawsuit was dropped because her parents got cold feet, and they went back to Philadelphia. What about Daniel? What about Charley? I imagine them this fall, off at school, saying their names, saying where they're from. She ruined their lives, or tried. And Charley's not much, but Daniel Stone is the nicest boy you'll ever meet. He lay down at her feet and let her walk across his back, and she says these things against him? "Slut" is kind, if you ask me. Girl gets caught having sex, says it wasn't her idea, puts it on the boy.

Sure, Tara, sure.

And now she's back. If she wanted to apologize, things would be different. But she's never going to admit she was wrong. Never.

The playhouse. The vacant lot where we held bonfires. The dumpster behind Langley's.

The snack bar at the pool. And now the Greene house, which no one wanted to buy. I bet it's insured. I bet it's insured for a lot of money. "Jewish lightning," my mother says the next day. I had forgotten the Greene family was Jewish. People made a big deal out of that, too, but it never mattered to us. And Tara got lots of extra holidays. I think she made half of them up. She was a liar, and that's what liars do: make things up.

* * *

I know what I have to do, but I don't want to do it. I don't want to go to the cops, tell them about Tara. The mud on her sandals the night after the rain, the fire at the pool. How I saw her standing outside her own house when it went up in flames. If I go to them, I'm a snitch. I'll be like her, only I'll be telling the truth.

Tara must know what's going through my mind, because she doesn't follow me home on Monday or Tuesday. Or maybe I start leaving just a few minutes earlier, now that Wendi's on time, since the pool closed down. But Wednesday, after I stop by the high school to make sure I'm not missing any major requirements, she's waiting for me at the edge of the lacrosse field, under the John and Adelaide Stone scoreboard, the one with the ad for Langley Seafood along the bottom.

Then she sees the state trooper's car, parked across the street, and she runs.

Two men get out. "Beth Ennis? Can we talk to you? Just a few questions. Can we talk to you?"

I look around. No one's there, no one will know if I talk to them. Tara might, but that's her problem, right? She was tagging after me, they saw her, she ran. They think I know something. But I don't. I can't know anything. I make up my mind that I'll talk to them but I won't volunteer anything. They teach you in kindergarten not to be a tattletale.

They take me to the state police barracks. In the car, on the way over, they ask me my age and I say eighteen. I guess they don't believe me, because I see them exchange a look and they ask for my actual birth date, like I can't do math. I turned eighteen just two weeks ago. My mom had the option to hold me back, so she did, so I wouldn't be the smallest in the class. The thing is, I'm kinda the biggest. I hit six feet at age fourteen.

"My mom held me back," I tell them. "So I wouldn't be the smallest. I mean, the youngest. I was never the smallest. But it wasn't like it was with Charley Boyd's parents. They wanted him to have an advantage when he tried out for football. They call that redshirting—which is different from Redshirts, which is a *Star Trek* thing."

I read a lot of science fiction and fantasy. "Speculative fiction" is the better term, I think. Because fantasies are that *Shades of Grey* stuff, about love and stuff. And science fiction sounds as if it's about science. When it's still about the people, you know? It's all what if. *What if?*

They ask me again for the year I was born and I tell them. ▶

"Five Fires" *(continued)*

* * *

At the barracks in Georgetown, they offer me anything I want from the vending machines—anything. I don't want to appear greedy, so I ask for a Diet 7Up and a bag of Utz crab chips. They're both really nice. Good cop, good cop. After all, I'm not a suspect. I'm just someone who knows things I wish I didn't know. The mud on Tara's sandals. Seeing her watching her own house burn. The thing she said about knowing how to make a fire from sticks. When I feel like I'm about to tell them something I shouldn't, I eat a big handful of chips, sip my soda. *The policeman is your friend. The policeman is your friend.* That old song comes back to me from kindergarten, back when I was normal size, right in the middle of the class when we lined up by height.

"You know the house that burned, right?" one asks me.

"Know of it, sir. I was never inside."

"And the playhouse? The snack bar?"

"Again, I know about those places, but they're not places I ever went."

"The vacant lot, the dumpster at Langley's."

They're not from Belleville. They need my help.

"Well, the vacant lot is where we have the bonfires in the fall. For pep rallies. And, and, for other things. Langley's is a seafood restaurant. It's owned by the Stone family. Daniel worked as a waiter there, modest as you please. He didn't need to work. But his family has what my mom calls good values. They believe in work. Daniel waited tables there in the summer. They have a really good fried oyster sandwich. My mom and I went there for her birthday once. But it was March, so Daniel wasn't working."

"So," says one of them. They look so much alike, they might be twins. Tan suits, short dark hair. "If you think about it, every one of these fires is tied to the Stone family or the Greene family."

"Well, not the vacant lot, sir. Everyone in the high school went there."

"Still, it's interesting, don't you think?"

I don't. I really don't. But I'm out of chips and soda, and I don't know what to do with my hands. I tent my fingers, then put my palms flat on the table. They're really sweaty, and now my fingers have that crab dust on them from the chips.

"Sirs? There's something I probably should tell you. I don't want to, and I would appreciate if you didn't let it get out. That I told you. Because, while I plan to major in law enforcement at Del Tech, kids can be very cruel. They'll say I'm a snitch. I'm not. I'm the opposite. But Tara Greene is back in town. I've seen her. I don't know where she's staying, but I see her every day, almost. She was at the school just now. Did you see her? She ran away when she saw you. She walks home with me from the deli. And the day after the fire at the pool, there was mud on her sandals, and I saw her, at the fire at her house. I don't know why she would burn down the snack bar, although I think she and Daniel first started flirting there"—Wendi told me that—"and I don't know why she would burn down her house, although her parents can't sell it; maybe she thought they would get insurance money—"

They interrupt and say: "You know, we probably should call your parents."

* * *

My mom is getting ready to go to work, and she's pissed. But when she comes in, she says, "Let's make this quick."

I say, "Mom, I had to tell them. Tara did it. Tara started all those fires. And she's been following me around for weeks now. I didn't let her in the house, although she kept asking to come in. I don't owe her anything."

The cops do that thing where they exchange a look, then leave. My mom, so old, so used up, so not the pretty schoolteacher with the convertible that needs a new tire, does something that she hasn't done since I was eight years old. She takes me in her arms, although she's so tiny it feels odd. It's like if one of those birds who rides on the head of a hippo decided to give it a hug. Not that I'm that big, just that my mom is that small. By the time I was fourteen, when she had bad nights, I could pick her up and carry her, put her in the tub, put her to bed. I hated doing that, yet I miss it sometimes. She doesn't need me as much as she used to.

"Oh, Beth, oh Bethie, what have you done?"

"Nothing, Mom. I wasn't even sure until now that it was Tara. I—"

"Oh, baby," my mom says. "You *know* that Tara Greene's dead since last May. Killed herself a week before graduation. She drove down here from Philadelphia and slit her wrists in that playhouse. You know that. Everyone in town knows that."

The cops come back in. I bet they were listening to us all along. It's a one-way glass, usually, so they can see in, listen to what you say. Everyone knows that trick. ▶

"Five Fires" *(continued)*

"But she set those fires," I say. "Sorry, but she did. I don't want to tattle, but I saw her, I saw her—"

"Beth," the one cop asks me. "We need to go through where you were. Every night there was a fire, okay? Can you prove where you were?"

"She was home with me," Mom says.

"Are you sure, ma'am? Are you sure?"

I say, wanting to be truthful, wanting to keep Mama from looking like she's covering up for me: "I did go out the night of the fire at the Greenes' house. But only after I heard the sirens. That's how I know Tara was there. I went out my bedroom window. But I wouldn't go out to do anything bad. You know that, Mama. I would never do anything bad."

The two men in the tan suits look to my mom, who is crying now and rocking in her seat.

"Been working four to eleven since August 1," Mama says. "The night shift. The fucking night shift. I don't even look in on her when I get home. She's always in her room with the door shut. At least—I thought she was in her room."

My poor mom. I probably should call her sponsor tonight. It makes her so nervous when I'm at the center of things. She doesn't think I can handle it. That's why she had that bad night last fall. But I'm a hero, Mama. I'm proud. I'm righteous. I don't mind telling these police officers what Tara's been up to, if that's what I have to do. I'll help them catch her, too. That will be exciting, almost as exciting as last fall, when I was the face of Belleville. ❧